No Land For Heroes

A Gaslamp & Western Fantasy

Cal Black

Bearberry Studio

Published by Bearberry Studio 2022

Copyright © 2022 by Cal Black

Book Cover Design by ebooklaunch.com

First edition

For Mom, who always sent my stories back with edits.
For Anne and Char, who encouraged me to write about cowboy
elves, and for always being my first readers.

INDIGENOUS REPRESENTATION

I understand many readers are concerned about the portrayal of North American Indigenous cultures and would like to re-assure you that I involved indigenous voices both prior to and post-publication regarding what is and is not appropriate to include in a fictional world. These people come from a variety of backgrounds and I've had extensive discussions with them regarding the portrayal of the Ghost Eye Clan and if that portrayal is respectful. If you are an indigenous reader and have concerns, please reach out. I'm happy to listen and discuss potential solutions with you. If you are a settler, please respect the indigenous voices that have spoken.

It is important to note that I am not telling a story of an indigenous person, but showing that they were a significant part of the 'wild west' while deconstructing the tropes often found in those older portrayals. To remove the Ghost Eye Clan would be erasing the presence of indigenous people within the genre, which is harmful in a different but equal way.

I strongly encourage readers to pick up books by indigenous authors if you are interested in learning more about indigenous voices and stories. Plus, they're awesome books.

-Cal

The Butcher's in the Bayou!
The Butcher's in the Bayou!
Careful he don't find you.
Or you'll catch his axe
As the muskets crack,
And he'll butcher you in the Bayou!

—Amelian Nursery Rhyme

1

PLAYING WITH FIRE

THE NIGHT'S STEADY DRIZZLE didn't bother the stolen horse or its rider. The weather had been hot for the last two weeks and it hadn't rained in three, leaving the prairie in near-drought conditions. The rolling ocean of tall grasses around them had gone brittle, turning the Prairie's usual whisper into a dry rattle. Rain would be good, the elven rider thought. Both for reviving the land and for washing away any traces of the crime she was about to commit.

Mildred Berry pulled her wide brimmed-hat low to cover her white hair. It would be a dead giveaway if she was spotted: there weren't any other albinistic elves running around this part of the Prairie. Her long ears twitched against the hat's brim as she tried not to think about the consequences if she was caught.

Previously, she'd mixed coal dust with fat to colour her hair, but it had melted from the heat of her scalp, oozing black rivulets down her face and neck. Effective at terrorizing guards, but messier than the makeshift dye was worth.

Adjusting her poncho to keep out the rain, Millie gave the horse a solid pat on the neck. Max, a mustang gelding, was a frequent and willing accomplice to her crimes. He was always happy to stretch his legs, took payment in carrots, and would never snitch. This late at night, the local lawman—Max's owner—would be too drunk to notice the horse was gone.

Plainfield's lanterns glowed on the horizon. It was a weed of a town, springing out of the dirt with the arrival of the railroad. Half its buildings were built from wood that had yet to turn silver, and the other half were whitewashed to look presentable. It was a town hoping to become a city, and Millie hated it.

Plainfield was little more than a stopover for travellers. Most headed further west to Stonecreek's mines or south to the swampy rice fields. The north was dominated by thick forests and the fur trade. Very few travellers from Plainfield went east. East led to actual cities, where people called themselves 'civilized' and 'respectable' and looked down on people like Millie. Cities stank.

The new railroad brought more settlers to the Frontier, making it a little less wild, a little less free with each homestead established.

"How upset would you be if I burnt down your town?" Millie asked the horse.

Max snorted and flicked an ear.

"Relax, I was only asking," she said. She blew a drop of rain from the brim of her hat with a sharp puff of air. The town would be too wet after the rain. Besides, Millie planned to avoid killing anyone on the job tonight. Missing cargo was easily forgiven by Plainfield's drunkard Sheriff, but dead bodies would draw the attention of more competent lawmen.

A shrill whistle cut through the steady drizzle. The train was finally leaving, and soon it would chug into sight.

"Ready, Max?" she asked the horse, nudging him to trot in a little circle to warm up his legs. She'd kept both of them warm and limber, ready for work. Max snorted and pawed at the ground. He was ready to give this new train a run for its money.

Fresh off the West-Colfield train yard, the Blue Bullet was said to be the fastest locomotive in the west. The rumours were that it could outrun a dragon itself, but Millie doubted it. She'd watched the famous train come and go over the last two weeks.

While it was faster than the old clunker that used to run this route, the mustang should be able to keep pace with it.

The train whistled a second time and Millie watched the white dot of its headlamp pull away from the orange glow of Plainfield. Soon the blue locomotive chugged past, picking up speed. She pulled her bandana up over her nose and pulled on a set of buckskin gloves she'd kept dry inside her vest.

Millie clicked her tongue, and with the slightest nudge, Max took off. Plainfield's sheriff no longer galloped the mustang, but Millie made sure to whenever she was in town. They pulled alongside the train easily. Max's thundering hooves masked by the clanking of steel wheels and the steady chug of the locomotive. One wrong move and she could be thrown under the train. Its wheels would cut her in half in an instant.

Millie grinned under her bandana. Few things could compare to the rush of chasing down a train.

Looping Max's reins in a knot so he wouldn't step on them, Millie placed her hands on his withers and pushed herself up to get her moccasined feet onto his back. Max's gait held steady on the smooth ground. Millie held the crouch for a heartbeat, for two, waiting for the cargo car behind them to pull far enough ahead. When the one that followed came into reach, she leapt from Max's back to catch the iron rungs of the train car's service ladder.

Her gloves gripped the wet iron and held fast. The dry buckskin absorbed the water that made the rungs treacherous. Millie scrambled up the ladder and pulled herself up onto the roof of the boxcar. From her new vantage point, Millie could see that Max was still racing alongside the train, though the Blue Bullet was gaining speed and pulling ahead. She threw Max a thumbs-up. He'd wander back to town once he got tired, and find some tasty carrots waiting in his stall for his work.

Millie adjusted her hat against the rain and counted how many cars were ahead of her. Even at night, Millie didn't need a lantern. Much like a cat, her eyes could see the train just fine in the low light, a legacy of her long-dead father. Millie was crouched on the sixth, not including the locomotive and its twin coal cars. Turning, Millie scanned the rest of the train for guards but found none. On the caboose, the signal lantern swayed in time with the train, its shutters set to the 'all clear' position.

Keeping her weight low, Millie crept along the length of the car and leapt the gap to her target. While the locomotive was brand new, the boxcar was worn and familiar, just like every other car she'd broken into over the years. Swinging herself over the edge of the car's roof, Millie clambered down its side door. She unlatched it, and bracing one foot against the vertical beam of the doorway, shoved the door to one side.

It stuck. Millie grunted and shoved again. After a moment the door gave way and a human guard squinted out into the rain. Spotting Millie, the guard nodded and motioned Millie to get inside with a tilt of her head. The elf didn't need a second invitation, ducking under the tall woman's arm, she climbed into the car and out of the rain.

"Everything go alright?" Millie asked, helping her partner push the boxcar door closed and latch it in place. No wonder she hadn't been able to open it.

"Yes ma'am," Ryan Collins said, stepping to one side to avoid getting wet as Millie peeled off her poncho and hat, shaking the worst of the wet from them. Ryan's long, dark hair was pulled back into a tight braid that she'd tucked under the collar of her stolen uniform. She looked stoic, but Millie knew the tiny furrow on Ryan's brow meant she was worried. "The train was late leaving Plainfield. Coal delivery put them behind schedule. Max didn't have trouble catching us?"

"Caught it without breaking a sweat," Millie said with a tiny swell of pride. "I left some extra carrots in his stall for whenever he wanders home."

Ryan's worry disappeared, and she tried to cover a smile with a cough, but Millie caught the way Ryan's hazel eyes crinkled up in amusement. Tall, powerfully built, Ryan was many things, but a skilled actress she was not. Even after years of practice, she still held herself with a certain poise that demanded people's respect.

Millie frowned, playing at being grumpy. Ryan wasn't used to train robbery, and if pretending to sulk helped her friend relax, so be it. People made terrible decisions when anxious. Ryan had wanted this job to be bloodless, and Millie wasn't about to let her friend make a mistake because of nerves.

"Don't look at me like that," Millie muttered, stepping into the narrow walkway between stacked cargo crates. "I'm not going soft." Pulling a tomahawk from her belt, Millie slipped the narrow axe blade in between the crate and its lid. Leaning on the long handle, the elf pried the lid up with a dry crack as the nails gave way.

"I never said you were." Ryan said, suddenly the picture of innocence. She held her lantern over the crate and leaned in, just as eager as Millie was to confirm the crate had what they needed.

"You were *thinking* it." Millie shifted her axe and pried the lid again until she could pull it off completely. Golden straw gleamed under the lantern, but what they were after was beneath that. Reaching inside, Millie shoved the straw aside to reveal neatly packed boxes of bullets that gently rattled with the motion of the train.

"One day you're going to take Max home for real, and we'll have to explain that," Ryan warned. The faux argument died the moment Millie pulled out a handful of bullets. "Thank the Messiah," Ryan said, making the sign of the wheel over her chest.

Spotting it, Millie frowned. Ryan must be more anxious than she'd let on.

"I'll just say Max likes us better," Millie said gently, handing the bullets to her partner. They were rifle calibre, and wouldn't fit her revolvers. She'd left her rifle at home. Trying to climb around a train with a long gun was difficult, and Millie had no interest in repeating that experience in the rain.

"You remember the rest of the plan, right?" Millie asked quietly. "No last-minute change of heart?"

"Distract the guards. Stop to unload. We get what we need. No one hurt, no more hungry bellies back home." Ryan nodded and letting out a slow, deep breath. She straightened her shoulders and slipped the bullets into her pocket. "No change of heart. I set up the distraction on the caboose before we left the station. We should have another hour before it goes off."

A distant thud—followed by a whoosh.

The women unlatched the car door and yanked it open. Rain spattered onto them as the bandits watched the caboose go up in orange flames. The distraction had fired early, splashing burning oil out over the caboose's roof. The alchemical flames devoured everything in their path despite the rain. A fire-wreathed figure leapt from the caboose into the darkness with a scream.

Millie grimaced. So much for 'no one gets hurt'.

"Okay, so. We're a bit early, but otherwise, the plan stays the same," she said, throwing her pack over her shoulders. "Send the guards to the back of the train; I'll set those cars loose."

"Do you think that guard will survive?" Ryan asked, pulling the rifle off her shoulder.

"Well." Millie cleared her throat awkwardly. She didn't want to make Ryan feel any worse. She had been the one to plant the device, and it would be too easy for her to feel guilty that it ignited early. Millie might not bat an eye, but Ryan was different. She had morals. "He *could*."

Millie pulled her bandana up and shoved her hat back into place to cover her telltale pale hair. "Stay safe."

Climbed out of the boxcar, Millie climbed along the sides of train cars toward the caboose. She'd have to be careful: the wetter her gloves and moccasins got, the less they'd grip the slick iron ladders. Jogging across the roofs of the cars would be faster, and keep her gloves drier, but the guards crawling out of the train like ants would spot her easily. Best to leave the high road to Ryan and take the lower one.

The train was curved along a bend in the track, giving Millie a better view of the mess they had made. The orange flames engulfed the caboose entirely and licked at the lumber car linked to it. If left unchecked, the fire would consume the whole train and anyone left inside it.

"All hands: put that fire out!" Ryan's commanding voice cut through the chaos of guards yelling and the growing roar of flames. "Keep it from spreading!"

Reaching the last car, Millie tucked herself into the space just above the coupling between it and the first of the flatbeds carrying lumber. In the car behind her, Millie could hear horses shift and snort in fear as they heard the crackle of flames. Above, guards leapt from the stockcar onto the stacked lumber lashed to flatbeds. Someone was shouting a spell while others beat at the flames with their thick wool coats.

Ryan peeked over the edge of the boxcar and gave Millie a thumbs up. Returning it, the elf pulled out her tomahawk and slid the spiked end through the lynch-pin's ring. She braced herself as best she could on the narrow coupling and levered the axe until a jostle in the cars gave her the slack to pull the pin free.

Tucking her axe back into her belt, Millie tossed the lynch-pin out into the darkness, watching the lumber cars fall behind. When the abandoned cars drifted far enough back, Millie climbed the ladder to join Ryan on the stockcar's roof. She stretched, cracking her back. The burning caboose was fading into the distance and below them, the nervous horses grew calm once more.

Millie looked around to get her bearings. Patches of scrub now interrupted the tall prairie grasses and, off to the train's right, a massive boulder rose out of the plains.

"I'm sorry about the bomb," Ryan said. "I should have—"

"Don't do that to yourself." Millie reached out and took her friend by the shoulders, looking up into her eyes. "The train was late; we couldn't account for that. West-Colfield *always* runs on time. We had no way to know tonight would be the one time they ran late." Under her hands, Ryan's muscles were knotted tight. The job wasn't over, they had to stay level-headed to make sure the rest of the plan went off without a hitch.

"I suppose," Ryan muttered, looking down. Her shoulders relaxed and Ryan took a breath, about to say something. She looked at Millie and flinched.

"Eyeshine?" Millie asked, glancing down at the lantern that hung from Ryan's belt. Her father's gift: new world elves could see in low light, but their eyes reflected light at certain angles like draconids and cats. Most elf eyes shone green. Millie's shone red.

"Sorry," Ryan said, embarrassed. "You think I'd be used to it by now."

Millie shrugged and squeezed Ryan's shoulder before letting her go. Ry wasn't the first person to react like that and wouldn't be the last. Reaching into her vest, the elf pulled out a flask and held it out with a little shake. Liquid sloshed inside, long cold but still effective.

"Coffee?"

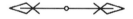

They reached the rendezvous point in good time. Millie reluctantly admitted to Ryan that the Blue Bullet was as fast as everyone said... once it was freed from a third of its cargo. A craggy pile of rock rose out of the scrub ahead of them, a long dead tree trunk sticking out of it at a precarious angle. Behind the rockpile waited the rest of their crew, ready to jump into action at Millie's signal.

After years of working alone, Millie had grudgingly admitted she needed help this time. She could eliminate the guards and take control of the train, no problem. But hauling several crates of ammunition across the prairie was a different story. Ryan hadn't joined Millie on the train because she was human, but because the other elf in their crew, Annie, had refused to. Their fourth, Sweetpea, was the only woman on the frontier that was more recognizable on sight than Millie was. A hat could hide Millie's hair, but Sweetpea had horns that refused most headwear. It was a shame, though. Having either mage would make sending the signal much easier.

Pulling a short bow frame from her pack, Millie strung it with a grunt and checked the string tension. It twanged, telling her that the string had remained dry despite the earlier rain. Neither she nor Ryan was a good shot with a bow, but luckily all she had to do tonight was aim 'up'. Millie pulled the signal arrow from her pack and unwrapped the scrap of oilcloth from its tip. The pungent stink of chemicals assaulted her nose immediately. Millie switched to breathing through her mouth to reduce the smell.

"Ready?" Ryan asked. She opened the lantern's hood to give Millie access to the flame. The flame flickered wildly in the wind caused by the train.

"Ready enough." Nocking the arrow, Millie touched the arrow's fuse to the flame. As soon as it caught, Millie stepped back and drew. She loosed the arrow, the tiny ember of its fuse arc up into the sky. The arrow was still climbing as it burst into bright red flame, bright enough to wash the train in an eerie red glow. But the flare revealed something else, too. The massive scaley bulk of a greater blue dragon, circling overhead.

"Oh." Ryan breathed.

The arrow struck the underbelly of the beast and buried itself into the dragon's skin. It shrieked in pain and its massive head snaked down to bite at the thing now stuck in its abdomen. The arrow didn't have enough power to hurt the dragon, but the extreme heat of the flare could melt her thick scales.

The train's engineer slammed on the locomotive's brakes as soon as he heard the dragon's scream. The railcar that Millie and

Ryan were standing on jolted back in response, sending them both staggering forward. Ryan caught Millie's belt, catching her before the elf tumbled over the edge of the car. The Locomotive's brakes kicked up twin curtains of sparks into the night, dazzling Millie's vision and ruining whatever night vision she'd had left.

Glancing back up as Ryan helped steady her, Millie saw the dragon rip out the offending arrow and toss it to the side. For a moment she lost the beast in the darkness, her eyes still dazed from the brightness of the flare.

Blinking rapidly, Millie pointed at the locomotive and shouted over the screech of train wheels grinding against the rails.

"Stop the brakes!"

Instead of answering, Ryan grabbed her up and threw both of them backward, onto the car's roof. Millie wheezed as the impact knocked the air from her lungs. Lying on her back, she watched the dragon swoop down, spewing flame at the shrieking locomotive. The yellow-orange fire spilled over the Blue Bullet and coal cars, its heat washing over where Millie and Ryan lay as flat as possible.

"Shoot the brake lever," Millie shouted again, voice nearly lost in the cacophony of screaming brakes and dragonfire. The coal had ignited immediately, and the roar of flames and the ping of rapidly heating iron warned of impending disaster.

"What?" Ryan looked at her, eyes wide.

"We need to detach." Millie squinted up at the sky, but the smoke and lit embers flying past them made it difficult to spot the dragon. She'd be back for another pass, though. The locomotive was still shrieking. "Shoot the brake! I'll get the coupling."

Ryan nodded, grim-faced. Living on the frontier, they were used to dealing with dangerous animals. Dragons this big were things you ran from until you found cover. There was no sense in fighting something as large as a locomotive and meaner than sin.

Millie's ears perked, catching the heavy flap of wings through the roar of fire. The dragon was climbing again, getting ready for another dive.

"Now!" she shouted, rolling to her feet.

Ryan got up onto a knee and sighted down the barrel of her rifle. Steadying herself, the woman took a slow breath in, and squeezed off a round. Millie couldn't stay to see if she'd hit her target. She was already scrambling down the car's ladder to get at the coupling. She pulled her revolver free, cocked the hammer, and fired. The bullet punched through the iron pin, dead centre. A second bullet knocked what remained of the pin free from its coupling. Overhead, she heard another sharp crack of Ryan's rifle.

"Jump!" she shouted, racing back up to join her friend. Ryan leapt from the train car. Millie dove after her, willing the locomotive to hold until it pulled away from the rest of the train.

It didn't get far. As Millie hit the muddy ground and rolled, the locomotive exploded. Super-heated steam tore the Blue Bullet apart as though it were nothing more than a firecracker. Wrapping her arms over her head, Millie pressed herself as flat to the ground as she could. Something hot and sharp bit into her back.

Gritting her teeth against the pain, Millie waited for another few rapid heartbeats before peeking out from under her arms. The dragon shrieked, wings flapping strangely as it retreated toward the badlands. Shrapnel must have hit it, too. Millie's relief was short-lived. The train's cargo cars slammed into the wreckage of the coal cars and remnants of the locomotive. The steel of the once-blue engine now glowed a dull red in the night.

"Move." Ryan hauled Millie to her feet and shoved her forward. Pain flared in her back but the elf got her feet under her, sprinting away from the wreck into the grass.

Each car that smashed into the others was a little slower, a little less catastrophic, but the sight still took Millie's breath away.

The locomotive's boiler was gone. Heating rods spilled out of the wreckage in crazy coils, twisted from extreme heat and the force of the explosion. The coal cars had scattered their burning fuel out into the prairie, where each lump set soaked grasses alight. The remaining cars folded into each other like hell's own accordion. The cars closest to the locomotive were already catching fire, and it wouldn't be long before the fire spread to the car that held the ammunition.

"The horses!" Ryan shouted and sprinted off back toward the back of the train.

"The what?" Millie gasped, pressing a hand to her back. Her glove came away sticky, but the heat of the shrapnel had cauterized most of the wound. A blessing, but it still hurt terribly. Ryan was running in the wrong direction. The ammunition was in the middle of the wreck.

Staggering back toward the train, Millie nearly fell over as a hawk swooped down from the night air.

"That one," she gasped to hawk-Annie, pointing at the car that held the ammunition. The bird tilted its wings and shifted mid air into a dark-skinned elf who hit the ground at a sprint. At the heart of the fire, Millie saw small clouds forming in the air and a deluge poured out of them onto the burning train. Sweetpea's work: the rain spell wouldn't be enough to stop the coal from burning, but it would slow the spread until they could get the ammunition out of the wreckage.

"Are you going to stand there and watch, or actually help?" Annie shouted over her shoulder. Millie was still catching her breath when a dog the size of a pony barreled out of the grass and ran up to Annie, ready to drag the heavy crates free.

"I'm coming," Millie panted. She braced her hands on her knees and tried not to think about how when she was young it didn't hurt this much to be a bandit. Then again, of all the robberies she'd committed in her life, this was the first to involve a dragon.

Straightening with a grunt, Millie ran after Annie and the dog. She could be old and achy once the ammunition was safe.

2

— · —

RED HANDS

THE TRAIN WAS STILL burning when the sun peeked over the horizon, painting the ugly clouds of smoke golden. The four women had offloaded the crates of ammunition and horses before the fire reached them. But now, exhausted and standing in the middle of a scorched patch of prairie, they watched what remained of the famed Blue Bullet burn.

"You've outdone yourself, Mildred," Annie said, sucking on her teeth. The dark-skinned elf rested her hands on her hips as she studied the wreckage. "I used to think Auntie's stories about you were made up, but destroying a whole train? Impressive." Annie's braids were pulled back, though one had caught a stray ember and smouldered where it rested against her broad shoulder. The smell of burning hair was masked by the heavy sulphur-musk of dragonfire and the far more pleasant scent of burning prairie. Either Annie hadn't noticed, or she didn't care.

"You shouldn't believe everything your aunt says." Millie winced as Sweetpea worked the piece of shrapnel out of her back and the elf scraped the heel of her moccasin against the crate she sat on, trying to get rid of the maker's mark branded into the wood. The stylized initials 'F', 'A' and 'R' were ones she'd hoped to never see again, but kept turning up like a bad penny. If she were younger, the feeling of 'getting back' at the owner of those initials would have been the best thing in the world. Now, a tired, scarred, weary, Millie wondered if she was inviting more trouble into her life. The town needed those bullets. It didn't matter who Millie had to steal them from.

"Now that's not fair," Sweetpea said, continuing to work on Millie's back. The arroyan woman's tail swished against her skirts as she concentrated. Somehow, despite all the fire, Sweetpea's ruffles remained unscathed. "Millie didn't *ask* the dragon to come attack the train." She paused and leaned around to look at her patient with her big mismatched eyes: one blue, one gold. Sweetpea's expression was warm and kind, despite the smear of Millie's blood across her pink nose.

"You didn't ask the dragon to help, did you?" she asked, lifting her eyebrows. High arroyans were interesting if you'd never met one before. They looked a little like elves and a little like orcs until you saw their horns and tails. Sweetpea's horns were delicately curled, like her hair. Other than her eyes, Sweetpea was entirely pink: her skin was rosy, her freckles a shade or two darker, and her hair was the softest shade of blush.

"No," Millie said slowly. "I did not plan on the dragon attacking the train while Ryan and I were on it." She looked over at Ryan. The human was no help, grinning at Millie from where she sat on another liberated crate with the massive dog leaning into Ryan like he hadn't seen her in years. His massive head rested on Ryan's shoulder while he was still sitting on the ground, his tail sweeping ash back and forth.

Fyodor was unnaturally big, even for a mastiff.

"In hindsight," Ryan said, patting her oversized baby of a dog. "It's a good thing the distraction went off early. Otherwise, things could have been much worse." Fyodor whined when Ryan stopped petting him and he shoved his face into her shoulder, nearly knocking her off the crate she sat on.

"It went off too early?" Sweetpea asked, mismatched eyes going wide. "What happened? The spell starts when you set it. Was the train late?"

"I thought West-Colfield always ran on time," Annie said, sarcastically. She was still staring at the tangle of metal that had once been the locomotive. Millie wondered which stories her aunt had told her if the other elf had thought they were just stories.

"New ownership," Ryan offered. "The train was late leaving Plainfield. They added the horses at the last minute and they had yet to update the manifest." Ryan glanced over at where the horses waited a safe distance away, grazing on what grass survived the flames. "Do you have enough room for them at the ranch, Annie?"

Annie's ears flicked at the question. Turning, she studied the new herd with pursed lips.

"Should be fine for a while, though we're not going to keep them all, are we?"

"It was fine, 'Pea. The charge worked like it was supposed to." Millie said, letting Ryan handle the horse issue. Right now, Millie was mostly concerned about the fingers that were still working on her back. "Could we please finish pulling that metal out?"

"Oh! Yes, sorry!" Sweetpea said, disappearing from Millie's sight. "It's caught a bit on an older scar, sorry Millie. This is going to hurt."

"I'll be fine," Millie said. She winced as Sweetpea dug her fingers in a little deeper to grasp the shard of metal. The pain of Sweetpea wiggling the shard loose from Millie's back was enough to make the elf suck in a breath and hold it deep in her chest. She compressed the air in her lungs until she felt the last bit of metal give up its hold on her flesh. A warm trickle of blood ran down her back, but at least now the metal was out and Pea could stitch her up.

"Here you go," Sweetpea said, cheerfully dropping the twisted piece of metal into Millie's palm.

"Oh," Millie said, staring at it. Whatever it had been, the metal was now twisted beyond recognition. It'd felt larger than it looked, too. "Thank you?" She tossed the bloody shard aside. Soon this would just be another scar, another story. She didn't need to keep a memento.

"You're welcome," Sweetpea chirped, settling in to stitch up the wound. She poured something over it that made Millie's eyes water from how much it stung. Whiskey, from the smell of it. Millie wrinkled her nose.

"This will stop the bleeding, but you should see if your grandm—"

"She's not my grandmother," Millie corrected. "It's her title. Like 'Sheriff', only 'Grannie'. I figure I'll stop by in a few days to see if they want any of our new horse friends. And get Grannie to look at my back while I'm there."

"Well, what do we have here?" a male voice called out. "The Scorched Bluffs ladies having high tea?" Millie's ears perked and twisted toward the sound. Dressed only in her camisole and with the wound in her back still open, she was not eager to entertain guests.

"Now if you'd all turn around real slow-like and put your hands up," the man continued. His voice sounded familiar, but it took a moment for Millie to place it. The strange drawl was something she heard most often at Plainfield. Usually in the saloon ordering drinks.

"I'll be taking them horses," Isaiah Willard said. Isaiah was the youngest and dumbest of the Willard Boys' gang. Millie waited a moment to see if any of his older, more dangerous brothers were around to interrupt him.

Ryan sat, calmly holding back Fyodor, who had stood and raised his hackles at the new arrival. His growl was low, warning the stranger to behave. Annie sucked on her teeth and watched Isaiah, hands on her hips. She didn't look impressed. Sweetpea, living up to her name, had lifted a bloody hand to wave hello.

Turning on her crate to stare at the Willard, Millie let out a tired sigh. Isaiah had gotten a growth spurt, most of it going to the Adam's apple at his throat and his legs, which ended in mismatched boots. Whoever had given him the confidence to try stealing the horses had done him a great disservice. But there he was, in his moth-eaten jacket and with a clunky revolver pointed their way.

"That won't be a problem, will it, Sheriff Collins?" Isaiah asked. He grinned, his attempt at a beard made him look like he had mange. "You keep your attack dog over there with your furry friend, and I'll be happy to pay you with a good time." He reached down with his free hand and wiggled his belt buckle suggestively. Ryan made a face at the suggestion.

"You bring a babysitter with you?" Millie 'the attack dog', asked.

"One man against four women. Odds are still good," Isaiah said. He looked at her and pulled a face as he noticed the heavy scarring on her back. "Messiah's tits, Deputy, do you fight bears for fun?"

"Not *bears*," Millie said, deadpan.

In a heartbeat, her revolver was in her hand, and firing a round straight into Isaiah's skull. The man staggered backward and crumpled out of sight into the grasses, mouth agape. One bullet left until they could unpack the crates back in town.

"Millie..." Ryan said reproachfully. "Was that necessary? He was just a kid."

Annie bit her lip, though her shoulders shook with quiet laughter. Sweetpea whistled softly, impressed at the accuracy.

"He knew who we were," Millie said with a one-sided shrug. "Isaiah's not smart enough to realise we were stealing this, but his brothers would be. Do you really want the smart Willards telling all of Plainfield that the sheriff and deputy of Scorched Bluffs were looting?" She tucked her gun back into her holster and reached for her shirt, only to have Sweetpea slap her hand away, leaving a bloody smear on Millie's skin. A moment later, the arroyan was back at work, sewing Millie's wound closed.

Ryan sighed and rested her chin on her hand, fingers tapping at her cheek. She looked at the grass where Isaiah had fallen.

After a moment's thought, Ry sighed again and her shoulders drooped.

"No," the sheriff admitted, patting her dog's neck. "You're right. So much for 'no fatalities', though."

"I mean," Annie said, still trying to keep a straight face. She coughed into her glove. "The Willard wasn't on the train, so technically he doesn't count?" When Ryan shot her a look, Annie cleared her throat. "Sorry, Sheriff. I'll go get the cart so we can load it up." She pressed her lips into a tight line whose edges wiggled as she hurried away, heading toward the hill with the crooked tree.

Fyodor had finally soaked up enough love to let Ryan go so he could sniff at the scorched ground. Blinking, Ryan stood and rubbed her eyes with the heels of her hands.

"The smoke?" Millie asked. Her own eyes were stinging from it, and while Annie's cough had been a poor attempt to cover a laugh, they would all be glad when they left the wreck.

"Yeah," Ryan said. "I'll be glad when we get out of here." She picked her way through the burnt grass over to where the Willard boy had fallen.

"All done!" Sweetpea said, patting Millie's shoulder. "Make sure not to tear them out before you visit your Grannie." The pink woman stood up with a swish of ruffles and wiped the blood from her hands with her handkerchief. Somehow, she'd managed to not get any blood on her skirt or blouse. Millie suspected there might be magic at play given how much red the arroyan had on her hands.

"Thanks 'Pea," Millie said, pulling her shirt back on, careful not to pull out any of the fresh sutures. Standing, Millie headed over to where Ryan stood. Fyodor trotted over, neatly intercepting her, and nudged Millie to the side. She tried to step around him, only to have a furry shoulder block her path.

"Fyo—" she said, trying to get around the dog. He licked at her chin and stayed stubbornly directly between her and the body in the grass. Millie could push past any normal dog, but this was Fyodor, a fancy breed of mastiff almost as tall as she was. Taller, if he stood on his hind legs.

"Ryan," the elf said, exasperated. "Your dog."

The sheriff glanced back, and Millie saw a smile crack through the worry on her face.

"He can't help it. He was bred to herd animals," Ryan said, laughing. "Especially with your hair right now. He probably thinks you're a sheep." The smile faltered and Ry called Fyodor to heel, finally allowing Millie to join her.

"Isaiah was a bad person, right?" Ryan asked, looking down at the dead Willard. He looked younger now that he was dead. His 'beard' was still pathetically patchy and the acne on his cheeks and chin was still angry and red even in death. One could easily forget what he and his brothers did for a living.

"He stole food, horses and anything he could sell for whiskey. He was not a good person," Millie said, pulling her gloves back on. She wouldn't lose sleep over a Willard, but Ryan was made of better stuff. If Millie could help her friend's conscience, she would.

"Did he deserve to die?" That was a different question entirely. "Maybe not yet. A smarter man would have left us alone."

"You don't think he did?" Ryan asked, raising her eyebrows. "You've told me what the Willards do to farms."

Nothing survived when the Willards visited a farm. Animal that weren't mounts or packhorses were slaughtered for meat. Food was stolen and crops were set alight. If the farmers were lucky, they were killed before the fire was set. If they weren't, the Willards just locked them inside the home. It wasn't the worst outfit Millie had seen operate, but it was needlessly cruel.

"You're right, he deserved to die." Millie nudged the body with her foot. "We could hang him up by Oak Creek. It'd be kinder than leaving him to the animals." Sooner or later, the other Willards would come looking for their idiot younger brother. It would be best if they found him far from Millie's corner of the frontier. There were plenty of people who'd shoot a Willard given half a chance. The sheriff and deputy of a tiny town in the badlands wouldn't even make the list of suspects.

"You okay?" Millie asked. Usually condemning a kid to death would elicit an argument, but today Ryan just looked thoughtful. Millie nudged her with an elbow, jolting the human from her fugue.

"Sorry, the dragon shook me up," Ryan admitted, running her fingers through the tail of her braid. "It had to be the blue cow from the canyons. Nothing else out here is that big. Why did she come so far out this way?"

Millie looked up at the western horizon. The sea of grass and shrub was beautiful this time of year, but the badlands beyond were a tangle of canyons and dusty mesas. That was a good question. Why *had* the Blue come so far out of her usual hunting grounds?

"Did you see the stamp on those ammo crates?" Ryan asked, changing the topic to something much worse than dragons. Millie scowled and crouched by the body, checking it over for anything useful.

"Yes," she said through her teeth, focusing on the body. The Willard kid had a flask of rotgut whiskey Millie tossed aside, some bullets that she pocketed. What had he planned to do with all those horses? And where had he left his own? There wasn't a town nearby, and Isaiah's boots wouldn't have survived travelling from Plainfield on foot.

"Are you sure?" Ryan asked, crouching next to her, shoulder bumping into Millie's as she checked Isaiah's revolver. "You didn't plan this specifically to rob *him*, did you?" She asked in a low voice.

"Sure didn't." Ryan was unconvinced, and Millie couldn't blame her.

"Millie—"

"No, I did *not* plan to steal from Rousseau," she snapped. "I didn't know who owned the crates and it wouldn't have mattered! We needed bullets, or we'd starve. I took the best opportunity we and now I feel sick knowing where they came from." She closed her eyes and sighed, pressing her thumb to her forehead. She'd kept her temper through a dragon attack, a train crash, and a Willard. But just a mention of Fred Rousseau and she lost it.

"I'm sorry," Millie mumbled. Ryan didn't deserve that.

"I wanted to make sure," Ryan said, pulling the elf into a gentle hug. "We'll burn the crates once we get home. You won't have to see them for long."

Millie leaned into the hug, resting a hand on Ryan's arm. The idea of watching Fred's insignia go up in flames helped. Ryan always knew what to say to make things better.

"I keep thinking I'm over everything, then I see his damn initials and realise I'm not. Is that how you feel like that about..." Millie trailed off and tilted her head back to the burning train wreck.

"A bit," Ryan said. She glanced back at the tangle of steel that had once been the famed Blue Bullet. "All the time, actually."

They stayed like that for a while.

"Let's put Isaiah into the fire," Millie said. "He might have deserved to die, but it'll be kinder to his family to find bones instead of buzzards."

3

GOLDMAN NATIONAL BANK

GOLDMAN NATIONAL BANK WASN'T truly national, not yet. However, the average client looking for somewhere safe to keep their money wouldn't know that. A fact the eponymous Mister Gilbert Goldman planned on keeping quiet for now. If all went well—and it had no reason not to—Goldman National Bank would be true to its name within five years.

Gilbert had cut his teeth working for international financiers in Newhaven, where he learned the trade of rubbing two coins together to produce a third. He could have chosen a life of comfort and security by staying the employee of one of the large firms, but why settle for comfort when he had a chance at luxury?

'Settling' only entered Gilbert's vocabulary when it came to two things: lawsuits and land claims.

A grouchy old man waited for him as Gilbert descended from his room that morning.

"When I was your age, I was up with the sunrise," Avrom Goldman said. "Didn't I teach you hard work? I have failed in my singular duty to raise you right." The old man heaved a dramatic sigh and took a sip of his morning coffee. Gilbert saw his father's eyes twinkle behind the pince-nez spectacles.

Avrom knew something.

"Good morning, Father," Gilbert said with a sleepy smirk. He wasn't about to allow the old man the satisfaction of controlling this conversation. "I was entertaining some new clients last night. I *did* tell you not to wait up, didn't I?"

"You absolutely did not," Avrom grumbled, waving away Gilbert's explanation with a wrinkled hand. "And why would I 'wait up'? Some of us still have a work ethic, you know." Avrom scowled behind his glasses, his bushy brows no less formidable than they were when Gilbert was a boy.

"Yes, well," Gilbert drawled, continuing the game as he picked up his own cup of coffee. "Do leave the poor woman alone when she wakes up. She lost her husband in the war. Terrible. She's still very torn up about it." If the Baroness upstairs had any feelings left for her troll of a husband, they certainly hadn't shown up last night. Or earlier that morning.

Avrom threw his hands up, exasperated.

"I raised you better than this. My own boy! My good, brilliant boy, taken advantage of by some rich woman. Again."

Gilbert saw nothing wrong with using his looks to his advantage. A giant of a man, he towered over most of Wyndford's population, including some of the orcs. His dark hair, swarthy complexion, and deep blue eyes earned him plenty of attention from Wyndford's ladies of society, and some of it's men. While his roster of lovers was extensive and well-rumoured, Gilbert never named any of them. To do so would be uncouth, and worse: bad for business.

"I merely offered a generous advance on her investment," Gilbert said with a chuckle. "And I would like to think it was a *mutual* taking of advantage. The war ended eight years ago, after all." Spread in front of the two men was a hearty breakfast: toast, poached eggs, fried potatoes and even a small platter of fresh fruit. Arnaud had outdone himself that morning.

Yes, Gilbert thought as he picked up his fork, life was very good.

"Bah! Discussing your lack of morals can wait," Avrom barked. He slapped the morning newspaper in front of him and slid it across the table to Gilbert. "You should read the paper."

Gilbert, a forkful of eggs almost to his mouth, looked over at his father. Eyebrows raised, Gilbert took his bite of eggs before he pulled the paper over to him. Immediately he frowned, realizing what had put his father into such a mood that morning. He forced his mouthful down, no longer enjoying breakfast.

Right under an article about the upcoming Wyndford World Fair was an engagement announcement. Bianca was getting married.

"Really, *Tata*?" Gilbert asked, looking up at his father. "You want to rub this in my face? Fine. 'Sir Giuseppe Montalto is pleased to announce the engagement of his daughter to Mister Harrold Colfield,' a gargoyle of an old man with thinning hair who she'll immediately cuckold."

"It doesn't say that," Avrom said, jabbing a gnarled finger at the paper. "Did that woman upstairs siphon out those brains of yours?" Gilbert's father barked a little too loudly. "This is important, Gilly boy. With a husband like Colfield she could—"

"A little quieter *Tata*. Please," Gilbert said, wincing at the nickname. The morning had already soured. The lady of the Goldman house had yet to wake up, and she didn't need to hear any of this. Gil skimmed the announcement again. Bianca had managed to snag the richest man in the West, the Colfield Rail manganate. Harrold Colfield, sole owner of half the iron works in Wyndford and a man so hated in the city that he was the only Colfield in the city's history without so much as a street named after him.

"Thank you, *Tata*, for ruining a perfectly good morning," Gilbert said. He stood up from the table, crossed the dining room to the hutch that held expensive liquor in crystal decanters. He pulled out the good whiskey and returned to the table with two glasses. He poured a finger's worth for his father, and then himself.

"*I* didn't ruin it, that Montalto harpy did," Avrom countered.

Bianca and Harrold-cold-hearted-Colfield. Gilbert stared at the glasses in front of him.

"You don't think she'll try to take Sarah back, do you?" He asked, unable to stand the thought. He would fight tooth and nail to keep his daughter, but with access to the Colfield fortune, Bianca could buy out every court in the city with a snap of her lovely fingers.

"A woman with any sense would leave that chapter of her life closed," Avrom said. He harrumphed and patted the table. "Bring that over here, would you, my boy? My knees ache this morning."

The problem with Bianca Montalto, Gilbert knew, was that she was more vindictive than practical. He'd have to walk a very fine line until she got a Colfield whelp on her hip, and forgot about the daughter she'd had dropped off on the Goldman doorstep three years ago.

"Arnaud?" Gilbert called for the family steward. He picked up the glasses of whiskey. He took a long sip of his before carrying the other to his father. "I'll be staying in today with Miss Sarah. Could you please get rid of the woman upstairs?"

The refined half-orc who entered the dining room frowned. His skin was sage green, his well coiffed hair minty, and his grey eyes narrowed at his employer. Arnaud would prefer to remain a chef, but sadly, the family finances didn't allow for a chef *and* steward. Until then, Arnaud ungraciously filled both roles.

"Surely, you are joking." Arnaud was almost as tall as Gilbert and was able to do what few others could: look Gilbert in the eye. "Instead, I will wake Miss Sarah and get her dressed for the day while you deal with the trollop you dragged home. A letter for you, sir." Arnaud held the envelope out to Gilbert, its yellow wax seal facing up. Only one person in Wyndford used yellow wax.

"That sounds like an excellent plan," Gilbert said with a smile. He had overstepped. Sarah would be inconsolable if the half-orc quit their service. Although the man was standoffish with the elder Goldmans, he was smitten with the little girl, and she with him. "Thank you. I will speak with the Baroness shortly."

Arnaud nodded and stepped away to go wake his favourite Goldman. Looking at the letter, Gilbert allowed himself a small sigh before he opened it. Its contents were ink-splotched and scrawled in haphazard loops, barely legible. There was only one person who would bother to send a letter in this state. A neatly written 'translation' underneath the illegible original confirmed as much.

'The Honourable Captain Frederic Albert Rousseau, Hero of the Amelior Union, requests your presence to discuss a delicate financial matter.'

Gilbert looked from the translation back to the original scrawl and was fairly certain that the translation was accurate only in spirit. He could spot at least three curse words that Rousseau's steward had omitted in his translation. Rousseau might be a drunk with a temper, but he was also the holder of the largest account with the Goldman bank.

"I'll need to go out," Gilbert told his father. "Our dear boy Rousseau requires some assurances about his investments."

"Surprised that man hasn't drunk himself blind yet," Avrom said. "Don't let him get his stink on you, Gilly. That man smells like a cheap tavern floor."

Looking at the letter in his hand, Gil wondered if maybe Frederic *had* begun to drink himself blind. It would explain the penmanship. A visit with Rousseau meant drinking with him, which Avrom soundly condemned. Gilbert had already started his day with a whiskey, and socializing was all part of managing difficult customers. Maybe a visit to Frederic would help him forget about the engagement. Once he had finished with Rousseau and washed off the smell of alcohol, Gil would take Sarah out to the zoo, perhaps. She liked seeing the tamed griffins the most.

"Give my apologies to Arnaud, would you?" Gilbert said, heading for the door. "It seems like he'll need to wake the Baroness after all."

Avrom's sharp laughter followed Gil out the door. Poor Arnaud, the man absolutely deserved a raise. If all went well with Rousseau, Gilbert hoped he'd be in a position to give it to him.

Frederic Rousseau's home was grander than Gilbert's. Built in the southern style, it was stuccoed brick with large pillars that supported a two tired porch. The Rousseau mansion stuck out among the gabled, dark brick mansions that dominated Wyndford's Golden District. Gilbert wasn't certain if Rousseau had paid for craftsmen to come up from Beaulieu to build it, or if he'd paid for the house itself to be brought up piece by piece. The story changed depending on what Rousseau was drinking when he told it.

Gilbert hopped down from the cab he had called and adjusted his jacket. One day, when the bank was doing well enough, Gilbert would purchase a tasteful brick home in the Gold district. Sarah would have her own nanny and the best tutors, and Gilbert wouldn't be at the beck and call of a drunkard.

"Mister Goldman," Rousseau's steward greeted him at the door. Lionel had served Rousseau since childhood and was more loyal than most dogs. No doubt it was Lionel who had written the 'translation' on Rousseau's letter. Personally, Gilbert wished he could deal with the steward instead.

"Mister Lionel, a pleasure," Gilbert said, greeting the man with a nod. "Dare I ask what today's emergency is?"

"Ah, the Captain has received some concerning news from Stonecreek, I'm afraid." Ever the professional, Lionel stepped aside to guide Gilbert inside. "He is in his study, please follow me."

"Lead the way." Gilbert buried his surprise under a winning smile. Stonecreek was a mining town experiencing a small silver rush. Gilbert had already invested some of Rousseau's funds in one of the legitimate outfits operating there. Stonecreek wouldn't be the first mining town to 'run dry' earlier than expected... but that shouldn't cause Rousseau to panic like he had when writing that letter. Gilbert knew better than to invest in mines. The real money was made in supplying those mines with equipment.

The outside of the manor was impressive but its interior was sparse. Lionel kept the place in good repair and clean, but there was perhaps half of the furniture that the home used to have when Gilbert first visited it. There remained only a handful of fully furnished rooms after Rousseau's years of gambling, drinking, and poor investments. That had been the bargaining chip Gilbert had used to turn Rousseau from a drinking partner to an investor in his bank. While the investments had begun to return excellent amounts of money, apparently it was not enough to outweigh the costs of the other two vices.

Gilbert's nostrils flared as he caught a whiff of whiskey as they approached Rousseau's study. From the sharpness of the scent, Frederic had chosen the kind of whiskey that got you drunk, rather than the kind you enjoyed.

Lovely.

Lionel knocked on the door and announced Gilbert's arrival.

"Took him long enough!" Whatever the years had taken from Frederic's home, they had taken nothing from his ability to bellow orders. Gilbert wondered if he was drunk enough that he'd forgotten he was no longer in the military, but Gilbert had only seen it happen twice.

Gilbert entered the study with a smile. It was one of the few rooms that retained its original furniture and the only one that had gained more over the years. Hunting trophies hung from the walls displaying Rousseau's greatest prizes: a small green dragon skull with double-point horns hung next to a head of a juvenile griffin with mottled feathers, and opposite was the skull of a swamp wyvern as long as Rousseau's desk.

Over that desk hung a portrait of the man himself, painted during his glory days. The handsome and heroic captain painted there was a stark reminder of what drink could do to a man. Underneath his better self sat the bloated, ruddy-faced man that had once won the south for the Amelior Union, betraying the men who'd raised him. But what made Fred a famous war hero was the capture of an infamous murderer who had terrorized all sides during the war. The Bayou Butcher was a soldier who had gone rogue, slaughtering indiscriminately until Rousseau caught him after the battle of Marigot.

"Gil, good to see you." Frederic said, lifting his glass up in greeting. It was half full and sloshed over the rim, falling onto the morning paper spread out on his desk. Frederic didn't seem to notice. "So-" He belched and had to pound his chest with a fist before he could continue. "Sorry about that harpy, saw the announcement in the paper."

Gilbert felt his smile calcify at its edges. This morning would get much better if everyone stopped mentioning Bianca's engagement.

"Old history," he said, waving it off. Gil joined Frederic at his desk, sitting in a comfortable chair whose velvet was balding. Just like Bianca's new fiancé. "Colfield is a good match for her, and past the age of most bachelors." He hoped the two had a long marriage and made each other miserable for every second of it.

"Not like you, eh Gil?" Frederic said, pulling a glass from his desk to pour Gilbert a glass. "Got plenty of time to find a wife who'll be willing to marry a Carpenter." Gil's smile grew dangerously brittle. It was early for Fred to be at the 'discuss religion' level of drunk.

"Luckily, women are allowed to follow the old faith of their own volition. Besides, I'm still young. I have plenty of time to find a match," Gil said, not rising to the bait. "Have you found someone? Is that what the note was about?"

Fred's face darkened at the question, and he shoved the glass at Gilbert. The whiskey in it sloshed over the side, landing on the mush-stained desk. Rousseau had plenty of lovers, though there were always rumours about the ones who disappeared. Not everyone could manage a man like Rousseau, though the current elf Gilbert had seen about seemed to be genuinely interested in the man. What was her name? Cygne? It started with a 'C'.

"Have you ever met a woman that makes all others pale in comparison?" Rousseau asked, his voice clearing of the mushy slur it held a moment before.

Gilbert thought about Bianca. There had been a time that he thought she was the sun itself. He'd been an idiot.

"You lost someone?" Gil asked instead. Rousseau would talk about the war, but he never talked about the things he'd lost. At least, he hadn't until now. What had happened in Stonecreek to prompt all of this?

"The best woman I've ever known," Frederic said, sagging back into his chair. He looked genuinely distraught. His eyes welled up, and the man had to clear his throat before he could continue. "I gave her everything, but the Butcher took her. I've tried, you know. Being a Hero of the Union meant there were plenty of offers. But..." he trailed off, staring into his glass. "There was only ever one of her."

"Good God, Frederic. I'm sorry. I didn't know," Gil said, heart dropping. No wonder Rousseau's life had fallen apart.

"We never found her. Not even a trace." Fred blinked rapidly and scrubbed the heel of his palm against his eyes. He shook himself, and the glassiness in his eyes returned. "No, the letter had nothing to do with any of that. Stonecreek," he said, reminding himself. "The train, that new blue one," he took a fortifying gulp of whiskey. "It never arrived. I had a shipment on that train. One you insured."

Fred leaned forward, resting his elbows on the whiskey-wet newspaper. It smelled sharp, with less peat than Gilbert preferred, but Frederic never drank for the taste.

"I can't afford to lose that shipment, Gil."

"If it's insured, you won't," Gilbert said. Something had Rousseau rattled. "If they haven't found the shipment when they find the train, we can start the process to reimburse you. You'll have the money in a month."

"I don't have a month, Goldman." Fred rubbed at his bleary eyes. "I need that shipment delivered or I need my money to refund the buyer. And I need it now."

Gil took another sip of whiskey and swished it over his tongue as he thought. When he'd set up Rousseau with the armoury company, he'd warned Fred about orders that seemed too good to be true.

"I'll need time to free up the funds, Frederic," Gilbert said carefully.

"Then you'd better go find out what happened to my cargo," Rousseau snarled. "These are not the kind of men to wait on money."

One day, Gilbert thought, he would punch Frederic in the face and enjoy it very much. But right now, he needed the man's name to attract other investors to the bank. So he smiled and tipped his glass of mediocre whiskey at the has-been war hero.

"Of course," Gilbert said. "I have a friend who's a detective with the Strattons. We'll find that cargo and make sure it reaches where it was headed."

Frederic downed the rest of his whiskey and leaned back, his chair creaking under the weight. The man could be both jolly or mean, but what kept Gilbert on his toes was how Rousseau could flip between being too drunk to stand straight and being clear-headed enough to see through bullshit with ease.

"Thank you for the drink, Frederic. I'll go get started on retrieving your goods." In God's name, he was a banker, not a merchant. He didn't need to go running after lost cargo. The moment the bank had more clients, Gil could refuse these ridiculous demands. "Would you like me to find you a wife while I'm out there?" he joked. It was always best to leave Rousseau in a good mood, or he would stew on any perceived slight until he erupted.

"On the frontier?" Frederic drawled. "Find your own out there. It's full of Wyndford's rejects." He belched again and waved Gilbert toward the door. "Lionel has the shipment information."

4

FAMILY TIES

THE FOUR BANDITS RESTED at a makeshift camp, using a weather-beaten hunter's cabin for shelter. The rescued horses grazed nearby. Millie would have been happy to linger at the camp, checking over the horses and enjoying the fresh air, but the wagon full of stolen ammunition wouldn't haul itself back to town.

After a nap and strong coffee, Millie packed up her gear and set out on her mule.

Sweetpea and Ryan would bring the wagon back to town, Annie would herd the horses to her ranch where they'd be safe, and Millie was to go find Grannie Whitewing and the rest of the Ghost Eye Clan.

Her argument to return to town first had been ignored, and Millie had found herself out-voted. She sulked as she rode through scrub and grass toward where the clan had last camped. Norbert, her pale grey mule, swivelled his giant ears back as she complained to him about how unfair it all was. Norbert was nowhere near as fast as Max the mustang, but he was a much better listener.

The closer they got to the encampment; the grouchier Millie got. The fresh sutures on her back tugged with each rock of Norbert's saddle and she could feel where the cotton of her shirt stick to them as they oozed.

If Millie could sneak into the Ghost Eye camp to see Grannie, she would. In fact, she had on one occasion and the whole camp had raised hell over it. Grannie was the best healer in the West, and Millie suspected she was the best in the entire Union.

She spotted the smoke from the camp's cook fires first, then the sooty tips of the tipis that poked above the grass. Catching the sound of grass rustling ahead, Millie and Norbert both perked an ear in the direction of the sound.

Norbert reacted first, stomping one hoof against the ground and snorting his annoyance at his walk being interrupted.

A white wolf, its fur tipped tawny brown, trotted out of the grass onto the path, pale eyes fixed on Millie as it lifted its snout to sniff at the air. Millie leaned against the horn of her saddle, unimpressed.

"Do I really need an escort?" She asked the wolf. She didn't bother looking around for the rest of the pack. There wasn't one. "Eyota, right? I snuck in *one time*. Years ago."

The wolf shifted into the shape of an elf, one that was tall and broad with the same pale hair the wolf had. Their pale grey eyes narrowed at Millie. Their skin was the same deep tan as other elves native to the land, which meant they didn't have to deal with the hell that was sunburned ears.

"How do you know it is me every time?" Eyota asked, crossing their arms over their chest. "Answer my question, then I'll answer yours."

"I asked mine first," Millie pointed out. She watched as Eyota's ears flicked down and back, giving away the other elf's annoyance.

"Yes, but you are hardly trustworthy, Mildred Berry," Eyota countered.

Norbert snorted again and stepped forward to walk around the elf that stood in his way. Millie held up her hands in a gesture to say both 'you got me' and to show she wasn't the one telling Norbert where to go.

"Well, guess I'll settle for having an escort then," Millie said with a dramatic sigh. Norbert reinforced her decision with a decisive flick of his overlong ear. That was another thing the fluffy mule had that Max didn't: loyalty. Also, really long ears that were made of the softest fuzz the world had ever known.

Eyota frowned, turning to watch Millie as Norbert passed them. Then, with an annoyed grunt, they turned and trotted past Norbert to lead the way.

"Grannie send you?" Millie asked.

"She dreamed you coming," Eyota said over their shoulder. "You're lucky you caught us. Tomorrow we move camp." They paused and glanced back at Millie with narrowed eyes again.

"What?" Millie asked, squinting back. "Did I offend someone by accident again? I make a point to only do that once per social taboo that no one ever tells me about until I break them."

Eyota sighed and turned back to the path, shaking their head.

"Grannie has been waiting for you to visit all summer. You make her sad by staying away so long," they said. "But the moment you are hurt, you arrive like a child with a bloody knee."

Millie squeezed her eyes shut and pinched the bridge of her nose. She hadn't even gotten to camp yet and the guilt had already begun. One day, she was going to drag Annie or Sweetpea along to show them why she was always reluctant to visit the clan. Actually, not Annie, Millie realised. The other elf would enjoy it far too much and would be positively gleeful if she got to watch Millie get treated like this.

"You're right," Millie said, rubbing at her aching shoulder. Some arguments weren't worth having. "I should have visited more, but we didn't get much rain this year. We needed to hunt more than usual, and that's my job back home."

"I thought your job was being a deputy sheriff."

"We can have more than one role, Medicine-person and clan-translator Eyota," Millie grumbled. The other elf flicked their ears in annoyance.

"Apprentice is the right word," Eyota corrected, though their tone was grudging rather than pleased. "Apprentice Medicine Person. I have yet to complete the rites required to become one." They turned to glare at Millie. "They are secret rites. Do not ask about them."

Millie lifted her hand up in confused defence. "I didn't, though?"

"Good. Don't."

Eyota was more combative than usual. Maybe they didn't want to escort Millie into camp, either. Next time, Millie would bring Sweetpea and let the arroyan woman charm the moccasins off Eyota and the clan while Millie sat Grannie down to sort out some expectations about her visits. Also, about the reason behind her visits. She was hardly there to steal secret rites about magic that she couldn't learn to do anyways. Magic fizzled around her. It was just how things were.

As they reached the edge of the encampment, a few Ghost Eye adults looked up from their tasks. The women were scraping hides while some men were repairing a tipi, the poles erected by the cover spread out over the grass as they patched where the hides had worn thin. To Millie's surprise, a small group of Osaugan traders were set up at the edge of camp. Their colourful shirts stood out against the familiar tan of the buckskin worn by the clan, and they wore their hair in braided mohawks instead of the twin braids that were common on the plains. What surprised Millie the most, however, was that the Osauga were human. As far as she'd known, the Ghost Eye clan didn't trade with them.

Millie lifted a hand to wave a greeting, but Eyota reached out and smacked it down. They shot her a warning glare that suggested greeting the humans was not allowed. More rules that no one told her.

"Auntie Berry! Auntie Berry," a little boy called out from the downed tipi, hurrying over. Eyota's younger brother had grown since Millie's last visit. Back then, he had been shorter than her waist. Now, he was at least an inch and a half taller. "How long are you staying?"

"That's 'Deputy Berry'," Eyota corrected. "She's not an Auntie."

Millie grinned at Eyota. "Oh, but I think I graduated to being one, right, Hotan?" The boy beamed, excited to have an ally. His sibling was always so serious, teasing them a little was practically required. Millie crouched and gave Hotan a careful hug, before whispering that she'd bring treats next time she visited if he kept calling her Auntie.

"Auntie!" Hotan agreed, easily bribed. Eyota glared at their little brother and chastised him in their language. Her knowledge of the Ghost Eye language was still fragmented, but she caught a familiar word that they liked to use for her. It meant 'Bad witch'. Hotan had his own opinion, however, and seemed to relish whatever Eyota said. His grin only grew wider.

"I'd better not keep Grannie waiting. Hotan, you take good care of Norbert, alright?" She said, interrupting the argument.

"You bet, Auntie!" The boy nodded, chest puffing out now that he was 'officially' in charge of the beloved mule. Millie pulled her saddle bags off Norbert's back and slung them over shoulder on her uninjured side. The mule soaked up Hotan's attention as if it were sunshine itself. Taking off his bridle so he could graze, she left him in the quite capable care of the boy.

"You shouldn't encourage him," Eyota muttered as they walked into the camp. While the children of the Clan were happy to see Norbert, their parents and grandparents eyed Millie with concern. As she walked, some left their cook fires to disappear into their tipi, while others greeted her with a small nod. Millie returned the nods and ignored the rest.

It wasn't their fault; she hadn't exactly made the best impression when she'd first met the clan. She'd been half-dead and ended up insulting the clan by disappearing after Grannie had healed her. Worse, she wasn't the powerful medicine woman the clan had expected her to be.

The Ghost Eye people were the spiritual powerhouse of their coalition of nations. Respected for being powerful healers and revered for being 'part spirit', their colourless hair and eyes were seen as physical manifestations of their abilities. So when Millie had shown up, as colourful as clear water, the clan had expected her to be the most powerful healer they had ever seen. They had also expected her to step into the role her father had abandoned decades ago.

Instead, they found out Millie couldn't do magic. She was so unmagical, that standing too close to a mage casting a spell would disrupt it. So far, only Grannie Whitewing had been able to find a way to work around that trait.

The elder herself stood outside her medicine worker's tipi. It was painted with depictions of powerful medicines and the spirits who had gifted those medicines to the people. Dragon and Stormbird chased each other around the peak of the tipi, while Bear and Bison walked the prairie along its base. A circle of six flames announced that the Ghost Eye belonged to the Council of Six Fires, the nation that overlapped with west Amelior.

"Mildred!" Grannie exclaimed with a warm smile. Although the Medicine Woman kept her hands clasped in front of her, her presence radiated out and enveloped Millie. Just being near the old woman was comforting. She was the only one who didn't treat Millie like a pariah. Grannie's hair was as pale as Millie's own, her skin nearly as translucent, only instead of lilac, Grannie's eyes were a grey that seemed to change depths each time you looked at her. Today they were the colour of woodsmoke. "You've hurt yourself again! Come in, come in, I have the stew ready for after I fix you up."

"Sorry," Millie said on reflex. "I should visit more often." She pointedly ignored the smug glance Eyota shot her way.

The apprentice pulled the tipi's flap aside for the two to enter, and Grannie waved them away as Millie ducked inside. The smell of fresh bison stew mixed with the scent of drying smokegrass braids greeted her. Millie's belly rumbled. It had been a while since she'd had a real meal. A bison pelt was laid out as a sickbed for those who needed Grannie's healing.

"Eyota can be so stiff in their opinions," Grannie said, and for all Millie knew, she already knew what her apprentice had said on the walk into the camp. The woman seemed to be the first to know of anything, no matter how insignificant. "Like one of those new train tracks, hmm?" Grannie said, her eyes catching the light of her cookfire and gleaming bright.

Millie, trapped by those gleaming eyes, managed to clear her throat. There was no sense in lying to a woman who had spirits whisper your secrets to her, but that didn't mean Millie would give her Elder the satisfaction of watching her squirm. She was pretty sure where Grannie was going with this, but not why.

"Oh?" she asked, hating that the medicine woman outplayed her in every conversation they had. "Tracks can still bend."

Grannie laughed, and Millie knew she'd made a mistake.

"Exactly! They can bend under the fire of a dragon, hm?" Grannie said, her smile widening until her face was all crinkled up in amusement. Millie's ears drooped, and despite being immune to Eyota's disappointment, found herself feeling like a little girl who was caught stealing. It was an uncomfortably familiar feeling. Not only was she caught, but she'd walked right into Grannie's trap.

Dammit.

"Dragonfire would definitely be hot enough," Millie agreed, unsure if further judgement was coming. Was Grannie letting Millie know that she knew about the train? Or would she start telling a story that had a lesson buried in it? Millie hoped not. She always seemed to get those lessons wrong.

"Speaking of dragons," the younger elf said in a bid to change the topic. "Do you know why the big blue has been so far out of her territory lately?"

"The same reason you were on that train, Mildred Berry," Grannie said. "She is hungry and there are bigger things than her that are just as hungry. Now, have some tea before I take a look at what you did to your back," Grannie said, gesturing at the pot that hung over the cookfire.

Knowing better than to argue with the elder, Millie set down her saddlebags and sat next to the fire with a pained grunt. The thin cotton of her shirt stuck to her back where the blood had dried, but the discomfort was minor compared to having Sweetpea stick her fingers in there to get the shrapnel out.

Millie poured two cups of the astringent tea and held the first out to the medicine woman. "You're not going to tell me I did the wrong thing?" she asked, unable to hold herself back any longer. "About the train?"

"Why? Would you listen to me?" Grannie asked with a laugh, easing herself to the ground next to Millie. From her close proximity, Millie could hear the elder's joints creak and she winced in sympathy. "Your people were going hungry, and I've seen you try to use a bow."

Millie made a face, her ears dropping low and getting hot. Instead of arguing, she blew the steam from her tea and took a sip.

"Oh, I know it's because of your shoulder," Grannie said, tapping the shoulder joint that had never quite healed right. It worked fine... until Millie had to draw a bow. Then it locked or clicked and would pull her aim off upon release. Grannie started to hum as she gathered the medicines she would need to treat Millie's shoulder.

"When you're my age, you'll feel that same ache in your hips and knees."

"I don't expect I'll live as long as you will," Millie said, watching the firelight flicker on the surface of her tea. Grannie reached out and flicked Millie's ear. Reacting on instinct, Millie jerked to the side. The reaction was a mistake. Millie felt the fresh sutures tug sharply, and a few gave way. Fresh blood welled up and slid down her back.

"What was that for?" she asked, pressing a hand to the offended ear.

"Tsk, now you've gone and opened your wound again," Grannie said, clucking her tongue. She motioned at Millie to finish her tea. "You don't expect many things," Grannie continued, "But you will not die as young as you keep thinking you will, Mildred Claire Berry."

Millie was entirely certain that she had never once, in her whole life, muttered her middle name aloud. The only people who had known it were both dead. One day, Millie was going to need to learn how to get spirits to keep their stupid spirit mouths shut.

"Your father was so optimistic, you know," Grannie continued, cradling her own cup to let the heat soak into her gnarled joints. "He might have been named after White Bear, but he always had his head up in the sky, that one. You do not have to force yourself to be his opposite by sticking yours into the dirt."

Millie's ears flattened back against her head. She scowled.

"I didn't get the chance to be optimistic," she reminded Grannie. "Or learn about your ways, your language." Optimism hadn't saved her father from getting shot when she was a kid. "I'm not one of you."

"No, you have not, and you are not," Grannie agreed. She took a tentative sip of her tea to check its temperature. Satisfied, the old woman took another, longer drink.

"But," the medicine woman said, setting aside the tea and taking up a golden griffon feather and braid of smokegrass. "You still found your way back to the family he left. You are still *my* family, Mildred. No matter what anyone else says."

Millie's throat grew tight. She knocked back the rest of the tea to chase down the emotions that threatened to well up. It was bitter and earthy, made from mushrooms and roots that Millie had yet to learn the true names of. A tingle spread down her throat as the tea numbed her nerves, physical and otherwise.

"Sorry your grandniece is a mess," Millie said, staring into the fire. A flame resembling the thick tail of a salamander crawled under a burning log. Squinting, Millie tried to see if there was actually a lizard in the fire, or if it had just been a trick of her eyes.

"Messy people are the ones who are not afraid to do what must be done, Mildred. You should have seen me when I was your age. Being a mess is as much a trait in our family as pale hair."

Lighting a bundle of smokegrass from her fire, Grannie swept the smoke over Millie from head to toe with deft flicks of the griffon feather. Millie closed her eyes, breathing in the sweet smell of the smoke. Her back was already growing numb, the tea doing its work.

But, Grannie said. Her voice was no longer in Millie's ear, but in her mind. You will need to c*ut yourself free of these scars before you can become who you are meant to be.* Millie knew Grannie wasn't talking about the scars that criss-crossed her back, though they might as well be a physical manifestation of the ones she was referring to.

"I need my scars," Millie mumbled. She had meant to say something else. "So I don't forget the lessons I learned to get them."

She could feel Grannie smile. *You learned those lessons in blood. You will not forget.*

Millie sank into sleep, soothed by the scent of smokegrass smudge and medicinal tea. She caught glimpses of the ghostly spirits that arrived, all pale golden white, all with pale eyes that glowed as she greeted them. Bear trudged in to settle by the fire, Eagle swooped down to settle on Grannie's shoulder... Salamander wreathed in ghostly flames as it skittered into the fire where it lay flat against the embers to bask in their heat.

Millie woke herself up with a sneeze. She was still lying on the buffalo pelt and some of its long hairs had tickled her nose. She sat up gingerly. The muscles in her back ached. Instead of the sharp pain she'd had since the train wreck, it felt like an old injury, one that ached with the approach of a storm the way her shoulder did.

"I was wondering if you were going to sleep all day," Eyota said, crouched by the fire. Millie glanced around, spotting Grannie on her own bed, sleeping after the healing rite. Running a hand up her back, Millie felt the smooth skin of a fresh scar where there had been a tangle of stitches and blood.

"How long was I asleep?" Millie asked. Her mouth was dry and tasted like dirt.

"An hour or two, not long," Eyota said, their eyes glowing with the cookfire's reflection. "Grannie said I'm to accompany you back to town. She said you offered the space around the ranch for us to camp at."

"Pretty sure I didn't," Millie said, rubbing the side of her face. She had certainly meant to, but Millie didn't remember actually mentioning that to Grannie. "I mean, I hadn't yet. We rescued some horses from a train crash—"

"You mean you stole them," Eyota corrected, giving Millie a sharp look.

"*Rescued*," Millie said firmly. If they hadn't, the fire would have burnt the poor animals alive. She had *stolen* the bullets but the horses would have been left on the train if the damn thing hadn't caught fire. "Annie can't take care of all of them on her ranch, and you and Grannie have been up my ass about me visiting more. So, this way everyone gets something they want."

Eyota squinted at Millie, their eyes golden in the campfire light. "Please tell me that is one of your expressions, 'up your ass'."

Ah, right.

"Yes. It means nagging me, but in a rude way," Millie said, feeling her ears get hot. Now that she thought about it, it was a dangerous phrase to use around someone who might take it literally. "Not that Grannie was rude, the expression is rude," she quickly corrected. Eyota was militantly protective of the

Elder, and Millie was too tired to get into more of an argument than she was already stuck in.

"Plus," Millie said, accepting the bowl of stew that Eyota passed her. "This way Grannie can visit the girls." And maybe Sweetpea could learn some basic healing magic, if Grannie would be willing to share it, though that was not a discussion to have with Eyota.

"How old are your girls now?" Eyota asked. "Three?"

"Four," Millie said. "Expect them to get into everything you have. I have yet to learn a knot that they can't undo." She blew the steam from her stew and tried not to think too hard about how long she had been away from her daughters. The answer was 'too long'. It was always too long.

"Four already," Eyota said. "Is that phrase appropriate to use around your daughters?"

Millie glared at them. "'Up my ass'? Absolutely not."

The apprentice's lips tugged up on one side, into a rare smile.

"Eyota, don't you dare say that around them," Millie said. Their smile grew. "*I mean it.*"

"Sure thing 'Auntie'," Eyota said, looking punchably smug. "Don't get 'up my ass' about it."

5

JEBEDIAH WILLARD

JEBEDIAH WILLARD HAD WAITED a full day for Isaiah to return to camp, but when his brother's horse came back alone, Jeb knew something was wrong. Every damn thing was going wrong. It was bad enough the damn train they'd set up to ambush didn't arrive, but Isaiah not coming back after he'd rode out to find out what happened made Jebediah's molars ache.

He turned and spat into the grass. His molars only hurt when bad things were afoot.

"He could've forgot to hobble his horse again," Elijah said. The second eldest Willard was hunched by their little campfire, roasting a scrub dragonet he'd caught earlier. The fat little things were as common as grouse out in the badlands, and there was good eating on them if you knew how to cut out the poison sacs in their belly.

"Naw," Jeb said, rubbing his jaw through his beard. "Something doesn't feel right about this. Di said the train's arrival was yesterday."

"Maybe someone else got to it first," the lone Willard sister said. Josiah was the only one brave enough to suggest that in front of Jeb. Anyone else he'd cuff upside the head, but he didn't hit ladies unless they hit him first. Jeb glared at his sister, but she didn't back down.

"You know Di's gotta eat, Jeb," Josie said around her pipe. "She sold that train manifest to anyone who had a way to pay her. Nothin' wrong on her part, Di's a smart woman. I'd do the same." Her sharp grey eyes settled on Jeb's jaw.

"Your teeth hurt?" Josie asked.

"His teeth always hurt," Elijah said from the fire.

"They only hurt when something bad's going on," Jeb said. "Something happened. If it was one of you, Isaiah'd already be saddled and ready to go."

"Yeah," the fourth Willard said. Zachariah had been quiet until now, holding the reins of Isaiah's horse. Jeb nodded in his direction. If Zach agreed, they'd be going. Jeb might be the eldest, and the leader, but he and his siblings trusted Zach's gut more than they trusted Jeb's teeth. "He would. Might be he lost his horse, but it'll be faster riding out to him than waiting for his sorry ass to walk himself back here."

Josie sighed, but it was one of resignation.

"Isaiah's an idiot," she said. "But you're right, he'd be out looking for any of us. C'mon Eli. You can eat that dirt turkey in the saddle."

"If he forgot about his horse... I'll be fixing to punch him," Eli grumbled. But he stood and pulled the roast carcass from the fire before kicking dirt over the embers.

"And ain't no-one here will get in your way if he has," Jeb said. "But if my teeth are right, it's someone else you'll be punching."

While the others packed up camp, Jeb took a last look at the ambush site they had laid out. It had been perfect: a pile of scrap wood soaked with oil and cloth built up on the tracks, ready to become a bonfire large and bright enough to force the train to stop. Once it did, Jeb, Eli and Zach would herd the guards off the train while Josie and Isaiah unloaded the horses and bullets. No witnesses, no survivors, pure profit. Enough so that he could finally tell Di she could retire from working at that damn saloon.

But no train showed up. Now Isaiah was missing, and Jeb's teeth hadn't stopped hurting since the night before. Jeb hoped that his idiot brother was just stuck on foot. The problem was, Jeb's teeth never bothered him near this bad any other time Isaiah'd lost his horse.

"Ready?" Zach asked, breaking Jeb's train of thought. "We'll find him Jeb. Don't you worry."

Jeb nodded and clapped his brother's shoulder in thanks. Who could you trust in this hard world, if not family? Even if some of your family was lazy or stupid. They'd pull through when it came time. They always had.

"I hope I'm wrong," Jeb admitted. "Let's go find that idiot."

They followed the train tracks east, passing through the edge of the badlands where the scrub outgrew the prairie grasses and where the rich black dirt became bleached and dusty by the sun. It was there that they first saw the smoke that smeared the horizon like God himself had reached up with a dirty thumb to wipe it against the sky.

"That ain't wood smoke," Josie said, sniffing the air. She was right, but Jeb didn't feel like talking. His teeth were only getting worse, and he clenched them together to keep from wiggling his jaw back and forth. Ma always said they'd hurt until he found the source of what went bad, and she was right. He needed to find that train and see what Isaiah had gotten himself into.

They passed the first piece of the train not long after. It'd been the locomotive's smokestack, torn off and its paint all bubbled and blackened. The edges of the plate it was riveted to were curled and sharp, as though a giant can opener had cut it free.

"Well," Eli said, guiding his horse around the piece of wreck. "If someone was able to do *that*, I'm fine with letting' them get the train first."

Jeb knew any of his siblings except Isaiah would have turned around the moment they found that smokestack. They'd have gathered the rest of the family and returned in numbers. But Isaiah was so certain he was a man, that his plans were successful because of his skill and bravado... and not at all because of how the rest of the family bailed him out when those plans of his failed. And they always failed.

Instead of answering, Jeb kicked his horse into a gallop, following the tracks straight to the main wreckage of the train.

It was horrific. The tracks had buckled and curled, bent by the same massive force that had sent the smoke stack flying hundreds of yards through the air. All that remained of the locomotive itself was the very base of it, twisted and scorched. The last time Jeb had seen any destruction like this had been during the end of the war.

There were no signs of life. No horses, no vultures feeding on the corpses of guards. Whoever had been driving the locomotive wouldn't have a corpse left to eat, but surely there had been others. West-Colfield Rail liked to brag about how many guards they had on each trip, protecting the train from men like Jeb.

"Isaiah?" Jeb bellowed, guiding his horse around the debris field. His teeth were unbearable now. "Isaiah, if you're playing, I'm gonna knock out all those pretty teeth of yours!" The threat did nothing. No idiot staggered out of the smoking wreckage with a dumbass smile on his face, hands held up as he laughed at his idea of a joke.

The rest of the Willards followed Jeb, silent. There were no more suggested explanations, and Jeb suddenly wished he had been wrong. But his teeth were never wrong, not when they hurt this bad.

"There."

It was difficult to see at first, half buried under a collapsed box car. Easy to miss if you didn't know what to look for. The burnt remains of a boot stuck out from under charred beams. Jeb's teeth stopped hurting the moment he spotted it. Jeb flung himself off his horse and grabbed one of the beams to lever it off the body. His gloves sizzled as the beam crumbled, exposing the glowing ember still inside of it.

"Fuck. Jeb, let me help." Eli was at his side, and Zach wasn't far behind.

The fire had gotten most of him, but the mismatched boots made the youngest Willard easy to identify. Pulling what was left free, Jeb stared down at the skeletal remains. A neat-as-you-please hole had been punched through Isaiah's skull, right between his eyes. Whoever had killed Isaiah had tossed him into the fire like he'd been nothing but trash.

Jeb felt someone put a hand on his back, but the sensation was far away. Like it belonged to an echo of himself.

"I should've gone," Eli said quietly. "I should've told him to stay put."

"He wouldn't've listened, Eli. You know that." Zach pulled Eli into a tight hug, his eyes red and watering.

"Jeb?" The question was still far away, but the gentle pat on his back helped bring his body back into place in the world. As the world snapped back into place, it knocked the breath from Jeb and he doubled over, sucking down air even though it was acrid and still thick with the smell of burnt body.

"Jeb?" They were all looking at him now. He could feel their eyes on him.

He'd made Ma a promise when she died. He'd look after their family, keep them fed and safe. And ever since then, he had. Five years of the Willard Boys living off the land. But now he'd fucked up. He'd let Isaiah go off and get himself killed.

"We bury him," Jeb said, spitting the taste of bile from his mouth. "We do the rites, send him off. Then we go find every other bastard who knew about this train." He sniffed and straightened, wiping his mouth on the back of his sleeve.

"Then?" Josie asked. She knew what he was going to say, but she also knew they'd all need to hear it out loud. Josie was as smart as Ma, and could read the boys nearly as well.

"Then we make an example," Jeb said. "Make sure anyone on this side of Wyndford thinks twice about raising a finger against any Willard. Hell, make anyone in Amelior think twice."

He looked up, meeting the eyes of his brothers. They nodded.

"Good," Jeb said, his gaze drifting back to his brother's corpse. "Whoever did this will wish their own mama had never been born."

6

— · —

HAL STRATTON

THE FIRST THING GILBERT did when he got home was rinse out the taste of Rousseau's bad whiskey with a mouthful of the good stuff. But only a mouthful. Seeing the former captain's deteriorating condition was a powerful deterrent against falling into a similar habit. Rousseau was hardly the first soldier to turn to drink after the war, but seeing the Hero of the Union grow cruel and petulant the more he drank... it was almost enough to turn a man to abstain completely.

"You stink," Avrom said, not bothering to look up from the ledger he'd spread out on the table where the newspaper had been. "Do they not bathe in the army?"

Gilbert stared at the whiskey for a moment longer than he meant to. He put it away and reached for the coffee instead. Pouring a strong cup for himself, Gil sat across from his father and surreptitiously sniffed the lapel of his suit jacket.

Damn. He *did* stink. The fine wool of his suit had absorbed the smell of Rousseau's bad whiskey. It would take a while to air it out. Gilbert wanted to go change, but he wasn't certain if the Baroness had left or not. Best not to risk an uncomfortable encounter until he'd had a chance to talk with Arnaud. Gilbert made a mental note to pay him a bonus this month. The man deserved it regardless, but if the Steward had handled the woman upstairs that had been above and beyond his duty. Still, better Arnaud, who had poor manners than Gilbert's father, who had none at all.

"We have a problem with the Bank, *Tata*," Gilbert said, blowing the steam from his cup. The enchanted carafe might have been a luxury, but it was one that paid off every time he poured from it and received coffee as hot as it'd been when it was freshly made.

"Really?" Avrom asked, looking over his pince-nez spectacles at Gilbert. "I think you have an investor problem. The bank isn't the one drinking its money away."

"We have an investor who is *causing* a bank problem," Gilbert snapped. He sighed and ran a hand through his hair. He hadn't meant to be that sharp, but men like Fred always followed up on their threats. "We insured a shipment of Rousseau's from Wyndford to Stonecreek—"

"Where's that?" Avrom asked, turning back to the ledger. He squinted at a line of sums. "A hole in the ground somewhere?"

"Technically, yes. Several holes in the ground. There's a silver mine." He was getting derailed by his father's tangent. Gil rubbed a hand over his face to scrub off the frustration Rousseau caused. It didn't work. "Regardless, the shipment didn't arrive. The whole damn train didn't arrive, and he's already drunk and refuses to wait until we can get the funds free to reimburse him." Gil sipped his coffee, expecting his father to continue asking about the mine.

Avrom carefully closed the bank ledger and removed his spectacles to rub at the bridge of his prominent nose. The pince-nez always left deep red indentations there, but Avrom rarely seemed bothered by it.

"That man," Avrom muttered. "Is a menace. He can't wait for his investments to grow, can't wait for insurance payments, can't wait for a natural death, so he's drinking himself there early." The old man rested his spectacles on the ledger and slid his coffee cup over to Gilbert for a top up.

"Anyone else and I'd be able to convince them to wait until we freed up the funds they need," Gilbert said. But his father was right. Rousseau was a menace when he was drunk. He'd be as likely to shoot Gilbert in the street as he would be to go to the courts and sue every last penny out of the Goldman bank and home. Gilbert had worked too hard to let some drunk bastard take his earnings and put his family out on the street.

"Maybe he'll choke on his vomit," Avrom suggested. "But while God is good, miracles don't happen every day."

"I'm going to hire the Stratton Agency," Gilbert said. He poured his father more coffee and passed the cup back, trying not to notice how gnarled his father's hands had gotten. Avrom was still as sharp as ever and was in remarkable health for a man his age, but how long would he last if Rousseau put them out of their home? No. Gilbert couldn't allow it.

"Do you remember Hal?" Gil asked. "He's one of them now."

"The Priest?" Avrom said, bushy eyebrows lifting in surprise. "Hah! A better fit for him, I think. He'll be better at digging up secrets than he was at burying them. I remember when you two blackmailed your headmaster." Avrom laughed, slapping the table with a gnarled hand. "I was never prouder of you than I was when you told me how you'd gotten those marks."

Gilbert's lips twitched up at the memory of him and Hal discovering the torrid and completely illicit affair their headmaster was having with the chaplain of the school's church. Both he and Hal received top marks that year, and every year after.

"Well, if you can get Halbert to help you, I'm certain you'll find those idiot's crates."

"It'll be good to see him again," Gilbert admitted, finally letting himself relax. It had been years, "And I think it's time to pick up old bad habits. Unfortunately, first we'll need to go out and find out what happened to that damn train."

Avrom choked on his sip of coffee, nearly spitting it out as he struggled to contain his laughter.

"You? Gilly, my boy, you've never been outside of a city!" Gilbert frowned, but knew there was no sense in interrupting his father when he got like this. "Most of the Frontier's not even mapped, and you're going to ride out there with your fancy coat and boots and find a missing train?"

"No," Gilbert said. His temper was shorter than it should be, but his father was being ridiculous. He had survived difficult situations before and wasn't rushing out to the Frontier without a solid plan. "I plan to ride out there with my fancy coat and shoes and set up a bank or two, hire locals to find out what happened to the train, and then decide what to do about Rousseau while he's a safe distance away." Gilbert sipped his coffee and arched an eyebrow at his father.

"Hm, that's not a terrible plan," Avrom admitted. "But you make sure Hal keeps you safe out there. If I get a ransom letter for you, I'll tell them they should be paying *me* to take you back!" Gilbert knew an empty threat when he heard one. There was a special kind of comfort in knowing Avrom had plucked him from the streets of Wyndford and taken him in by choice. There was never a question of Avrom's love, even if that love was expressed through sharp quips and long-winded lectures on the importance of compound interest.

The door to the kitchen burst open and a little girl marched out, carefully holding a plate with a messy-looking sandwich on it. Arnaud hurried after her, reaching down to help steady the plate so that the sandwich didn't completely slide apart.

"Papa!" little Sarah Goldman announced, her dark eyes sparkling with pride. "I cooked!"

"Miss Sarah insisted on making you lunch," Arnaud said, his professional expression firmly in place. Gilbert glanced at the clock that hung on the wall and smiled back at his daughter. It was still far too early for lunch, but his little storm cloud of a girl had cooked him something!

Scooting his chair back, Gil reached down and helped her place the plate onto the table in front of him. Scooping her up, he planted a kiss on her cheek and settled her on his knee.

"It looks delicious. Thank you, Miss Sarah," Gilbert said. "Will you help me eat this wonderful lunch?"

Sarah nodded eagerly, then wrinkled her tiny nose.

"Papa, you stink."

The thin hope Gilbert had of Rousseau forgetting the urgency of his request was dashed when the captain sent a letter the next morning with a train ticket enclosed. Worse, it was a second-class ticket, scheduled for the next day. Gilbert allowed himself to feel insulted. A single ticket out to the Frontier where outlaws robbed rich men, and drunks killed anyone they didn't like the look of. While that might technically also happen in Wyndford, Gilbert knew the local villains and what their prices were. God only knew how long it might take to build up relationships with a whole new set of thieves and crooks. It'd take longer than Rousseau was willing to give him, that was certain.

The first thing Gilbert did was exchange the ticket for a pair of first-class seats, leaving one day later. He paid the difference himself, writing Rousseau a note thanking him for the tickets but explaining he had to wait for a Stratton Detective to arrive and would leave the following day. Somehow, it'd been enough to get the bastard to leave Gilbert alone.

Avrom could run the bank in his absence, and Arnaud would care for Sarah. Hal, now Hal Stratton, was meeting them at the train station. Gilbert had spent every free moment either poring over the insurance agreement he'd signed with Rousseau or with his little storm cloud daughter.

Gilbert couldn't afford a vengeful Frederic Rousseau. The insurance agreement was ironclad and had multiple signed copies that stipulated Gilbert had a reasonable time period in which to pay out the compensation. However, some things were more powerful than a legally binding contract, and Fred had access to all of them: high society, government officials, and back-alley leg-breakers.

He tried to push his headache aside as he navigated Wyndford Central station. Gilbert had a plan, and soon he'd have help from a loyal friend. There were worse situations to be in. As soon as Gilbert resolved this mess, Rousseau would find himself dumped as a client. Each investment would be cancelled and paid out and the captain could go bankrupt under his own steam. Gilbert estimated Rousseau would be insolvent before the year was out.

"It's nice to see some people haven't forgotten what a hard day's work means," Avrom said, dodging a pair of porters who were carrying a steamer trunk stacked high with hat boxes and parcels. There was even a small cage with a fur stole in it. The fur barked as it passed them by, startling both Avrom and the little girl perched on Gilbert's hip.

"Papa, what's *that*?" Dressed in a green gingham dress with ruffles, Sarah Goldman finally dropped the sulky air she had been wearing all morning. Little girl curls bounced as she looked from the departing furball up to Gilbert.

"I think it's a puppy, Buttercup," Gilbert said, kissing his daughter's cheek. Soufflé-soft, he made sure to tickle it with his beard. Dark-haired, with a button nose and large eyes framed by long lashes, Sarah certainly looked like her papa, though her eyes were grey instead of blue. Those eyes were the only thing Sarah's mother had given her before dropping this smallest, brightest infant at Gilbert's doorstep three years ago. Gilbert's storm cloud deserved a beautiful life full of smiles, ruffles, and the best tutors so she could talk any ill-intentioned suitors into knots. No, unlike her mother, Sarah would never have to marry a rich old man to support herself.

"Never understood the appeal of those things," Avrom muttered, adjusting his spectacles. They had grown foggy from the steam of the nearby locomotive. The elder Goldman looked every inch the respectable banker today. Dressed in a smart grey suit, blue cravat and with a top hat perched over white hair, "They're no better than loud, fluffy rats."

Gilbert stepped into the space the porters had left in their wake and followed them through the crowd toward his car. With each step, he could feel small hands tighten around him until Sarah couldn't take it anymore.

"Papa, why do *you* have to go?" She asked, eyes far too sad for such a little girl. "Stay here."

"I'll be back before you know it, Buttercup," Gilbert said, pecking her cheek. "I'll be on a train home the moment I finish up my business. Promise you'll be good for *Tata* Avrom."

His little girl, his Sarah. So solemn, so serious as she looked back up at him through her long lashes.

"I promise," she said. Sarah was working very hard on pronouncing her words, but when she was distraught, a wayward 'r' still turned soft. "Papa, you need to promise: don't let a mean dragon hurt you. Or... or I'll be real upset!" Her lower lip trembled, and Gilbert tried not to let her see how hard it was to leave as he tucked a stray curl behind a small ear.

"I promise, storm cloud."

"I'll keep him safe, little lady," a familiar voice added. Gilbert turned to see Hal approaching through the crowd. The dark-skinned man was dressed in a dark blue suit and red wool vest. In one hand, he held a small bouquet of daisies and in the other, a valise. Pinned to his chest was a silver badge announcing that he was a detective with the Stratton Agency. The detective dodged an old woman dressed in mourning black and smiled warmly as he joined them.

"Why, you must be Little Miss Goldman," Hal said, tipping his bowler to Sarah to reveal neatly trimmed coily hair. "Apologies for my tardiness. These are for you." He held the daisies out for her with a small flourish. Sarah took them with a shy smile, hugging the flowers tightly.

Gilbert took the moment to pry Sarah from his hip and passed her to Avrom. For a man who complained so much about aches, Avrom never seemed to mind carrying his granddaughter. Freed, Gilbert smoothed the wool of his black suit and adjusted his tie but couldn't resist bending down to kiss his daughter on the cheek one last time.

Being a Stratton suited Hal more than clergy did. Hal had always been broad of shoulder, but in the last year before attending seminary he'd started standing in a way to make himself smaller: curling his shoulders in and hunching as if that made him less intimidating and more priestly. Now he stood like he once had, shoulders back and an easy smile showing off white teeth against his dark skin.

"Hal, are you sure you don't need to get adopted too?" Avrom asked, as he had many times over the years when Hal joined Gilbert over school breaks. Gilbert realized with a small pang in his chest that he hadn't seen his friend since he'd left for seminary school. That had been before Sarah had been born. "You're a sensible young man, and I could use *one* son who knows the value of a hard day's work."

"Your offer gets more tempting as time goes by, Mister Goldman," Hal said, tipping his bowler hat at Sarah, who smiled into her daisies. Gilbert allowed himself to relax as his daughter's mood improved. "But my father has grown used to complaining about his son who left the Church to join the Strattons. Would you take away that man's lone comfort?"

"You want another son, old man?" Gilbert asked, placing his hand over his heart in feigned insult. Hal would make an excellent brother. As a boy, Gilbert had often hoped that his friend might say yes to the offer. "Am I not enough?"

"You're enough of a *headache*," Avrom barked. "Detective, try not to let my idiot son get into *too* much trouble. You know what he's like. Especially around women."

Hal laughed, and he clapped a hand on Gilbert's back. Audibly. He seemed more amused than the request warranted.

"I'll do my best Sir," Hal said. "Out that far, there isn't much that isn't scaled, furry, or both."

"Are we still talking about the women?" Gilbert asked in mild horror and moderate fascination. He'd heard rumours about harpies. The real kind, with feathers and nicer dispositions than Sarah's mother. Avrom glared at his son and covered one of Sarah's little ears.

"Shall we?" Hal asked and nudged Gilbert with an elbow. "If we miss boarding this train, we'll be walking to Plainfield."

Gilbert said his goodbyes and followed Hal onto the train. He took a moment to peek into a second class car and frowned. He would never have fit into those seats. Rousseau was an asshole for thinking so.

Vindicated in his decision to exchange the tickets, Gil settled on his cushioned first-class seat at the window.

"I appreciate you coming on such short notice," he said as Hal settled in the seat opposite him.

"You only have to ask, Gil," Hal said. The detective set the valise on his knee and rummaged through it, pulling out a copy of the morning's paper. "You and your father have always been good to me. I'm happy to help. Besides, how could I possibly turn down an opportunity to investigate a dragon attack?"

"A what?" Gilbert asked. He blinked, and took the newspaper Hal thrust at him.

The final whistle blew, and Gilbert looked out the window to wave to Avrom and Sarah. As the train pulled away from the station and they disappeared from sight, Gilbert looked at the paper he'd been handed.

"'Majestic Blue Bullet attacked by dragon,'" he read. A few locals looking for their missing brother had stumbled across the wreckage. "Well shit, if a dragon attacked the train, the bullets and dynamite in that shipment would have torn that train apart." Gil pulled his hat off and ran his hand through his hair.

"Maybe," Hal mentioned, lacing his fingers together. "But you said your insurance agreement covers theft and misplacement. I didn't see 'dragon' listed there."

Gil raised his eyebrows, looking up at his friend. "This is true..." he said. "All we need to do is prove the dragon destroyed the shipment and have a court declare it an act of God."

Hal grinned and tipped his head forward.

"Then we can focus on the second half of this case," he said, brown eyes dancing. "If you're sure you want to go through with it. Targeting a war hero is a risky choice."

Gil folded the paper and set it aside for the moment. Reaching into his coat, he pulled out a book bound in yellow.

"You can't be serious," Hal said as soon as he read the title. 'The Hero of Amelior: How Frederic Rousseau Saved the Union.' "The man's own autobiography? You know that it'll just be him building his own mythology. Why bother reading it?"

A slow grin spread over Gilbert's face. "Well, I happen to have a second book I've acquired to compare it to. I want to know what this man is afraid of people finding out."

"Please tell me it's not that horrible trash about the Butcher."

Gilbert pulled the second book from his jacket and waggled it at the detective. It was bound in faded red canvas, with a simple title stamped onto it in black ink. It was already dog-eared, its corners worn pale. 'The Bayou Butcher'. It was absolutely trash, and entirely about the notorious soldier that went insane during the war and killed innocents and enemies alike.

"I found the banned version," Gilbert said, looking at it proudly. He'd managed to track down the last surviving copy in Wyndford, maybe in all of the Union. "Which means that it has something in it that Rousseau doesn't want people to know. Also, it has the naughty parts kept in."

Hal groaned, sinking back into his seat. Without saying another word, he held out a hand for the red book.

"Aha! I thought so," Gilbert said, passing it over.

7

SCORCHED BLUFFS

"MOST OF THE ELDERS think you're a bad witch." Eyota said. Until that moment, Millie had been enjoying the peace of being out on the trail. The prairie grasses swayed, revitalised by long overdue rain. Even the cicadas began their humming song, signalling that the latter half of summer had begun. Then Eyota's statement ruined it.

Millie squinted at the horizon. They'd been on the trail for a few hours, judging by how low the sun sat in the sky. She lifted her gaze, looking for any dark shapes in the sky. Greater Dragons usually hunted at sunup and sunset, but the Blue's behaviour had been erratic lately. Millie didn't want another surprise visit. There were only two equines today and no train, but there were some things in life that you didn't take chances with. Greater Dragons were one of them.

"Mildred, did you hear me?" Eyota asked, turning to look at the sky in case Millie had seen something. Their ears dipped when they realised there was nothing there. No doubt they were going to think this was Millie playing a joke on them, a trick instead of genuine paranoia.

"Yeah." She sighed, reluctantly looking at the other elf instead of keeping an eye on the sky. "I heard you. But it wasn't a question, was it? So, some Elders think I'm a bad person or an evil witch." Millie lifted an eyebrow. What did Eyota expect her to say?

"I thought you would argue, given your nature," Eyota said, ears flicking between checking behind them and remaining upright. It seemed to Millie that her paranoia was catching. "Normally you argue about everything."

Millie groaned, twisting in her saddle to stretch out the tight muscles in her back. Although Grannie's healing was miraculous, she always felt stiff afterwards. Like the newly mended parts needed breaking in to match the rest of her. This conversation felt exactly like her back right now: stiff, awkward and too new to feel right.

Eyota was waiting for an answer to another of their non-questions.

"Fine, I argue a lot. But the Elders can think what they want about me," Millie said, looking Eyota in the eye. They were, unfairly, a good two heads taller than Millie perched on their mare. Norbert wasn't a small mule, but his ears didn't make up the height difference between him and a full-blooded horse.

"I can't do magic, but I have done a lot of things, good and bad. Aside from fucking up a lot of customs I'd never been taught, I've done well by the clan," she said, scanning the trail ahead for any sign of dragons. "These are hardly the first people who have decided I am a 'bad' person, Eyota."

"Was keeping your daughter away from her father doing right by the Band?" Eyota asked. Their voice was neutral, but the question was anything but.

Millie felt her ears get hot, and they snapped down flat against her head. She kicked Norbert into a trot to circle in front and cut Eyota's mare off. Norbert's own long ears pressed back, matching those of his rider.

"I am going to say this once," Millie snarled up at the apprentice. "So, you'd better perk those fucking ears up and pay attention. Fenna is my daughter, and I will raise her how I see fit. Her father died *years ago*. Do you really think she'd have a better life in the Clan where she hears terrible stories about her mother all the time? You think I don't hear them talk when I get into the camp?" It was one thing for her to be called names. But her daughter deserved a better life than that.

"I thought you didn't speak our language?" Eyota stammered, leaning back. Their eyes had gone wide, but Millie was too furious to care. All their posture did was urge the thing in Millie's chest to attack. She bit the inside of her cheek to hold back the instinct that snarled inside of her.

"I know the words for 'bad witch' and 'murderer'," Millie snapped. She took a deep breath and let it out slowly, forcing down the sudden fury back to where it lived at the base of her spine. "My daughters deserve a life growing up together, not split apart because one looks Ghost Eye, and the other doesn't."

The thought of separating her girls twisted in her gut. But what if Fenna would be happier growing up surrounded by people who looked like her? Millie flexed her hands in her gloves, trying to work out her anger. She consciously lifted her ears into a more neutral position, though the scowl stayed put.

"The other girl could learn our customs. She could become Ghost Eye. But if they stay in your town, what will your girls do when they hear about—"

"If you finish that sentence, you will never be welcome in town again," Millie said, staring at Eyota. The world flattened around her, and the cicada song faded into a dull ring in her ears. "You can come with the rest of the Clan to choose the horses at Annie's ranch, but you are not welcome in town until you think about how badly what you were about to say might hurt two four-year-old girls."

Eyota's ears dipped, and Millie knew she'd struck home. She wanted to twist the verbal knife, make Eyota hurt badly enough that they would never ask that question again. She bit back the worst of it.

"They are *four*, Eyota," Millie snapped. "I'll tell them about my sins, but when they are old enough to understand. If you take that chance from them, from me, I will never forgive you. Do you understand?"

The apprentice medicine person opened their mouth, but closed it again, saying nothing. Their lips pressed together into a thin line, and slowly, they nodded.

"I apologize, Mildred. I do not want to see the little girls hurt."

No, Millie thought. *Just me. You just wanted to hurt me.*

"So, we're understood," Millie said, straightening in her saddle. She rubbed Norbert's neck, letting him know he could stand down. "And for the record, I try not to be a bad person anymore. It's not easy." Casting a last dagger of a glare at Eyota, Millie nudged Norbert to resume walking along the trail.

As the thudding in her chest slowed, so too did the ringing in her ears. The cicadas hadn't stopped singing, and the steady buzz was reassuring. They wouldn't be singing if the dragon was around.

"Mildred... stop."

They'd barely gone ten minutes when Eyota spoke again.

Exasperated and tired, Millie turned in her saddle, letting Norbert pick his path forward.

"What?"

"I *am* sorry," Eyota said, nudging their mare ahead to walk alongside Norbert. "I... struggle with some things. Cultural things that aren't part of formal teachings. I didn't understand why you seemed unbothered, or why you never brought Fenna to visit the Clan. I did not mean to question your dedication to Fenna, or your other daughter."

"Rasha," Millie interrupted.

"What?"

"Her name, Eyota. My other daughter's name is Rasha." Millie watched Eyota through half-lidded eyes. The council the Ghost Eyes belonged to welcomed anyone who would learn their ways, but Eyota and others only seemed to care about the girl that looked like them. Rasha was always an afterthought.

Eyota frowned, looking down at the grasses around them, their ears flicking as they thought that correction over.

"Ah," they said after a moment. "You are bothered that Rasha is not wanted, because you were like her when you lived among the settlers. You said your father died young, correct?"

Millie sighed, pinching the bridge of her nose. Eyota almost had it right.

"I never said anything about my father. I'm sure Grannie told you about him," she corrected. "But yes, he died when I was young. But people looked at me strangely and were afraid of me because of how I looked, not because of who I was," Millie said. That came later.

"Because you are half spirit?" Eyota asked. "There are many animals that look like you do. We revere them among the peoples here."

"For the sake of not getting into another argument, let's say I am half spirit and not a normal person who gets too many sunburns," Millie said, ears dipping. She didn't want to get into this again. "Your people revere the spirit people like Grannie, like my father... like me. The settlers think I'm undead or cursed or something." She'd stopped counting how often she was mistaken for a ghost a long time ago.

Eyota snorted, ears flicking upward in amusement.

"That is *stupid*. Undead beings are grey and often fall apart."

"Yes," Millie said. "And generally, they smell terrible, which is why I was always insulted when people asked if I was one." As unkempt as she'd been while living on the streets, Millie had never smelled *that* bad. She was pretty certain she hadn't, anyway. There'd always been corpses around that made her nose wrinkle.

"I am sorry that people thought you looked dead," Eyota said, reaching out to pat Millie's shoulder. The smaller elf allowed it. It had been a long day and there were still a few hours left of riding before they arrived in town. Millie didn't want to spend all of that time arguing, not without having access to coffee.

"When I said that word meant 'bad witch', I believe I misspoke. It means broken, not evil," Eyota said. "People call you a broken witch."

"Well," Millie said reluctantly. "I don't see how that's any better, but I guess it's not wrong."

Slowly, Eyota's questions and apologies percolated through Millie's mind, and she realised why Grannie had sent the apprentice along with Millie instead of arriving later with the entire clan. Eyota wasn't sent to help set up camp at Annie's ranch. They were sent to learn more about the world. To learn how to become more flexible in their thoughts. And Grannie had basically told Millie as much, back in her tipi. 'Eyota was stiff, like a train track'. And what had Millie just caused to get uprooted and twisted out of shape?

Train tracks.

Tilting her head back, Millie let out a small groan. The old woman had outplayed her again.

"Oh, *goddamn it.*"

It had been a series of very long days for Mildred Berry. As she and Eyota saw the first glow of Scorched Bluffs' lanterns emerge from the darkness, a warmth welled up in Millie's chest that made the back of her throat ache.

Scorched Bluffs was a strange town, built and rebuilt, nestled against the titular bluff: a plateau of tan and red rock that once held a silver mine. Now it was held together with multiple spells and struts that the miners put into place. The bluffs themselves blocked the town from the elements and offered shade in the sweltering summer months. Normally, there were small garden plots that grew hardy crops that did well in the dusty soil, but the recent drought had caused all but Sweetpea's succulents to die off.

"It is both smaller and larger than I thought it might be," Eyota said, looking at the ramshackle cabins that served as homes, and the once-proud hotel that still had soot on its bricks from the time Scorched Bluffs earned its name.

"It used to be larger," Millie said. "Not as big as Plainfield, but more homes, more people. More smithies to turn the silver into usable ingots." She motioned at the dull glow of the remaining blacksmith's shop.

"That's Nylah's, an orc. She's one of the first residents who moved here after the fire. In the morning I'll introduce you to everyone, but at this hour most folks will be asleep already." Sleep, something Millie was very much looking forward to.

Eyota nodded, stifling a small yawn of their own.

"We have a few mages, but no healers. I'm sure they'd be happy to teach you a bit of what they know if you're willing to do the same." Millie stifled a yawn, leading the apprentice toward her own shack. She had built it away from the main grouping of buildings, put together from scavenged wood beams and old mining equipment. It was a modest thing, but it had a porch with a bench on it that was perfect to sit outside in the mornings and a patch of scrub grass that Norbert eyed eagerly.

A lantern waited in the window; its wick turned down low to conserve oil. The girls would be asleep by now, but at least someone was there with them.

"I believe I can teach a few things," Eyota said carefully. "Things that aren't as sacred."

Millie nodded, rubbing her eye with the heel of a hand. Spirits, she was tired. It was getting harder to stay awake for days on end with each year she got older. At least she still had a stash of coffee at home.

"Only what you'd feel comfortable sharing," she said, unable to stifle the second yawn. "We can talk about it tomorrow. For now, sleep."

But sleep needed to wait for the horses to be turned out into the small scrub patch, rubbed down after the long ride, and watered. As Millie was carrying Norbert's tack to the porch, the door to the cabin opened.

"Oh! You brought a friend!" Sweetpea whispered, slipping out of the cabin with a swish of skirts. She was surprisingly quiet on her hooves, something that always had Millie curious about how she managed that.

Eyota froze in place, their eyes going wide at the sight of Millie's babysitter.

"Are they alright?" Sweetpea whispered to Millie, her luminous eyes fixed on Eyota.

"Long ride," Millie said, pulling her friend into a hug. "Also, I think you're the first high arroyan they've met."

Sweetpea blinked, opening her eyes even wider, her mouth forming a soft little 'oh'. She gestured at the horns and mouthed 'these?'. Millie, too tired to prolong an already awkward situation, nodded. The horns, the tail, the hooves. The pink skin. It could be a lot if you were used to the earthen tones of other beings.

"I am sorry," Eyota said slowly. "We do not have a word for your people, yet."

"Oh, that's okay," Sweetpea said with a cheerful little giggle. "We have plenty of names for ourselves. But you can call me Sweetpea for now, like the flowers."

"Are the girls asleep?" Millie asked, setting down Norbert's saddle on the porch railing. "They didn't give you or Lyddie any trouble?"

Sweetpea looked at Millie, her mismatched eyes full of reproach.

"Millie, when have your girls *ever* given me a hard time?" She asked. When Millie opened her mouth to answer, Sweetpea interrupted her and pressed a finger to Millie's lips. "Shh, shh, we don't talk about the sugar incident. They're asleep. You two go in and get some rest."

Flashing Eyota a gleaming smile with sharper than usual canines, Sweetpea turned and set off for the General Store and her apartment that was attached to it.

"Is that one always like that?" Eyota asked, following Millie up onto the porch.

"No," Millie said. "Normally she's much perkier. She probably didn't want to scare you any more than she already had." This time it was Millie to put a finger to her own lips, signalling Eyota to be quiet. Opening the cabin door as silently as she could, Millie managed to get a full step inside before two sleepy elves threw themselves at her.

"You two are supposed to be asleep," she said, prying the little ones from her legs long enough to crouch to their height and pull them into a tight hug. Each got a kiss on the cheek, and Millie closed her eyes, breathing in the smell of their hair. They smelled like soap and sleep, and the warmth in Millie's throat returned.

"We were," the little blonde mumbled. Blonde was... an incorrect description. Her hair was white like her mother's, though golden instead of silvered, and her darker skin made it stand out all the more. The second one nodded, sending red curls bouncing against her freckled ears.

"Okay, well," Millie said, "I'm going to join you in a moment, I need to get a bed ready for our guest. They're an..." She looked up at Eyota, lifting an eyebrow. "Auntie isn't the right word," she said, feeling the exhaustion steal words from her mind. "From Grannie's Clan. This is Eyota."

"Cousin," Eyota said, and lifted up a hand in greetings to the two little ones. "Cousin Eyota."

Two sets of sleepy eyes pulled themselves away from their mother to stare up at the new elf in their home. In the light of the lantern, Fenna's eyes shone golden and Rasha's silver. Millie couldn't resist pulling them back into a tight hug at the sight. Her little sun and moon.

"Cousin like Auntie Annie's your cousin?" The redhead mumbled.

"Mhm," Millie said, shepherding her girls back into the cabin. It was simple, but over the years, Millie tried to make it comfortable. A lone bed sat near the wood stove for warmth, the wool blankets and furs the girls had peeled back as they climbed out.

"You two get back into bed to keep it warm for me, okay?" Millie kissed both faces again and shoo-ed them back to bed. If they were awake for much longer, it'd be hell to get them back to sleep.

Catching her sister's hand, Rasha trudged back toward bed. The shyer of the two, Fenna, glanced back at Eyota with wide eyes. The stare didn't stop as the girls climbed back into bed. Millie knew her little owlet of a daughter would continue to stare until Fenna decided Eyota was safe.

"It's a bedroll, but it should be warm enough," Millie said, keeping her voice soft and calm. She didn't want to wake the girls up any further. Climbing the ladder to the cabin's small loft, Millie pulled the spare bedroll free, along with a few ratty blankets and furs, to keep her guest warm. On the prairie, the ground held the day's warmth. But out in the badlands, nights got cold.

"It will be fine," Eyota said, taking the bedroll from Millie to spread it on the wooden floor. "Thank you." They kept glancing back at the little girls, although one had already fallen back asleep, her red curls acting as cover for her sister to hide behind.

"Tomorrow," Millie said. She wasn't sure if she said it to herself or to Fenna. "We'll explain everything tomorrow."

With Eyota set, Millie pulled off her boots and vest and climbed into bed with her girls. She was too tired to change, and Fenna wasn't the only one who felt uncomfortable around strangers in their home. Eyota was a guest and had never given Millie any reason not to trust them, but it wasn't Eyota's fault that Millie felt like her hackles were up. Eyota hadn't been the dragon that almost killed Millie a few nights ago. Eyota wasn't a Willard who burned down farms. Eyota was just... rigid.

"Good night, cousin," Fenna whispered, feeling brave now that her mother had climbed into bed with them.

Millie pulled them close under the covers and pressed her nose to Rasha's curls.

She didn't remember falling asleep.

8

PLAIN OLD PLAINFIELD

THE FIRST THING GILBERT did upon disembarking at Plainfield was stretch out his back. The cushioned seat had helped, but trains weren't made for men of his stature. Twisting slightly, Gilbert grunted as something in his spine popped back into place.

Around him, the passengers milled about on the plain wooden platform that passed for a train station. Further down the train, labourers started unloading crates of cargo under the watchful eye of armed guards. The strange thing was, Gilbert couldn't tell if the guards were protecting the cargo from potential thieves in town, or from the labourers themselves.

"So," he said, turning to Hal, who joined him on the platform, valise in hand. "What's the plan, Detective?"

"I'm still not used to *you* calling me that," Hal said with a laugh. Like Gilbert, Hal noticed the armed guards, and his eyebrows rose. Shaking his head slightly at the sight, Hal turned to point at the town's freshly built buildings. "We'll stay here for the night, buy horses and supplies, and see what we can find out from the townsfolk. The men that reported the dragon attack did so here, so with any luck, they'll still be around."

Hal rubbed his chin, thinking.

"Think we should hire them?" Gilbert asked.

"Let's see what kind of men they are first," Hal said. "There are plenty of folks out here who wouldn't hesitate in taking your money, leading us out to the middle of nowhere, robbing us blind and leaving us to die out there."

Gilbert took a deep breath in. The smells of dirt, dust, and horseshit greeted him. "Ah, that makes me feel a little more at home."

"People robbing you blind makes you feel at home?" Hal asked, raising his eyebrows in surprise. Gilbert grinned back.

"I might be a city boy, Hal," Gilbert said, tipping his hat. "But I wasn't born into the lap of luxury, remember? Certified former street urchin right here, and banking is a ruthless business." He motioned for Hal to come with him to pick up what little luggage he'd brought.

"Right, well. Today we prepare, tomorrow we ride out on the old road. There's a small town that's close to where the train wrecked called Scorched Bluffs. *Real* small, practically a ghost town now, but the locals might know how to avoid that dragon." Hal sniffed, rubbing his nose. "I'd trust a guide from there more than from Plainfield."

Gilbert nodded. As much as he didn't want to encounter the beast up close, he couldn't help but hope they saw it at a safe distance. A dragon, big enough to destroy a train. Avrom's stories of the old world always said the dragons were gone... but here in the wilds, they survived. They thrived.

"Is the dragon why it's called *Scorched* Bluffs?" Gilbert asked, eyebrows lifting slightly.

"Maybe," Hal said with a shrug. But the question had piqued an interest in the detective. "I certainly *hope* not. They build most buildings out here from lumber. Regular towns regularly go up in flames. I'd hate to see what might happen to one built close to a dragon's hunting ground."

"So, first we prepare," Gilbert said, picking up his own valise from the first-class steward. "To the saloon?" From the corner of his eye, he spied the steamer trunk from Wyndford, along with the caged pup who pawed at the bars. Glancing around for trouble, Gilbert reached out and flicked the cage's latch open.

In a flash of fox-orange, the fluffy thing was out of the cage, down the trunk, and racing off into town.

"I'll pretend I didn't see that," Hal said, watching the direction the puppy ran off to. He sniffed again, rubbing his nose with the back of his hand. "I thought I smelled a dog on the train."

Gilbert smiled and held his hands out to either side, a picture of innocence. Draping one arm over Hal's shoulder, Gilbert turned them both to look out at the town called Plainfield. It was terribly plain. The buildings were whitewashed, the people respectable looking, and there was even a bank. Once they'd sorted out the business about Rousseau's missing cargo, Gil planned on buying that bank out and establishing his own. If he was going to be Frederic's errand boy, he'd make the trip worthwhile.

"Dogs don't belong in cages," Gilbert said, walking toward the town's hotel. "If he's loyal, he'll show up again."

"That's *why* I'm pretending I saw nothing," Hal said. He hesitated before patting Gilbert on the back. "We should arrange the horses first, then worry about booking rooms."

"I have another idea," Gilbert said. "Why don't you see about the horses, and I'll speak to the Plainfield Sheriff. He might have more information about the wreck and where to find the men who found it." Gilbert brushed a stray speck of dirt from his lapel. "Afterwards, I'll meet you at the hotel's saloon where we can rest, get a good meal and maybe moderate company before we set out in the morning."

"Alright, alright, don't go losing *my* pay in a crooked card game," Hal said with a chuckle. Gilbert grinned and released his friend.

"Hal," Gilbert said, pressing a hand to his heart in mock insult. "When have you known me to lose at cards?"

Parting ways, Gilbert arranged for their things to be sent to the hotel and headed straight for the town jail. All of Plainfield felt new in a way Gilbert was unfamiliar with. Wyndford's financial quarter was one of the oldest in the city, with well over a hundred years of buildings, streets, even gaslights. Out here, everything was fresh-cut wood and whitewash.

The jail matched the rest of Plainfield: freshly whitewashed and built from Wyndford-milled lumber. Gilbert knocked on the door after he was unable to find a handle. Gilbert blinked in surprise as the wooden door swung inward, revealing a weathered man's face with an impressive moustache. With the man's appearance came the stench of unwashed bodies, old beer, and older piss. Somehow, this jail smelled worse than Rousseau's study.

"Ah! Hello, I'm looking for the Plainfield Sheriff," Gilbert said with a friendly smile. "Would that be you?"

The man squinted up at Gilbert, then nodded as if he needed to remember that yes, he was in fact the Sheriff.

"Someone steal something of yours?" the Sheriff asked, stepping back and holding the door open for Gilbert. "You'll wanna duck. This building wasn't made for men your height. Half-orcs hit their heads all the time and they ain't even as tall as you."

Gilbert glanced at the doorway and noticed a faint wear pattern in the centre of the crossbeam. He ducked, placing a hand on his hat to hold it in place as he entered the jail.

"No, no one stole anything from me, Sheriff," Gilbert said. It took a moment to be able to see in the dimly lit jail after the bright afternoon sunshine. The only light inside came from a sputtering lantern on the wall and a single barred window. The jail had three cells, of which one was occupied by a figure who lay on the ground, snoring loudly. By the greenish tint of its skin, Gilbert figured a half-orc. Maybe the one that hit its head on the doorway often enough to leave a dent.

"Then whaddya need a Sheriff for?" The man asked and belched. "Did Max get out again?"

"I'm afraid I don't know who Max is. I'm here to look into the train wreck," Gilbert said, gesturing at the door with his hat in hand. "The one caused by a dragon. I was hoping you might be able to tell me who reported it, so I can ask them some questions."

The man looked Gilbert over, running a dirty hand over his moustache. His bleary eyes lingered on Gilbert's fine wool suit and clean shoes.

"It was them Willard Boys who found it, Jeb Willard's the one you'll want to talk to, if he's willing." The Sheriff rubbed his hand over his mouth again, scratching at his unkempt moustache. "But if you're planning on going to the wreck itself, you'll be heading to Scorched Bluffs," he said, and nodded to himself. He turned and spat onto the jail's floor. "That's a cursed town, it is. I should prepare ye for what you'll be seeing. Course, I could use a drink. It's dry as hell out here these days. Ain't rained in weeks."

Gilbert was quite certain it had rained on the night of the train wreck, as the papers specifically mentioned the weather in their reports, and Plainfield's dirt streets were still muddy. Instead of arguing, he put on a bright smile and pushed the door open for the Sheriff.

"Well, allow me to buy you a drink for your trouble. I'll be meeting my partner at the saloon and I'm certain that he would be interested to hear what you have to say." Lawmen were the same everywhere. Gilbert's smile widened as the Sheriff hurried out the door. He was well versed in this kind of payment.

By the time Hal found them at the saloon, the Sheriff had fallen asleep on the table with a half-empty bottle of whiskey clutched in one hand. Gilbert had moved his chair away from the lawman and had a cute redheaded elf perched on his lap who was drawing a map on the back of an old sheet of music. Engrossed in learning about the dangers of the wilderness from the pretty saloon girl, Gilbert only looked up to greet Hal when he heard him pull a chair out from their table.

"I've always been in awe of how fast you make friends," Hal said, shaking his head. He set his hat on the table and leaned back in the chair, making it creak.

"Miss Diamond, darling, would you be so kind as to get my friend some refreshments?" Gilbert asked the girl on his knee. With a smile at Hal and a whisper to Gilbert, 'Diamond' hopped down and hurried off to get a fresh round of drinks. Gilbert watched her go, noting that she ignored a table with a pair of grubby men that tried to get her attention. Poor thing had to live off pioneers and men that believed soap was the work of the devil. No wonder she was so attentive.

"Did you even go looking for the sheriff?" Hal asked, interrupting Gilbert's thoughts. He blinked, looking over to see his cousin watching him with an arched eyebrow.

"Looked for *and* found him," Gilbert said, patting the sleeping man on the shoulder. The Sheriff startled and fell off his chair, spilling whiskey on himself. The star badge glinted in the saloon's dingy light.

"A shining example of the Frontier lawman," Gilbert commented, dryly. He was too excited to keep still and leaned over to Hal with a broad grin. "While the Sheriff was largely unhelpful, our dearest Diamond here has a sister out in Scorched Bluffs and knows the place well. As a result, we now have a map and we know that town is a place that scares the piss out of most Plainfield residents, our Sheriff friend included."

Hal took a closer look at the map Diamond had been working on. Inexpertly drawn, with notes in Gilbert's handwriting to indicate specific landmarks, the map was far better than nothing.

"So did you find out why it's called 'Scorched Bluffs'?" Hal asked, and Gilbert savoured the impressed expression on the Stratton's face.

"*Yes!*" Gilbert said, lighting up. "The town used to be called 'Bare' Bluffs until four years ago when the whole thing burnt down. It was mostly empty by then but the Sheriff died in the fire and the person that replaced him was a woman. The whole town is women."

Leaning back in his chair as Diamond returned, Gilbert felt giddy. This was shaping up to be a much more exciting trip than he had first expected. A town full of women with a lady sheriff and lady deputy. Mysteries about a train, about what happened to all the outlaws. If it weren't for the promise of company for the night, Gilbert was ready to set out that very moment.

"Any outlaw that goes *near* the hellhole is strung up," Diamond said, catching the tail end of the conversation. Setting down a glass in front of Hal and one for herself, she filled each from a fresh bottle of whiskey. "Jeb and his boys won't go near the place. They call it cursed." Diamond settled back onto Gilbert's knee and he wrapped an arm around her waist, enjoying the smell of perfume after the Sheriff's moonshine stink.

"Jeb?" Gilbert asked, looking at the freckles that spattered 'Diamond's' nose. "That wouldn't happen to be one Jeb Willard, would it?"

Diamond blinked, but her quick smile almost covered up her surprise before Gil spotted it. He was certain that Diamond was an excellent poker player.

"Why yes, but what does a fine, *upstanding* man like yourself want with Jeb and his boys, Mister Goldman?" She asked, batting her eyelashes at him.

"Well," Hal said, rolling up his sleeves so the table's surface wouldn't get his sleeves dirty. "We're looking into that train wreck, ma'am." Hal shot Gil a look, and the easy smile was back on his face. "If Goldman's asking about him, I'd wager that Jeb was the one who reported it."

"Hal's a Stratton Detective," Gilbert mock-whispered to Diamond. "Worth every penny."

Diamond's flirtatious act slipped a little, and she sighed and slipped off Gilbert's knee to sit on the remaining empty chair at the table. Hal's eyebrows shot up and he exchanged glances with Gil. What had they said that prompted *that* response?

"Jeb's not an evil man," Diamond said, leaning in so the two sober men could hear. "But it's hard to make a living out here, y'know. He and his boys were out scavenging when they found it." There was more to the story. Even Gilbert could see that.

"But...?" Hal prompted.

"The youngest of Jeb's brothers, Isaiah? He got caught up in the attack. Jeb's been a mess since. They're off burying him tonight, but he should be back by morning." She nibbled on her thumb, thinking. "I don't know how much he'll talk about it; he barely said a thing to me about it."

"And I take it that normally he tells you everything?" Hal asked. Diamond answered with a half-hearted shrug.

"I'm a bit sweet on the guy," Diamond admitted. "He's real kind and takes care of the rowdy customers for us. Keeps the drunks like the Sheriff in line. He tells me a lot."

Gilbert took a sip of his beer and thought over the new developments. They'd planned to ride out in the morning, but if this 'Jeb' got back before they set out, maybe they could get a quick conversation in with him.

"When he and his 'boys' do get back, can you tell him that we'd like to speak with him?" Gilbert asked. "And please pass on our condolences regarding his brother. I imagine it must be difficult for him right now."

Diamond melted, and she nodded eagerly, causing her red curls to bounce where she'd pinned them up atop her head. The flirtation was over. Gilbert wasn't about to bother a lady who had a beau.

"I'll let him know soon as they get back," she said. "Now, let me get you two boys something to eat."

"Oh, Miss Diamond," Gilbert said, catching her as the elf stood. "Might I ask who Max is and why he keeps escaping?"

Diamond's lips twitched, and she burst into laughter.

"Max is the Sheriff's horse," she said, wiping at her eyes to keep the tears from ruining the kohl she'd drawn around them. "The old drunk always forgets to latch the stall, so Max gets out *all the time*. He always comes back, eventually." She sniffed, still giggling to herself. "Alright, food. I'll be back in a moment."

9

ONE LESS WILLARD

JEB'S DAY PASSED IN a fugue of hard labour and grief. They'd ridden out to the old farm where Ma had raised them, and dug a grave next to her own. The men worked in shifts until the grave was deep enough while Josie tended to the family rituals off to the side. A proper Rota Sanctus burial would need a priest's blessing, a ceremony symbolizing the rotation of the Wheel as one life ended and a new one began. But the Willards weren't no proper Rota worshipers. Old Nan had left the old country because their beliefs were called heretical. Here, in Amelior's fringes, the Willards could practice the rites of the Wheel the real way.

Josie had removed Isaiah's ring fingers from his corpse and the bones were boiling clean over the funeral fire. Tending the fire and the body was crucial if Isaiah was to be reborn within the family, and it was a job that was trusted solely to women.

Leaning on his shovel, slick with sweat and covered with dirt, Jeb glanced over to where his sister fed the funeral fire with the first of two wheel effigies. Woven from smokegrass and other pungent herbs, the effigy caught in the flames and smoked, carrying the spirit of Isaiah up toward the heavens.

Josie looked over at the brothers, all four of them. Jeb, Eli, and Zach stood by Isaiah's shrouded body, waiting. Standing, Josie carried the second herb wheel over to the body, tucking it into the shroud over Isaiah's heart.

"We lived, we die, we will live again," Josie said, pressing her hand onto Isaiah's body. "Come back to us, Isaiah Folsom Willard, when it is your turn to be reborn." She made the sign of the wheel, and Jeb and the others followed suit.

"We lived, we die, we will live again," Jeb said with his brothers.

Josie stood and stepped back. She prayed as they buried him until the wheel of herbs finished smoking in the funeral fire. Once it had, Isaiah was no longer trapped within his own corpse. It became an empty body, a reminder that Jeb had failed Isaiah this time. Next time he wouldn't.

Taking his brother's body by the shoulders, Jeb and the other men lowered him into the grave. They were lucky that his bones survived the fire. Without Isaiah's remains, the rite of rebirth was impossible, and the rite kept Isaiah in God's great cycle of life. Without it, he'd be abandoned to nothingness, left to go insane with no connection to his family or the God that left him behind.

It was the worst thing a person could do, take away not only a man's life, but all lives he had ahead of him. That was the fate that waited for whoever shot Isaiah. Jebediah tried to be a good man, but all Isaiah had been doing was scouting, to be killed for such a thing… to be put into a fire that nearly destroyed the remains so he couldn't be properly buried… it was an evil act. One that had to be answered with an act just as vile.

Jeb thought about the evenings he'd spent teaching Isaiah how to shoot. The first time he took the boy out on a job, how strong Isaiah had been after shooting his first man. He hadn't even cried, strong in his faith that the man would be reborn at some point so long as his body was left behind.

He'd been a handful and a half, a little stupid, but who hadn't been when they were young and full of life? Jeb remembered his own mistakes, how invincible he'd felt as he headed off to fight in the war. Isaiah wouldn't get the chance to grow out of that. Not in this lifetime.

They patted the fresh mound down with their shovels.

Josie rose from the fire, the now clean finger bones in her hand. They steamed in the evening air, still hot from being boiled clean.

"He will live again," Josie told Jeb, placing a knuckle bone in his hand. "Take and protect this bone so that he may find you when it is his time to be reborn." Jeb knew the significance of the finger bones. He wore a small leather bag around his neck that held the bones of Ma and Pa. But speaking the significance aloud was part of the rite. It tied Isaiah's spirit to the bones themselves.

Jeb nodded and closed his hand around the fresh yellow knuckle.

"He will live again," he answered, completing the invocation.

Josie repeated the ritual with Eli and Zach, each gifting them a finger bone. Finally, she took her own, whispering a private affirmation into her hands where she held it. Jeb knew better than to try to learn the rites of the women. Jeb had been a boy when Ma had explained how women held a different connection to God and his Cycle. A far stronger one, as they bled for him, and carried the lives he returned from death. Women's magic was something Jeb knew not to fuck with.

"It is done," Josie said, tucking her own piece of bone into the pouch around her neck.

Jeb stared at the flattened mound that covered the corpse that had once been his brother. He felt numb, a welcome relief from the raw grief he'd been struggling with since they'd found what was left of him.

"It's time to head back to town," he said. "I need to speak to Diamond about who else knew about that goddamn train."

Eli started walking to where the horses were grazing in the old corral. But Josie and Zach looked at one another.

"I'll rest here," Josie said. "You and Eli go back to town. There's a few more prayers I want to get done. We'll meet you the day after tomorrow in town."

Jeb looked them both over. They were angry at Diamond, he knew. They didn't want to be there when he spoke to her, but didn't want to cause Jeb any more discomfort. In turn, Jeb didn't want to cause them further pain by speaking that truth aloud.

"Alright," he said, dipping his head. "Zach, you take care of her, now."

Josie had a right to be angry at Diamond; she'd raised Isaiah since Ma died. The last woman of the family left to remember all the prayers and keep the boys in line. They'd all done their best with Isaiah, but it was Jeb who'd let him go scout for the train. Jeb, who hadn't asked Diamond who else had been told about its expensive cargo.

It was up to Jeb to make things right.

Placing his hat back onto his head, Jeb tucked Isaiah's finger into the pouch that hung from his neck. By the time he joined Eli at the corral, his brother had both horses saddled and ready to go.

"You alright?" Jeb asked.

Eli's eyes were rimmed red, but they were usually like that. His stare was a touch more glassy than normal, his eyes less focused as he looked at the horses.

"Not yet," Eli said, clearing his throat. "I should've been the one to go." He sniffed aggressively and spat away from the horses. "No matter how many times we told him-"

"Isaiah's head was thicker than a buffalo's," Jeb told his brother. "Some men gotta learn their lessons in one life to be better for the next."

Eli's eyes snapped up to fix on Jeb, surprising the elder Willard with the anger there. Normally, the thought of rebirth helped with losses, but today it had been the wrong thing to say. Pa would have been furious at the slight doubt Eli showed, but Jeb wasn't his Pa. He wasn't about to get angry for saying the wrong thing to a man who was hurting.

"I apologize," he said, resting a hand on his brother's shoulder. "C'mon. Let's go find out who could've done this, and have a few strong drinks until it hurts less."

"First good thing you've said all day," Eli muttered. He clapped a hand over Jeb's and gave it a small squeeze. "It wasn't your fault either, Jeb. But we'll make it right."

Jeb released his brother and swung up into the saddle of his horse. It didn't feel right leaving Josie and Zach behind, but they would rejoin the family when they were ready.

They arrived after dark. Plainfield's lanterns and the sounds of drunken revelry greeted Jeb and Eli as they rode into town. The Sheriff was already passed out on the steps to the Saloon, an empty bottle of whiskey near his limp hand.

The Willards dismounted and hitched their horses next to the snoring Sheriff. Normally, Jeb wouldn't think twice about leaving his things outside in the saddlebags. Plainfield knew better than to steal from a Willard, or so he'd thought. But someone had killed Isaiah. Someone who'd been in Plainfield to find out about the train's cargo. But Jeb didn't want to be seen carrying in his things; it would set a bad precedent. Suggesting that there was someone around that he was afraid of.

"You go get yourself a drink," Jeb told his brother. "I'll find you after speaking with Di."

Eli nodded and went inside, leaving his saddlebags in place. Jeb reached in and pulled out a small bundle he'd kept safe for the few days, and followed.

If anyone did get bold enough to steal from him, they'd join the killer in becoming an example of why you didn't fuck with a Willard.

The Saloon was rowdy at this time of night, full of travellers who were stranded after the train wreck, pioneers who planned to carve out a home on the prairie, and opportunists looking to make a quick buck. The faces changed nightly, but the regulars knew who Jeb was. Even drunk, they offered somber nods to him as he waded into the cacophony of laughter and drinking songs.

Diamond found him first, looking pretty as a peach with her red curls piled up on her head and wearing that blue dress he liked so much. Seeing her made his heart feel a little lighter, and he took off his hat as she approached.

"Evening Miss Diamond," he said. He wanted to pull her into a hug, to tell her how he felt like a failure, how he'd let his youngest brother get killed. Instead, he cleared his throat. "Do you have time to talk?"

Her lovely face creased in worry, but as she took his rough hand in her soft one, Jeb knew that worry was for him. She wasn't afraid, and he hoped to God that she would never have to feel afraid of him.

"I'll make time. Come up to my room, we can talk there," she said. She gave his hand a little squeeze and led him upstairs to the bordello. Di didn't take on clients much, Jeb made sure she never felt like she had to. He admired how good she was with people. He wanted to make sure she never went hungry. Never felt like she had to do work she didn't feel like doing.

Her room was decorated with fine shawls and trinkets he'd given her over the years. It always made his heart warm to see the very first gift he'd given her hang above her bed: a sterling wheel strung on a leather cord. The night he'd given it to her, he'd stammered through an apology that it wasn't gold, that it was plain instead of jeweled, and Di had hung it up right then and there. Said it was special because it was from him.

"Are you okay?" she asked as soon as they were inside. She pulled him into a hug, and Jeb let himself melt into the embrace, wrapping his arms around her narrow shoulders. She smelled of soft perfume and flowers and he buried his nose into her curls to shut out the noise and stink of cheap beer that wafted up from the saloon below.

"No," he admitted. "We buried him, did it right, but..." he trailed off. He didn't want to have this conversation. He wanted to curl up with her and talk about when they were rich enough that he could buy Di her own saloon, dreaming about the day they could live together for good.

"What is it?" Di might not have been raised like a Willard woman, but her senses were as sharp as Josie's. She placed her hand on his cheek, stroking it gently. "Jeb, you know you can tell me anything."

He sighed. Taking her hand in his, Jeb stepped back and hated himself for it.

"Someone else knew about the train, Di," he said, watching her face. He could feel his already grieving heart begin to crack. "Isaiah wasn't killed by the dragon. He was shot. Who all knew about it?"

He watched her lovely green eyes widen. He prayed that she'd tell him, that she'd be honest, that he wouldn't have to add her to the list of people that had to pay for Isaiah's murder.

"Jeb... I'm so sorry," she said quietly. "I told a few people, not many. Locals." She took his other hand, holding them both in front of her. "I don't know if *they* told anyone else after they found out... but there're some men downstairs that might be able to help. They're here about the train. They want to find out what happened to it. One's a Stratton Detective-"

Jeb felt his throat seize up. He leaned back instinctively, but didn't let go of Diamond's hands.

"A Stratton? Here?" he asked in a hoarse whisper. "Shit, Di, what if he decides to try to clean up Plainfield?" Suddenly things were worse. Jeb never pretended he was a law-abiding man, and the thought of a Stratton arresting what remained of the Willards in a single swoop was terrifying.

"Jeb, breathe," Di whispered, pulling him back close to her. She placed his hand on her cheek, her lovely eyes fixed on his. "Strattons don't work for free. He's here with a banker, something about the train's cargo. You didn't take anything from the train, did you?"

"Wasn't anything left to take," Jeb whispered.

She smiled, soft and gentle. "Then you don't have nothing to worry about from him. In fact, I bet you two could help each other. The Stratton already wants to find that cargo, and you want to find out who was there at the train wreck."

God, Jeb loved her. Diamond was brilliant in ways that he wasn't, and once again her understanding of people shone. He leaned in and kissed her, soft and sweet. When he pulled back, both of them were smiling like stupid teenagers.

"I'll tell you who all I told," Di said, stroking his hand. "But... well. I don't know who did it. If I did, you know I'd tell you straight away."

"I know," Jeb whispered. "Di, when this is over..." he reached into his pocket and pulled out the little bundle he'd taken from his saddlebag. "I've been holding onto this for weeks, not sure when, not sure if-"

"Yes," she answered before he got to the question. "I will."

"But..." he stammered. "You ain't even seen it yet."

She laughed, and Jeb felt his heart mending at the sound.

"Jebediah Willard, you could propose with a scrap of tin, and I'd say yes," Diamond told him.

It was some time later that Jeb pulled the necklace from its bundle and helped her put it on. It was a fine little chain, a simple locket that she could tuck into her corset to keep safe. Inside was a pressed little rosebud. Her favourite flower.

He kissed her shoulder and held her close. Eli wouldn't mind if he was a little late to come back down to the saloon.

10

SLEEPLESS NIGHTS

MILLIE CROUCHED BEHIND A fallen tree, keeping low to avoid getting picked off by secessionist sharpshooters. A storm was blowing in from the coast. She could taste salt in the air and the stink of mud was thick in her nose.

A sharp crack split the air, but it wasn't thunder. A cannon ball smashed through the ground next to the downed tree, kicking up mud and grass as it skipped across the battlefield on its way to the Union forces spread out behind her.

Millie swore, scrambling along the log to where one of its limbs reached up like a dying man's arm, begging to be saved. She tucked herself down against the mud and rested her rifle against the trunk. Being out in the middle was dangerous, but the outcome of this battle would decide if the 43rd Irregulars could eat that week. Supplies had been blocked up for a month, and this was the last blockade to clear.

Squinting one eye closed, Millie focused down her sights, lining up her shot. Taking a deep breath in, she slowly let it out and squeezed the trigger. Her bullet punched through the arm of a secessionist, who screamed and dropped his lantern by the stores of black powder needed to fire the heavy guns. Millie didn't watch what happened next. She threw herself as deeply into the mud as she could, arms over her head.

There was a half-heartbeat of nothing, and then the night lit up like it was noon, the thunderous explosion leaving her ears ringing and the downed tree riddled with shrapnel. Unable to hear more than that deafening ring, Millie poked her head up over the log to see a crater in the ground where the heavy artillery had once been.

The union bugle sounded the advance, and the Irregulars sprinted across the field. Elves, orcs, and everything in between, descended on the secessionists and tore them apart. Sometimes, literally.

The dream reset.

Millie ducked to avoid the sharpshooters as it looped over and over, each time getting more difficult to hit the man with the lantern, to avoid getting shot, to storm the enemy. Each time, Millie struggled to move, the mud getting thicker and deeper.

Eventually, her body jerked in its sleep and woke her. Heart thudding and tight in her chest, Millie sat up in bed and scanned her one room cabin. It was still dark. The girls were still asleep. The town was quiet. Eyota was lying in front of the banked wood stove.

Millie took a deep breath. The air was arid, not swampy. The night was quiet, with only the soft sounds of Fenna's snores filling the air. Looking down at her girls, Millie willed her heart to slow. Gently, she stroked the soft ears of her little girls, watching them flick in their sleep like kittens.

The earlier excitement of her return home had exhausted them, and for the moment, not even the light ear touches woke them.

Careful not to disturb her daughters, Millie slipped out of bed. Nights like this usually required roughtooth tea for her to be able to fall back asleep. Millie had hoped that as tired as she'd been, she'd sleep the night through. But tonight, not even little-girl snores and the exhaustion of being awake for nearly two days straight could quiet her dreams.

Pulling on her boots, Millie snagged her poncho and gun belt on her way out the door. The night air was frosty, turning her breath silver as she emerged from her cabin's warmth. For a moment, Millie stood out in the chill, feeling it sap the warmth from her skin and, with it, the last remnants of her dream.

She hadn't had a dream that vivid in a long time. It bothered her. Had it been the train robbery that dredged old memories out of the muck? Or was it seeing the insignia that branded the crates of bullets? Hell, it could be anything, and it could be nothing at all. Nearly ten years on, and the dreams came and went like they had a mind of their own.

Millie pulled her poncho on; the cold air having done its job. She buckled on her gun belt and checked her revolver to ensure it was loaded. The single bullet remaining from the train robbery was where she'd left it. The water pump wasn't far, but Millie didn't take those kinds of chances. Not anymore. There were too many wild things out on the Frontier. At least with the animals, you could scare them off with a warning shot. Millie didn't waste bullets on warning shots when it came to outlaws.

The water bucket wasn't by the porch where it had been when she'd arrived home. Frowning, Millie looked out at her small town. Had Sweetpea taken it when she'd left? But no, there it was, turned upside down in the middle of Scorched Bluff's lone road.

The overturned bucket was moving, skidding along the dirt until it stopped and moved in a different direction. Most buckets didn't run away on their own, but most buckets didn't have two curious four-year-olds who used them as cages for 'pets' they liked to find in town.

Millie approached carefully, her hand on her pistol. At least it wasn't a rattler. Those wouldn't move if stuck under a bucket. The moment they were in the dark, the horned snakes stayed quiet and only struck out when disturbed. That didn't mean whatever was under the bucket was friendly, though. Most critters had a nasty bite when cornered. Millie hoped that whatever it was, it was non-venomous.

Using her boot, Millie tipped the bucket back toward her, creating an opening between dirt and the bucket on its opposite side. A squirrel-sized lizard scurried out in a flurry of legs, leaving behind a thick tail that immediately began to smoke. She kicked the bucket up into her hand as the dropped tail burst into bright yellow flames.

"Shit," she hissed. Spotting the tailless salamander as it made for the nearest cabin, Millie sprinted after it and leapt, slamming the bucket down to trap it again. She landed in the dirt with a grunt. Scrambling to her feet, she checked the bucket to make sure she had it contained.

A nest of frightened salamanders could burn the town down, and Scorched Bluffs had taken great care not to let the pesky lizards near the wooden buildings. How one ended up under a *wooden* bucket... it had to be the girls. How her daughters had managed to trap a salamander without it igniting was a question that could wait. Millie pinched the bridge of her nose. First, they'd caught ground squirrels, now salamanders? Next thing she knew, they would be catching rattlesnakes and asking to keep them as pets.

Under the bucket, Millie could hear the salamander scratching at the wood as it tried to escape. She'd need to scour the bucket out before it'd be usable for water again. Salamander oil was precious for lanterns, but tasted terrible.

Holding the bucket down, Millie looked around for something to place on top of it to keep the salamander from escaping. Her saddle bags were back on her porch, illuminated by the still-burning salamander tail left behind.

Spotting a brick by the side of the road, Millie darted over to grab it. The moment she let go of the bucket, it started to scoot along the road again leaving a trail of burning oil. Hurrying back, she put the brick on top of the bucket and checked if it was heavy enough to keep the bucket in place. The scrabbling of the salamander's claws was audible against the wood, and she could smell its fire from where she stood, but the bucket stayed put.

The tea had to wait.

Jogging down the road to the town jail, Millie wondered if Ryan had better luck sleeping.

Squat, square, built with plastered logs, the jail was only one in name. The last time anyone had been locked up was before the fire. Instead, it served as the Sheriff's office, and home. It was a place to store spare equipment or weapons that weren't needed that day.

Millie knocked but didn't wait for an answer. She slipped inside, trying to be quiet. The main room was the official jail, with an iron cage forming two cells along the right side of the building. To the left-

"There was a salamander in the road!" she said, ducking under the swing of the Sheriff's fist. It clipped the tip of her ear and Millie whistled softly in appreciation. "You're getting faster. You almost hit me that time."

Ryan, wearing a nightshirt and slacks, squinted at the elf. Her long hair was loose, dark waves and nearly reaching the human's waist. In the dim light cast by a lantern in the Sheriff's office to the left, Millie could see her face change from grim determination to exhausted annoyance. Next to his owner, Fyodor yawned. He had smelled the elf, and now, rather than greeting an interloper with teeth, he trudged over and leaned against Millie, tail thumping against the wall.

"Millie. It's the *middle of the night*," the sheriff groaned. Her sleepiness evaporated as Millie's words sunk in and Ryan straightened up, eyes flicking toward the door. "Wait, salamanders?"

"Salamander," Millie confirmed flicking her ear a few times to shake off the sting from Ryan's punch. "Just one, luckily. I've got it trapped under a bucket. Pretty sure I need to sit the girls down and have another talk about why catching dangerous animals is dangerous." Millie reached out, greeting the giant dog with a pat. Fyodor sat down and leaned into Millie, knocking her sideways into the wall.

Ryan rubbed a hand over her face. Millie would bet ten dollars on the fact Ry was awake for the same reason she was. No one in town would take that bet. Very few Scorched Bluffs residents slept well at night.

"Did they tell you where they caught it?" Ryan asked. "Fyodor, heel." The mastiff whined, but obeyed. Freed, Millie followed the pair into Ryan's office. It was cramped, a wood stove butted against one wall and the evidence safe sat next to it, doubling as a table. The rest of the room was filled with Ryan's desk and a pair of wooden chairs. The door leading from the office to her bedroom was closed.

"No, they're still asleep. I'll ask in the morning." Millie squinted out the jail's barred window at the night sky. "Later... in the morning, anyways. Did I wake you up?" She asked, eying the closed door.

"I want to say yes so that you stop showing up this late at night," Ryan answered, stoking the fire in her stove. She already had a kettle filled with water sitting on the element. Hopefully that meant coffee, or roughtooth tea. "But no, I was already awake. I was thinking about the train when Fyodor heard you coming."

The big dog leaned back into Millie with his big head, nudging her to one of the wooden chairs at Ryan's desk. Millie sat in the chair and found her lap immediately filled with his head.

"He's a good boy, aren't you? Such sharp ears you have!" Millie cooed at Fyodor, whose tail immediately became a tripping hazard, from how hard it started to wag. Her lap would be full of drool in a few moments, but there were worse things to get stained with. Salamander oil was one of them.

"He is," Ryan said, glancing over her shoulder at the dog. "And to think you used to be scared of him."

Millie huffed, her ears flicking in annoyance. "This dog is twice my weight and taller than I am if he stands up, Ry. I wasn't afraid. I was outclassed." She leaned over and kissed the big guy's forehead. They hadn't exactly met on the best terms back then.

"So, the train?" Millie said. "Do you want to talk about it?"

Ryan was quiet for a moment, fiddling with two tin mugs.

"I'm worried," she admitted. "You were right about the Willard; he would have made things dangerous for us. But sooner or later they'll realise he's missing..."

"...and they'll come looking," Millie said, finishing her friend's sentence. "Yeah. I've been thinking that over. As terrible as they are, they care about each other." She chewed on her lip, scratching behind Fyodor's ears as she mulled that over.

"But," Ryan said, leaving the stove and joining Millie at her desk. "More than that, I'm worried about whose name was on those crates. Did you know that there was dynamite in there, too?" Ryan rested her chin on her palm, brow knitting into a frown.

"Dynamite?" Millie repeated, eyebrows shooting up along with her ears. "That's great!" Ryan's frown deepened. "I mean: no, I didn't know, *but* it'll be really useful. The manifest I saw listed bullets and a few rifles; I would have mentioned it if I saw dynamite listed there." Millie leaned back in her chair, resting her hands on the dog's head in her lap. His skull was larger than her own.

"You would have," Ryan agreed. She sighed, letting her head sink down onto the desk with a quiet groan. "But dynamite is expensive. What if his company sends someone to see what happened?"

"A dragon happened, Ry," Millie said gently. "You saw it happen. Dynamite doesn't explode without the blast cap stuck in there with the fuse. I'd be shocked if they shipped them with-"

"The fuses were in place," Ryan answered, her voice muffled from the desk.

"Oh," Millie said. She took a deep breath and let it out in a huff, thinking about how close they'd all been to dying. "In that case, we're double lucky we didn't die. From the dynamite, and from the dragon," she said. "Or from the Willard. Triple lucky."

Ryan lifted her head from her desk and looked at the elf from behind strands of her hair. She tried a smile, but it didn't quite reach her eyes.

"Last I heard," Millie said, squirming out from under Fyodor. She walked over and crouched next to her friend. The dog joined her, resting his jaw on Millie's shoulder. The breath on her ear tickled, and she tried to hold it up and out of the dog's whiskers. "Last I heard," she repeated. "The owner of that munitions company was a useless drunk who could barely stay upright. In a few years, he'll drink himself to death."

She took her friend's hand and gave it a squeeze. "And then we can all celebrate."

Ryan smiled and, while it was still sad, it was a little more genuine than the first.

"Shouldn't I be the one giving you this talk?" she asked. "Are you really okay with all of this?"

"I'm absolutely not okay," Millie whispered. "So, I'll need you to repeat all of this back to me later today, word for word. But maybe with a few more cusses in there."

"Deal," Ryan said, reaching out to ruffle Fyodor's ears. "So. Coffee or tea?"

Millie glanced at the window again and saw the faint blush of sunrise touch the tip of the bluffs that hung over the town. Soon her little girls would start waking up, and she'd need to be back and ready to get them fed.

"Coffee."

11

THE OLD ROAD

MORNING CAME TOO EARLY.

Gilbert opened one eye, spotting the sunlight streaming in through the hotel's window. Still early, the sky was losing the last tinge of gold as the sun crept higher into the sky. Detangling an arm from the woman next to him, Gilbert rubbed crust from his eyes. His companion groaned and buried her face deeper into her pillow.

Poor thing, not everyone was an early riser.

Careful to keep from disturbing her further, Gilbert got up and collected his things. His clothes were scattered around the small hotel room, but his watch, hat, and gloves waited neatly on the bedside table. His wallet was tucked inside his hat, and Gilbert counted out a few bills, leaving them on the table for his delightful companion. Making sure he had the remainder of the funds he began the night with, Gilbert tucked the wallet away and finished getting dressed.

Hal was waiting for him in the saloon below, which was now cleared out of last night's patrons and looked far dingier in the light of day. A trail in the floor's sawdust told Gilbert that the Sheriff must have been dragged out from his place under their table at some point, though it hadn't been before Gilbert had retired last night.

Hal wasn't alone, much to Gilbert's surprise. Next to his friend sat a tanned man who was shorter than both of them, but with shoulders as broad as Hal's and a chest that put most bulls to shame. Spotting him, the tanned man smiled, eyes crinkling. Clean-shaven and wearing a fine layer of dust over his chaps and vest, the stranger lifted his mug in Gilbert's direction.

"You weren't kidding. He really is a giant," he said to Hal.

"Morning'," Hal said with a nod. "This is the marshal around here. Gil, meet Allan Douglas."

Gilbert smiled back, taking a seat across from the two. The Marshal? How fortunate! After the lacklustre Sheriff he'd met, Gilbert was glad to get a chance to talk with a sober lawman. Maybe this one wouldn't start sobbing into his bottle about how his horse kept running away.

"Pleasure to meet you, Marshal Douglas," Gilbert said, reaching out to shake the man's hand.

"Call me Allan," the marshal said. His hands were deeply callused, and his grip was stronger than Gilbert expected. "The only reason I'm a marshal is because the last one died and I didn't run away fast enough." He sighed, looking genuinely unhappy for a moment. With a twitch of his shoulders, Allan seemed to shake the mood off, and soon his friendly smile was back in place.

"Gilbert, right? Your friend was telling me all about your trip to Scorched Bluffs," he said. "I'd travel with you, but *some* sheriffs don't know how to hold their liquor. The one in Scorched Bluffs. She's not like that." His eyes grew dreamy, and Gilbert raised an eyebrow at his friend. Hal smiled and tilted his head toward the Marshal.

"What is she like, then?" Gilbert asked, motioning for the waitress to bring him a cup of coffee as well. "This Sheriff of a town that burnt down?"

Allan leaned back in his chair, looking down as he fiddled with the leather strap wrapped around a wrist. His cheeks grew bright, and Gilbert watched in a sick fascination as he realized the man was blushing. Good God, where had they found this lovesick boy?

"Well, she can read real good," Allan said. "Teaches the little ones out there how to, too. Keeps the peace like a real lawman should. It's not just handcuffs and roughing people up-"

"I rather *like* women with handcuffs who aren't afraid to get rough," Gilbert said with a devilish grin. It disappeared when someone kicked his shin sharply from under the table. Gilbert winced and reached down to brush the dirt from his pant leg. Hal shook his head ever so slightly.

The marshal seemed unaware of Gilbert's implication, and his dopey smile had widened. His ears were red now, the tips faintly pointed. Allan was a half-elf, Gilbert realized. He hadn't noticed at first because of how broad the man was, though the native clans of elves were taller than most of the ones from the old world.

"Oh, she can handle herself. I'm not worried about that," he said. "She'd make a better marshal than me, but she's turned it down. Says the Bluffs need her more right now."

"What's her name, Allan?" Hal asked, clearing his throat.

"Sheriff Ryan Collins, but she lets me call her 'Ry'," Allan said, suddenly bashful. As if the nickname suggested they were more than acquaintances. Gilbert was certain that if this lady Sheriff ever kissed the marshal, the man would self-combust.

"I was hoping, given you're headed out that way," Allan said, clearing his throat. "That you'd be kind enough to deliver some letters. Mostly business, bounty announcements, law changes, that sort of stuff. I'd planned to deliver it myself..." the marshal sighed, much of the animation disappearing. "But someone went and killed one of the Willard boys. They'll be out for blood, and the Plainfield Sheriff is no good at keeping them in line."

"These are the same Willards that found the train?" Hal asked. He glanced at Gilbert. These were the same men that the saloon girl had encouraged them to speak to, though they sounded like a far greater problem the way the Marshal was talking about them.

"Yessir," Allan said, turning his mug of coffee in place. "Nasty bunch, the oldest isn't so bad, but when he's not around, the others cause all kinds of trouble. But it's hard to hold them to it. They're slippery and no one'll ever speak up against 'em. But I'd advise against talking to them outside of the town limits if you can avoid it. Even the nicer one'll rob you if he gets the chance."

"We'll keep that in mind, Allan," Hal said. "You recommend contacting Sheriff Collins instead?"

Allan nodded. "She'll know about whatever's happened out there. The deputy's one of the local elves and has an eye sharper than a damn hawk's." He shuddered. "Mean, though. You won't get no warm welcome from her, that's for sure."

"We'll make sure Sheriff Collins gets the mail, marshal." Hal said with another of his amiable smiles. "And I'll tell her you send your best regards."

Gilbert sat back, watching as his friend charmed the marshal. It was interesting to watch, although Allan was certainly their senior in age. He seemed so hopeful and boyish. How, Gilbert wondered, had that innocence survived out on the Frontier?

"Great! I mean it, really. Thank you." The marshal looked relieved. "I still have to figure out how to get the news to all the other small towns, but they're less-" Gilbert waited, certain the Marshal had begun to say 'less important'. Instead of continuing, Allan stood and put on his hat.

"I'll be getting those letters," the marshal said.

Gilbert waited for Allan to leave and then looked at his friend. Hal was rubbing his chin, dark eyes fixed on the departing lawman. A small, thoughtful crease between Hal's eyebrows replaced his smile.

"Hal," Gilbert said, interrupting his friend's thoughts. "Two things: One, where did you learn to manipulate poor lawmen like that? And two: If I *ever* act like that over a woman, shoot me."

Hal laughed, loud and genuine. Somewhere, from a corner of the saloon, a man groaned as Hal's voice cut through a terrible hangover. Gil leaned in his chair to try to spy who it was, but he didn't recognize the collapsed lump there. Hal glanced over his shoulder and winced in sympathy.

"I learned it from you, Gil," Hal said more quietly. "All those years of watching you get out of trouble. But if I live to see the day where you act like the Marshal over a woman, I'm documenting it for prosperity. Your father would pay good money to see it."

Gilbert rolled his eyes. Where was his coffee? Where was the waitress who had gone to *go get* his coffee? Why had this morning turned into making fun of him? Gilbert stood, determined to go find something to do while he sulked. It wasn't Hal's fault, but it felt odd to be the one who people were *less* interested in talking to. Then again, Hal was a detective now. He had a shiny badge and maybe that attracted other lawmen, like a coin attracted magpies.

"We've got a long ride today," Gilbert said, placing his hat onto his head. "I'll go make sure our horses are ready. If the waitress ever comes back, can you get that coffee for me?"

Hal raised his eyebrows. He nodded, not trying to argue. No doubt he'd sensed that shift in roles as well.

"The horses should be in the hotel's stables," Hal said. "I'll meet you out front."

Hal had *definitely* noticed the shift in roles, Gilbert thought. Tipping his hat with a smile to show he held no hard feelings; Gilbert made his way outside to the stables.

An orc filled nearly the whole doorway to the stable, an impressive feat given that it was a door to be used by horses instead of people. Tanned to deep mossy green, the man had several pockmarks on his forearms. The scarring was pale, some marks still bright pink and new.

His hair was pulled back into a tight topknot and the orc's beard was neatly trimmed. It wasn't often that Gilbert felt small, but this man was massive. He glanced up at Gilbert before going back to his work, carefully braiding the mane of a draft horse. The horse snorted, greeting Gilbert before the orc did.

"Ah, hello?" Gilbert called out. "My friend Hal Stratton paid for some horses yesterday."

The Orc looked up from his work again, this time eying Gilbert closely. Gil had to resist the urge to snap his heels together and salute. No doubt it wouldn't go over well out here.

"The detective?" The orc said, his voice gravelly. Oddly, he had a touch of an arroyan accent, but as far as Gilbert could see, he didn't have any horns. The empire had opened its borders to orcish folk generations before anyone else, but he'd yet to meet anyone that had actually grown up within the empire.

"That's the one," Gil said with a smile. "If you could point me toward the horses we've paid for, I can get them saddled."

The orc pulled back, looking insulted. What had Gil said wrong this time?

"You know how to saddle a horse?" Oh. Gil wondered if he should throw some dirt onto his jacket to make people less bothered by his appearance.

"It's been a while, but yes," he said. "I'm Gilbert Goldman." He held out a hand to shake, but the orc took the offered hand and put it on the draft horse's braid.

"Nash Strongpaw," he said. "Hold this, so Buttercup doesn't shake it out again. I'll go get your horses for you, Mister Goldman."

"Alright," Gilbert said, looking at the man's handiwork. Despite Strongpaw having hands the size of shovels, the braid was neat and tight. "Can I ask you something, Mister Strongpaw?" Gil said as the orc headed deeper into the stables.

"No 'Mister', just Strongpaw," the orc rumbled. "And you can ask, but I might not feel like answering."

"Fair enough. Please, call me Goldman," Gilbert said, patting Buttercup's neck. She was a pretty palomino, with hooves the size of dinner plates that were neatly trimmed and shod. Gilbert continued the braid. The task made easier with Buttercup's straight mane compared to the curls of his little storm cloud daughter. A pang of homesickness struck, and Gil wondered if his girl was doing alright. Arnaud would keep her well fed, and Avrom was the best grandfather a girl could want, but... Gil had never left her for longer than a day.

"What is it that I'm doing that's making so many people out here avoid me?" Gilbert asked. Buttercup might have a straight mane, but his little girl was a little more patient. The draft horse tried to crane her neck to the side to see what Strongpaw was doing. "Not you, too," Gil muttered under his breath. Not even horses out here liked him.

"You look like a banker," Strongpaw said from inside one of the stalls.

"I am a banker."

"That's your problem," the orc answered. "Lotta people out here need loans to get started. Farms, businesses, it all takes money. Most loans to Frontier Folk are... difficult to repay."

Ah. Gilbert thought about the loan system he'd set up. He'd done his best to make it honest and easy to understand, while still turning a profit. But he didn't run the banks out here (yet), and he could imagine the impossible interest rates being sold as 'insurance' on a 'risky endeavour'.

"Did you know about this?" Gil whispered to Buttercup. She snorted and tugged at the lead that was tied to keep her in place.

"Well, if it helps, Strongpaw," Gilbert said, finishing off the braid. He looked around for something to tie the braid off with, and spotted a length of ribbon resting on a hook next to Buttercup's lead. Taking it, he tied off the horse's braid tight enough so that the horse wouldn't be able to shake it loose again. "I don't currently have a bank out here, though when I do, I plan to resolve that issue. I prefer to make my money off the rich, not the people who need it."

The orc leaned out of the stall, squinting at him. Gilbert smiled his best friendly smile, even though it had been failing him consistently since they'd gotten off the train. Strongpaw responded with a grunt, and lifted up a hand that held a bundle of fox fur with straw bits stuck in it.

"Sure," he said, noncommittal. "This yours?"

The bundle barked, surprising Gilbert. His smile widened into a genuine grin. It seemed that the liberated puppy had managed to find a safe space after all. Patting Buttercup one last time, Gilbert walked down the alleyway to take the little puppy from Strongpaw.

"Why yes! Yes, it is," Gilbert said. He wasn't entirely lying. "Where did you find it?"

"He was sleeping in one of the saddlebags," Strongpaw said, gently placing the tiny thing into Gilbert's hands. "Thought it was one of the barn cats for a second, never seen a puppy that's all... fluff."

"Ah, he's an orman spitz," Gilbert said, carefully plucking bits of straw from the puppy's fur. "They stay all fluff, and quite small too." The puppy wagged his tail, licking desperately at Gilbert's fingers. Poor thing must be hungry. Gil knew there was jerky in the saddle bags, once he had the horses, he'd pull some out to give the pup.

Finishing up with the first horse, Strongpaw moved onto the second, a tall black stallion who snorted a greeting to the stable hand. Staying with the first horse, a bay gelding, Gil pulled some jerky out of Hal's saddlebag and held it up for the pup. Sniffing at it, the dog started licking at the bit of meat before scarfing down the bit Gilbert pulled apart for him.

"What is that?"

Looking up, and feeling like when he used to get caught reading a naughty story in school, Gilbert saw Hal at the door of the bay's stall.

"This is your horse!" Gilbert said, ignoring Hal's pointed look. "Did you get the coffee?"

Hal held up a canteen.

"Excellent! Well, we should get going, now that everyone's here," Gil said, tucking the tiny puppy into the pocket of his jacket. Somehow, the tiny thing fit. "Thank you so much for your help, Strongpaw." Gil slipped out of the stall and patted Hal on the shoulder on his way by.

The orc grunted and held out the reins for Gilbert to take.

"Banker," Strongpaw said, holding the reins firm as Gilbert reached for them. "Scorched Bluffs burnt their bank down." Letting go of the reins, the orc clapped a hand as large as a shovel onto Gil's shoulder. It knocked him a half step sideways. "You try to set up there, they might burn you down, too."

The black stallion sniffed at Gil's shoulder. Uncertain whether to thank the stable hand or ask how he knew where they were going, Gilbert watched Strongpaw disappear into the back of the stables. In his pocket, the puppy wiggled and barked. Reaching down to scratch the tiny, fluffy head, Gilbert led his horse into the street to wait for Hal.

"I'm not even going to ask what that was about," Hal said once he'd led his bay outside. "You can't keep the puppy, Gil."

"I don't know that I could tell you even if you did ask." Gilbert glanced back at the barn, trying to sort through Strongpaw's message. If the orc didn't like bankers, why warn him about a speck of a town? Had the fire that swept through that place been started at the bank? "The Puppy was in your saddle-bags. He found his way back to us: it's fate."

Hal gave him a look that told Gil exactly how little he bought any of that story.

"You're a Carpenter," Hal said. "You explicitly *do not believe in fate*." Ah, Strongpaw's warning had rattled Gil more than he'd thought. Using 'fate' was a mistake when feeding a story to a former priest. Gil mounted his horse, careful not to disrupt the puppy's place in his pocket.

"So I am! And I still think fate doesn't exist, but that personal choice does. And the puppy chose to sleep in your saddlebag and deserves a fair shot at a life not spent in cages. Don't you think?" Gil asked, adjusting his hat. "Don't tell me *you* don't believe in fate anymore, Brother Halpert Thomas?"

Hal rolled his eyes and grimaced at the use of his old name. Gilbert knew he'd won when the now-Hal Stratton climbed up into his own saddle.

"I still believe in God and his Messiahs," Hal said, gathering up his reins. "I just think I misunderstood Their plan for me. I can help more people doing this kind of work, compared to being stuck inside a chapel all day, every day."

Gil's mouth twitched as he tried to maintain his serious air. Not trusting himself to say anything without breaking into laughter, he only nodded and gestured for Hal to take the lead. He wondered if Hal realised he'd admitted he found the priesthood boring. Judging from how grumpy his friend looked, Gilbert felt reasonably certain that he had.

"You chose to take a new path?" Gil asked, scratching the puppy's head.

Hal groaned and nudged his horse into a trot. Gilbert pressed his lips together and wondered which story about Scorched Bluffs he should believe: Marshal Allan's, where the town was rough but just; or Strongpaw's where they burned down banks and bankers alike.

12

MISTER RIVERS

JEB NEVER DID MAKE it back downstairs that night. Jeb wanted to be selfish for a single night and stay with his now-fiancée before he and his siblings hunted down Isaiah's killer. Spending time with Diamond was worth Eli's annoyance, though Jeb knew he'd need to head down to speak with him before Zach and Josie arrived in town.

Most of the people that Di had told wouldn't cause issues, but one of them was a real big problem that would need to be discussed amongst the whole family.

"You're not going to go after all of them, are you?" Diamond asked, running a hand over his back. Jeb was sat at the edge of her bed, pulling on his boots. She was still in her night shift, though she'd be getting dressed real soon to be ready to work the lunch hour. With her red curls loose around her shoulders and her face free of makeup, Jeb thought she was the most beautiful woman he'd ever seen.

"We'll have to find out who did it," he said quietly. Reaching out, he caught her hand and brought it to his lips. "But I don't plan on taking too many chances now that I have someone to come home to." He watched her smile bloom and felt his heart grow in kind.

"Good," she said and gave his hand a squeeze. "You'd better go check on Elijah. You know how he gets when he drinks."

Kissing her hand one last time, Jeb stood and grabbed his coat and hat on his way out the door. The smells wafting up the staircase from the saloon proper were familiar: fresh sawdust, vomit, spilled whiskey. It was a wonder that Di's room never seemed to smell like that.

Ordering a beer on his way past the bar, Jeb headed straight for the corner his brother usually chose. Eli was still lying on the ground, an arm draped over his eyes to block out the sunlight that streamed in through the saloon's windows.

"Mornin' Jeb," Eli groaned. He didn't bother moving his arm.

"C'mon up now," Jeb said. He grabbed his brother under his arm and hauled Eli up into a chair despite his weak groans of protest. "You sober yet?"

Pressing a fist to his chest, Eli belched to the side. Jeb leaned back, expecting vomit to follow. When none did, he took a seat next to his brother, ready to steady him if Eli looked like he was about to fall out of his chair.

"Unfortunately," Eli groaned. "The marshal's been marching in and out of here all morning. I didn't feel like dealing with him yet, so I stayed put."

Before Jeb had a chance to ask why the kid marshal was in town, someone thunked his beer down in front of him. It sloshed and fizzed, the head spilling over the stein's lip onto the still-sticky table. Jeb looked up at who was bold enough to bother the elder Willards, and found himself staring into the craggy face of a complete stranger.

The man's greying hair was cropped short, and a scar ran along the side of his face, dipping behind a black leather eye-patch that covered whatever remained of his eye. Jeb's teeth immediately started to ache. Instead of jumping to his feet to ask who the hell this man was, Jeb sucked on his molars and leaned back in his chair to get a good look at the interloper.

"You Jebediah Willard?" the man asked, his accent strange in a town of migrants. Jeb had heard plenty of accents in Plainfield:

orcish, old world, new world, dwarven, even arroyan from that giant stable hand. This was an accent he hadn't heard since the war. This man had come from the Bayou.

"You've come a long way from the swamp," Jeb said, looking the man over. "Have we met before?"

"No," the man pulled out a chair and sat without asking. "But I have been told you are the man to hire if I have a messy job."

"Sounds like my kind of work," Jeb said, taking a drink of his beer. "Whatcha need done?"

"I need some vermin taken care of. Big kind, get into all kinds of things they shouldn't." The man with one eye folded his hands together on top of the sticky saloon table. "I work for a man who pays well, who is reliable. He has offered to cover the cost of this work, and is willing to provide a bonus for proof of a job done."

Jeb set his beer down lightly and glanced at his suffering brother. Eli was holding himself very still, sweating and pale. Jeb slid the beer over to him, knowing it would help with the hangover.

"I'm listening. But you know more about us than we know about your boss. You and he got names we can call you by?"

The man smiled, and Jeb recoiled at the sight of his teeth. He'd filed his top teeth into points. They'd been hidden behind his moustache until the smile, and Jeb hoped the man never smiled again. No one sane ever did that to themselves.

"Call me Rémi," the man said. "As for my boss, let us call him Mister Rivers. I have the first instalment of your wage. The second will be provided upon completion of your work. Do you agree?"

"You got a description of those vermin?" Eli asked, revived by the beer. "Lotta rats pass through these parts. We'd want to make sure we get the right ones."

"Ah, it talks," Rémi said with another menacing smile. "Yes. A giant human, a banker. Dark hair, fancy clothing. The other is a Stratton. The only one this far west of Wyndford, I believe."

Jeb felt a chill trickle down his spine. These were the two men that Di had wanted him to speak with. The banker would be no problem, but the Stratton... Stratton Detectives had a reputation for being hounds. They were best avoided, and the risks taken by killing one required some thought.

"I see you are concerned." Rémi reached into his pocket and pulled out a pouch. He tossed it onto the table with a thud. "Allow this to be the negotiator that I am not. This is half of the payment." He leaned back in his chair, his single eye watching Jeb without blinking.

Jeb opened the pouch and closed it immediately as soon as he saw how much money was inside. This one job would pay for a wedding and for Di to get her own saloon. Hell, it might pay for the one he was sitting in.

"Done," Jeb said, tucking the money into his coat. "We'll set out first light tomorrow."

Rémi's eye narrowed. "So late? These men have already left for the next town."

"We're waiting on the rest of the posse," Jeb said. "And we know where the vermin will be headed. We can head 'em off on their way there." The two men were going to the train wreck. Even if they took the long route past Scorched Bluffs, Jeb knew he and his family could head them off and lie in wait at the wreck.

"Ah," Rémi seemed to consider this, then nodded once. "Good. I would advise not to run off with that payment, Jebediah Willard." He leaned over the table and smiled again, revealing those horrid teeth. "My employer is not the kind of man to steal from."

The saloon was full. The entire population of Scorched Bluffs had gathered for the town meeting. Sweetpea had baked fresh bread for the event. Annie had come in from her ranch and was talking to Lyddie the barkeep about horses, and Millie had her old guitar out, playing a simple song as the rest of the townsfolk got settled. Her girls, sullen after a day of learning letters and reasons why they shouldn't catch flammable wild animals, sat on the floor, playing with some yarn dolls while Eyota watched.

Ryan had just walked up to the small riser at the front of the saloon to begin when Fyodor began to bark, deep and loud. The room stilled and as one; the residents turned to look at the hotel's front door.

Millie set down her guitar on the table, next to the lantern that held a tired, tailless salamander. The girls had already named it, and so 'Stumpy' had been adopted.

"Sounds like they have a bigger dog than you do," a man said, stepping through the doorway and into the saloon's interior. Dark skinned with neatly trimmed hair and a beard, he wore a badge on his chest that made Millie's throat tighten. A Stratton. What the Hell was a Stratton Detective doing in Scorched Bluffs?

Following the detective was an even taller man, one who had to duck slightly to get through the hotel's doorway. For some inexplicable reason, the giant had a tiny red puppy tucked into his vest.

Both men had sharp eyes and easy smiles.

Both men wore clothes that actually fit them.

Both men *stank* of having too much money, and Millie hated them on sight.

"Hello!" the taller one said, sweeping his hat from his head. The pup in his vest barked twice in greeting, his beady little eyes fixed on Fyodor.

"My name is Gilbert Goldman, and this here is my friend, Halbert Stratton. We're looking for a room, a drink, and a 'Sheriff Ryan Collins'." He smiled a cocksure grin that set Millie's teeth on edge. He seemed to sense her discomfort, and the bastard looked directly at her and *winked*. "Then maybe some company?"

Some of the women in the room looked at Ryan, while others watched the men with wary expressions.

"Eyota," Millie said quietly. "Take the girls home."

13

STRANGERS

WELL, THIS WAS DISAPPOINTING. The Scorched Bluffs' saloon had far too much clothing and too few drinks on the tables. Strangely, the room was full of the smell of freshly baked bread instead of old ale, though he wasn't certain what he'd expected from a town full of women. More alcohol, at the minimum.

The collection of townsfolk was a strange mix that Gilbert had never seen gathered in one room before. The table nearest to him was a family of elves, while a dark elf in braids was sitting next to an orc, who seemed to be missing an eyebrow. Hell, there was even a pink-skinned arroyan all dolled up in a blue ruffled dress and had a yellow ribbon tied around one of her horns. Noticing his attention, the high arroyan smiled and waved. A friendly arroyan was *also very weird*.

Gilbert looked back to the family of elves. A small elf who looked to be drained of all colour was glaring daggers at him, and had her ears pinned back against her head. The other adult elf in buckskin gathered up a pair of itty-bitty baby-girl elves in shapeless dresses and moccasins. Both girls were watching him with giant eyes and opened mouths. Gilbert noticed their ears wiggle when he smiled at them. The girls didn't seem to be sure whether the smile was exciting or frightening.

"Why hello there. I don't believe I caught your names," Gilbert said to the little girls, walking over to crouch in front of them with a smile. In his vest, the Pomeranian barked and wiggled, trying to climb free and make new friends.

"Because we didn't give them," the pale elf said. Her voice was sharp and cold. "You said you were here to speak to the Sheriff. These two sure ain't the Sheriff."

Blinking in surprise, he looked up at the seated momma. From his angle, he could see the faint red of a sunburn on her ears and the remains of kohl smudged around her strange eyes. He'd heard about people with albinism, but had never met anyone with it in person. Were they always this angry?

"These ladies aren't sheriffs?" Gilbert asked, unable to keep from verbally prodding the angry woman. He was aware of the eyes on him, and the way multiple bodies around him shifted their weight. Plainfield had a rough and tumble feel, but this place was coiled tight. Although he could put it down to the dragon's recent attack, Gilbert had a gut feeling it was more than that. He hadn't become so successful by ignoring his intuition.

"Is that a *fox*?" The little redhead piped up, pointing at the Pomeranian still tucked into Gilbert's vest. The pup strained forward, licking desperately at the air near the small finger.

"This is a puppy who *looks* like a fox," Gilbert said, reaching into his vest.

The quiet click of a revolver's hammer being pulled back was almost lost among the small dog's barks and whines. But close as he was, Gilbert heard it and froze.

He looked up from the redheaded girl to see momma elf levelling a revolver on him. Hand steady, almost relaxed, she watched him with cold lilac eyes. This wasn't the first time Gilbert had faced down a gun, but usually, it was drunk rich men who could barely focus on him. They could be talked down with the promise of a drink. The look on this woman's face told him she wouldn't hesitate to shoot. She didn't even look bothered. This must be that 'sharp' and 'mean' Deputy Allan had mentioned.

"Ma'am. Please," Gilbert heard Hal say from behind him. He was using his calming voice, the one they taught him at seminary school. Gilbert had heard it on more than one occasion, which—come to think of it—had also involved drunk rich men with guns. Perhaps Hal could teach him how to use the priestly voice before this trip was through.

"I believe my friend is freeing the dog. *Right, Gilbert?*"

For once, Hal's seminary voice didn't seem to work: the elf didn't stand down and so Gilbert didn't move. This was the most interesting thing to happen in weeks.

"*Millie.*"

Gilbert glanced over to see a tall human woman walking toward them. Dressed in a plain shirt and suspenders, the woman had a rifle strapped to her shoulder, a mastiff at her heel and a shiny tin star pinned to her chest. It seems he had found both the angry deputy and marshal Allen's Sheriff. In a moment of absurdity, Gilbert both wanted to congratulate the Marshal on his taste and gently tell the man to be a bit more realistic about potential love interests. The Sheriff was far, far, out of the poor man's league.

The pale elf huffed. 'Millie' flicked the hammer back into place and spun the revolver back into her holster. She kept her eyes on him and smiled tightly, suggesting that she would have much preferred to keep the gun trained on him. Gilbert felt a shiver of interest prickle along his spine. How did someone end up this angry, ever?

"Yes! That's exactly right," Gilbert said, ever so slowly pulling the tiny wiggly pup from his vest. "My pup wanted to make friends, so who am I to keep him from two small, lovely ladies?"

Too excited to wait to be set down, the fluff ball squirmed in his hand. The moment he was released, the puppy zoomed around the little elflings, over their laps, around their feet, licking every hand in sight. The squeals of giggles the girls let out made Gilbert feel a pang of homesickness. He'd thought to bring the puppy home to Sarah, though if the little girls here liked him, Gilbert could always find another puppy in Wyndford for his storm cloud.

"There," Gilbert said, standing and brushing some stray fox-red hairs from his vest. "The dog is happy, the girls are happy, and I won't tell anyone that your elf threatened to shoot me."

He flashed the momma a winning smile, watching the elf's face with great satisfaction as lilac eyes narrowed.

"I'm Sheriff Collins," the Sheriff said as she joined them. "And this is my deputy: Mildred Berry. Despite misunderstanding the situation, she was acting within the rights of her position."

"As she is allowed," Hal said, tipping his head in the sheriff's direction. Gilbert was certain he could *feel* his friend's annoyance. They'd been in Plainfield, a town full of ruffians and outlaws, and no one had pulled a gun on them *there*. But here the Deputy was ready to shoot over a puppy. "Our apologies, *Deputy* Berry."

"A Deputy? Well, good for you, not letting your height limit you-" Gilbert said, interrupted by a fist that caught him on the jaw. Head snapping to the side, Gilbert took a step back from the elves. He placed a hand over where he'd been struck and frowned at the aggressor. It was the dark skinned elf, furious on the pale one's behalf.

"Ow." Gilbert worked his jaw to make sure the blow hadn't knocked anything out of place. He'd done a little boxing back while in school, but that punch had landed harder than any he remembered.

"Don't ever call her anyone's elf ever again," the elf with braids snarled. "Eyota, Girls. Come with me." The other elves gathered the little girls (the blond one refused to let go of the puppy) and left. The tiny pale deputy remained; arms crossed over her chest. It looked suspiciously like she was trying not to smile.

Almost in unison, chairs scraped against the floor as the townsfolk stood. A few whispered to the Sheriff on the way by, some stared, while others left in silence, avoiding any eye-contact with the two men. The arroyan slowed as she reached them, smile still in place as she paused to whisper a friendly 'hello' on her way out.

Gilbert smiled back, rubbing his jaw. At least someone in this hell town was friendly. Allan had warned them about the deputy, but he hadn't mentioned the rest of the town was just as angry.

"Lyddie, can we get a couple of pints and some water?" Sheriff Collins asked once the saloon was emptied. "Gentlemen, with the promise no more guns will be drawn on you tonight, why don't you take a seat?" She gestured at the table where the Deputy was, though the elf had stood when everyone was leaving.

The elf took the guitar off the table and reached over to pull a spare chair over, lifting it up to keep it from scraping along the floor. Gilbert realized that there was no sawdust in this saloon, a bit of dusty dirt, but that had blown in through the door. The universal result of drunkards not holding their drink seemed to be missing.

"Thank you, darling," he purred, taking the chair from the deputy.

"I would have shot you if you hurt them." She said it in a whisper so quiet, Gilbert was half certain that it was imagined. But no, the smile on her face was too hard and tight for that to have been anything but an intentional warning.

"As you should have," he replied, his smile dropping for a moment. "But I don't hurt *little girls*." He watched her watch him, her eyes flicking over his face. He had nothing to hide at that moment, and while he tried to smile, Gilbert knew it didn't quite reach his eyes. Odd, normally he didn't have a problem smiling. Maybe the sight of the little elflings had made him more homesick than he first thought.

Whatever she found there, she found to be satisfactory. Gilbert watched her ears tilt up ever so slightly, and her smile relaxed into a neutral expression. It was like watching someone let out a long, slow, breath; only she did it silently. He got a nod, simple and brusque.

"I would have shot your shoulder first," she said instead of an apology. The deputy seemed to hesitate, shifting her weight onto her right foot and held it there. "I'm sorry Annie punched you. Unfortunately, the concept of belonging to someone is a sore spot among many of us."

"Well, it hasn't been a full decade since the war," Gilbert said. "Although it was meant only as a turn of phrase, I can understand how it would be taken otherwise. I apologize... but," he said, his grin back. "You can kiss my bruise better if you'd like," he offered with a purr.

The sheriff cleared her throat loudly. The mastiff, hackles relaxing, barked gruffly in agreement. Gilbert noticed the elf's ears turn a brighter red that had *nothing* to do with sunburn, and didn't hide his smug grin from her. Oh, this trip might be fun after all.

"Sorry, business first. Pleasure after?" He suggested, setting the chair down at the table.

"Nope," the deputy said firmly. "Just business."

"I apologize for my friend," Hal said, scratching at his beard. "Feel free to punch him again. It might knock some sense into him."

Gilbert noticed movement in the corner of his eye and flinched back, a hand held up in defence. It seemed, though, that the deputy was simply moving to take a seat. Aggressively, deliberately, to make him flinch. What an aggressive, horrible, *interesting* woman.

"He was joking! My god, you *are* angry," he sputtered. With a sigh that feigned annoyance, Gilbert took a seat and nodded a thank you to the barkeep as she set down a pint of pale beer in front of him. Half-elven, with red hair, she looked familiar, though the facial features were broader, and her hair lighter.

"Are you Diamond's sister?" He asked. "She was very helpful in Plainfield."

"She goes by 'Diamond' now? She would," Lyddie said with an expression of disgust. "Well, glad she's still alive, I suppose." Grumbling to herself, Lyddie finished setting down the drinks and disappeared into the back of the saloon. Gilbert opened his mouth to speak, but heard something hard hitting wood. Repeatedly.

"Diana owes the town a significant debt," Sheriff Collins said with a serene smile, unphased by the sounds coming from the kitchen. She took a seat and rested her forearms on the table, focusing speckled hazel eyes on Gilbert. "So naturally, she's been staying well away. I *do* hope that you're not here to collect her mother's 'inheritance'. This would be the third time we've had to explain that there is none."

Gilbert caught his friend looking at him with lifted eyebrows. Gilbert shrugged. He and Diamond hadn't exactly talked after they'd left the saloon back in Plainfield. At least not about inheritances or finances. Gilbert frowned, gingerly prodding his jaw with his thumb. He could feel that the skin was hot, and he would likely bruise.

"No, we're not here about inheritances at all," Gilbert said. He lifted the glass of beer and placed it to his jaw, letting the cooler glass pull the heat from his skin. It helped less than he had hoped it would. He took a sip from it instead. For being so far out on the Frontier, the beer was surprisingly good. Cool and refreshing, hardly the warmed-over piss they served at Plainfield.

"I represent Goldman National Bank and its clients," Gilbert said. He set the glass down. "There was cargo on that train that was insured with my bank, and I would prefer if we're able to find it and return it with no further dragon encounters. Marshal Allan suggested we come here to find out what happened."

The Sheriff listened thoughtfully, while the deputy leaned forward, eyebrows raised.

"You did hear that part about the dragon attacking the train, right?" she asked. "What do you expect to find out there to return? Ashes?"

Gilbert nudged his friend with his elbow. So far Mister Stratton had been too quiet and not nearly helpful enough. Time for him to earn his keep. Well, his retainer fee.

"Well Deputy," Hal said, clearing his throat. "If we aren't able to recover the cargo in question, we'll need to confirm it's destruction. If we only find ashes at the site of the attack, that should satisfy Mister Goldman's legal agreements."

"Do you know where it is?" Gilbert asked.

The two women glanced at each other, then nodded.

"I was out hunting and stumbled across the wreck. Still stank like dragonfire even though the fire had mostly burnt itself out by then," the deputy said, wrinkling her nose. Gilbert wondered if he should comment on how cute it was, purely to annoy the woman. But that could wait, Gil noticed a strange lack of fear on their faces. Shouldn't a dragon attacking trains concern a town mostly built from wood?

"Are dragon attacks a regular occurrence out here?" He asked. Partially to satisfy his curiosity, partially because *what if dragon attacks were a regular occurrence out here?* Sarah would never forgive him; she was terrified of dragons in her bedtime stories.

"On trains?" The deputy asked. "No, but they painted this one blue, right? The big dragon out in the badlands near here, she's a Greater Blue. Could have thought it was a threat. It's nesting season." She shrugged, and Gil noticed it was ever so lopsided.

"Well, that's excellent," he said, clapping his hands together in excitement. "Could either of you escort us out to the wreck in the morning? It would all go much faster if you show us where the wreck is." He watched the elf's face harden in the passive expression she had been wearing. It was ever so faint, the way her eyes narrowed, and the way her lips pressed tighter together.

"Of course," the deputy offered, smiling back. She did not want to be their guide; Gilbert could see that much. "I would be *happy* to."

The sheriff raised an eyebrow, looking over at Deputy Berry. Whatever she saw was enough to keep the Sheriff from arguing. Collins nodded and reached for her beer. Gilbert did the same, raising it in a quiet toast to the strangest lawmen he'd ever met.

"Well Gentlemen," the angry deputy said. "Welcome to Scorched Bluffs. May you find what you're looking for, then get the hell out."

14

ATTEMPTS MADE

EVERYTHING WAS TERRIBLE. THERE were men in town who were smarmy and rich and *handsome,* and Millie had agreed to escort them out to the train wreck. That meant leaving the girls behind with Sweetpea again, even though the arroyan was gracious enough to pretend like it wasn't a problem. But as lovely as Millie's girls were, they were full of trouble.

Which led to what would surely be Millie's least favourite part of an already crappy evening. The girls had held onto the rich man's puppy and Fenna had refused to give it back, saying the puppy had 'chosen' them and it was only through appealing to the four-year-old's sense of empathy that Millie had managed to argue that the tall man might miss his puppy, so it should go back.

The guilt over that conversation weighed heavily on her shoulders as Millie stepped into the empty saloon. A four-year-old shouldn't be that good, shouldn't care that much about strangers that would be ready to sell the whole town out in a heartbeat.

Millie found Lyddie in the saloon's kitchen, sitting by the stove while knitting a pair of small socks. The wooden table used to cut meat had some dents that Millie would bet ten dollars were caused by the cast-iron frypan that lay nearby.

"So," she said, the tiny puppy in one hand. "'Diamond' still gets under your skin."

Lyddie looked at the table's fresh dents and then back to Millie, the tips of her faintly pointed ears turning pink.

"Better the table than anyone's face," Lyddie said. "I'm surprised you don't hate her more than I do."

Millie shrugged, lifting the frypan in her free hand and turning it to examine if it had suffered at all from its role in the table's abuse. It was ridiculously heavy and seemed to have survived unscathed. Too often, people underestimated the prowess of cooks, a mistake Millie had made sure to only make once.

"I do hate her," Millie said quietly. "But she also gave me one of the best parts of my life. I don't feel right killing the woman who gave birth to my daughter." She gently set the frypan down, and the puppy yipped at it, defending his new friend from the strange object.

"I might have gotten upset if you killed my sister," Lyddie admitted. "I'd have understood why, but still been upset."

Millie smiled at her. "I would have asked you first, probably." She nodded toward the half-knit socks. "Those are for Rasha, aren't they?" She asked. The girls had a town full of aunties, but Rasha was lucky enough to have one by blood, as well. "She'll love them."

"They are, though I'll make a pair for Fenna too," Lyddie said, tugging at the knit tube. The loops were tight and even, the wool dyed blue using roughtooth roots. "You aren't here just to check up on me, are you?"

Damn. Millie would much rather continue talking to her friend than going to find the person who owned the dog she carried, but Lyddie could practically smell procrastination on a person.

"Which room did you put the giant man in?" she asked with a sigh.

The bartender raised a single eyebrow very slowly, then looked at what Millie was holding. The fluffy red puppy was ecstatic to be held, and his little tail was wagging so fast his whole body trembled in Millie's hands. The puppy licked his nose and kept looking up at the elf who carried him.

"Do... you want a bottle of whiskey to bring up?" Lyddie asked. "It might not be wine, but we've got enough to spare."

"Lyddie, this is about returning the dog," Millie said, voice flat. Maybe if she glared hard enough at the other woman, Lyddie wouldn't notice how hot Millie's ears were getting.

"I'm just saying you don't have to pretend with me. It's awful late and–"

"I am holding. The dog. It is his dog." Millie held up the puppy, who barked. He was the dog!

"I'll get you some of the better whiskey," Lyddie said. "How long's it been? Before you had the Fenna? You work so hard; you deserve to let yourself have a little fun. He'll be gone soon and probably never come back. What's the harm?"

"You know what? I bet I know which room it is," Millie said, stalking out of the kitchen. Sure, the last time she'd spent the night with someone had been when she's conceived Fenna. Which, in Millie's opinion, gave her more reason to keep this visit entirely about returning the puppy that her little girls had stolen. The last thing Millie needed from city men was to get pregnant by one of them. The Clan still wanted Fenna to live with them. She could only imagine what rich asshole types would do if they heard they had a child.

The hotel wasn't used much for guests anymore. Built of brick, it was the only building that had survived the fire and wore the scorch marks on its exterior to prove it. During the rebuilding period, those that stayed lived in the hotel. These days, the town used it for storage, though a few rooms were kept up for any new arrivals.

Jogging up the steps to the second floor, Millie steeled herself for having to deal with overly friendly strangers. A single lamp lit the hallway, hanging on the wall between a pair of rooms that no longer had dust on the doorknobs. Perking an ear, Millie looked from one to the other, debating which she should knock on. The Stratton seemed to be more pleasant to deal with, but he was a goddamn *Stratton Detective*. The less attention those bastards paid her, the better. Then there was the banker, all... sleazy flirting and unnecessarily tall.

Millie heard footsteps from the room on the right and sighed. Fuck it. Whoever this was, they were awake at least. She knocked.

There was a pause, then she heard the man cross the room inside.

"Sorry to bother you so late," she said, watching the door open. She was met with an ungodly amount of chest. Ah, the giant was in this room, then. She looked over his bare shoulders and chest, then up to his face, where he looked both surprised and pleased. For a banker, he was remarkably fit. There were even a few small scars on his arms and ribs, though Millie was careful not to look too long.

"I'm surprised, deputy," Goldman said with a slow smile. He stepped back and motioned her inside. "I'd given up hope you'd come visit after you sulked through our meeting tonight."

Millie blinked, ears tilting to one side.

"I wasn't going to *steal your dog*," she said, patting the puppy she followed Goldman into the room. "I'm sorry my girls took him. They like to adopt stray things." And name them. And get attached to them.

She took two brusque steps in, crouched and set the dog down by the foot of the bed. It immediately tried to climb back up her leg.

"*My* dog?" Goldman said, the surprise in his voice causing Millie to look up at him. The man was standing by the bedside table, a bottle of whiskey in one hand and a glass in the other. *Strange, shouldn't he have emphasized the word 'dog'?* Millie thought. *Why place it on 'my' instead?*

"This dog is yours, yes?" Millie said slowly, rubbing the pom's belly. "You had him tucked in your vest when you showed up earlier tonight." She paused. He was looking at her strangely. "Is he... *not*... your dog?"

"Nope," Goldman said, pouring a dram of whiskey into the glass. "Not mine. That pup is a stowaway from Plainfield where he escaped from some horrid woman who had him in a cage."

Millie looked down at the spitz, who was grinning up at her, his tiny tongue hanging out of his mouth. He wiggled on his back, demanding more belly rubs. He was a tiny thing, smaller than some varmints she saw while out hunting. The wildlife of the Bluffs would, quite literally, eat this thing alive.

"If you stay with me, Fyodor will step on you and then you'll be a very flat spitz," Millie told the puppy. He answered with a yip and pawed at her leg. She sighed.

"I think he's yours now," Goldman said, kindly. He held the glass of whiskey down to her. "Or your girls', if you prefer. I had thought about bringing him back for my daughter, but he seems to have chosen yours."

"Your daughter?" she asked, standing. Millie eyed the whiskey and then took it, sniffing at the glass. There was no dusty coating, no oily sheen to the drink, but she would never not check a drink poured by a stranger. Satisfied, she took a small sip. One of the good bottles Lyddie kept in reserve. The whiskey was smoky and strong and for once she didn't feel sick at the thought of its smell.

"Sarah, she's three," Gilbert said. "Around the same age as yours, I think?" He refreshed his own glass, still on the bedside table, and set the bottle down. Walking over to her, he held his glass out in a toast.

"To tiny daughters and to a fruitful expedition tomorrow," Gilbert said. "Cheers."

The sooner these men were done looking for their item, the sooner they would be gone. The sooner they were gone, the safer everyone would be. Millie smiled up at Gilbert, clinked her glass to his and took another sip, nose wrinkling at the sharp smell.

"Cheers," she said, clearing her throat. "What are you looking for, anyway?"

Goldman sipped his own drink and set it aside. He leaned back against the wall, a slow smile spreading over his face as he looked at her. He looked very... annoyingly pleased. Shirtless men that looked like that shouldn't be calm, they should go be calm and handsome somewhere far away from her.

"What?" she asked. She refused to let some rich boy from the city make her feel self-conscious.

"Your nose," he said. "You scrunch it up whenever you sip the whiskey. It's cute, but you don't need to drink if you don't want to. The whiskey's feelings won't get hurt."

Millie scowled and pressed her ears back against her skull. She knocked back the rest of the whiskey in one go, and coughed at the fire it left down her throat and the warmth that spread through her chest. Ugh. Even Lyddie's better stuff was nearly impossible to get down.

"I'm not cute," she snapped. "I'm old and grouchy and I'm going now."

Goldman shrugged, holding out a hand for her glass. She held it out, but froze as she spotted a pair of books on his night table next to the whiskey bottle.

"You're kind of cute. But we both have a long day ahead of us. I'd invite you to stay, but then neither of us would get any rest." Goldman leaned forward, gently taking the glass from her hand. He followed her gaze to the books and he glanced back at her, curious.

"Do you read?" he asked.

"Yes, I can read," Millie snapped. She crossed the rest of the room to pick up the books, looking at each. Their titles made her blood run cold, and she flapped her ears to try to distract Goldman from noticing how the blood had drained from her face.

"But this is a whole bunch of bullshit," she said, waving the autobiography of Frederic Rousseau at him. She slapped it down onto his night table, tucking the red book into her vest when she had her back turned to him.

"Oh? How do you know that?" Gilbert asked. She heard him get off the bed, and Millie's ears swivelled back to keep track of his movement. Turning to look at Gilbert, Millie crossed her arms over her chest.

"A lot of the war's veterans end up out on the Frontier," she said. "They talk about the so-called Hero of the Union. All the awful shit he did. If you hang around Plainfield long enough, you'll hear their stories."

"Ah," Gilbert said, his long eyelashes framing dark blue eyes that had no right being as pretty as they were. "You mean like letting the Bayou Butcher run amok for so long."

"Sure," Millie said cautiously, ears dipping low. "He only stopped them after they killed a unionist family, right? We all know the stories. The Butcher is a bogeyman for children now, but he knew they were out killing non combatants for years. What kind of hero does *that*?"

She knew she'd said something wrong the way his eyes seemed to sharpen on her. The problem was, which part of what she'd said had he picked up on? This man was smarter than she'd given him credit for, and Millie was beginning to regret finishing the whiskey out of spite. Her chest felt warm and her tongue seemed to be a touch too loose. Worse still, he hadn't given it to her to loosen her up. He'd said she didn't have to drink it.

"You tell your daughters about the Butcher?" Goldman asked.

"No," Millie admitted. She took a deep breath and let it out slowly, focusing on the words she wanted to say. She was far from drunk, but she didn't want to give Goldman any more information by accident. "I tell them stories about the men like Rousseau that let bad things happen if it means it'll make them richer. And stories about dragons. We all prefer the dragon stories, to be honest."

They watched each other for a few heartbeats, and Millie felt her ears growing warm again.

"We have a long day ahead of us on the trail, you should get rest," she said, her voice overly sharp even to her own ears. She saw the banker's lips twitch up, and she pressed her lips together into a tight line.

"We leave at dawn, and I am *not* 'cute'," she said, turning on her heel. She scooped up the puppy her daughters had named Freckle and stomped out into the hall. Her ears twitched back, catching the banker's faint chuckle. She scowled harder and told herself she was *not cute*. She was fierce and tired and grouchy and spirits only knew why some stupid young city boy was getting to her.

Millie headed straight for the Jail. She knocked once before opening the door, ducking out of habit even though Ryan didn't greet her with a punch this time. Instead, Fyodor came barreling out of the Sheriff's office, a stick in his mouth. Smelling the puppy, the mastiff greeted the small dog with a whuff of air.

"Ryan?" Millie called, pushing past Fyodor to get into the office.

Her friend looked up from some letters, the faintest blush on her cheeks but one that faded the moment she saw Millie pull the stolen book from her vest.

"We have a problem," the elf said, tossing the book about the Bayou Butcher onto the desk. "We have a *huge* fucking problem." Unable to stand still, Millie set the puppy down and began to pace the tiny office, followed by one giant dog and one tiny one.

All colour drained from the Sheriff's face as she picked up the small red book and read its title.

"Why would a banker have this?" Ryan asked, watching Millie pace. "Isn't this edition banned?"

"Absolutely banned," Millie said, scrubbing at her face with her hands. "He even had Fred's fucking autobiography, too, sitting out on the nightstand. There's no way that they have those two specific books with them and then come here just to investigate lost cargo."

Millie fell into a squat, wrapping her arms over her head and stifled a scream against her knees.

"Hey, hey," Ryan said, and Millie heard her chair fall back as the human woman leapt up and hurried over. Strong arms wrapped around her, pulling Millie into a comforting hug. "We'll figure this out," Ryan whispered. "You're taking them out to the wreck. While you're gone, I'll get the town ready. With the bullets, we're better prepared than we've ever been."

Chest tight with nerves, Millie nodded. She felt ill. The taste of whiskey on the back of her tongue felt more like bile than special reserve.

"Okay," she breathed, trying to slow her racing heart. "Okay. You get the town ready; I'll take them out to the wreck. I'll give them the chance to find whatever they're looking for and send them back to Plainfield. Give them a chance to be what they say they are."

Ryan didn't ask what would happen if they weren't. She didn't need to.

"If that Stratton is real, we're in for trouble," Ryan said instead.

"If they work for Fred, the Strattons will be the least of our worries," Millie whispered.

15

GRAVEDIGGERS

TRYING TO FIT A six-and-a-half-foot tall man into a regular sized bed did not make for a good night's sleep. Gilbert gave up when he saw the sky lighten through the hotel room window. His late-night visitor hadn't stayed, which was a shame, but he was entirely convinced after his restless night that the narrow mattress wouldn't have had enough room for a second body, no matter how tiny that body may be.

Rolling out of bed, Gilbert stood and stretched, his hand hitting the low wooden ceiling before he was able to straighten his elbow. This whole town was built for tiny elves, he was certain of it.

Tiny, angry, cute deputy elves that had gone as pale as a ghost at the mention of the Bayou Butcher, or paler than a ghost in this specific case. Gilbert wanted to know why; why'd she'd recognized the books he'd had on his nightstand without being close enough to read the covers? Marshal Allan had been right about her. She was mean, but she had also been on the defensive last night, and something she'd said kept sticking in his mind. She didn't tell stories of the Butcher to her girls to scare them into behaving. She'd said she told them stories about the men like Rousseau.

How the hell did a tiny angry deputy elf know what Rousseau was like? More interesting still, when he'd tried to pack the

Butcher book into his saddlebags that morning, it was gone. Gilbert wasn't even mad that the deputy had swiped it. He was impressed *he hadn't noticed her do it* when she'd been within arm's reach.

Once he dressed and packed, Gilbert stepped out into the hallway to find it pitch black. The lantern that had hung on the wall last night was either gone or had burnt out. Reaching out, Gilbert felt the slightly pebbled finish of the hotel's wallpaper, and after some searching, a bare nail. Not burnt out, then.

"Sneaky elf," he muttered. "Tiny, angry, cute and *vindictive* elf." Using the wall as a guide, Gilbert felt his way down to the ground floor.

The saloon was empty and the fireplace, banked for the night, cast no light into the room. Gilbert could see the faint light of the pre-dawn sky through the saloon's windows. Heading toward them and the door, Gilbert bumped into at *least* two chairs on the way, sending one clattering to the ground. He stood there for a moment, staring at the dim shape by his feet and deciding whether to try to pick it up or edge around the damn thing.

The door to the saloon opened, Gilbert blinked at the sudden brightness of the lantern that was thrust inside.

"You alright, Gil?" Hal asked, peering at the otherwise empty saloon. "I didn't think you'd be up yet." The Detective was fully dressed, and it looked like he'd been up for some time. Unlike Gilbert, Hal looked well-rested.

It seemed the elf was not the lantern thief after all, a fact that Gilbert found disappointing. He would have liked to hold a petty act like that over her. Maybe even use it to find out how a town ended up filled with women who could identify an orman spitz on sight, or sheriffs who owned a purebred moorland mastiff. The cost of a single moorlander puppy could feed a working-class family for years. Most owners insured their dogs the way an average person might insure their home.

Gilbert righted the offending chair. "I was attacked by a chair," he said. "Don't worry though, I won." Adjusting the front of his suit and brushing invisible specks of dirt from his lapels, Gilbert used the lantern's light to avoid further mishaps on his way to the door.

"Well, good thing we're celebrated chair hunters," Hal said with a grin, the lantern casting his chin dimple into deep relief. "I was coming to get you. The baker is brewing some coffee and then we can set out. Deputy Berry is already at the General store." Hal paused, glanced outside over his shoulder and then leaned in, his face growing serious. "Something's off here. Did you see the Sheriff's dog?"

Gilbert nodded. "I asked the old man for a moorlander when I was a boy and I got a lecture about how one of those could pay for my education. 'Dogs can't accrue interest'." Gilbert rolled his eyes. Dogs could accrue interest if they were proper pedigree and were intact. While he hadn't gotten too friendly with the Sheriff's dog, he was certain it was both.

"Right?" Hal said under his breath. He sighed, relaxing back into a less conspiratorial posture. "I asked for one too. Percy got one when he got married, but-" Hal shook his head as if to clear it of lingering familial duties.

"The deputy had a strange reaction last night," Gilbert said quietly. Hal rolled his eyes, clearly assuming the worst.

"Turning you down is not a 'strange reaction', Gil," Hal said, rolling his eyes.

"Hah, funny," Gilbert muttered. "No, not that. She tried to return the puppy last night, and she spotted those books I'd brought. And she froze. She knows something about Rousseau. If we can get her to tell us, we might have what we need to blackmail him into leaving the bank."

Hal scratched at his jaw, thinking that over.

"You said he likes blondes, right?" Hal said. "Hard to get blonder than being albino."

It felt like the floor shifted under Gilbert, and his stomach dropped. If the Deputy had an encounter with Rousseau, that would be enough to explain her behaviour. The reaction to whiskey, the open hatred of wealth and hostility about the books.

"Well," Gil said, trying to recover his internal balance. "We'll have the chance to talk to her on the ride. I think... it's worth trying to find out what she knows."

The Deputy in question was waiting by an outdoor stove, clutching a mug to herself as if it held aqua vitae itself. *Maybe it did*, Gilbert thought as he caught the aroma of very strong coffee. She had her back to the wall of the general store, ears perked and eyes shone red in the lantern's light. She looked like she was some sort of hell cat. Next to her, the arroyan's eyes shone yellow and blue. Colours that, in theory, were much less unsettling than red when it came to eyes.

"That's creepy," he muttered as they approached the two women. "Does everyone's eyes shine like that here?"

"Nope," the arroyan said happily. "It's our glowing person-alities shining through." It took Gilbert—still uncaffeinated–a moment to realize it was a pun. The elf snorted into her mug, a sound that was suspiciously close to laughter.

"I'm Sweetpea, by the way," she said, holding out her hand. "You can call me Pea, or Sweetpea, or Miss Sweetpea. Your friend already asked me to send a telegram back to Wyndford for you." Sweetpea smiled and her sharp canines glinted in the dim light. The whole visual of a horned arroyan in ruffles and lace was terribly off-putting, but Gilbert took her hand and kissed her knuckles as manners dictated. So far, friendly faces were hard to find in Scorched Bluffs. He wasn't about to alienate the only friendly resident that was over the age of five.

"It's a pleasure, Miss Sweetpea," Gilbert said. "I would have arrived sooner, but someone took the hallway lantern." He looked pointedly at Hal.

"Oh! I can fix that!" Miss Sweetpea gestured for Gilbert to lean down and lifted herself up onto the tips of her hooves. For a moment her eyes glowed, *truly* glowed, and she murmured an incantation that Gilbert felt rattle and buzz at the base of his skull. Then, with a pleased smile, Sweetpea tapped her index finger against Gilbert's forehead. He blinked and pulled back, surprised. Then blinked again, taking a step back as the world was suddenly bright and easy to see. Everything was grey, but he could see the small lizard warming itself under the wooden stove, the bags under the Deputy's eyes, even the cabins out at the edge of town.

"Well, Miss Sweetpea, aren't you full of surprises?" Gilbert murmured, looking back at Miss Sweetpea in awe. He could see her every freckle as clear as if they were under a noon hour sun. "Thank you."

The arroyan mage repeated the spell for Hal, and Gilbert watched his friend's pupils dilate. Hal blinked, then blinked again rapidly as he adjusted to the newfound ability to see. When he looked at Gilbert, Hal broke into a grin. Gilbert grinned back, like some idiot schoolboy.

"Is this how you see all the time?" Hal asked Sweetpea.

"No," Sweetpea said with a cheerful smile. Gil waited a moment, expecting an explanation. None came.

"Well, now that you two won't trip on your own feet," deputy Angry-Elf said, "We're heading out in fifteen minutes. The sooner we get to that damn wreck, the sooner we can get you fellas on your way." She pushed herself off the wall, finishing off her coffee in a single gulp. Eying Gilbert, then Hal, deputy Berry narrowed her eyes.

"Go on then, your horses ain't gonna saddle themselves."

Heavily armed with a repeating rifle slung across her back and a revolver at each hip, Deputy Berry would have cut a grim figure if not for the ridiculous mule she rode. A grey with a fluffy mane that had been braided back and forelock trimmed so he could see. Each ear could have belonged on a rabbit instead of an equine, and it took Gilbert genuine effort not to laugh every time the deputy and her mule heard a sound in the distance. Their ears would swivel in tandem. Next to the two men on their taller horses, the deputy seemed even tinier. Gilbert had tried to figure out how she fired the rifle without being knocked over and settled on the idea that she carried pistols for that very reason.

Despite his best efforts, the elf responded to his questions in as few syllables as possible or ignored them completely. Her ears had slowly pinned back against her head as he asked about the rifle logistics and offered to shoot him so he could see how it worked first hand. That was the point where he had allowed the silence and watched the landscape around them for dragons instead.

There was beauty to the plains: the grasses whispered in the breeze, the sky was clear and blue, and the air was full of cicada song. As beautiful as the land was, Gilbert couldn't say the same about the *smell*. The wind changed direction some time ago, bringing with it smoke and rot. There was an underlying muskiness to the smell that only got stronger as they rode on. Gilbert realized that was likely from the dragon. He had never considered that dragons had a *smell*. They were big and burned things.

"Up ahead," Deputy Berry said, interrupting Gilbert's thoughts. "You can see some of the cars piled up in the middle of the burn."

Gilbert didn't see any train cars at first. Miss Sweetpea's spell had worn off hours ago, leaving him mildly annoyed that his eyes were back to their normal ability. The tall grasses had been burnt away, leaving a large dark patch of ashes and dirt on the horizon. As they continued forward, he squinted, barely able to make out a pile of rectangles folded up against each other like an accordion.

"Oh," Berry said, looking to one side. "There's part of the train." She pointed to a patch of flattened grasses. As Gilbert and Hal came alongside her, they stared at a hunk of twisted metal. Its two-inch thickness had bent outward, almost hiding the headlamp that had once been fixed to the front of the locomotive.

Gilbert tilted his head, torn between hoping that Rousseau's cargo had burnt up and he didn't have to deal with the man ever again, and the cargo being recoverable.

"Do you think there's a smaller piece I could have brought back to Wyndford?" He asked brightly. "It would make a lovely piece in the bank for my clients. I could have it mounted in the lobby. It would tell everyone that 'Goldman National goes to the edges of the world itself to insure your items'," he said, motioning with his hand to make an invisible marquee in front of him.

The elf watched him from her mule, deeply uninterested.

"If you want to haul it back, sure," she said. "Be my guest." She nudged her mule forward, and Gilbert let his smile fade. Next to him, Hal leaned over in the saddle and patted his shoulder.

"A chunk of the train wouldn't be a bad idea," Hal thought out loud. "It would prove the complete destruction of the cargo."

Ahead, the Deputy tensed, ears flicking directly up. Gilbert nudged his friend and gestured at her with his chin. They both looked up, expecting to see a giant shadowy beast bearing down on them. The blue sky remained broken only by a stray fluffy cloud. Nary a dragon in sight.

Odd.

"Is something the matter, Deputy?" Hal asked, nudging his horse ahead. Gilbert followed. "You look alert."

"It's fine," the elf said, shaking her head. "I saw a rattler in the grass, but it was heading away from us." She looked at Gilbert over her shoulder, saddle creaking under her. She smiled, all sharpness and no warmth. "You should go for a piss in that patch of grass, right there. Maybe roll around a bit in the grass for good luck."

"Ah, did you want to see more of what's on offer?" Gilbert asked with a friendly smile. "Deputy, how *scandalous*."

Her smile dropped immediately into a look of disgust. Looking from Gilbert to Hal, she wrinkled her nose at the Stratton. "I don't know how you haven't shot him yet."

Hal grinned, throwing a shrug Gilbert's way. "It crossed my mind, but he's basically family." The elf cast a last glance at Gilbert before turning back around. She flicked her right ear a few times. The friends followed at a walk, letting her pull ahead.

"Did you see a snake?" Gilbert asked in a murmur.

"Nah. But after the spell wore off, it feels like I can barely see anything at all," Hal grumbled. "We should have invited Miss Sweetpea along."

"We should have," Gilbert agreed. "She's far better company."

He could see the train properly now, at least what was left of it. The accordion-folded remains of cars butted up against the sharply bent rails that lifted to the sky at strange angles, like the talons of some grounded beast. Thrown off to the side of the railway were burnt out husks of rail cars and at the very front, thrown to its side with its boiler peeled completely open, lay the remains of the locomotive.

Dark shapes huddled around one of the burnt-out cars, and the Deputy pulled free one of her revolvers. Squeezing off a shot into the sky, she sent buzzards and rock dragonets scattering into the sky with protesting screeches.

"And you saw this happen?" Hal asked. "From where?"

Gilbert listened, catching the verbal trap Hal had laid for the Detective.

"I didn't see it happen," deputy Berry answered, neatly avoiding it. They passed from the tall grasses into the barren patch where the fire had turned everything living to ash. "I think I heard when the locomotive blew, though. I was camped further to the north. There's a small shack there. When it was dawn, I came down to see what made the sound and smelled the dragon." She sniffed the air.

"You can still smell it, actually." She frowned slightly. "I thought the musk would have faded by now. It's late in the season for her to be in heat."

Gilbert split off from the two, riding toward a burnt-out car that the buzzards had been at. He thought he knew what he'd find there, but was surprised to find the buzzards had been at foodstuffs whose cans had burst during the heat of the fire.

Dismounting, Gilbert put a hand over his nose and mouth to reduce the stench of rot. It would smell far worse, he told himself, if not for the birds. It still smelled horrible, and he could feel his eyes watering. Walking down the line of ruined train cars, he stopped at the one that had been carrying Rousseau's cargo.

"Hal, what happens when bullets end up in a fire?" Gilbert called out.

"Uh," Hal said from somewhere behind him.

"Have you ever seen popped corn?" Berry asked, walking over. "Bullets cook off, and eventually the casing explodes, but it's not near as dangerous as if fired from a gun unless you're standing right next to the fire."

She joined Gilbert by the very empty remains of a boxcar. It didn't have any bullet holes visible in the charred remains of its walls, though if the Deputy was telling the truth, it wouldn't. He watched her face as the elf stepped into the wreckage and kicked some of the ashes aside.

"There should be the remains of casings and the bullets themselves, though," Berry said with a frown.

"So, someone stole the cases of ammunition," Gilbert said, tucking his hands into his pockets. He kept his eyes on the deputy, even as his heart sank. He was hoping they'd been destroyed. The cargo hadn't been insured against dragons, but it *was* against theft. The deputy didn't seem the type to take bribes to look the other way, which made his life harder.

"Who would steal bullets and leave behind food, though?" Hal asked. The deputy's ears dipped slightly at the question. How fascinating.

"Everyone," she said, looking up from the ashes to the two men. "Bullets are lighter, easier to sell, more useful. Bandits want them to steal from honest folks. Honest folk need to hunt and to be able to scare off the bandits.

Gil looked at Hal, raising his eyebrows in a silent question. Did that seem accurate? It sounded logical to him, but it would make finding the damn crates near impossible.

"Whoever did it must have been the same ones who killed that Willard kid," Hal said. "His brother got drunk back at Plainfield, mentioned whoever shot him put a round right between his eyes."

"The Willards are bad news," Berry said, her voice even. "I imagine the surviving ones are already out for blood. If it was anyone else, I'd suggest following their trail to find your thief, but they don't leave witnesses."

Gilbert looked over at her, noticing she was holding her ears at a neutral angle.

"You didn't smell the body?" Hal asked.

"I didn't get close," Berry said, tipping her chin up at him. "And I didn't go digging through a burning wreck for bodies. Call me a bad deputy if you want, but I wasn't sure if the dragon would be back."

Oh. Gilbert glanced at Hal. Neither he nor Gilbert had mentioned the Willard boy had been put into the fire... so how did the Deputy know that's where the body was?

16

— · —

THE LITTLE RED BOOK

MILLIE AND THE MEN left before dawn, with Sweetpea seeing them off. Ryan had watched the small party set out from the jailhouse's window, cradling a tin mug of coffee. She hadn't been able to sleep well since the train wreck, but it was the arrival of the banker and Stratton that had caused full-blown insomnia.

The small red book Ryan tucked into the jail's safe the night before might as well be a stick of dynamite. She had skimmed through it with Millie that night, searching for any notes in the margins, any underlined passages that would offer them insight on why the men had brought that particular book to Scorched Bluffs.

The book was salacious, describing the murders attributed to the Butcher in gory detail and presenting the armies as bumbling oafs who succeeded primarily by luck instead of any actual skill. No wonder it had been banned. If that's all the book had been, they would have returned it to the men's bags before they noticed it was missing. But there was a problem.

The book spoke about Millie. It was distorted through pulpy words, but anyone who spent time with the elf could spot the similarities. The prime suspect throughout the book was 'Ghost', a pale elf who had no name and grew up in the wilderness. The author had gotten the gender wrong and described

Ghost as tall and lean with his hair spiked into a mohawk, but the rest was accurate. Ghost fought with tomahawks. Ghost had a bad temper and was fearless.

The author didn't really explain why Ghost was suspected of being the Butcher, falling back on a tired excuse of Ghost being an evil albino elf.

The book stayed in the safe as Sweetpea saw the group off and made her way over to the jail. Ryan heard her knock on the jail door, then adjusted her skirts with an audible rustle. Fyodor heaved himself up to his feet and trotted over to the door to greet their guest with a deep bark.

"Oh, stop it," Ryan said, leaving the window to pull Fyodor from the doorway. The door was too narrow to allow someone through when he stood in the way. "It's just Sweetpea." Stepping over her dog, Ryan opened the door to let the baker inside.

"You're up early," Sweetpea said with a smile. "Good morning. I saw you snooping and thought I'd check in."

Fyodor shoved his head past Ryan's hip to sniff at Sweetpea's pocket. Licking his impressive chops, Fyodor's attempted begging was interrupted by Ryan's hand as she pushed his snout back out of the way. Ignoring his soft whine, Ryan tilted her head toward the jail's interior.

"I've got some coffee on, want some?" Ryan shooed her dog back to the office. Fyodor reluctantly obeyed, but made sure Ryan knew he was sad about it. He hung his massive head low and let out a deep sigh.

"That would be wonderful, thank you!" Sweetpea said. "So do you want in on the pool?"

Ryan paused; weight already shifted onto her back foot to head back into the office. She frowned slightly. Sweetpea's face was cheerful, empty of any mischievous glint, but Ryan had learned over the years that the arroyan's definition of 'mischief' was more aligned with Millie's than anyone else's. That was to say: it often involved fire and other dangerous materials.

"What pool?" Ryan asked, eyes narrowing slightly.

"The betting pool," Sweetpea said, slipping past the Sheriff with a swish of skirts. "Annie thinks Millie will kill both men. I think she's just going to shoot one. But like, in the leg." She dipped her hand into a pocket of her skirt and pulled out a dog treat, slipping it to Fyodor on her way past. Ryan would have missed it if she hadn't been watching the arroyan for that very action. She deeply regretted ever agreeing to Millie's suggestion of teaching Sweetpea how to pick pockets.

"Don't you think creating a betting pool about someone's life is a bit morbid?" Ryan asked, closing the jail door with a small groan. "These two could cause us a lot of trouble if they had half a mind to."

Sweetpea perched on the visitor's chair, folding her hands delicately into her lap. She thought about Ryan's question for a moment, pursing her lips and tapping her hooves lightly against the wooden floor.

"No?" she asked, more than answered. "I mean, we're not trying to kill them, right? I think that Hal guy seems pretty nice. Maybe if we ask him nicely, he won't tell his other Stratton people about us. And if he says no, *then* we can kill him."

Ryan squeezed her eyes shut and pinched the bridge of her nose. Taking a moment, she weighed the benefit of explaining why killing a Stratton detective would be a bad idea against the likelihood that Sweetpea already had thought of *why* it was a bad idea and judged those reasons to be inconsequential. The latter won out.

"What are you all betting with anyways?" Ryan asked, changing the topic. Rubbing her eyes, she crossed the room to her stove and the pot of coffee that sat on top of it. It was a shame that they had to make the coffee by reusing grounds so frequently.

"Babysitting duties," Sweetpea said. "I'll be taking them this time, since last week they filled Nylah's forge with salamanders. It was sweet of them, but the salamanders didn't really want to stay put in the furnace..."

Ah, that's where the salamanders had been coming from. Ryan poured a fresh cup of coffee for Sweetpea and refilled her own mug. She'd indulged and used a fresh scoop of the stuff that morning. Coffee was more precious than gold out in Scorched Bluffs, and they all tried to make it last by reusing dregs, but it was never the same as a fresh pot.

"Who do you think those men are here for?" Sweetpea asked.

"Millie, I think," Ryan said, passing a full mug to the arroyan. Her reaction was immediate. Sweetpea's face lost its permanent smile, and her brows knit tight in concern.

"Is it safe for her to be out there with them?" Pea asked. "I could catch up with them if I left right away."

Ryan shook her head, sitting on the edge of her desk. Blowing the steam from her mug, she took a light sip of coffee. Bitter, a little watered down, but still caffeinated. It was just what she needed.

"No," she said gently. "Millie can handle it; we spoke about it this morning. We can't be sure they really are here for her, or if the train story is genuine. She'll take them out to the wreck, and then hopefully they get what they need and leave." If not, the wreck was far enough away that Millie could take care of the pair without interference.

Sweetpea sighed, deflating in her chair.

"Okay," she said, staring down into the coffee Ryan had given her. "But we should get ready, right? In case they are here for more than the train."

Ryan nodded. It was a grim thought, but it would be best for everyone if they prepared for nothing than if they were caught unawares.

"Are you going to be okay if we have to fight?" Ryan asked, her voice gentle. She'd never seen the other woman look so upset. Not even when Millie's girls had ruined a whole batch of bread by adding sugar to the dough.

"Oh, pshaw, of course I will," Sweetpea said, flipping her curls over one shoulder. "It's just, this is Millie, you know? She pretends like it doesn't bother her, but I saw her face back at the train. Something's bothering her. She didn't even make a joke about the Willard kid's boots." Sweetpea sipped her coffee and sighed.

"It's unsettling to see her unsettled," Ryan agreed. She had seen more of the elf's fragile side than anyone else in town, but that had been years ago. Since their arrival in town, Millie had been steady and strong, if abrasive. They were both shaken up after the dragon, but finding the books in the banker's possession seemed to chip away at Millie's composure.

Doubt crept in. Maybe Ryan should have been the one to take the men out to the wreck. She trusted Millie more than anyone, but had they made the right choice?

"Can you keep an eye on Eyota and the girls today?" Ryan asked Sweetpea. "I need to talk to Nylah about the mines. I want to make sure they're ready in case we need them."

Sweetpea saluted, perking right back up now that she had a task.

"Yes ma'am! Eyota's kind of scared of me for some reason? So, it should be easy to keep them doing stuff and out of your hair."

Ryan's lips twitched up into a small smile. Poor Sweetpea, the friendliest of all the townsfolk and the one that always scared any visitors.

"Sounds like a plan," Ryan said, finishing her coffee. "And put me down for the betting pool. Millie won't shoot either of them."

17

———

STORM CLOUDS

A STORM WAS BLOWING in. The breeze was still gentle, but Millie could feel the subtle changes in the air. The wind changed direction, growing a touch colder. The pressure in the air lessened, making the old wound in her shoulder ache and setting one ankle bone abuzz.

Crouched in the ashes of the box car she had robbed only days before; Millie spotted a single burst cartridge. Reaching out, she plucked it from the thick, drifting ash that had covered it. Turning it over in her hand, she blew on it to clear the shrapnel of dust. A few bullets must have fallen out of the opened crate in the derailment and cooked off when the fire finally reached the box car where the bullets had been.

"Who'd you say this client of yours was?" she asked, looking up at the two men. She stood, grunting as her ankle complained about the changing weather. Holding out the scrap of brass to the banker, Millie tilted her chin at it. "Popcorn," she said, dropping it into his hand. "Careful, it's still sharp."

"Ah, well our client shouldn't matter," the Stratton said, plucking the bit of metal from her hand before his friend could hurt himself on it. "What matters is that someone stole something that wasn't theirs." He pulled out a small magnifying glass from his coat and examined the still-intact blast cap, turning it this way and that in the sunlight.

Millie watched him, her face and ears set in an expression of mild curiosity. This was why she hated Strattons. They were always getting into things and figuring out mysteries that should be left alone. Millie slowly arched an eyebrow. She didn't have the right angle to see through the magnifying glass, but she could see a maker's mark stamped into it with her naked eye. She knew who she'd stolen from, but that didn't mean these two needed to find out about any of that.

"You mentioned not looking for survivors in the fire," Goldman said, too casually, too effortlessly for his statement to be anything but the lure in a trap. "But you said you didn't get close to the wreck. How did you know there was a body in the fire?"

"Someone had to be driving the train, right?" Millie said, her ears flicking back. "You saw that locomotive. I don't think anyone could have survived that, but West-Colfield's been telling anyone who'll listen that they doubled their guards." That much was true. She wasn't sure why the company had bothered sending a flyer to Scorched Bluffs, of all places, but a month ago, they had.

She frowned, making a show of looking around.

"I don't see any bodies," she paused and sniffed the air. "I don't smell any, either."

She could feel both men watching her now, and she wasn't sure why. She had given nothing away, had she? Millie prided herself on being a good liar, but had she lost her touch over the years of living honestly in Scorched Bluffs? Years of raising little girls that could smell an untruth a mile away, and being bold enough to call her on each and every one.

"What?" she asked, scowling at the banker and detective, both.

"The youngest Willard had been put into the fire after he was killed," Goldman said. "Just curious how you mentioned not checking the fire for survivors."

Oh.

Shit.

"The Willards burn down farm houses with people inside," Millie said, letting her voice get flat and hard. "Animals too, sometimes. I've found more than one homestead they left like that. Sounds like whoever killed them thought it would be a fitting way to get rid of a body. Not that much firewood out here, aside from the train itself."

She watched the tiniest of frowns appear on the Stratton's brow. Doubt.

"We were told that they weren't lawful, but that they weren't awful," the detective said. "But considering the source, that might have been a biased account. How many homes have they burnt down?"

Too many. Far too many.

"I've discovered three, personally," Millie said. "I'd imagine there are more the closer you get to Plainfield. It's the younger ones that do it, usually while the oldest stays in town." Millie chewed on her lip, thinking. "It was the youngest that was killed, right? I was thinking he'd stuck his face where it didn't belong, but now... maybe someone's had enough of their shit." Millie sure had.

"You think someone would hunt down a band of outlaws that burns people alive?" Goldman asked, raising his eyebrows in disbelief. "That's quite a risk, isn't it?"

Millie shrugged, stepping out of the ashes and brushing her palms clean. "Sure. But out here, family is everything. If someone took mine from me by burning them alive, there's not a thing in this world that would stop me from returning the favour to those that did it." She looked up at Goldman and smiled.

"You have a daughter; how far would you go to avenge her? Protect her?" She was rewarded with a deep scowl, though it wasn't directed at her. She had her answer, and had given him something to think about that wasn't how she knew there had been a body in the fire.

It wasn't a bad idea. When these two were gone, it'd be easy enough to track down the rest of the Willards one by one. As terrible as they were, the only stupid one was now dead. Sooner or later, they'd find out who else knew about the train's cargo. Scorched Bluffs had burnt down once already, Millie didn't want that to happen again.

"You were asking who the client is," Gilbert said. "That doesn't matter, but the crates would have been stamped with a mark like this." He pulled a letter from his coat to show the familiar three letters that had been stamped onto it. There was also a wax seal, it's coat of arms one she knew by heart.

A lion rampant stood over a field of waves. Above its head floated a single feather and below the motto was composed of three words: *liberté, férocité, fidélité.* Liberty, ferocity, loyalty. The motto of House Rousseau.

The world grew dim around her, the sounds of the cicada song turning to thick cotton in her ears. Millie stared at the emblem, then looked up at Gilbert to see him watching her with a familiar expression. This man was too sharp, too aware. Too good at the game of redirection and lies. Goldman was too smart for Millie's health.

"Well. Better get to work before the storm blows in," Millie said, her voice distant. "There must be tracks if someone stole crates of ammunition." She couldn't afford to lose control right now. She took a deep breath and forced herself back into the present. The smell of dirt and ash, the breeze on her ears. Focus.

"Storm?" Gilbert asked, frowning. He looked up and around, settling on the growing cloud bank to the south. "Oh. Yes, I suppose we should."

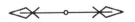

The hammering rain on the railcar's tin roof was deafening. It drowned out everything except the crack and rumble of thunder.

Millie could smell the ozone and charred flesh. Every flash of lightning burnt the tableau in front of her deeper into her mind. A mage, a slave bound by iron shackles, who called lightning down on his own line of soldiers. Over, and over, and over again.

The men and the horses were settled on the far side of the railcar, one of the few untouched by fire. It was jackknifed between its neighbours. The barn door on its side damaged from where Ryan had used a hatchet to free the horses inside.

Dirt hung frozen in the air, joined by crackling lightning that framed the man's face. He was serene, at peace in a way that his minders were not. In a way that Millie was not, as she inhaled rain, struggling not to scream.

The Secessionists had dragged him and other enslaved mages out to the muddy field after Millie destroyed the heavy artillery. She had been directly responsible for the suffering that man embraced, and she had watched him scorch himself black, taking out the entire company with him. He had died, smiling.

She never dreamt of him, but during storms everything came back as vivid and cruel as if she was back in the thick of the battle. The smell: salt, ozone, burnt flesh, mud. The smell was always the same.

Night had crept in under the cloud cover, and not even elven eyes could pierce the gloom without the help of lightning flashes. The railcar was lit by a lantern Stratton had in their corner; its wick turned low to keep it dim. The men, formerly huddled over some papers, now lay on straw, asleep.

Millie watched them through three flashes of lightning and the following rolls of thunder. Only then did she get up, slowly creeping over to where they lay. Pulling the pilfered gun from her belt, she held it at the ready. They were working for Rousseau; they were here and knew who she was. Why else show her the letter from Fred himself? These men had to die. When better to kill them than in a storm, and where better than at the site of a known dragon attack? Old urges were difficult to stamp down, but Millie wasn't ready to draw down the attention of the full Stratton Agency yet.

Still, she slipped the detective's gun from his belt with light fingers. Best for everyone if she held onto that. Humans couldn't see well in the dark and she didn't need anyone shooting at her tonight. Easing back over to the banker, she carefully fished out the letter he had shoved in her face earlier. She watched for any sign of the man waking, but he seemed to be fully asleep, unaware of her presence. Letter freed, she rocked back to sit on her heels and open it.

A photograph fluttered out, landing on the straw in front of her. Millie picked it up, looking at the family there. An old man in a three-piece suit and top hat stood next to a younger looking Gilbert who was seated on a leather chair and holding an infant in a white lace dress. She had round cheeks and a serious face with dark eyes that stared out from the little image. Millie turned the photo over, reading the words inscribed on the back.

Avrom, Gilbert, Sarah Goldman. Dated two years prior. Millie tried not to think of how sad the little Sarah would be if her father didn't return home. There was no mother in that photo to cushion such a blow. She looked at the letter itself, expecting familiar, neat handwriting. What she found instead was a mockery of a letter, scribbled in large looping letters and splotches of ink that made the letter nearly unreadable. But it was his handwriting alright, Fred Fucking Rousseau.

As far as she could make out, there was no mention of elves. No mention of Scorched Bluffs. It only mentioned the insured cargo.

Millie frowned, staring at the paper in her hand. It didn't make any sense. Why would Fred care about a shipment of ammunition that small? Why the threat hidden between the lines that he would ruin the banker if Goldman didn't pay out?

"Find what you were looking for?"

Millie jumped, pressing the Stratton's pistol into Goldman's side. Gilbert looked up at her and smiled.

"You're not very good deputy material, are you?" He said, barely audible over the sound of the rain. "Stealing guns from Strattons, books from bankers, and rifling through people's personal effects when you think they're asleep. What would the Sheriff say if she found out about that?"

Millie pulled the pistol from his side and felt a strong hand grab her wrist from behind. Hal firmly took his gun from her hand, and Millie felt cold metal wrap around her wrist with a familiar 'click'. She said nothing as Hal took her other hand and brought it around to cuff behind her.

"Mildred Berry, you are under arrest for theft until such time you can be remanded to a local authority," the Stratton said. "I will search you for weapons now, ma'am. I apologize if that offends."

"I told you she knows something about Rousseau," Goldman said to his friend.

Millie closed her eyes, ignoring the feeling of her gun belt being removed. She focused on the rain, the smell of ozone and charred flesh, and not the knife being taken from her boot. The rifle was hung off her mule's saddle, her hatchet too. Disarmed and bound, Millie sniffed at the air again.

The smell of ozone and burnt flesh wasn't just in her mind, she was *certain* of it. The musk of dragonfire had been a warning, one she had stupidly ignored.

"Put the lantern out," she hissed, head snapping to the crack in the railcar door. "That's her."

"Who?" Hal asked, shuttering the lantern. Millie could still feel one of his hands on the cuffs holding her in place.

A heavy flap of wings answered him. The horses shook their heads and pawed at the straw on the floor, sensing the predator nearby. The heavy rain had muffled the sounds of her arrival, and now it was too late to leave. Through the crack in the door, illuminated in a flash of lightning, Millie saw scales glisten.

18

BLUE'S SKIES

FOR A HEARTBEAT, EVERYTHING around Millie froze. The two human men on either side of her, the gleam of cobalt scales on the other side of a cracked wooden door, the horses and mule hitched behind her.

The elf didn't dare move, but her mind raced through the different outcomes of the scenario she found herself in. Goldman and Stratton were pawns, unaware of who they worked for. That ignorance made them dangerous. That ignorance sealed their fate, but they didn't realize it yet. These men had a family who were innocent. And Millie didn't want more innocent blood on her hands.

The dragon. She was a distraction, a threat, a tool. If she had to, Millie could use the dragon to obliterate everything held inside the railcar, including herself.

Especially herself.

Millie closed her eyes, listening to the hushed breath of Hal behind her, the din of rain on the railcar roof, and the nervous shuffling of the horses.

"You need to uncuff me," she said in as loud a whisper as she dared. "Or that dragon will kill us all."

"Why would I do that? You might try to get away," Hal said. Millie felt the words more than she heard them.

"Because," she said, speaking slowly and enunciating every syllable. "If the choice is being turned over to Rousseau, or being burnt alive, I will scream and fight until the dragon outside melts the ground under us into glass." Millie took another breath, holding the air in for a count of three heartbeats. She could feel her pulse slow, the adrenaline coiling up tighter and tighter in her muscles. Slowly, calmly, she let out the air and opened her eyes, turning around to look the Stratton in the eyes.

Gilbert had crept up closer to the door, his eyes wide as he looked from the dragon outside to where Millie and Hal stood.

"The lady makes a compelling—if concerning—argument," he said and looked at his friend. "Better let her go."

Millie felt Hal fumble at the cuffs in the dark, removing from her wrists with as little sound as possible. Even with the rain muffling their scent and sounds, none of them wanted to risk drawing the dragon's attention.

"After the dragon has gone, we can revisit the fact that a deputy stole my firearm from me," Hal whispered. "Sheriff Collins will need to revoke your badge."

"A conversation we can all have together in the jail when we get back to town," Millie agreed. She rolled her shoulders and bounced a little in place to prepare for what was coming. First, her hat came off, then her poncho and vest. Millie set them down by the doused lantern and pulled her knife and hatchet from where Hal had set her weapons.

"If we all make it out of this," she heard Goldman say. "I would really like to buy you a drink and hear how a deputy elf knows Captain Rousseau well enough to recognize his family's coat of arms."

"I told you," Millie said, "A lot of veterans come out to the Frontier." She walked past where the banker crouched, studying the railcar for options.

Aside from the sliding barn door that Gilbert was watching the dragon through, the livestock car had three other exits. Two, the doors that lead from one car to another, were useless because of how the train's cars had jackknifed together in the crash. Even if the men were strong enough to get one of those doors open, the dragon would hear them.

Millie stopped under a hatch that was installed on the car's roof. Meant for easily refilling the feed trough on long journeys, it was the safest option. She tucked her hatchet into her belt and motioned the banker over.

"I need a boost," she said to Gilbert. "Lift me up." She expected him to argue, but it wasn't the banker that had objections.

"What's going to stop her from leaving us here with the dragon?" Hal asked. He was looking at his friend as Gilbert stood. "Do you trust her?"

"She could have shot us earlier," Gilbert answered, reaching out to where he had heard Millie's voice. "Also, not a lot of options right now. Dragon outside, elf inside. I choose elf."

Realizing he couldn't see her, Millie reached out and took Gilbert's hands, guiding him over to stand under the hatch. *Spirits, thank whoever made this man a giant*, Millie thought. Without him, she'd need one of the horses to reach the hatch, and dragons spooked even the most reliable of mules.

"Lift me straight up, okay?" She said, putting the banker's hands together. He laced them into a stirrup. "Then stay here until I come back to get you, or until morning when you can see if the dragon is gone."

She stepped into his hand, holding onto his shoulders as he lifted her upward.

"What if you don't come back?" Gilbert asked. "You'll break my friend's heart if he can't arrest you. And mine, if I can't buy you that drink."

Millie reached up and pushed on the hatch door. It moved a little but was stuck. Pulling her knife free from her belt, Millie slid the blade through the gap between the hatch and its frame, wiggling the blade against the wooden latch that held it closed.

"If I don't come back, it's because I'm dead," she whispered. "Apologize to my girls for me, if that happens." Just a little more... the latch moved aside, sending down a dribble of rainwater as the hatch door moved. *There.*

Millie placed the knife back into her belt and pushed. The hatch door lifted and the sudden onslaught of rain drenched her. Under her, Gilbert gasped at the cold water, but there was no time for apologies or snark. She grabbed the frame tight and hauled herself up and through. The hatch door thudded against the back of her head and the tin roof was slippery. With a grunt, Millie pulled herself out into the storm.

Out in the relative brightness of the night, Millie could see the big blue curled up in the debris field, less than fifty feet from their railcar. Head tucked under a massive wing, the dragon had wrapped her tail around her to conserve heat, the way the smaller rock dragonets did when it was raining. It made sense that the larger species had similar habits... although the sight of the blue doing something so mundane seemed impossible.

Millie lay on her belly on the tin roof, watching the dragon for any sign that it had heard her. The very tip of the dragon's tail flicked, but the beast didn't raise her head from under her wing. Millie waited for a few more heartbeats to be sure, the chilly rain plastering her hair and shirt to her skin.

There was no time for second thoughts. Millie knew she didn't have another choice. She might be able to negotiate with these two, but if they died in the railcar, Fred would send more men. Men that might be less interested in protecting tiny girls from their mother's past.

Millie slithered over to where the next car butted up against the one she was on. Using the other car's roof as a handhold, she slipped her legs over the edge and lowered herself down as far as she could. Hanging for a moment from the slippery roof, Millie looked down at the gravel tracks under her.

Pushing off the car with one foot, she jumped clear of the rails and landed in the mud beyond. Something popped in her knee, and Millie felt heat bloom inside the joint. But it would have to wait. Everything had to wait until that damn dragon was gone.

"You think I made a mistake?" Gilbert whispered. After he heard the elf jump from the roof, he crept over to the cracked door once more. He could barely make out the shape of the dragon in the darkness. It had stopped moving, turning into a dark mound. If not for the lightning that occasionally lit the beast up, he could have convinced himself that the dark shape was only a pile of rubble.

"I didn't say anything," Hal whispered back, creeping over to join him. Gilbert heard his friend's breath catch as a flash of lightning lit up the debris field. Curled up like a giant cat, the blue dragon had tucked itself away from the rain.

Gilbert thought back to when he had sat at the breakfast table with his father, reading a buttery newspaper, and had wondered how a dragon could destroy a freight train. Now, as he watched the wing the size of a sail flick off rainwater, Gilbert wondered how anyone had survived living in dragon territory. Cobalt scales shone in the brief flashes of light, darker on the thing's back and speckled with a deep red in lateral lines across the dragon's side.

"I thought they were exaggerating," Hal whispered, crouching next to Gilbert. "I thought maybe it had been a bomb, not an actual dragon that attacked the train."

Gilbert watched the dark shape, an afterimage dancing in his vision after the lightning. "Did you see her face?" He asked. "When Deputy Elf saw Rousseau's coat of arms. Did you see the look on her face?"

He felt Hal sigh, but couldn't look away from the dragon outside. It was mesmerizing, and Gilbert hoped, the only chance he would have to see such a beautiful and terrifying animal up close.

"I did. But you know the man better than I do. What could cause that kind of reaction to a war hero?"

"Everything," Gilbert answered. He rubbed the stubble on his chin, hand still wet from the elf's escape. "Everything I know about him is the opposite of those plays, his books. That look means she must have met him in person. He's got a thing for blondes, blonde elves especially."

Something about that didn't sit right. What were the odds that of all the places for Frederic Rousseau's cargo to go missing, it was next to a town where elves reacted like they knew the man? A town where purebred dogs ran around that cost more than the entire town? And what were the odds, that the elf who seemed to know Frederic was blonder than any of the other blonde elves that Gilbert had seen rotate through Rousseau's mansion.

"Hal," Gilbert said quietly. "I think we just found the woman that broke Rousseau's heart."

Jebediah Willard didn't like thunder. He didn't mind rain, or snow, or any other kind of weather, but he did not like thunder. Huddled inside a tiny one-room shack with the rest of his siblings, he tried to hide the way he flinched every time a crack or boom rumbled across the sky.

If Isaiah were here, he'd make a stupid joke and then Jeb could have been angry instead of afraid. But Isaiah was dead and Jeb was stuck in an old hunter's shack that was leaning so badly, he was certain it would shake itself to pieces with every crack of thunder. It was scant protection from the storm, but that was the thing about storms on the prairie: there was precious little to hide under. Thunder struck whatever was tallest and if you were outside in a storm, often times the tallest thing nearby was you.

"Zach's almost back," Josie said from where she leaned against the doorframe. He'd told her not to stand so close to the outside, not to lean on the door, but Josie refused to move from her post. She was twice as stubborn as her brothers, and fearless when it came to storms. "He's coming up the road now."

"Good," Jeb said. He straightened, squaring his shoulders as if it might help steel him against the threat of thunder.

Zach ducked into the shack, pulling his hat off and shaking it at the doorstep to get the worst of the rain off.

"Found them at the train wreck. The two men and a kid elf. Probably a tracker they hired," he reported, steely eyes glinting in the lantern light of the shack. "Three total, shouldn't be no problem to take them down... Except for that blue dragon from way out in the Badlands, she showed up right after the storm started."

The Willards looked at each other, and Jeb frowned.

"Grounded?" he asked. Zach nodded. Jeb's frown deepened.

"You think it's a stormbird?" Josie asked, putting a cigarette between her lips.

"What else would ground a full-grown blue?" Jeb said, holding out his hand to her. Josie sighed and handed him a spare cigarette. Jeb tucked it between his lips. "We wait until the storm breaks. Any luck and that blue takes care of those boys and we can get paid for it."

There wasn't much in God's great cycle that could scare a dragon, except a stormbird. Jeb had never seen one and had hoped to die without ever having to. Regular storms were bad enough, but a bird that ate dragons and threw lightning from their eyes and thunder from their wings was a thing of nightmares.

"I hope the dragon clears out after," Zach muttered. "That thing is big, even for a blue."

19

DIRTY DEEDS

THE COOL RAIN SOOTHED the swelling in Millie's knee and kissed at her skin when she peeled her shirt off, tearing it into strips of wet cotton to wrap around her hands. She needed a pair of lanterns that wouldn't get doused by the storm.

Millie had found jars when she and Ryan had been looting the wreck. They had taken one crate but left the rest. Finding a pair of unbroken jars didn't take her long, and Millie used her knife to punch holes in the tin caps. It was a gamble to rely on there being a salamander nest in the wreck, but Millie figured the heat of the dragon's fire would have attracted any nearby salamander clutters, and before long, she was proven right.

Nestled against a plate of steel that must have held the heat of the fire for days, she had found a nest of salamanders with orange spots down their backs. Millie reached out and scooped one of the adult antsy lizards into each jar. The process felt too easy. The lizards only lighting themselves up once they were inside the jars. At least until the matriarch of the nest got hissy. Larger than the rest, the queen lunged forward and locked her jaws onto Millie's forearm. With a muffled grunt of pain, Millie smashed the butt of her knife into the queen's head, dislodging her just as the queen ignited, setting the smear of salamander oil on the elf's arm aflame. Millie doused it by shoving her forearm into the mud, wiping her arm against her boot as she pulled it free of the puddle. The bite was angry and red, but the burn was minimal, at least.

"Sorry guys," she muttered and picked up her two jar-lanterns. "But I need to see."

The second part of her plan was a little less certain. How could she possibly scare away a dragon? The manifest had listed TNT for the mines at Stonecreek, but Millie hadn't memorized which car that crate was on. Searching for it, lizard lanterns in hand, Millie had heard a familiar croak, followed by a warning hiss. One lizard froze in the jar, and she carefully set both lanterns down in the mud. Circling around carefully, she squinted into the darkness under one of the jack-knifed cars. Red eyes stared out, fixed upon the lantern lizards. The one that had frozen in place was no longer feeding its fire, the residual oils on its skin slowly burning off.

Millie knew she'd only have one real chance to get the thing that was under the railcar, and if she didn't... the city men were as good as dead. She might be fine, but- the little girl in the photograph with serious eyes would lose her papa. Fred would come looking for his missing banker and the Strattons would come looking for their lost detective.

It was safest to save the men, and then impress on them how important it was that they never, ever tell their patron about her existence.

Laying down in the mud, Millie squinted into the darkness under the car. The two salamanders provided enough light for her to make out the silhouette of a large lizard. Its muscular tail was in reach, and thankfully the thing's head faced away from her, focused on the trapped salamanders in front of it. Whispering a prayer of thanks to whichever spirit had lured the lizard to the train, Millie reached out and grabbed the tail, wrapping both hands around it and pulled. She scrambled up to her feet, closing her eyes as she dragged the lizard out from under the car, holding on as it hissed and threw itself side to side to escape. Unlike the rotund salamanders, this thing was all muscle and couldn't lose its tail. Its primary defence was nullified by Millie's closed eyes, though it could still scratch her up good if she let it. Pinning the thick Basilisk's tail between her thighs, Millie worked her hands upward along its thrashing body to grab its face. Placing a hand over its bulging eyes, she breathed out a sigh of relief as the lizard stilled.

Opening one eye, careful to look at where she held its tail between her legs, Millie cautiously glanced at the rest of it. The size of a dog, the basilisk had slipped into a kind of stasis, unwilling or unable to move in case it damaged its eyes, which were now covered by a wet hand wrapped in cotton shirting. The sound of the struggle might have woken up the dragon, and Millie had a few fresh cuts in her leggings from its hind feet, but at least she had a way to get the men out of the wreck. She pulled a strip of the cotton off her free hand, wrapping it carefully around the basilisk's head to cover its eyes. Much like a frog, the giant eyes stuck out from its skull while open, but retreated into the skull for safety when the thing swallowed or when a tired elf grabbed it and dragged it out of its den. Tying the cloth in place with a careful slip knot, Millie allowed herself to take a deep breath, and listen for the sound of the dragon.

No gout of flame spewed down onto her, only the cold rain. Raindrops sizzled and popped as they dripped past the jar's perforated covers to land on the salamanders' fire.

Freed of the Basilisk's hypnotic stare, the second salamander was still dazed, its fire slowly sputtering out. That was fine, that one could stay put out for the moment. Millie used a strip of her shirt to tie around the jars at each cap to make handles. She looped the dimmed lantern through her belt to keep it out of her way.

Scooping up the basilisk under her arm, Millie picked up the second lantern, whose inhabitant was very much still upset and on fire. Creeping forward, Millie slid through a cracked railcar to the other side of the train. She estimated that she had a hundred feet of bare field between her and the dragon. The long grasses had burnt away, and the debris wasn't large enough to use for cover. She'd have to creep forward as silently as possible and hope the spirit who put the basilisk under the train was still around and worked on dragons too.

"Alright, sorry buddy," she muttered to the basilisk under her arm. It was probably not going to survive the following encounter, but that was part of nature. Basilisks ate the small draconids like Salamanders, big dragons like the blue ate the basilisks. Circle of life, miracle of nature, the Messiah at work and shit.

The dragon either hadn't heard the earlier scuffle or had and didn't care enough to look up. She was still curled up like a cat, head tucked under one massive wing. Millie crept forward, using cover as best as she could until the final stretch. The railcar with the men and horses was in sight, not more then twenty paces past the dragon. On this side of the door, the wooden car looked painfully flimsy.

Taking one last deep breath to calm her hammering pulse, Millie left her last piece of cover—a half crushed crate that had once been full of hay—and moved forward. Her feet squelched in the sooty mud, her heart was hammering in her ears, and the basilisk was starting to twitch under her arm. At least the salamander was still on fire, lighting her way across the mud until she was thirty... twenty... fifteen feet from the dragon.

She was beautiful up close. Cerulean and cobalt scales glinted in the light of the salamander lantern, and a lateral line of red scales curved along the dragon's neck and side. This close, Millie could see her chest rise and fall, her wings shiver to shake off the rain... and her tail twitched as the dragon smelled something familiar. Millie glanced down at her leg. The blood from her struggle with the Basilisk had soaked through the front of her trousers.

No time to waste, then.

Millie threw the salamander jar at the dragon. It bounced off her neck, glass clinking against scales before landing in the mud. Thick flying muscles bunched under the dragon's skin, and her head whipped out from under her wing. In the middle of certain death, Millie thought the dragon looked more indignant than angry. She huffed and shook her head, sending water scattering from her neck. One of her eyes had been damaged by the train wreck, Millie saw. It was weeping and crusted shut.

"Uh, hi," Millie said and pulled the strip of cotton from the Basilisk's eyes. "I brought you a snack." From the light cast by the salamander jar, the small elf watched the dragon's slit pupils widen until the blue's eyes were nearly black. Recognizing the look of a hypnotized animal, Millie slowly set the basilisk down on the ground. Backing away, Millie pulled the spare lantern from her belt and hurried over to the railcar door.

Her arm hurt. Her knee hurt. Her leg hurt. She was tired and chilled, and in no mood to deal with any argument.

Millie opened the door and shook the lantern to get the salamander to catch fire once more.

"Get the horses."

The men got the horses, and Millie bundled her things, tying them into Norbert's saddlebags. Pulling on her poncho, she led her mule out of the car and away from the dragon. Casting a glance over her shoulder at the dragon, Millie was relieved to see the big girl still frozen in place, although the very tip of her tail seemed to tremble.

It wouldn't be long before she shook off the hypnosis.

"Deputy, might I ask how you distracted the dragon?" the banker asked, hurrying after her. "Or where you might have gotten such skills? Or maybe—"

"We'll talk when we're out of her hearing range, okay?" Millie said, striking out toward the lone shack. It was the closest safe-house, even if it wasn't terribly safe. Still, it was a shelter, and it had a fire pit to warm themselves up at. Better still, whiskey and medicinal herbs waited in her cache of supplies.

By some miracle, the dragon didn't follow them. The storm slowly lessened, and dawn finally brought light to the far horizon where the first hint of clear sky teased a respite. That didn't stop Millie from compulsively checking the skies behind them.

"We're almost there," Millie said, glancing behind them. The lingering storm clouds painted the sky red as the sun crept above the horizon. "And then we can sit down, and have an honest conversation." If they weren't here for her, why the fuck did they work for Fred?

"I did promise you a drink," Gilbert said, his hat keeping the rain from his face. Hal followed behind, squinting out at the horizon. He seemed to frown. Why–

Thunder cracked in the air and Gilbert took a step back. He blinked, surprised, and then looked down at his chest, where a hole was punched into his coat. The rainwater dripping down the wool grew red.

"What?" He whispered.

"Get down," Millie hissed, running over to him. No, no, no. She had gotten them to safety, they had all just gotten away safely. Millie tackled Gilbert, only to feel him stagger back rather than fall. "*Get down*. Please." Another crack rent the air and one of the big horses spooked, sprinting past Millie and the giant human.

Gilbert nodded, slowly collapsing onto the ground, then lying down on his side.

"Getting shot hurts," he muttered, pulling something from his coat pocket. A book, a familiar book bound in faded yellow canvas that had a hole in the middle of it. Millie frowned at the book, then looked back at Gilbert. The wound was shallow, and while it was bleeding, it wasn't life-threatening.

"That is the first good thing that book has ever done," Millie muttered. "Stay like this until I whistle the Union Choral, okay?" she said, taking Gilbert's hand and pressing it against the wound to slow the bleeding. "I need to go kill some people." She looked up, peeking up from the tall grasses to see the Willards emerging from her safehouse.

"Who... are you?" Gilbert asked, trying to catch her hand. Millie looked back down and patted his chest on the non-injured side.

"Didn't you read the book?" she asked with a smile. "I'm a Ghost."

20

STANDOFF

JEBEDIAH SQUINTED OUT THROUGH the rain at the sorry excuse for an elf who now stood alone. The big horses had bolted,
and the men were down in the grass. Zach had spotted them first
and put a bullet right into the big bastard's chest. All three had
dove into the grass, but it was the small elf who stood up, hands
lifted to show she was unarmed. Bloody and muddy where the
rain hadn't washed her clean, the elf was just in her undershirt
and trousers.

"That's no kid elf," Jeb muttered to Zach. "Fuck." He knew
exactly who this was, and it was a big problem. A huge problem.
"Don't shoot until I tell you to," he warned his siblings.

Walking out ahead of them, Jeb held his hands out to his sides
to show that he wasn't reaching for his gun.

"Miss Berry?" He called out. He wasn't sure if he should look
directly at her. With her hair stuck to her head and long ears
drooped, she looked like a half-drowned kitten. It would be
hard to believe what Diamond had told him, if it weren't for the
scars he saw all along the elf's arms and shoulders. It looked like
someone had cut her up and sewn her back together.

"Jebediah Willard," the elf answered. "Your boy just *shot* at
me."

Jeb slowly reached up and pulled his hat off, holding it to his
chest in a gesture of apology. He could feel Zach and the others

staring at him. He hadn't told them yet, but he would once they were safely away from the cursed thing he was talking to.

"I apologize, Ma'am. My brother didn't realise that was you. Our business here is with those two men, and we aint got no quarrel with your fine self." He tilted his head toward the mule that waited by her shoulder. "We'd greatly appreciate it if you left us to our business, Ma'am."

"I haven't been paid yet, either," the elf said, her voice carried across the rain stronger than Jeb had expected. He tried not to flinch. She looked like a dead thing. The only colour on her was the blood on her pants and arm. It was unholy, is what it was.

Jeb looked over at Zach, who still held his rifle, though it was pointed down at the ground. The Stratton had to be crouched in the grass near her, but the rain made it difficult to tell where he was.

"We don't want no trouble," Jeb said. "Diamond's spoken highly of you. We'd be happy to give you some of our fee…"

"The hell we will," Eli sputtered, stepping forward. Josie's hand snapped out and cuffed him before Jeb could react.

"Look at her, Eli. She's a dead thing," Josie hissed. Jeb looked back at the elf, hoping that she couldn't hear what Josie was saying. "It's bad luck to kill them. Nan said they'll haunt you for the rest of your life, feeding on your soul at night." The mention of Nan Willard had a sobering effect on the men around them. Momma Willard had her rules, but Nan had been the wisest woman any of them had ever met.

A cunning woman from the homeland. It had been Nan who taught him about the stormbirds, how to survive them and how to make sure none caught his scent. If she had told Josie about Ghost Elves, then Josie would be the expert. Jeb knew they were dangerous. Which made the tiny woman standing in front of them far more of a threat than even Diamond had known.

"Fine, but let me keep the bodies," the ghost elf said. "You get the credit, and leave my cut with Di at the saloon." Then, quick as a flash, she turned, a pistol in her hand that hadn't been there a moment ago. Without so much as a breath of hesitation, the elf fired into the grass where the Stratton boy had disappeared into. The grass rustled and Jeb sucked on his molars, listening to the man's death groan.

Goddamn.

"Well, uh, we'll need proof they're dead," Zach said, his rifle back up at the appearance of the elf's pistol. Jeb reached over and slowly pushed its barrel down again, unwilling to let his brother bring down a curse on them all. They'd lost enough of their family already.

"Yeah, yeah, hold on." The elf ducked down, disappearing into the tall grasses again. When she stood, her hands and undershirt had blood smeared on them. The elf started walking forward to the Willard posse without fear, red hands high.

"Zach, if you shoot and I get haunted because of your twitchy finger, I'll murder you myself," Josie hissed. Jeb glanced over to see his brother had lifted his rifle back to his shoulder. Zach was scowling, eyes fixed on the elf.

"Jeb—"

"Put up the goddamn gun, Zachariah," Jeb snapped. "The elf finished our work for us. Leave her the teeth. Our pay will be more than any gold teeth she finds."

The elf was a full head shorter than Josie, silver hair speckled red with the human blood. Her eyes were worse than Jeb had thought. Not just pale, but an unnatural purple. They couldn't hide her true nature as a dead thing. Josie edged backward at the elf's approach, making the sign of the Wheel in front of her to ward off any death the elf carried with her.

"Here," the ghost elf said. She held out a bloody tin badge with the words 'Stratton Detective Agency' on it, and then a folded letter that was half stained red. A hole punched through one corner, the size of a bullet. It had a wax seal attached to it.

Jeb looked over his family and motioned to Eli, whose hands were free. The haggard Willard backed up a step, shaking his head. "I don't want to touch it; she might've cursed it! Like Josie said!"

"I didn't say that! I said we'd get haunted."

Jeb watched the elf frown and fear rose up in his throat, cold and tight.

"*Elijah Hettnam Willard*," Jeb snapped. "Go get the goddamn badge and letter and apologize to the lady." He glared at his younger brother until Eli stumbled forward to meet the elf, reaching out to pluck the items from the elf's hands. Quick as a snake, the elf caught Eli's forearm, holding onto him tight. Jeb was too far to hear what she hissed at him, but he watched his brother turn pale.

"You curse my brother, and I'll shoot your leg out from under you," Zach snarled. But Jeb noticed that this time, Zach's rifle stayed pointed down at the ground.

"Sorry to hear about your brother," the elf said, letting go of Eli to wipe her bloody hand on her hip. "I hope you find who killed him." She levelled her eyes straight at Jeb, and he could swear she stared through his very soul. "After all, family is everything out here."

Throat tight, thinking of what Diamond had told him, Jeb nodded quickly.

"It is. Thank you, ma'am. We'll be going now." Jeb grabbed a fistful of Eli's coat and hauled him toward the horses.

"What did she say to you?" he whispered. Eli shook his head, still clutching the proof of the two men's deaths to his chest.

"She said she didn't kill him, but she'd kill all of us if we didn't leave," Eli said. His eyes were wide and bloodshot. "Who is she? She could do it; I saw it in her eyes."

"I'll tell you on the way back to town," Jeb said. "The sooner we leave, the safer we'll be."

Gilbert lay on the ground, one hand pressing the deputy's poncho to the bullet hole in his chest to staunch the bleeding. Wet, cold, and in an incredible amount of pain, he sucked in quiet breaths and listened to Deputy Berry's voice in the distance.

"Hal," he whispered, grimacing at the pain that talking caused. "I think our deputy might be the most terrifying person I've ever met."

Hal, lying in the grass next to Gilbert, looked over at him. There was a splatter of mud on his friend's cheek from where the deputy had shot the ground by Hal's face, and a faint stipple of dirt that buried itself into the cartilage of his ear. Hal, now stripped of his badge but otherwise unharmed, nodded carefully. They had watched as the deputy smeared the stolen badge against her injured leg, leaving her own blood on it instead of Hal's.

"I'm starting to agree with you, Gil," he whispered back. "How are you doing?"

"I would like to revise my earlier request," Gilbert said. "About women, and asking you to shoot me if I fall for one." He swallowed, glancing down at the poncho that was now quite red, and the book that had been discarded to one side, the thing that had probably saved his life. Once the outlaws were gone, he had a long list of questions for Berry.

"Yeah?"

"Yeah. *Please, don't*. Getting shot hurts a hell of a lot more than I thought it might."

The men lay in silence after that, listening to Deputy Berry return, her boots squishing on the wet ground. Beyond her, the Willards argued among themselves. Some believed Berry was a demon, while the eldest was doing his best to haul his family out of her path.

"You're both dead," Mildred said quietly to Hal and Gil as she passed by. "Sorry." She patted her mule and gave him a light kiss on his nose before digging into his saddlebags.

"You almost shot me," Hal muttered, rubbing at his ear.

Gilbert felt horribly overlooked, certain that *actually* being shot deserved more attention than merely 'almost' being shot did. He was the one bleeding and in a significant amount of pain, after all.

"I shot the ground," the deputy said, and Gilbert caught a brief smile on her face. "Don't worry, I need you two to do something for me. Stay 'dead' until I tell you they're gone." She looked up, over in the direction she'd come from. The men waited, Gilbert trying to bite back a groan as he unconsciously held his breath and discovered that it hurt quite a lot to do in his current situation.

"They're leaving," Millie murmured, finally. She pulled a few things from the saddle and walked over to crouch next to Gilbert, a pair of pliers in her hand.

"I don't have gold teeth," Gilbert said, eying the pliers. Then offered her his best smile, showing off his natural white teeth. "See?" He was rewarded with a small laugh from her, muffled into her shoulder. She wasn't actually going to take his teeth, was she?

"Soon as the Willards are out of hearing range, we need to take care of that bullet," Millie said, her smile fading. "It's going to hurt. A lot."

Gilbert looked at Hal, who seemed as worried as he felt.

"Ma'am," Hal said. "I believe you owe us an explanation."

"About what?" Millie asked, pulling her revolver from her belt. She opened it and pulled out a single bullet from the drum. "About those boys out there? Fred sold you out. I don't know why he sent you two here, but it doesn't matter. He wants you dead and isn't afraid to pay for a whole damn posse to take care of the job."

Gilbert watched her frown. He knew he should be worried about why she took out a bullet, but the revolver was safely tucked back into her belt again. Unless she planned on throwing the bullet at him, Gilbert wasn't sure what she planned on doing with it.

"How do you know so much about Captain—"

"Don't call him that," the deputy snapped, glaring at Hal. "He's a drunk with big pockets and everyone gets up his ass about winning the goddamn war."

Gilbert ran his tongue along the back of his teeth, suddenly and uncomfortably aware of the position of each in his mouth. His mind didn't stop working, and through the pain and concern over his smile, a connection snapped into place.

"You served with him," Gilbert murmured. "You knew him from the war. You're the first blonde elf. But he said the Butcher took you..."

He watched her body go rigid, her eyes snapping to focus on him as her ears drooped low. For the first time since he'd met her, Mildred Berry looked afraid. She swallowed hard, visibly pulling herself together from whatever memories Gilbert had brought up.

"There never should have been more," she said quietly, taking the poncho from his hand and removing it from his wound. "I hate that there were more." She unbuttoned Gilbert's shirt, peeling the fine cotton back from the bullet wound.

Seeing it, Gilbert felt lightheaded, like the ground under his body shifted under him. Blinking rapidly, he looked away, focusing on Berry's face.

"I appreciate the interest," he murmured. *What was she doing?* "But is now really the best time? Being shot and all, I can't promise that I'll be up to my usual standards." Gilbert glanced at Hal, but his friend was already moving to hold down Gilbert's arms.

"Hal, I love you, but I'm not certain-" Gilbert said, interrupted by a leather glove being placed between his teeth. Normally, he'd be quite pleased with that development, however. The pliers were back, and Hal was holding him down quite strongly.

"Sorry," Millie whispered. "Try to be quiet. I'll do it quick."

She hadn't lied. It hurt, and it hurt badly as she stuck the pliers into the wound. A shock of heat rolled through his system, preceding the worst of the pain by a split second. The pliers pried the wound open as they gripped the bullet, and then... then... it was out. Gilbert sagged into the wet ground, grateful for the cool rain that fell on his face. It kept him awake.

"Don't let go yet." Her voice was a little soft and sounded further away than normal. "We still need to stop the bleeding."

Gilbert blinked, watching as Millie wiped the pliers clean on his shirt, and used them to open the bullet she had pulled out earlier. He hissed, biting on the leather glove again as she sprinkled gunpowder into the bullet wound. Gilbert had read very little about medicine, but he was certain gunpowder was not a pain reliever. Nor was it something one usually put into open cuts.

The Deputy straddled him, sitting on his belly to keep him pressed down to the mud. With an apologetic glance at him, she struck a match and held it to the wound. The gunpowder flashed, and Gilbert screamed into the glove, and a small rough hand that pressed to his mouth. His body shook, shot twice in the same square of flesh. The rain felt like small pin pricks over his skin, his nerves suddenly too awake.

"Sorry," Millie whispered again, patting his cheek gently. "You did good, Gilbert." She slipped off him, and Gilbert was faintly aware of Hal helping him to his feet. The mule brought over to help steady him. He tried to walk, dazed and unable to feel his hands or feet.

The deputy and Hal were talking, but Gilbert was too occupied trying to keep from tumbling forward in the long grass. The stalks kept catching at his feet. The mule and Hal got him to a small shack, and Gilbert was never so grateful to lie back down. The shack's floor was wet, but it was still a welcome change from the colder ground. Coals of an old fire burned in a fire pit, and Gilbert closed his eyes, letting himself focus on breathing for a while.

"Here," Gilbert opened his eyes to see Millie holding a small brown bottle in one hand. Laudanum? Where had *that* been when she burnt a hole in his chest?! "Open your mouth. This will help with the pain. Then, I believe I owe you a story."

"About the war?" Gilbert asked, opening his mouth. The familiar taste of opium and whiskey touched his tongue, and he swallowed down the drops Millie fed him. Almost immediately, his tongue tingled and grew numb. Soon, the pain eased, softening with each breath he took. God bless non-bullet-based medicine.

"I thought he sent you to kill me," Millie whispered. "He killed the rest of us. One by one, every soldier in my company that survived the damn war... because he didn't want anyone to find out the truth."

"What's the truth?" Gilbert murmured, his words soft and mushy from the medicine.

"Fred Rousseau didn't win the Battle of Marigot," Millie said quietly. She sighed, glancing down at her hands. "I did."

21

BIGGER FISH

HAL WASN'T SURE HOW he had ended up here. Everything had made sense until a certain, tangible point: Gilbert needed help, so Gilbert hired him to find missing cargo and blackmail someone. They arrived in a tiny town that was weird even for the Frontier. The Deputy was angry and stole his gun and then... the dragon arrived?

Everything after the dragon had gone sideways. The elf was not just a deputy, but some unnervingly capable war veteran who had served under the man who they were working for and he wanted her dead? She had frozen the dragon in place? Alone? Then pretended to kill them instead of *actually* killing them when the Outlaw gang had presented her with the opportunity. Not only that, the gang of assholes who burned people alive ran away from her. Instead of letting them die, she saved their lives, treated Gilbert's gunshot wound and was watching over the banker she previously hated while Hal tried to chase down their horses.

Ahead of him was a pile of stones that rose out of the grassy plain, and if he got on top of it, he could look for the trails of flattened stalks left behind by the panicked animals. A small thought popped into his mind as Hal reached the rocks and climbed. It was crazy, sure. But what other explanation did this all have?

What if Rousseau wanted *someone to rob that train?* Hal frowned, boot slipping on the muddy rock underfoot. It had stopped raining for the time being, but everything was still wet. The ground, the grass, him. Even if Rousseau was a drunkard, there were signs of a rational plan among the chaos. Rousseau wanted the insurance payout, that much was clear. But why target Gilbert while committing insurance fraud?

Reaching the top of the stone pile, Hal looked around him, wiping his gloves on his coat. It was already muddy from diving to the ground earlier. A little more mud wouldn't hurt it any.

The prairies were beautiful, daylight breaking through the clouds in glorious smears of gold. It looked like one of the seminary's stained-glass windows of when the Messiah had preached from the fount of knowledge or led the People to their promised land. Only, this was real. The air was fresh and the smell of dirt thick, though it still carried with it a hint of sharpness from gunpowder and dragonfire.

Reassuring himself for the umpteenth time that the elf was unlikely to kill Gilbert while he was gone, Hal looked out at the surrounding plains, spotting a few trails through the tall grasses that led first in a straight line, then slowly curved to the blue ribbon of a creek that flowed past the shack and rock pile both.

Hal pulled one of his gloves off, placed two fingers between his lips, and whistled sharply.

Where the trails of flattened grass dipped down toward the creek, he saw a black head appear, ears perked. The horse's head bobbed as it started heading toward him. Hal saw the second head appear before long and muttered a short prayer to the Saints that both the horses were alright. The mule might be sturdy enough to carry Gilbert, but it would be faster if they all rode. They *needed* the full-sized quarter horses to get back to Scorched Bluffs safely.

Taking another deep breath, Hal whistled again.

It died on his lips as a dark shape burst out of the clouds, swooping down toward the horses. Clouds streaming from its wings, the enormous bird extended its talons and snatched a horse from the ground. Hal covered his ears at the crack of thunder its wings unleashed. The sky lit up with lightning, and the grasses around it flattened by the sudden burst of wind.

The stormbird shrieked, carrying its catch back up into the clouds like Hal's half-ton horse weighed little more than a rat.

Hal stood there, ears ringing. Slowly, he lowered himself to sit on the rocks and stared at the patch of ground that smouldered from multiple lightning strikes, their paths through the grasses marked by scorched-dry stalks and steaming leaves.

Well.

For a moment, things had almost made sense. Now he was back to being lost, a Stratton without his badge and a man with no horse. The surviving animal had bolted off again, this time heading further away from the shack. He didn't blame it. First a dragon, and now a stormbird. He'd been half convinced those didn't even exist until now.

Hal pulled a flask from his coat pocket and unscrewed it. He took a long drink, then poured out a few droplets onto the rocks under him. A small offering, but hopefully the Messiah would take pity on him, and... he wasn't sure. What could they do in the face of something that was as powerful as that bird?

"Need help?"

Hal jumped to his feet, hand reaching for the pistol at his side. Muddy stones shifted underfoot, and he went tumbling down into the grasses. The flask went one direction as he went the other, a hand clasped to his belt to keep his gun in place. He wasn't letting the elf get it off him again. Even if it meant getting some scrapes on his way down the rock pile.

Hal groaned, pushing himself up onto an elbow, looking up to see who had snuck up on him. Perched on the rocks behind where he had been sitting, crouched the androgynous elf from town. The one that had been with the deputy.

Eyota.

"You shouldn't sneak up on someone like that," Hal muttered, getting back up to his feet. "I could have shot you."

The elf lifted their eyebrows and stifled a small smile. Hal noticed their long ears twitch.

"I saw stormbird take your horse. Do you need help getting the other one back?" They asked, tilting their head (and ears) toward the direction the horse had taken off in. "I can go get it for you. It'll be faster than if you try to walk over." Hal frowned for a moment, then let out a heavy sigh.

"I would greatly appreciate your help..." he paused and decided he should just ask. "Miss? Mister?"

"Eyota," they said, twitching a shoulder to shake off the titles. "Apprentice Eyota, if you need a title." That didn't help Hal out much, but he wasn't willing to jeopardize the help this healer offered. He nodded, taking off his hat.

"Eyota," he echoed. "Deputy Berry is at the shack down the creek. She's tending to my friend; we ran into some bandits."

The mage's head tilted; ears perked right back up. "Is Mildred alright?" they asked, a small frown forming on their face.

"Yes, she's fine," Hal stammered.

"You get the horse," Eyota said sharply. They leapt up, a burst of water droplets and feathers raining down, and then a pale hawk fluttered away, leaving Hal alone once more.

Hal sighed. Slowly, he reached down to pick up the dropped flask, shook it, and took another long drink. It was still half full, better than he could have hoped for with how the day had gone. Screwing the cap shut, he tucked it back into his coat and started walking after the horse.

No whistling this time, in case that was what brought the bird. Find the horse, get Gilbert to safety, and get out of this goddamn place, Hal thought to himself. When he was back in civilization, he wanted nothing more than a strong drink and a hot bath.

22

·━━ ◦ ━━·

SEEING GHOSTS

"BECAUSE YOU WERE ALREADY *bleeding too much,*" Millie said, exasperated. She crouched in front of the shack's fire pit, trying to coax the kindling into flame. The Willard gang hadn't left the coals glowing, and someone had drenched the ashes with piss. *Assholes.*

Millie had propped up Gilbert's legs with some spare firewood and his coat under his head, before clearing out the piss-soaked ashes in the firepit. The injured banker watched from where he lay to her side, his blue eyes boyishly wide from the laudanum's effect. Millie had been able to tell when the drug started working because he started to complain that he hadn't gotten any earlier.

"Is that true?" Gilbert asked, watching Millie blow gently on the flame she had gotten to catch. "I thought you were being mean."

"I was not 'being mean', it's true." Millie added some kindling to the tiny flame. "You probably would have survived, but the sooner we stopped the bleeding, the better off you'd be." She rocked back to sit on her heels, looking over at Gilbert. He had gone into shock, but was remarkably resilient for a rich city boy.

"No, no," Gilbert said, shaking his head. His skin was pale, but the fire would help keep him warm until his body recovered. "Is it true *you did it to save me?* I thought you hated me."

She stifled a small smile, realizing that the smarmy persona melted away to reveal someone endearingly earnest. Pulling her poncho over him, Millie checked the wound for the tenth time since they'd arrived at the shack. The bleeding had stopped, but the skin was angry and red around where she'd lit the gunpowder. Even as far as battlefield treatments went, the powder was a nasty fix. Effective, quick, but brutally painful.

"I didn't save you," Millie said. "That stupid book of yours did. Without it, I wouldn't have been able to stop the bleeding at all." She fed a few more twigs of kindling into the fire and pulled the battered and bloody book over from where it sat next to her saddlebags.

"Are you in it?"

Millie froze, fingers resting on the canvas cover. One side was still canary yellow, but the other -the one she touched- was stained red with Gilbert's blood. She ran her fingers over the bullet hole in the cover as she tried to decide how to answer.

"I don't know," she said, picking the book up. "I never managed to get past the first chapter before—"

Millie stopped as she felt the fine hairs on her arms and the back of her neck lift on their own. The prickling sensation gave her only a split second of warning before the sky outside exploded with light. The elf threw herself over Gilbert, curling over him to shield him from what came next.

Rapid-fire claps of thunder shook the derelict shed, rattling the rotted walls around Millie, and she curled tighter around Gilbert's chest and head, trying to shelter him from the incoming...

...cannonball that smashed into the ground, kicking up a spray of mud as it skipped across the battlefield. It smashed through the orc to Millie's left and continued through the ranks. Millie stared at the air where her Corporal stood a moment before, her face warm with the mud and blood splatter the ball left in its wake. She dove forward, tucking and rolling behind a downed tree.

Artillery and muskets rained lead upon her cover. She knew it would't hold for long. Scrambling forward, she levelled her rifle between the tree's limbs and took a steadying breath. Letting it out slowly, she squeezed the trigger.

"Deputy Berry?"

The soldier dropped his lantern into the stocks of black powder. Millie threw herself flat a heartbeat before the artillery line detonated. The boom was deafening, and shrapnel tore the tree apart. Her shoulder burned, and as Millie tried to push herself up to her feet, her left arm struggled to hold her weight.

Blood bloomed through her coat, staining it black as the blood dripped down her arm. Tucking it against her chest, Millie rolled to her feet and shouted for the Irregulars to charge.

"Deputy? ...Millie?"

Blinking, Millie looked around the shack. The far side had collapsed, the three remaining walls strong enough to hold the roof up for the time being although the wooden slats that acted as shingles were already starting to bow down, softened from the earlier rains.

"What?" she asked, glancing down at the man under her. "Are you okay?" Had something fallen on him? Gilbert's face was still pale, and there were faint beads of sweat across his nose and forehead. Millie realized he had wrapped his arms around her during the thunder, and looked over her shoulder at where one rested on her back. Her ears flicked.

"As much as I am flattered to finally get your attention," Gilbert said, wincing as he gently rolled them both to the side. "I was just shot. Maybe later, when elves jumping onto me doesn't hurt so much."

Millie's ears flicked back in annoyed embarrassment.

"I jumped because the roof looked like it was going to fall," she grumbled. Pushing herself back up to a crouch, she rolled her left shoulder out of habit. Its range of motion was the same as it had been since the battle. Fine, but not great. Goldman's wound, however, had been tugged too hard by her attempt at saving him. The angry red burn had split open again and while it wasn't bleeding much, an open wound was vulnerable to infection.

"Shit," she muttered, pulling her saddlebag over. She still had a few bandages left in there, but she also needed enough to get Gilbert back to town where Sweetpea or Eyota could take a look.

"Besides, I would hate to disappoint you our first time," Gilbert mumbled, rolling back flat with a small groan. Millie rolled her eyes, but she had figured out the bravado at this point. Being shot for the first time, seeing a dragon, all so far from the city he lived in... no wonder he was trying to be brave.

"I'm going to check on your friend," Millie said, pressing a wad of gauze against his chest. "Hold this here until I get back."

"Wait," he said, dutifully holding the gauze in place. The bravado had slipped a little, and his face showed his worry. "What was that? Will Hal be okay?"

"That was probably a stormbird. They nest in the badlands sometimes, but normally they don't come out this far. And I'm sure he's startled but fine. He's too scrawny for a Stormbird to take." Unless one of the lightning bolts had hit him.

Millie grabbed her rifle and ducked out of the shack's doorway, aware that it was probably the sturdiest part of the half-collapsed building.

She was greeted by sunshine, hawk feathers and sharp talons swooping toward her face. Still twitchy from the thunder moments earlier, Millie punched the bird out of her way, knocking it to the ground. Too late, she realized that it was all white.

"Did you punch a *bird*?" Gilbert asked from behind her. Millie's ears drooped low, and she crouched to check on it. "That's not very nice, Deputy. Birds can't punch back. They don't have hands."

"I'm sorry! I'm sorry!" Millie sputtered, picking the dazed hawk up and setting it back onto its feet. It screeched angrily, and Millie winced. "Yeah, I know, but you surprised me." Her eyes widened, and she scooped the hawk up again, tucking it under one arm like it was a chicken. It screeched again, but wasn't able to flap its way free.

Millie set it down on the ground in front of Gilbert, who looked from her to the bird and back.

"Do... do we eat it?" He asked.

Millie prodded the hawk. Ruffling its feathers, the hawk did a side-stepping dance back and forth, head bobbing. It seemed less than pleased, but Millie made a solid connection when she'd hit it. With a small burst of wind and fluttering feathers, Eyota crouched where the hawk had been.

"Oh," Gilbert said. "Hello, other elf."

Eyota pressed a hand to one eye and glared at Millie the other. "I will forgive this Mildred, but only because I did not announce my arrival." The healer turned away from her and looked at Gilbert's eyes, examining the contracted pupils, and then felt the temperature of his forehead with their wrist.

"Laudanum," Millie said. "I got the bullet out, but-"

"Go help the other human," Eyota said, waving her away. "Before he loses the other horse." The healer huffed in annoyance, muttering in their own language under their breath. Millie was only able to catch a few of the words, but it was enough to know they were complaining about her.

Grabbing her hat, Millie stepped back out of the shack. She found the Stratton easily. He was standing in the middle of the stormbird's strike, staring down at the ground. The grasses were flattened in a circle and patches of scorched ground still steamed where the lightning had melted the sandy soil into thunder-glass.

"I," Hal said, looking up at Millie's approach. "I don't quite know how to process what I just saw. But we're short a horse."

Millie looked around, noticing that they were *short two horses, actually*. She adjusted her hat to keep off the sun and walked over to the detective, patting his arm gently. The stormbird's presence in the area explained why the blue was so far out of her normal range, but damn if the bird wasn't already making Millie's life hard enough without stealing horses.

"Eyota is treating Goldman," she said. "Take off your shirt and we'll go find the other horse. Then you three can head back to town and warn them about the Willard Gang."

Hal cleared his throat, eyes wide.

"I'm sorry, what?" he asked, extremely politely. Millie could see a faint flush on his dark cheeks.

"Take off your shirt," she said, fluttering her eyelashes at him. "I don't have one and Strattons are supposed to be gentlemen. You have a coat and a vest, and I'm out here burning up under the sun in what fancy ladies call 'unmentionables.'" Hal glanced at her shoulders, which were already turning pink under the sun.

"Fine," Hal said, pulling off his coat. "But to get the shirt, you need to answer one of my questions."

"Fine. What's your question?"

Hal tossed her his coat to hold and Millie caught it one-handed. It was still heavy and wet, but the wool would keep him warm through the night. It would have to, if they were going to walk back to Scorched Bluffs to get Gilbert to safety and warn Ryan.

"What was a Ghost Eye elf doing as far east as Marigot? That's right on the coast."

Millie swallowed; her smile gone. She watched Hal, who waited for her answer, eyes boring into her while his hand hovered at his tie. For a moment, she debated choosing the sunburn over the answer, but Millie knew she had to be in fighting form if the Willards came back. When they came back.

"The clan used to live further ease. They migrated out here when they realised a war was going to break out," Millie said. "My father was Ghost Eye, I'm not. He met my mother in Marigot and then he died." She blinked, holding her other hand out for the shirt.

"Anything else?"

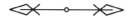

Jeb wiped the silvered badge clean on his pant leg. He turned it over, studying the letters stamped into it, darkened by weather and blood. The elf killed a Goddamn *Stratton Detective* like it was nothing, and all she wanted was a cut of their pay. Di had warned him she was ruthless, but he hadn't been prepared when he saw her in action. She hadn't even blinked when she pulled the trigger.

"Jeb," Zach caught his attention. The younger man spurred his horse into a light trot to catch up to him. "You need to tell us who that was." Zach was frowning, and Jeb could see he'd been picking at his lips again. They were chapped and bleeding, a sign that the younger Willard was worried.

Looking back over his shoulder, Jeb made sure the lone shack was out of sight and there was no undead elf stalking them.

"The way she killed that Stratton like he was nothing more than a varmint, I think she might be the one that killed Isaiah." Zach probed at the bleeding crack on his lips with his tongue, watching Jeb closely. "She's a killer, ain't no bones in my body say otherwise."

"Josie, Eli," Jeb called out, motioning for them to fall back so they could all hear what he was about to say. "I need to tell you why we're not going to go after that woman back there. Even if she was the one who killed Isaiah."

Zach opened his mouth to argue, but Jeb held up a hand to stop him.

"I told you stories when I got back from the war, remember?" They nodded, and Jeb sucked down a deep breath. "I didn't see much fighting in it. Joined too late, was too far from the Bayou when Captain Rousseau took it. But that woman back there, she was in the thick of it. She's the deputy at the Bluffs these days. Di knows her."

"How does Diamond know so much about a Marigot veteran?" Eli asked, still shaken from his experience with the elf. "And Zach, she said she didn't kill Isaiah. I believe her. She could've killed me right then, and she didn't."

"The pale elf moved into town before Di left," Jeb said, interrupting his brothers before they could get into an argument. "Di refused to tell me much more, other than if I wanted to keep y'all safe, it'd be best to avoid her. The elf knew about the train, but Di said she only warned the town because there'd be bandits lurking around when it came through."

"This is bullshit," Zach snapped. He jabbed a finger in the air at Jeb. "You're too soft about your pet elf, believing everything she says. That, back there? She wasn't undead, she was just a short weird looking woman. I could've taken her down with a single bullet if you'd let me. And you saying she knew about the train? Hell, Jeb. You can't be that stupid, ain't no one in Plainfield who will sell that town bullets because they can't pay for 'em."

Jeb felt his neck grow hot. Zach might not be wrong, but he didn't want to lose the rest of them. He said nothing, knowing it was a mistake. His teeth started to ache again, but that wasn't enough of a reason to tell Zach to shut up. What if the pale elf *was* the one who'd killed Isaiah?

"If she was the one who killed him," Josie said, breaking the silence, "We'll need to know more about her and her town before we return the favour. Luckily, there's someone who can tell us more, and that someone's about to become a Willard. Speaking of which, you'd better apologize to Jeb for insulting his lady like that."

"She said yes?" Eli asked, straightening in his saddle.

Zach muttered what could have been an apology, slouching.

"She did," Jeb said. He didn't want to impose on Di, but... hell. She was going to be a Willard, so she might as well start getting involved in the family business. A ghost of a smile lit up Eli's face and it warmed Jeb's heart. When they were done with Isaiah's killer, Jeb wanted nothing more than to go back to the old farm for a month and spend time with his family, including his wife-to-be.

"Di's a sharp woman," Josie said. "She'll help us."

Later, as the Willards rode into Plainfield, the townsfolk grew quiet and watchful at their arrival. Something was off, more than usual. The locals knew the Willards. They knew not to get in the way, knew not to ask too many questions about where all that money came from. Plainfield was never a target, and the townsfolk knew it. They were respectful around the Willards, but now they were acting like cowed dogs.

Sucking on his molars, Jeb let Elijah and Zach ride ahead of him, both making a beeline to the saloon. Josie hung back, watching the townsfolk as intently as Jeb was.

"Josie, Keep Elijah out of trouble while I get the rest of our pay," Jeb said to his sister as they let their horses walk through town toward the saloon.

Josie pressed her lips together tight and nodded. Jeb gave her a pat on the back and adjusted his hat before he followed her into the saloon.

Elijah was hugging Diamond, who smiled nervously over his shoulder at Jeb. She gestured with her eyes to the rest of the Saloon. Half the room had been taken over by stone faced men who turned to look up at Jeb in unison. Many wore scars from the war, the kind of scars you could *only* get from war.

Feeling like he had stepped into a rattler nest, Jeb scanned the room for the swamp man that had hired him. Rémi was at the back of the saloon, standing next to a boulder of a man who dangled a blond half-elf on one knee. The one eyed man nodded to Jeb and leaned down, whispering something to the man he stood next to. After an imperceptible nod, Rémi motioned for Jeb to approach.

He did so with measured steps, reaching into his pocket slowly to pull out the letter and the badge.

"Jebediah Willard," the swamp man said, his pointed teeth glinting in the saloon's dull light. "We were not expecting you to be back so soon. Please, have a seat. This is... Mister Rivers."

The man seated at the table pushed the girl from his lap and looked up at Jeb with bloodshot eyes. The half elf hurried away, passing him with a ducked head.

"Did you see—" Zach whispered to Jeb as he passed.

"Ignore it," Jeb muttered.

"Mister Willard, I trust you to return quickly out of success and not failure," Rivers said. He had the look of a drunk, but his swollen face and bloodshot eyes lent the man no softness. Some men, like Elijah, drank to forget. To let themselves be soft in a hard world. Men like this, Jeb knew, got more dangerous the more they drank. They were broken glass, quick to anger and impossibly unpredictable.

"Rémi told me you were the right man for the job. He is rarely wrong. Is that your brother?" Rivers asked, looking at Zach.

"Yessir. Zachariah's the sharpest shot out here," Jeb said. He set the letter and the badge down on the table and took a seat across from Rivers. Consciously, Jeb rested his hands on the table, in clear view of the two men. He didn't want trouble. "He took care of the varmints you were asking about."

Rivers picked up the badge first, studying it carefully. Like Jeb had done, he turned it over in his hands and squinted at the maker's mark. Satisfied, Rivers tucked it into his coat and picked up the letter. As he opened it to read, Jeb watched a dark smile spread across the man's face. Jeb knew how to read some, but the contents of the letter surprised him. It was a mess, full of ink splotches and fingerprints.

"Marvellous," Rivers said. He tucked the letter away as well and pulled a small key from a cord that hung around his neck out from under his shirt. With a quick yank, Rivers snapped the cord and held the key out to Jeb. "The coin's all there, just too heavy to carry around. The Sheriff is holding it safe for you boys in one of his cells."

Jeb motioned for Zach to come take the key and to go check on the promised payment.

From a few tables away, Elijah had finished his first drink and began telling Diamond about encountering the ghost elf. Di was trying to get him to shut up, but before Jeb could intervene, Rivers stood abruptly, knocking his chair to the floor with a clatter.

"Another bottle," Rivers called out. Diamond looked at Jeb, eyes wide. But what could he do? Rivers' men filled the whole damn saloon. "You," Rivers boomed, pointing at Eli. "C'mere and tell me about this ghost elf." Jeb's molars ached at the hungry look in Rivers' eyes.

Elijah was still too shook-up to recognize Jeb's warning glare, or maybe the promise of a free drink was enough for the idiot to ignore it. The ache in Jeb's teeth spread to his jaw as Eli hurried over and held out his arms to show the small bloody handprint on his shirtsleeve.

"She grabbed me, see? Had the eyes of a killer, that one. The only colour on her was blood. Not like the Clan up north, they're pale sometimes but—"

"What did she look like?" Rivers interrupted. "Was she small?"

Jeb cleared his throat. "Eli, maybe it'd be best to leave this gentleman to himself."

"Small like she wasn't full grown, but she had scars like I've never seen," Eli said, eyes wild. "All up her arms, all kinda scars. Told me she—" the crazed Willard yelped in surprise as Rivers exploded into motion, grabbing the smaller man by the collar and hauling him across the table, knocking aside the half-full whiskey bottle and sending it crashing to the floor.

Jeb drew his gun and, in the sudden silence of the saloon, the click of his revolver's hammer echoed a dozen times over as the surrounding men pulled out their own weapons. This was not a fight he could win, but he couldn't let a stranger beat up his brother right in front of him.

"I apologize for my brother, Mister Rivers. Let him go and nobody needs to get hurt," he said calmly. "He ain't in his right mind today."

"Her eyes," Rivers hissed, ignoring Jeb completely. "Were they blue? Or purple?"

"P-purple, sir," Eli sputtered, his voice strangled and afraid. "They were purple." Immediately Rivers let Elijah go, and the idiot scrambled off the table, rubbing his throat. The skin on his throat was red where the fabric of his shirt had been pulled tight. Jeb was sure if Rivers had wanted to kill Eli, it would only have taken the beast of a man little more than a flick of his wrist to snap Eli's neck.

"Sit down, boy," Rivers said. "If you found her, you're lucky you're all still alive. And double lucky, since I have a new job for you. You're going to find this elf for me, and you're going to help me get her back. Alive."

Jeb looked over at Rémi, and was caught off guard by how dark the swamp man's expression had become. Slowly, Jeb sank back down into his chair, his gun resting uselessly in his lap. He was certain that whatever he'd stumbled into was well over his head.

23

A MATTER OF TIME

Now THAT LAUDANUM EASED his pain, Gilbert could focus on the things happening that didn't make sense. The deputy had punched a bird and now there was the elf from the Scorched Bluffs Saloon crouched over him, with a growing black eye.

"Are you her cousin?" The question bubbled up, the laudanum removing any filter he might have had. "You're much taller than her."

"Mildred? No, but yes," Eyota said. This close, Gilbert noticed small differences between them and the Deputy. The deputy's ears were a tell, though she seemed to take care to control them when she noticed people were watching, but the healer's ears flicked and swivelled without any conscious thought. They were slightly longer, too. "There are honorifics in my language that do not exist in yours. A cousin is close, though I am an apprentice to her great-aunt."

Gilbert blinked. "Why doesn't she live with you, then?" He licked his lips, wondering if the water flask had gone with the Deputy. He hoped not. Laudanum gave him terrible cottonmouth. "Is it because she's... sharp?"

The healer frowned, in the middle of mixing some tea. For a moment, Gilbert worried that time had stopped, and he'd gotten stuck.

"No," Eyota said, un-sticking time for him. "She wasn't raised with us. She doesn't know our language, our customs. There are those who would not want her to be a part of the Clan. They see her as too much of a settler. Though, the more I learn about your people, the more I think she is not like them either."

"Mmn," Gilbert said, closing his eyes. "My people. I'm a Carpenter, not a Wheel follower. There's not that many of my people out here. We like cities where we can build things like our lives. Our destinies. I think my father is afraid of open fields, actually."

Maybe that's why he liked her. She wasn't quite part of the people she lived with, either. He'd been targeted for being so tall during school, and he imagined that growing up with her colouring would not have been an easy thing, especially if she wasn't around others who looked like her.

"You make buildings?" Eyota asked, and when Gilbert opened an eye, he caught them looking at his hands. "You do not have hands that look like they build things."

Gil laughed, then winced as the burned flesh tugged on his chest.

"No, no, not that kind of Carpenter. We follow the old religion, at least the old one, back where we're from. The Wheelers call us Carpenters because we prefer to build our own fates, rather than accept a decided outcome." he reached up to rub at his chest, and had his hand smacked away for his trouble.

"The Wheelers, they are the ones who get reborn, correct?" they asked, stirring the tea as it heated on the little fire.

"Some of them think they do," Gilbert said. He noticed Eyota was frowning. "Did I talk too much about gods?"

"No," they said. "Mildred stopped the bleeding in your wound, but made scars that I cannot get rid of." Eyota looked at Gilbert, their frown deepening. "You are a vain man. This will bother you, won't it?"

Gilbert laughed, then groaned as the movement tugged at the still-healing muscle in his chest. Grimacing, he lifted his right hand and waved the assumption off. He might be vain, but he was also practical.

"I'd rather be alive than handsome and dead," he wheezed, clutching his ribs. "Now, when I get back to Wyndford, I can tell everyone about how I almost died." The sudden thought of home, the realization of how close he had been to death, punched through the soft blanket of laudanum. Gilbert sucked in a deep breath. He didn't want to think about how his little Sarah would have taken the news that her Papa was shot by a smelly Outlaw.

"She's afraid of the dark," he murmured.

"Mildred?"

"No, no. My daughter, my little girl. She's afraid of the dark, but she's so brave. Sometimes we go into dark rooms with a single candle so she can show me that she's not afraid, even though she is." He smiled, looking up at the sagging, rotted roof of the shack overhead. It was a far cry from the sculpted plaster over his own bed.

"She sounds like a brave little girl," Eyota said. "Even if she's afraid, she is determined to face that fear, and prove it has no power over her. There is much strength and honour in that. You should be proud."

Gilbert glanced at Eyota, eyebrows lifting. He smiled slightly, but he knew it didn't reach his eyes. It was kind of the healer to say, but he missed his home. He missed *Tata's* grumpiness, Sarah's serious hugs. He even missed Arnaud's pervasive ennui.

"Thank you, she is. She's a very brave girl," he said. He needed to change the topic or he might sink deeper into homesickness.

"Mildred is not afraid of the dark," Eyota said, taking the tea off the fire. "But she is afraid of her dreams. They scream at her for things she did, but mostly for things she did not do." They poured the tea into a shallow bowl to let it cool slightly. "There are ways to heal the heart, but... I do not know how to do that yet. Grannie—our medicine woman—knows, but she says that Mildred must do most of the work herself."

Blowing the steam from the tea, Eyota murmured a blessing over it and slowly poured the liquid onto Gilbert's gunshot wound. It stung for the first breath, and then slowly a numbing warmth spread down from his skin to the aching muscles below.

"You will need to rest for a while as your body accepts the healing. You should sleep," Eyota said, and placed their hand over his eyes.

"I'm not—" Gilbert remembered slipping down into warm darkness and then nothing until voices drifted down into the darkness, Hal's rumble and the sharp grumbles of the deputy, though he wasn't sure what they were saying. He followed them up, back to his body, which was now covered with something scratchy and warm.

Gilbert forced his eyes open, reaching up to rub the crusts from his eyelashes. His entire body ached, every muscle complaining. It felt like he'd fought multiple matches of boxing in a single evening. With a groan, Gilbert pushed himself up to his elbow and peered out the doorway.

It was sunset, he saw. The cloth door pulled back and Hal ducked into the small shack. His friend looked worried, and something else. Something was off...

"Where's your shirt?" Gilbert asked, frowning. Hal was in a vest, but bare-chested underneath. "Show-off."

Hal grinned, relief flooding his eyes as he crouched next to Gil. "The Messiah is good. I'm glad you're awake. I was wondering what Eyota did to make you sleep so long. How are you feeling?"

"Shit, mostly," Gilbert said. "Where's your shirt?"

Hal chuckled and gestured over his shoulder to the doorway. Outside, Gilbert could hear the two elves speaking in low, hushed voices. How considerate of them not to wake him up, though Gil was certain he could have slept through a thunderstorm after that spell. Glancing down at his chest, he saw the angry red of the Deputy's field medicine had faded to shiny pink scar tissue.

"I plan on going back to town with the Healer," Hal said. "Deputy Berry will wait with you until morning and you'll ride the horses back to town. Rousseau is up to something, but I don't know what yet." Hall rubbed at the stubble growing on his chin. "The deputy is scared, which concerns me. She faced the dragon like it was nothing more than a big dog, but something about Rousseau has her frightened." Gilbert watched Hal's face in the fading light. He looked grim, his jaw set and eyes narrowed. He knew that expression.

"You want me to do something?" Gilbert said. "You want me to seduce the deputy? Hal, *I have been trying*. Unfortunately, she's interesting rather than interested."

Hal snorted, and a flicker of a smile returned. He shook his head, glancing over his shoulder again. He seemed nervous, but Gil didn't understand why.

"No, no. If you want to keep trying, then good luck. I need you to find out why she's afraid. She's still not telling us everything, and I think if we have to, we'll need to know who she is. We may need to negotiate with Rousseau, I would rather do that with something to negotiate *with*."

For a moment—just a moment—Gilbert thought Hal was asking him to turn the elf over to Rousseau. He blinked and reached up to rub his eyes again. No, that was the exhaustion of nearly-dying that was muddling his thoughts. Hal wanted to find out who the Deputy was.

"Alright, I'll get her to open up," Gilbert said. "But where is your shirt?"

The blond man was still sitting at his table. A fresh bottle of whiskey had replaced the shattered one. He had a fresh glass next to him, but barely touched it since gathering the other Willards at the table. Diamond had disappeared from the saloon, no doubt to check on the blonde elf who had been attending Rivers earlier.

"Mister Willard, do we have a deal?" Rivers asked. The amount of money offered was staggering, enough to tempt a man to turn in his own mother. But Jeb's teeth were still aching. Something wasn't right.

"Almost," Jeb said, running the brim of his hat between his hands. "I have a question about this elf of yours. You said we were lucky to get away alive, but not why. If we're going after her, we'll need to know what she's capable of, sir."

Rivers looked deep into his glass. He took a gulp of the whiskey and set it down, staring into the amber liquid like it was a crystal ball.

"Tell me, Jebediah Willard," he rumbled. "What do you know about the Battle of Marigot?"

Di mentioned the elf had been around for that fight, but when it came to history, Jeb's education was lacking. "Well, sir, it was the last big battle of the war, wasn't it? Out in the Beaulieu Swamps. I joined up too late to be involved. Captain Rousseau won the battle, and the war after it."

Rivers' eyes crinkled in a strangely tight smile.

"Well, you're partially right. If you don't know about the battle, you won't know about her." Rivers took a deep breath, and then knocked down the whiskey he had let sit in his glass for over half an hour. "We called her the Ghost. She signed up early in the war to be part of the militia, fighting against the slavers. She was young and hotheaded. We needed bodies to fight with and bodies to block bullets with. My Commanding officer and I... we thought for certain she would be the latter."

Rivers pressed his lips together, looking back down into his glass.

"She wasn't. Born wild, she taught the other militiamen how to track, how to hide in the fields and swamps. She would have captured more men than I did, but she killed them. Every last one of them." Rivers wiped his mouth with the back of his hand, no longer watching Jeb.

"She had a habit, you see," Rivers continued. "Of picking off the enemy one by one. If they surrendered, she'd line them up, get them onto their knees, and slit their throats. She'd take an ear from each human. The sub-humans, she wouldn't bother with those."

Jeb sat extremely still. Isaiah had been badly burnt by the fire. He hadn't checked if Isaiah's body still had ears or not.

"Plenty of men die in war," Jeb said, cautious.

"In battle," Rivers said. "But this was slaughter. The Commanders ignored her actions until Marigot. She defied orders, rushed into the city with her regiment. They slaughtered anyone they could find. It didn't matter. Men, women, children...

"After Marigot, I found her in the middle of some black magic sacrifice. She'd had some greenskins nail O'Leary's second in command to a door. I got there before she could finish the damned rite, but I'll never forget the state she'd left that man in." Rivers shook his head. "They called her the Butcher, after that. Messiah only knows what she's been up to since she escaped from prison years ago. I thought at first that the dragon attack was a coincidence, but with the magic she's learned I wouldn't be surprised if she called down the beast to hurt my business."

Jeb sat stock-still now. The Elf had arrived at the tail end of a storm, marked up like a hellion and already bloody. He swallowed. She'd wanted to keep the dead human bodies of the banker and the Stratton. Diamond was terrified of her. Rivers' story would be unbelievable in most circumstances, but the damn dragon seemed to follow the ghost elf wherever she went. Josie was right, the elf was an unholy monster.

"And you plan to take her alive?" Jeb asked.

Rivers smiled, eyes focusing back onto Jeb.

"I do," he said. "She deserves to face true justice for what she's done, Jebediah. These men around us, they're still loyal to me.

Some are mages, some other soldiers who knew her. Fought her as we threw her in jail. I'm not the only man who wants her caught. I think, Jebediah, that the Messiah himself sent you to me. A family of faithful, ready to do his work. And the Wheel must work," he said, making the sign of the holy wheel.

"And the Wheel must work," Jeb echoed, returning the blessing. The words stuck in his jaw, burrowing in and aching in the spaces between the roots of his teeth. There was no way out of this without joining Rivers. He knew there was something wrong about Rivers' story, but neither he nor his siblings were in a place to walk away.

"Well, sir," Rivers said, holding a hand out to Jeb. He took it. "I believe we have an arrangement. The prairie will be a safer place once we catch the Bayou Butcher."

24

OLD WAR DOGS

"Eyota, I need you to leave," Millie said, as Hal stepped back into the shack. "Find Sheriff Collins and tell her what's coming." Millie looked up at the apprentice. "And I need you to tell the clan to hide in the hills until it's over."

"*What* is coming?" Eyota asked, their eyes narrowing.

"You've seen my scars. The man who did that," Millie whispered. "He's the same man who hired the outlaws that shot the tall human. Those outlaws will tell him about me, and he will come looking. We need to be ready," she said, her voice falling into a whisper. "Because men like him don't come alone."

Eyota's eyes widened. "All of your scars?"

"Most of them," Millie said. "I need you to go warn everyone, and I need you to do it right now. We all need time to get ready."

"Do not let him take more of you," Eyota said, cupping Millie's face in their hands. "It is better to be a broken witch than become hollow from hate. Stay Mildred." Eyota pulled their lips into a smile, but it didn't reach their eyes.

"I won't," Millie said, touched by the gesture. The promise already tasted like a lie, saccharine and foul. The healer had already shifted back into a hawk and climbed into the sky with powerful wing strokes. The smaller elf watched them go, unsure if she had told Eyota enough. Ryan could fill them in, if it was necessary.

Hal must have heard the heavy flap of wings, she thought, watching the Stratton stumble out of the shack and stare at the pale hawk flying off without him.

"What was that? I thought I was going to return with them?" He asked, looking over his shoulder at Millie.

"They had an important message to carry," she said, running a hand over her hair, trying to press the flyaway strands flat to her braids. It was fruitless, and she gave up. "I'm sorry. I told them to go."

"More important than speaking to the Sheriff?" Hal asked, frowning. "What did you tell them?"

Ah, Strattons, always too smart for their own good. Millie walked over to the shack, patting Norbert on the way by. The mule nuzzled at her shoulder, checking for carrots, and when he found none, flicked his tail at her. Mentally apologizing to the mule, Millie gave his neck a last pat and continued on to the detective and shack itself.

"The same thing I'll tell you," she said. "But I only want to re-live it once, so you'd both better pay attention." Millie adjusted the rolled-up sleeves of the shirt he had given her, pushing it to her elbow. It almost immediately fell back, halfway to her wrist.

"As much as I appreciate the offer of your shirt, couldn't one of you two be smaller?" she muttered. The shoulder seams hung down to her elbows and while she had belted the shirt around her waist, Millie felt like she was wearing a whole damn sail. "Thank you, though." Millie ducked inside. Gilbert was propped up on an elbow, and she immediately frowned. Why was he pushing himself up like that? "You should be lying down," she said. "How are you feeling?"

"Oh, *that's* where the shirt went," Gilbert said, but his voice was tight. The laudanum would have worn off by now and Millie knew from experience that wounds treated with magic still hurt well after the flesh had mended. Eyota said it was something about the mind not being able to accept the pain was over. Millie thought, privately, it was the body's way of telling the mind that dumbass decisions had harsh consequences.

"I didn't offer it," Hal grumbled, following her into the shack. "You asked for it."

Millie, dangerously on edge, grinned at Hal.

"I *always* ask for it," she said. The Stratton's face creased in confusion, and she felt no need to explain what she meant.

"Do you?" Gilbert asked.

Ah, yes. With the ease of the laudanum's softness, his bravado had returned. Millie sat by the fire pit and pulled her saddlebags into her lap. Eyota left the fire banked, ever thoughtful about others. Already the horizon blushed pink, the scattering clouds of the storm lit up in brilliant colour.

For a moment, Millie watched them through the collapsed side of the shack.

"Laudanum first," she said, mostly to herself. "And then it's time I tell you the story of why Captain Frederick *Fucking* Rousseau wants me dead." She pulled the dark-tinted bottle from her bag and handed it to Gilbert. "Two drops, no more," she said.

Gilbert took three just to spite her.

She took the bottle back, staring at it for a long moment. She took a deep breath and then took a single drop of laudanum. From the corner of her eye, she saw Hal watching. She held up a single finger to forestall any proselytizing about the sins of laudanum.

"Are you going to share?" Hal asked, taking a seat near them. He shrugged off his coat with a grimace. "I forgot how much wool itches," he muttered.

Feeling the soft warmth of the opium creep up her cheeks, Millie held out the small bottle to the Stratton. She tried not to notice the thickly corded muscles that flexed under his skin or the faint scarring on the back of his shoulder. She knew that kind of scar. Lashes. Someone had been a naughty boy. Funny, she'd thought these two were soft, but under their fancy clothes they had scars just like everyone else.

"Alright, but I'm hiding this later in case you two are addicts," Millie muttered. Her lips felt pleasantly soft from the inside out. "I'd expected a sermon," she admitted. "Laudanum is evil, blah blah, the Messiah hates drugs."

Hal's lips pulled into a poorly suppressed smile and he took a lone drop of the medicine. "Naw, I don't preach anymore. Not about the Messiah, at least. I found I could do more good outside of the Church than as a part of it."

Gilbert laughed, clutching at his chest. Millie realized her face must have soured, her ears drooping in disgust. She could feel her ears get warm in embarrassment, and flicked them rapidly to get rid of the extra blood that no doubt was turning them red.

"That, that ear flap thing, that's adorable," Gilbert said, his voice softened. The idiot had taken three drops of laudanum. He would be useless before long. Millie glared at him, getting more annoyed as his smile grew wider.

"You said you were going to share your story?" Hal prompted, taking two drops for himself. "About Rousseau?"

He was magnificent. Dressed in a linen suit of blue, his blond hair shone in the sun. A neatly trimmed moustache almost hid the sneer of contempt he gave the soldiers he had caught throwing stones at a young, frightened elf. A houseless elf without the sigil of an owner on her plain dress.

"Do you think this is bravery?" He snapped.

She could taste blood. It was something that would follow his presence for a decade to come. Whenever Fred was nearby, she would taste blood. Early on, it was her own blood that stained her tongue. As years passed, the blood on her tongue became someone else's.

He was a hero back then, a demigod from the stories her mother once told her. All golden and strong and good. One of those things was true, she learned. Only one.

"She attacked us first."

Millie couldn't remember the face of that man anymore. It blurred, adopting features of future encounters until he was an amalgamation of humans that preferred cruelty to understanding. And there was a legion of them, ready to step into line to replace fallen comrades.

Millie blinked, looking down at the kindling in her hands. Her eyes felt hot and gritty, and it was still too early to allow tears. She clenched her jaw to keep her emotions in check and fed the twigs into the hot coals.

"I was his slave, but I didn't start out that way," she said. "My father was Ghost Eye, like Eyota. My mother was a free elf in Marigot that worked with a furrier. I was born in the city, and for a while, things were alright. We didn't have much, but we didn't go hungry often. Papa had a way of singing the fish up to his boat." She shook her head, trying to rid her ears of the haunted song her mind tried to play for her.

"After my father died, my mother began to drink. She sold me to Rousseau when he asked." She pursed her lips, thinking about how much to tell them.

"I wasn't good at being a slave. Fred bought me with a reason in mind. I'd cut one of his soldiers after they gave me trouble." A lie. She'd stabbed him, then slit his throat. "He bought me and paid the soldier damages for what I'd done. He trained me to be a soldier, to protect his family." That part was the truth.

She got the kindling to catch and blew gently on the tiny flame, coaxing it into strength.

"I thought Rousseau fought *against* the slavers?" Gilbert asked. "He's never mentioned owning any slaves."

"He wouldn't," Millie said, solemn. "I can't imagine the official history talks about it much, but long before the Battle of Marigot, the Unionists were winning. They'd choked off the land supplies, the shipments of iron and steel and gunpowder. Marigot was starving before the war even started. It was easy to see which side would win, and Fred sided with the Union, knowing if he helped them win, he would get to keep his head and his fortune." She fed another twig into the fire, watching the sap snap and spit as it caught.

"When he defected, I stuck with him. I was stupid. He promised freedom to any slaves who fought with him. It was impossible to save up enough money to buy our own freedom at that point." The word tasted bitter in her mouth. Worse than any amount of laudanum. She ran her tongue over her teeth as if she could scrape it clean off the damned thing. 'Freedom'.

"Did he free you?" Hal asked.

"He wouldn't," Gilbert answered for her, using her words. "Rousseau is a liar and a cheat. Worse than all that, he's a sore loser. He can't stand letting people know he's in debt. I can't imagine he'd be willing to let anyone go who was the hero he wanted to be."

Her lips tugged up at their corners, and Millie tilted her head at Gilbert. "He was a young lieutenant back then. An Officer on the rise. When he switched sides, we gathered together a squadron of irregulars. Elves, orcs, dwarves, any non-human who knew Marigot and was willing to fight." This part was in the yellow book of Gilbert's. She wondered if she was in it. "We took anyone. We knew that if we encountered an ambush or a rout, we wouldn't have any brigade riding to our rescue. Slavery or not, the Unionist army was distrustful of a bunch of Swamp men trying to fight the old society."

"But you won," Gilbert said.

The Secessionists brought the mages in to replace the destroyed artillery. It was a logical decision, but a poor one. Cracks of thunder split the air as mage after mage called the storm down on themselves and the soldiers around them. Mages she had promised to find protection for. Mages she had met in dark cellars, some from childhood games in the Marigot slums. They used the iron shackles to funnel the lightning across their lines, electrifying the men who had enslaved them.

Millie pressed on, desperate to end the battle. To save anyone she could.

"We won," Millie said. She watched the little fire grow, consuming each twig she fed into it. "We lost nearly everyone, but we won."

O'Leary, the secessionist general, pulled back, retreating into the city of Marigot. They closed the gates, but gates didn't last long against the fury of Marigot's abused children, finally coming home to confront their masters. Delilah, a half-orc, had shattered the gates with a single spell. She caught a bullet to her face a heartbeat later.

The Irregulars continued their charge.

"We'd kept in contact with most of the slaves and non-humans in the city," Millie said. "In exchange for helping us, they would be freed for their service." Her throat grew hot, and she was suddenly aware of how tight it was.

"And when the time came, they did. They did what they had promised to," she said quietly. "Fred did not."

The city erupted all at once. Lightning, gunfire, and steel built into a cacophony of death and pain. The irregulars pressed deeper, carving their way to the heart of the city, where the Beaulieu Governor's seat waited. Fortified and with good vantage points over the rest of the city, the Governor's office would be the regroup point for the secessionists. That was where O'Leary was headed. So that's where the Irregulars were headed, too.

They heard the screams the moment they breached the building. Wild, inhuman, coming from the councillor's room a few floors up. They rushed in, guns cocked and steel drawn.

They found the young man nailed to the heavy wooden doors to the councillor room. Arms and legs outstretched, head hanging low. The door was painted with red symbols, while others were etched into the wood with a knife.

"We found O'Leary in the middle of summoning a demonic spirit. A few minutes later and he would have been successful, the thing would have torn through us."

Hal recoiled, and Millie nodded grimly. Human sacrifice was heresy to the Messiah's cycle. It was breaking the wheel for unholy power. There was no sin worse.

The man on the door groaned, and while O'Leary and his men surrendered, Millie walked over to the intended vessel and slit his throat. It was a better fate than what the Secessionists had planned for him. She remembered that taste as his blood splattered on her face. It was only when the fighting stopped that Frederic finally arrived at the scene, his personal guards levelling rifles at her.

"Witch," Rémi had snarled. "Heretic."

Frederic's face told Millie everything she needed to know. The world wouldn't hear who truly captured O'Leary. The world wouldn't hear that a human general, respected despite his position in the war, had been captured by a company of elves and orcs. No one would know that O'Leary had resorted to sacrificial magic in a desperate bid to win the battle.

"Mildred Berry, you are under arrest for crimes against the Amelior Union," Frederic said. She had thought he was saving face. That after the war was won, after everything was settled, she would be let go.

"I was arrested," she said, poking at the fire. The faces of those early human soldiers might have blurred into anonymity, but Millie could remember the freckles and knotted brow of the young man on the door as clear as day, every day. "It would be bad for reconciliation if word got out that O'Leary resorted to heresy. So they blamed me, because I looked funny." A bitter smile spread across her lips, and Millie looked away from the fire to meet Hal's eyes.

"But why kill the Irregulars?" Gilbert asked.

Millie shrugged a single shoulder. The other itched, deep in the joint where old shrapnel still lived. She reached under Hal's shirt to rub the scar there.

"You said it yourself," she said. "Fred is a liar and a cheat. He wanted to be the hero of the war. So that's what he became, killing anyone who knew different." She fed a log into the fire now that it was finally hot enough to handle the larger piece. "He spared me for a while because I was compliant. He had trained me to be his little soldier from the moment he bought me, and that kind of training takes a while to shake off."

Millie chewed at her lip, unsure how to explain the rest. Should she even bother?

"I escaped, eventually," she said with an unhappy smile. "I went west and didn't stop until I found Scorched Bluffs, a town so small and so remote that I knew Fred could never find me."

The two men were silent, watching her with soft dark eyes.

"How do we know you're telling the truth?" Hal asked.

She wasn't, not all of it at least.

"Look," she said, twisting and undoing her belt. Lifting the shirt and her undershirt up to reveal an old scar, a tangle of old burnt skin, Millie let them look. An F, A, and R, intertwined. It was the same brand that was burnt into every crate of bullets that she had stolen from the train. Despite him saying that he'd free her, Fred had still marked her as one of his possessions. At the time, young and dumb, she had thought it would give her protection.

She felt gentle fingers trace over the scars and looked over her shoulder to see Gilbert had pushed himself up to sit again, his hand outstretched to explore the old marks.

"People aren't property," he said quietly. "And dogs don't belong in cages."

She didn't understand what any of this had to do with dogs, but she agreed with the idea. People weren't property. Dogs shouldn't be caged unless they were rabid.

"Maybe some of us should be caged," she whispered.

Blood on her lips, on her cheeks, on her hands. Always blood, always tasting blood until she couldn't stand it anymore. When she escaped, she slaughtered everyone in her way without a second thought, leaving behind a trail of blood that led out into the wilderness.

"Some war dogs only know old tricks," Millie said, letting the shirt fall back into place. The brand had been only one scar of many. "I spent years trying to become someone else. Someone with a good life, and it didn't matter." She blinked back hot tears, thinking about her sins. She'd had the opportunity to kill Fred once, and she hadn't taken it. She'd let him live, and he'd continued hurting people. "None of that mattered, because he's coming and he's going to try to take everything from me."

"Well, I don't believe that," Hal said, resting a hand on her shoulder. "A fight is coming. Maybe, maybe an old war dog is what your town needs right now." Millie looked at him, his dark eyes no longer trying to be cheerful and warm. He'd let down his mask after she'd done the same.

She'd run for years, and it didn't work. She had hidden for years, and he'd still found her.

"Maybe you're right," she said.

25

THE PATH AHEAD

MILLIE DIDN'T EXPECT TO sleep. She expected to lie awake and relive the horrors of the war. The horrors of one Captain Frederic *Fucking* Rousseau. Maybe it was the laudanum, maybe it was the giant of a man who had reached out, pulling her into a gentle hug, but as she lay in the half-collapsed shack with two human men, stroking the hair of the Banker she kept trying to hate, she felt almost comfortable. Almost safe, although *that* was certainly the laudanum at work.

"I have a little girl," Gilbert murmured, still propped up against the sturdier wall of the shack. His arms draped loosely around her, one hand occasionally reaching out to brush her braids, as if to check that they were real. "Back home. She's so good, so serious. I promised I'd get home safe."

"Tell me about her," Millie said. He had mentioned her at the hotel, but talking about family was better than talking about Fred. Hal lay next to them, his hat resting over the top half of his face. Millie let him think she believed he was still asleep.

"Her name is Sarah, and she is the most precious little storm cloud. She made me promise I wouldn't get hurt and now-" Millie reached out, brushing her fingers through his hair to calm Gilbert before he could follow that trail of thought any further. He melted under her hand, nuzzling into her palm like a puppy.

"You're safe," Millie said. "I'll keep you both as safe as I can." She had more to ask, more questions that gnawed at the back of her tongue until they came rushing out, freed by the laudanum. "But I need you to promise me something. If I die, probably while protecting you and your friend, promise you'll watch over my daughters. It's only fair."

Only fair, that he would live, her girls would live, and she wouldn't. Millie hummed a few bars of a lullaby, thinking that she would be sure to sing her girls to sleep before Fred arrived. One last good night.

"Only," Mumbled Gilbert into her palm, his voice already getting soft with sleep. "Only if you take care of my Sarah if *I* die. Only fair."

Millie wanted to say he would survive, but she had seen too much war to make stupid promises like that. Stupid deaths took good people all the time. Instead of saying anything else, Millie brushed her thumb over his cheek and continued humming. *Go to sleep, tall banker. Sleep off the drug that makes you soft and kind.*

"Be her momma," Gilbert mumbled. "If I die, promise you'll be Sarah's momma." The last word turned into a light snore. Millie waited to see if he would wake, but he slowly settled to the ground, still holding her hand to his face. Glancing over at the Stratton, Millie saw his posture had relaxed and she could hear the deep, slow, breaths of a sleeping man.

She let out a frustrated sigh, still too awake to sleep, too sleepy to do anything beyond planning the day ahead. They would set out for Annie's ranch, pick up a few spare horses and ride the rest of the way to town. From there, Millie would kiss her girls, grab a coffee, and head out to retrieve the stash at Annie's Ranch. Whatever Fred was planning, she knew she would need it.

Millie dreamed of Marigot that night. She dreamed of Fred, and of the lost friends who had become family. She dreamt of that crushing moment that she realised Fred wasn't going to let her go free. That he never would. She dreamt of his hands around her throat like the iron collars of Marigot.

Arms tightened around her and Millie jerked forward, her elbow pistoned back into a very solid chest that grunted in pain. The grunt didn't sound right; it was too deep. Too surprised.

"Is that how you greet everyone you sleep with?" Grumbled the man who held her, his arms loosening. "No wonder you're still alone, ow."

Shaking off the last webs of her dream, Millie looked around. The sagging roof of the lean-to shack, the groggy Stratton who startled awake at the sudden sounds and the long arms that were letting her go.

"Oh shit, did I hit the bullet wound?" Millie whispered.

Gilbert grimaced, but his hand was pressed against his ribs instead of his chest. Millie let out a sigh of relief and threw her arms around the banker, hugging him tight. It lasted only a moment, a series of confusing heartbeats, before she pulled away, rolling to her feet and into a crouch. Millie watched the groggy banker with wary eyes, forearms resting on her knees. Her head hurt, her veins itched, and she had a terrible case of cotton-mouth, but she was alert, which was more than either of the men could claim.

"No," Gilbert grumbled, reaching up to rub his face. "But you have unnaturally pointy elbows." He squinted at the empty side of the shack, where the sky was starting to lighten. "Is it morning?" he asked with a grimace.

"How much do you remember from last night?" Millie asked, squinting at Gilbert.

"Did we have sex?" He mumbled, looking over at her. Then smiled, waving his hand. "Relax, I'm just joking. You snore, though. A lot."

Her eyebrows shot up. It seemed the asshole banker had returned. For a moment, Millie debated drugging him for the remainder of the walk back to town. Ultimately, the benefits were outweighed by the potential of causing an addiction that would hurt a stormy little girl. Instead, she shrugged and smiled.

"No, but you asked me to be your daughter's momma," she said, smile growing wider. "That's quite the proposal, sir."

Gilbert froze and looked at her. She watched him look past her to Hal for reassurance.

"Yeah," Hal said, stifling a yawn. "You asked her to be Sarah's mom. Sounded an awful lot like a proposal, Gil."

Surprised, but amused at Hal's support, Millie smiled and held up her left hand, wiggling the fingers on it as if to show off a ring that wasn't there.

"I accept. I ain't no fancy lady, don't need no shiny stones. A simple ring since we have an honourable witness." She watched Gilbert look from her to his friend, the faintest panic creeping into his expression.

"I will get a ring," he said in a too-measured voice, "*After* we get Rousseau taken care of."

Millie smiled and shook her head. She would take care of his daughter if anything happened as promised, but she knew she couldn't expect any reciprocation. Millie, Fenna, and Rasha, the elves were on their own as elves always were. Once they got back, she would speak to Eyota, make sure the clan would be willing to take them in if anything happened.

"Come on, I'll get some coffee going, then we'll need to set out. It's going to be a long walk for you two, even trading rides on your horse," she said, standing. Short as she was, she could stand up straight even with the bowed-in ceiling. "I'd offer Norbert, but you both have longer legs than I do."

26

BAD NEWS

RYAN WAS IN THE middle of playing hopscotch with the little Berrys when Eyota returned. Fyodor barked as a pale hawk swooped down to land on the hotel's wooden porch. She felt her eyes go blurry for a moment and Ryan blinked to try to clear the sensation away. As her vision cleared, Ryan saw the apprentice was back in their elven skin, brushing off a few stray feathers that clung to their arms.

Something was wrong. Eyota had a black eye, and their movements were quick and nervous.

"Girls, go inside to see if Auntie Lyddie needs help," Ryan said, shooing the tiny elves toward the hotel's door. Fyodor, sensing an opportunity, hurried over to help herd the little girls inside. It was only with his help that Ryan could forestall the thousand questions that Rasha and Fenna wanted to ask.

"Fyo, bring them to Lyddie," Ryan told her dog. Millie might get annoyed that Ryan used her dog to herd the girls, but it was easier.

"What happened to your face?" Ryan asked, turning to Eyota. The swelling wasn't terrible, but the elf's bruise was already quite dark. It would be a while before a bruise like that faded naturally.

"Mildred happened," Eyota said, probing their cheekbone with careful fingers. "I caught her by surprise."

Ryan winced. The nice marshal was still terrified of Millie after he'd made the mistake of waking her up from an accidental nap. She'd put a hole right through his hat, and only apologized after she'd had a full cup of coffee. Ryan had tried to explain to Allan that spring that the girls were teething and Millie had had little sleep, but he'd seemed to take her reaction as a personal affront.

"I'm sorry. She's twitchy like that," Ryan said, motioning for the apprentice to follow them to Sweetpea's shop. "Sweetpea should be able to help with the swelling."

"That's not why I'm back," Eyota said. "Mildred said the man who gave her those scars is coming."

Ryan felt her blood run cold, draining from her face to pool in her boots. She turned back to face Eyota, stepping closer so she could keep her voice quiet.

"Tell me exactly what she said," Ryan whispered. So, the two men had been working for Rousseau, the book hadn't been a coincidence.

"She said that the man who gave her those scars was coming and would bring others. That you needed to know so the town could get ready," Eyota said. "That I should tell the Clan and get them to move into the hills to be safe. The Man Who Scars hired outlaws to kill the Tall Man, and they saw Mildred with him."

Ryan's thoughts derailed, and she shook her head to clear her mind. Had she heard that right?

"Wait," she said, "The tall man, and the Stratton weren't working for Rousseau? I mean, the man Millie is warning us about?" Then why did they have the book? Why were they working for him? Why did they show up in Scorched Bluffs, of all places?

"Sheriff Collins," Eyota said, face grave. "I need to go speak with my clan. They should be setting up camp at the ranch now, and this…" They frowned, hesitating.

"This is not your fight," Ryan said for them. Eyota nodded, apologetic. "Please, go tell them. I'll follow with Sweetpea to pick up spare supplies from the ranch. I can try to answer any questions they might have when I arrive."

"I will tell them. Thank you, sheriff," Eyota said. They stepped back and, once again, Ryan's vision blurred. Ryan rubbed at her eyes, wishing that magic didn't feel so strange. Blinking away the last of the spell's effect, Ryan jogged over to Sweetpea's shop and knocked on the door. She didn't wait to be greeted, and stepped inside to find a surprised Sweetpea setting down a tray of fresh cookies.

"Rousseau is coming," Ryan said. She could feel her chest growing tight. "We need to get that extra ammo from Annie's. Can you get the cart ready? I'll grab the girls. If I know Millie, she'll stop by Annie's before coming here." Years ago, Millie stored something on the ranch that she would need if Rousseau was on his way. Ryan knew it would be difficult to explain, so she didn't.

"Why bring the girls?" Sweetpea asked, frowning in worry. She was already pulling off her apron and getting her shawl for the trip. "Shouldn't they stay here where it's safer?"

"Millie will want to see them." Ryan felt her stomach twist. These might be the last days her friend had. She should spend them with her daughters. Guilt gnawed at Ryan as she thought of all the hunting trips, the trips to Plainfield to steal supplies, to rob a train, all that time the elf had spent away from the two things she loved the most for the benefit of the town. "She'll *need* to see them," Ryan said, correcting herself.

27

THE BAYOU BUTCHER

MILLIE HEARD THE THUNDERING of hooves first, but the whistle that followed was what put her on high alert. Ears perked straight up, she stood in her stirrups to look down the path behind them. She had a hand on her rifle, and counted the number of hoofbeats. More than one horse usually meant more than one rider. Neither Millie nor the human men were expecting company, but the whistle had been to get her attention.

"Scary Lady, don't shoot!" Allan shouted as soon as the he was in range. The rider had one hand lifted up, his hat having long fallen from his head and now hung from its strap around his neck, floating behind him like one of Sweetpea's kites. He rode one horse, but was leading two others. One was Max, who hadn't even broken a sweat. "Don't shoot! It's me!"

Next to her, Gilbert turned his horse around so he could see who it was. He squinted, then looked over at Millie.

"He warned us you were mean, but I didn't expect him to call you 'scary lady'," Gil said, his face finally cleared of the fog left from the night before.

"He learned the hard way that waking me up is not appreciated," Millie muttered. "I didn't shoot *him*; he just keeps making a big deal out of it." Still standing in her stirrups, she waved an open hand, showing the Marshal that there was no gun in her hand.

Hal, still on foot, shrugged. He couldn't see much through the tall grasses, some of which reached past his own hat. He had, until now, been following the trail broken by the horses to save energy. Smart man figured it out himself without even needing Millie to suggest it.

"We made friends in Plainfield," Gilbert answered. "He's quite smitten with your Sheriff."

"Oh, I know," Millie said. "Ryan will figure it out eventually." There were worse men that could court her friend. A hapless but kindhearted idiot was one of the better options out on the Frontier.

That made the men look at each other, then back toward the incoming marshal. Slowing his horses to a trot, Allan fixed his hat in time to tip it to Millie. His cheeks were flushed, but his ears were pale, she noticed. Whatever he had chased them down for, this wasn't about Ryan.

"I'd like to say I have two witnesses that can confirm I haven't killed anyone recently," Millie said. Max the mustang trotted toward her, tugging on his lead when he reached the end of it. Norbert flattened his ears back and snorted, establishing who was Millie's favourite.

Allan squinted at her, then looked at the two human men. "Uh, thank you for confirming you haven't murdered anyone? However, I admit to being concerned about the way you qualified that with 'recently'." The marshal trailed off and looked back at Millie. "It's a good thing I brought spares, since she hasn't killed you."

"It's not for lack of trying," Gilbert said.

Millie snatched a bug off a nearby blade of grass and threw it at him. The bug, a beetle, tumbled halfway before spreading its wings with an audible buzz and flew off in a dizzy line.

Damnit.

"The Willards shot the banker," Millie said, ignoring Gilbert's laughter. "I pretended to shoot the Stratton so-"

"It was all very brave, Allan," Gilbert continued. "Then she set a bullet off in my chest under the pretense of—"

"It was battlefield medicine!"

"—and I quote, 'battlefield medicine', and then we all had a nice sip of Laudanum and slept it off," Gilbert finished, her interruption not even breaking his train of thought. Millie felt her ears flap down and back in annoyance. She also noticed Allan nudge his horse sideways, a few steps away from where she sat on Norbert.

"Well, I'm glad that no one is actually dead," Allan said. "Yet. But here's the rub: there's a slimy man in town. The one who hired Jeb Willard to kill these two. He, uh, found out about you." Allan trailed off, looking uncomfortable.

Cicada song filled the silence between them.

"Are you going to arrest me?" Millie asked quietly. "If you know who I am?"

"Naw," Allan said, shaking his head. "As soon as Diamond told me what was happening, I bought out the farrier's horseshoes and, uh... 'requisitioned' these two horses. I figured it might not stop who's coming, but it'll slow them down a little." He held the reins out for Hal, who was still on foot.

"*Diamond* told you? And Marshal Allan Douglas," Millie said, blinking. "You stole horses? I'm impressed."

As Hal mounted up, the Marshal sputtered and fiddled with his own reins. Millie nudged Norbert forward, unwilling to let any more time slip away. They had to get back to town.

"I have a question, actually," Hal said, grunting as he swung into the saddle. "Why would you get arrested if you didn't kill anyone? Especially if you haven't killed anyone *recently*."

Millie glanced over her shoulder at Allan, whose face had fallen. No more jokester. Millie always suspected he was smarter than he ever let on, hiding behind jokes and snark the way she hid behind snarls and glares. He looked at her, then tilted his head toward the other men.

"How long have you known?" she asked him.

"A while," Allan said with a one-shouldered shrug. "I figured if Ry thought you were fine, you were. Scary, but fine. Now I wish I'd paid more attention. Maybe we could have hidden you, or sent that slime hunting in a different direction or—"

"It's fine," she said. "I told them most of it last night. I thought if Fred was coming, it was only fair that they knew what problems that'd bring."

"Did you? I don't recall you telling us you were the Bayou Butcher," Gilbert said, crossing one arm over the one holding his reins. "Or was that the Laudanum that omitted that bit?"

Millie's ears dropped, and she looked over at the banker, startled. He remembered the story about Marigot and he had figured her out. Telling them about the sacrifice, that was it. That was how they'd stopped the Butcher in all the books, wasn't it? Fuck.

"What? It was hardly my first opium den," Gilbert said, rolling his eyes. "I was quite within my abilities last night. You *are* in it, you know," he added. "The book, I mean. It took a while for me to realize it. The author neglected to mention how tiny you are and the author thought you were a man." He shook his head. "But you're in it as a few different people. The Ghost, the Butcher."

Breathe in, breathe out. She whispered it to herself like a mantra as she crept forward through hardwood floors, past glowering portraits of white-bearded old men and diamond-encrusted women. She was not alone tonight, but the others had already moved into their positions. They hadn't been kept in a cell for the last year, barely fed. They had stamina that she didn't.

Breathe. Move. Breathe.

"Goldman, stop," Millie whispered. Her belly twisted at the names. Once badges of pride, now they just made her sick.

"But there's so many more!" Gilbert said. "My personal favourite was the Silver Bullet. I'd thought, see, that it was because you used silver bullets? But I realize now." he gestured toward her pale hair.

"Gil," Hal muttered. "I think that's enough."

"Oh, no! Not at all, my dear friend," Gilbert crowed, nudging his horse into a trot to come up alongside Norbert. "Would you like to hear how some of her earlier battles went? Well, these were *hardly* battles. More like slaughters, really. Battles involve other soldiers, don't they, Ghost?"

The floors were freshly waxed and shone in the home's light from the mansion's exquisite gas lamps. Her bare feet didn't make a sound on floors too well built to creak. The doors were oiled, the soft whisper of the gaslights smothered any sound Millie made as she slunk into the first room.

Her heart leapt into her throat, choking off all breath. The room was beautiful. Moonlight streamed in through lace curtains, and a girl was in the four-poster bed, sleeping peacefully. At her feet lay a dark shape, a dangerous shape.

A dog that stirred at the scent of a stranger.

"Mister Goldman, please." Allan tried to stop him. Bless his heart, he was trying.

"She killed *families*," Gilbert snapped. "Children."

Her ears twitched, but Millie was still stuck far away and long ago.

The knife was so heavy in her hand. When she looked down at it, Millie started, horrified at the skeleton's claw that held the handle. Skin, sinew, bones, nothing else. A skeleton, barely held together, barely able to hold the knife in its grip.

She fumbled, catching the knife by the blade and cutting herself. As quiet as she tried to be, a slight hiss slipped out from her lips. The dog was up, knocking her to the floor with a single leap. Slavering jaws hovered over her throat, and Millie closed her eyes and tilted her head back.

Please. End it.

Please.

"This isn't the time!" Allan was growing exasperated. He was the marshal here. He was supposed to be the one in charge.

"I think it's the perfect time. What about the families that don't get to send their little daughters to sleep every night? What about them, marshal?"

How long had she been afraid of dogs? And here she was, about to be killed by one. She waited for jaws to close on her throat, but they never did.

"Fyodor?" a sleepy voice asked. "Fyodor who is—who are you!?" The girl from the bed. Millie felt the dog being pulled away, and a pitiful sound caught in her throat. No, no. Please. Please don't stop it.

The girl was beautiful. Dark hair, soft and sleek where it draped around her shoulders, pale eyes indistinguishable in colour in the darkness of her room. Strong hands reached down, pulling Millie up to her feet, although the world tilted under her for a moment.

Millie held a bloody finger to the girl's lips and breathed a soft 'shhh'. The knife had fallen somewhere. The dog was growling, and in the rest of this beautiful house, people were dying.

"I was supposed to—I can't—" Millie babbled. She felt feverish. "You need to run. I'll try to hold them off." But how could she, in such a state? Underfed, overworked, she was little more than a ghoul unable to hold on to a knife. She knew she wasn't supposed to survive the night. This was Fred's way of closing off loose ends, wasn't it? The Bayou Butcher, finally caught and killed after murdering the most prominent family in Wyndford.

"I don't understand," the girl said, looking from Millie to the door the elf had shut behind her. "My parents—" She let go and made for the bedroom door. Millie caught her by the sleeve of her nightgown, clawed fingers still strong enough for that at least.

"No." The elf dug in her heels, dragging the girl from the doorway toward the lace-curtained window. "No. They're gone. We need to go, girl." She was never sure if the dog had helped, or if some instinct had welled up inside of her, giving Millie enough strength to get Ryan to the window.

To get her out.

What Millie did remember, in crystal clarity, was leaving the knife on that beautiful floor.

"I did it," Millie said, slowly coming back to herself. Lips numbed; she could barely feel the words as she said them. "All of it. I killed the towns full of people, local leaders, families. I burnt the silos of grain. Salted the ground. I did all of it."

She blinked, realizing she had been looking down at her hands. Among the burns from the salamanders only nights ago, among all the other scars and calluses, there was a single white line from a night many years ago.

That night, she thought she was changing her life. She'd promised not to kill any more innocent people, but here she was, the killer of an idiot outlaw, soon-to-be killer of the three men around her once Fred found them. Killer of the whole goddamn town she had worked so hard to rebuild.

Killer.

Sadist.

Butcher.

"Why?" Gilbert asked.

"I knew nothing else," Millie said, looking up with a small shrug. "I thought that was the only way to survive. And, for a while, it was. I thought I was saving the people no one else stood up for. Then they were slaughtered anyway. Like I said, nothing I did made a difference: Fred is coming and I have to face everything I've run from: Fred, who I was, what I did."

She felt far away. Her hands held Norbert's reins, but she couldn't feel them. They weren't skeletal anymore. Years of rebuilding herself had turned them strong and capable.

"And now you're just a loving mother?" Gilbert asked. "How could you possibly reconcile those two lives?"

She couldn't. She had been trying, but she couldn't. Wasn't that why she could never sleep? Never dream without watching that battle over, and over, and over again? Wasn't that why she woke up with a start some nights, heart pounding so hard she had to step out into the night air to be sick?

"I promised," Millie whispered. "On the only godly things I know, I promised I would save lives. It won't be enough to save *me*, but it'll be enough to help the other families." She straightened her shoulders. "And that's why we need to get back to town. Annie, Ryan and the others need to get ready."

She frowned, unwilling to let the heat in her eyes turn into anything more.

"I can't go! My family—"

"—are already dead. But you *aren't and neither am I," Millie hissed, cupping Ryan's face in her hands. The one she'd cut bled red onto the beautiful skin and the sight of it made Millie want to cry. This girl was older than she had been when she had killed her first man.*

"Do you know what's kept me going?" Millie whispered, searching the pale eyes of the young Ryan. "Getting stronger so I can kill the motherfuckers that did this to me. And I can help you. But you need to come with me."

"Does the Sheriff know?" Hal this time. Still disoriented, but clawing her way back into her body, Millie looked over at him.

She was crying. They both were. Salt stung the cut in her hand, but Millie waited until the girl nodded.

"We'll get him," Millie whispered, pulling the girl into a tight hug. "But not tonight. Tonight, we run." It could have been any-one. Anyone that had been in that room. But it was a girl, with pale eyes and dark hair, who had been too kind and pulled her dog away from Millie's neck.

"Okay."

"Of course she does," Millie said, coiling herself up inside. Using the tension inside her to hold herself in place. "She's known who I am since the day we met."

"And who is that?" Gilbert asked. "Are you Deputy Berry? Or the Bayou Butcher?"

"Both," she said, looking Goldman in the eye. "I've been both the whole time."

28

— . —

SCORCHED EARTH

THE GROUP PASSED THE rest of the ride in uncomfortable silence. Gilbert refused to let Hal catch his eye. Both the Marshal and the Detective had tried to stop him from asking questions, but they were questions that needed to be asked. He would have thought that two men of the law would understand. Hal especially, since he'd been the one to ask Gilbert to find out more about the deputy.

Soon, a very dangerous man would be riding into the town of Scorched Bluffs. Gilbert needed to know what kind of woman Mildred Berry was. Was she the murderer of innocents from the book? Or was she the tender mother who had tried to return a puppy and sung lullabies when softened by laudanum?

Gilbert had pushed and prodded with sharp questions meant to bait the woman into reacting. She had the other times he'd provoked her, but this time... he didn't understand. It was like she had gone somewhere else, her answers quiet and after-thoughts.

He still didn't have a bearing on her. She could be a protective mother or a war criminal. Hell, she said she was both, and he was inclined to believe her. That didn't make his decision any easier. He couldn't stand aside to let Rousseau take her, not after the bastard tried to get him and Hal killed... but what happened after that? Would he leave the town to be on its own? Or would he report that he'd found the Bayou Butcher and have her go to court for her crimes?

He would talk to Hal and Allan once they were in town, Gilbert decided. Maybe they had caught something he'd missed, although it was unlikely. A banker made his trade by reading people as much as he read markets. That the deputy remained a mystery was irksome, to say the least.

"I need to stop by the ranch," the Deputy said, interrupting hours of uncomfortable quiet. When Gilbert had been pestering her, she'd looked and sounded distant. Now she sounded firm and certain again. "You three can continue on to the town."

"No, no, we'll wait for you," Gilbert said. "I don't feel comfortable leaving you around hapless ranchers." He heard someone kick their horse into a trot and turned to look just in time for Hal to punch him in the shoulder.

Gilbert winced, leaning away from his friend as he reached up to rub his upper arm. "Ow, that's the side where I got *shot*, Hal."

"That was two days ago," the deputy said, finally turning in the saddle enough to look over her shoulder at the three men. "Get over it." She looked Gilbert over and her lips pulled into the kind of smile that made him shift uncomfortably in his saddle. Women that butchered villages shouldn't be allowed to smile like that. It was dangerous and seductive, and entirely too effective on poor bankers like himself. Gilbert frowned.

"It was less than two days ago," he said, then looked at Hal for confirmation. "Right?"

"The woman that has yet to shoot you out of some unexpected reservoir of saint-like patience is correct, Gilbert." Hal was glaring at him, and Gilbert wasn't sure why until his friend leaned over and hissed under his breath: "You meet a war criminal named 'The Butcher' and your plan is to *insult her?* What is wrong with you? Are you trying to get shot again?"

Ahead, the path—for surely this was no road—split off to the right. The gnarled tree that Gilbert had come across on his arrival stood tall, looking like it might as well be a gallows tree. Would they all be strung up there upon Fred's arrival?

"Is something wrong?" Berry had turned in her saddle when she realised the men had pulled their horses to a stop. She lifted her eyebrows.

"Did you shoot the Willard kid?" Hal asked, his brows drawn into a tight knot.

"Yes."

She looked from Hal to Gil. There was no remorse in her face. She had looked upset earlier when he'd been pestering her, but at the mention of killing the Willard there was nothing. "He was the one who liked to burn the farms down. The youngest, but one of the worst." She scratched the side of her nose and frowned when she noticed it was sunburnt. "He also spotted us unloading the bullets from the train. It would have caused us a lot of frustration if he went back to his big brothers and told them."

She waited for their judgement; eyebrows raised. Next to Gil, Hal was scowling at the ground.

"Are you going to arrest me?" Millie asked, holding out a hand toward them, the inside of her wrist pointed up at the sky. "You can, though I'd appreciate if you do it after we deal with Fred."

"Isaiah was a dick," Allan agreed. "As far as I can see, you were defending yourself, and self defense isn't murder. Where do you think I could help the most, deputy?"

"Good man," Millie said with a bright smile to the marshal. Reaching up, she adjusted her hat, tipping it Allan's way. "Annie could use some strapping young men on the ranch." She kicked her mule into a gentle trot, taking the path to the right.

Something seemed off to Gilbert, but he wasn't able to figure out what. Was it her overly sharp smile? Or the flippant way she had admitted to killing the Willard kid? Good God, he was turning into a Stratton. As much as he could admit a thrill for catching someone red-handed, Gilbert was uncertain if he felt comfortable aligning himself with the two other lawmen. After all, a certain amount of banking was about making deals on the verge of legality and learning how to keep a secret.

"To the ranch it is," Gilbert said, kicking his horse into a trot. At least the road was wide enough to catch up to the ridiculous mule the elf rode. "We'll keep you company. I would hate to get lost trying to find your speck of a town." He eyed her, waiting to see what her reaction would be this time. This woman made no sense. Under the guise of loving mother deputy Berry, she had repeatedly threatened to shoot him. Now, exposed as the Butcher and repeatedly provoked, he got nothing.

Deputy Berry looked over at him with a raised eyebrow. Gilbert noticed her ear closest to him flicked, as though to shake off a fly. Gilbert squeezed the reins in his hands so he didn't reach out to tickle the fidgety ear.

"Well, Allan knows the way," she said. "But hell, you should meet Annie again, anyway. She was the one who punched you back at the hotel." With another sharp smile, the Deputy nudged her mule into a canter, leaving the men behind.

Ahead of her, the ranch came into view. The fence was barbed wire, the tall grasses of the prairie cropped short by the herd of horses that grazed there. It was a strange sight, draft horses grazing next to stout pit ponies. A few of the horses trotted over to the fence at the deputy's approach.

Gil looked up at the ranch's gate as they passed under it. Built from withered logs planted deep into the ground and a third lashed across the top, the gateway was a crude thing. It was the decoration that had Gilbert's attention. He and Hal had ridden past a ranch or two on the way from Plainfield. Those had a sign on their gate or a cattle skull wired to the crossbeam.

Annie had tied streamers of faded cloth and painted rope in knots, hanging in loops from the crossbeam. Each swag of decoration was punctuated with a bleached skull. One, Gilbert recognized as deer, another he guessed was a bear, but the largest, strapped to the centre of the crossbeam, was that of a dragon.

It was much smaller than the one at the train wreck, but a very real, very dead, dragon.

"Deputy," Gilbert said, craning his neck as they approached the colourfully morbid gateway. "What on God's Green earth is wrong with the people here?"

"Annie's Auntie taught her orc magic," Millie said. "Humans can't use it, but some elves can. Apparently, it makes our ears get all itchy on the inside if we do too much of it. The spell on the gate keeps the big dragon away."

The main buildings of the ranch were ahead, but so were a full village of tipis painted with strange eyes and animals. The people among the tipis largely ignored their arrival, but a group of people emerged from the farm house. A large dog and a tall woman were first out the door, but the two little elves that followed quickly overtook them as they rushed to greet their mother.

"Looks like the whole town's here," Gilbert muttered. "Time to get some answers." He kicked his horse into a canter, leaving the two men behind.

Gilbert hadn't realized how right he was until he neared the gathering and was greeted by another pair of women leaving the house. Sweetpea, the lovely woman who did lovely magic, was wearing a dress of faded blue stripes and ruffles, while the other woman who stepped out of the house was indeed the woman who had punched him at the town meeting. Her actions made much more sense, now that he knew the deputy had once been a slave. He would have punched himself, too.

Tall and broad-shouldered, Annie was dressed in leather chaps and a flannel shirt, her dark hair pulled into tight braids decorated with beads and feathers. Spotting Gilbert, Annie narrowed her eyes and wrinkled her nose. It seemed her original opinion of him hadn't changed.

"Why'd you let the humans come?" Annie asked, eyes not leaving him as Gilbert slowed to a trot as he approached. "You should have sent them to town."

To his surprise, the Sheriff seemed to perk up as she spotted Hal and Allan coming up the road. A smile flitted across her face, but it was quickly quashed as she noticed Gilbert watching.

"You made it!" Sweetpea, the lone friendly face of the crowd, said, throwing her hands up to wave. "I *told* you Millie wouldn't kill them. Annie, you lose!" Sweetpea grinned at the rancher, her canines glinting in the late afternoon sun. Gilbert blinked, trying to understand the conversation. Had the lovely Miss Sweetpea made a bet that the deputy wouldn't kill them? That was awfully cavalier with his life.

Annie rolled her eyes and crossed her arms. "Fine. I'll take the Berrys next time Millie leaves."

The deputy, having dismounted and thrown her arms around her daughters, looked up with a small frown. Gilbert was certain he heard a puppy squeak from the centre of that embrace.

chore," Annie muttered, looking away from the family. "Auntie always says, never bet anything you aren't okay with losing. Or doing." Pursing her lips, Annie looked back at Hal and Allan, who were taking their time in riding up to join everyone.

"Is she here?" deputy Berry asked.

"My aunt?"

"Yeah," the deputy sputtered under some loving kisses from her daughters and their new dog. Carefully setting the girls down, she straightened, the spitz tucked under one arm. It was vibrating happily, and Gilbert felt a pang of betrayal. The puppy hadn't even greeted him. Traitor.

Annie hesitated before she answered.

"No," she said, shooting a concerned glance at sheriff Collins. "She's still in Marigot. Are things *that* bad?"

"It's all hands on deck," the deputy said. That phrase, whatever it meant, changed the entire mood of the women. Each head, human, elven, and arroyan, snapped to focus on her, their expressions grim.

"What'd I miss?" Allan asked, as he and Hal finally arrived. Glancing over at him, Gilbert noticed the normally friendly expression the man wore was troubled. "Ry?"

The Scorched Bluffs sheriff was frowning, watching her deputy. After a moment of silence, only interrupted by the sound of dogs panting, she looked over at the marshal with an expression that Gilbert was certain contained regret.

"We need to talk," Sheriff Collins said, her voice soft. "All of us. Sweetpea, can you?"

"On it!" Sweetpea said with a smile. "Little Berrys, I have some treats to feed the ponies. Will you come help?"

The girls, both clinging to their mother's legs, looked at the arroyan woman with suspicion. The blonde one seemed the most tempted by the offer, while the redhead hugged her mother's leg tighter.

"I'll come with you," the deputy said, glancing at her sheriff. Ryan nodded, which was even more confusing. Gilbert was certain that the phrase 'all hands on deck' had been a cipher. Whatever it meant, the women all seemed to understand that it was a grave situation. Did they also know about the deputy's past?

He felt at a loss. The last time he'd been so unsure of how to act in a situation was when a little storm cloud of a baby had been delivered to his door. Nothing made any sense right now. Glancing at the two other men, he noticed that while Hal seemed equally adrift, the marshal looked as grim as the women did.

What was going on?

The horses were taken by the baby elves and Sweetpea, with deputy Berry helping to corral the small girls toward the barn. Left with Sheriff Collins and Annie, the men waited awkwardly as the little ones disappeared into the barn.

"Millie told you about who's coming?" Collins asked, looking at Gilbert, then at Hal.

"Well, Rousseau sent people to kill us. So yes, she did," Hal said.

"I got shot," Gilbert added. "And figured out who she really is." He watched the Sheriff's face for anything, any hints that she knew about the elf's past. The blink and slight lift of the Sheriff's eyebrows told him that she was surprised, but not at the suggestion the elf had a past. The deputy had mentioned the sheriff knew, but Gilbert had thought it was a bluff at the time.

"You did know," he said.

"Lyddie and a few others were here when Millie and I arrived years ago," Collins said, reaching down to pat the head of her giant dog. "This was before the fire. We lived on the edge of town, pariahs in a town full of them." The sheriff sighed and looked up at Gilbert and Hal.

"Ry, you don't-" the marshal said quietly.

"She does," Annie said, crossing her arms. "All of you are probably gonna die. You should know why, before it happens."

Gilbert felt slightly insulted at the assumption, but an icy whisper in the back of his mind suggested that if Rousseau didn't kill him, perhaps Berry would.

"Men from Colfield Rail came," Collins said, scowling now at the memory. "They offered the sheriff money if he gutted the town. The line between Wyndford and Stonecreek was going in, and Colfield Rail wanted to ensure that they owned the only way in and out of the new mines there. Some townsfolk left, taking the money. Some, like Millie and I, had nowhere else to go."

Annie turned and spat onto the ground, her sole contribution to the story. It was enough.

"We rebuilt after the fire. By the time we had shelter again, the railroad was nearly finished. No one came looking." Collins didn't spit as Annie did, but her expression told Gilbert enough.

"What caused the fire?" Hal asked from Gilbert's side.

"The previous sheriff," Collins said. "The Hotel was built from brick. It didn't catch, though he tried. Millie saved us by bringing us to the cellar and we waited him out. After that, it was Lyddie, Diana, Millie, and myself. Annie was out here on her ranch, and the coward that he was, the old sheriff didn't bother trying to run her out."

Annie grinned. It was not a pleasant smile, nor was it warm.

"Forgive me," Gilbert said, holding his palms up to the women watching him. "But please explain how a war criminal became a deputy, even in a town of five people."

Collins' lips tugged up at one corner, then the other. "I deputized her," she said. "And we were down to four people by then. Di had left, and Lyddie and Annie weren't about to argue. And that day we laid down a plan to make sure no suit-wearing *sunnavabitches* would ever take what we built." Collins glanced at the marshal, and Gilbert noticed a faint flush of colour touch her cheeks. "Not you, Allan."

Gilbert rolled his eyes. Good God, the sheriff was as bad as the marshal. If they survived Rousseau, he would be shocked if there *wasn't* a little law-abiding baby on the way in a month.

"So, Millie trained us," Collins added with a small shrug. "She was a sergeant in the war, you know. They always leave that part out of the stories. She was a good one, too. While we trained, we also prepared."

"Millie isn't the only woman here that has trouble looking for her," Annie said with a nod. "We all had our reasons to learn."

"Ah," Hal said. "You are right, the books did not mention she was a Sergeant."

"Or that she was 'she'," Gilbert added. "Or one individual."

"Anyway," Annie said, rolling her eyes. "When she's back, I need her to check the traplines. I don't trust anyone else to do it, no matter how many times she says we're ready. You three, on the other hand," Annie said, gesturing at the men, "are going to help me load up the wagon."

"I need the marshal," Collins said. "We should go warn the others and get started on setting up the welcome party."

Gilbert opened his mouth, but a swift elbow to his ribs from his dear friend Hal, turned his deliciously rude comment into a grunt.

"That's fine," Annie said. "We'll meet you after sundown. Ride safe, sheriff."

Collins tipped her hat at the rancher and headed over to get her and the Marshal's horses. That left Gilbert and Hal alone with Annie, who was now eying them like they were livestock. Not unfamiliar with the feeling, Gilbert smiled back. The wrinkle of Annie's nose and the twist of her lips told him it didn't work.

"Follow me," she said.

She led them to a shed that was closed with a thick chain and padlock. Gilbert watched as the elf placed her hand on the lock and murmured a few words in old orcish. The air flickered, and Gilbert tasted metal for a moment, and then the lock opened, letting the chains fall to either side.

"Did you taste metal?" Gilbert murmured to his friend.

"Yes."

"Orc magic doesn't agree with humans," Annie explained, pulling the heavy chains from the door. "It's why no half-human orc can do traditional magic."

"But elves can?" Gilbert asked. Next to him, Hal spat out a bit of blood.

"Elves with some orc blood in 'em, sure. Not Mildred, though. She dampens any magic if she stands too close. Drives me crazy when that happens."

Annie threw one door to the shed open. The shed itself was packed full of crates, each painted with the title of what they carried. Ammunition. Gunpowder. Dynamite. Some crates, the ones holding ammunition, carried the Rousseau Armory stamp. The others were from different companies, some of which had gone out of business years ago.

There was enough firepower in that single shed to level a full quarter of Wyndford. Gilbert swallowed, eyes flicking from one crate to another, and another.

"Where did you *get all this?*" Hal asked.

"Mildred is real good at scavenging," Annie said. "We've been stockpiling since the fire."

29

SECOND SKINS

DEPUTY MILDRED BERRY, BAYOU Butcher and mother of two, sat in the hayloft of Annie's barn with her chin in her hand. In front of her was a metal trunk that she hadn't so much as looked at for nearly four years. The metal was covered in dust and bits of hay from the bales that had hidden it from curious little elf hands.

Despite herself, Millie smiled. Her girls were curious and smart and got into all kinds of trouble, like she had at that age. Which was exactly why she had hidden away the box holding her past at Annie's ranch, buried under bales of hay. As much as she wished the girls would have more time to be free and innocent of who their mother was, Millie knew that Fred wouldn't wait.

He knew she was alive. He knew she was here. He would be coming for her.

The wooden stairs that lead up to the hayloft creaked. Head snapping up, Millie stood from the bale she'd been sitting on and stepped in front of the trunk. She wasn't ready to talk to Goldman about what she'd done. Almost, but not yet. If she had more time, Millie wanted to tease apart why she felt so much more shame at the idea of answering to him instead of herself, but time was a luxury none of them had.

To her great and visible relief, the person that appeared on the stairs was Annie, not Goldman.

"Found it," Millie said, tapping the trunk with the side of her foot. "I owe you for keeping it away from the girls. Thank you."

"It's just a box," Annie said, walking over to sit next to her. "Hiding it is hardly a hardship."

"It's more than *just* a box," Millie said, looking down at the trunk at her feet. She tried to see it as nothing more than a container. A box. But she couldn't. It held her past, something she had tried to keep hidden from the people she cared about. There was some human myth about a woman who opened a box, wasn't there? She'd let out everything bad upon the world. It felt like Millie was about to repeat that woman's mistake.

"Mildred, I'm not my aunt. I don't have a wise saying ready for every situation, but sometimes a box is just a box." Annie kicked it with her boot. It clanged: a dull sound muffled by the contents it held. "I can't tell you what you should do, but the Mildred I know is not someone who is afraid of a box. Don't let Rousseau get further into your head than he already has."

Millie chewed on the corner of her lip, thinking that over. She'd lied to herself about why she'd hidden the box. Yes, partially to keep curious little hands out of the contents, but also because it was easier to pretend none of it was real if it was hidden away. That by ignoring it, maybe her life as a mother and deputy would be the only part of her life that mattered.

"By the way, your grandma is now in the farmhouse, so come get her when you're done," Annie said, clapping Millie on the back on her way to the stairs.

"She's not my grandma," Millie called after her.

Annie waved, heading back down the steps. Ears perked, Millie listened to Annie's boots descend the wooden stairs and step outside onto dirt. Only then did Millie pull her lock picks from her pocket, crouching in front of the trunk. Years ago, she'd thrown the key into the creek near the smuggler's shack, never to be used again. In hindsight, it seemed ridiculous, but at the time Millie wanted to ensure her girls wouldn't get into the 'box' without her knowing about it. Millie wished they could have had more time. More years of giggles and bed time stories.

With a jiggle and twist, the lock clicked, and the lid of the metal trunk relaxed upward. Millie lifted the cover, listening to the hinges creak. Her nose wrinkled a moment before she sneezed, sending dust up into the beam of sunlight that streamed in from the hayloft's window. Ugh. *Hay.*

A bundle of oilcloth lay on top. Pulling it out, Millie unwrapped the pair of tomahawks. They were sheathed in leather, but would still need to be sharpened before Fred's arrival. She had expected to find rust on the spikes that protruded from each sheath, or the blades cradled within, but they'd been stored in the arid badlands instead of the dank swamp. The steel shined on each axe blade, remarkably sharp after the years of disuse. This pair were the originals. Made from steel instead of iron, their blades were etched with a durability enchantment that had faded the moment she'd picked them up.

Under the tomahawks lay a pair of silver-plated revolvers. Each grip was inlaid with mother-of-pearl pulled from St-Gerald's Bay, renowned the world over for its lustrous pearls. The silver had tarnished, but the internal workings of each gun were steel. Millie knew that after a good clean, the revolvers would shoot just as straight as they had when she kept them polished to a white shine. The guns suited her better like this, showing their age. Millie was no longer a shiny, bright thing, either.

Beneath the weapons, her coat waited.

The navy-blue wool of the Amelior Union infantry had faded over the years. She'd spent many evenings over the course of the war, sewing in patches of wyvern skin to help deflect bayonets and fireballs. The coat used to be something she was proud of, with beaded chevrons on her shoulders and each tear carefully mended. There had always been plenty of wool to use for repairs, cut from the coats of the dead. Pulling the folded coat from the box, Millie ran her palm over the wool, catching on the only tear she hadn't mended. The wool was still stained dark from her blood. The shrapnel that made it was still buried in her shoulder, making the joint ache whenever it rained.

She continued to unpack the trunk, pulling out the razor and mirror, the kohl pot, the half-chaps still with blades of long-dried grass stuck to them.

Annie was right. This was just a box. The memories Millie thought she had packed away had lived in her head. Locking the coat, the guns, the axes away... that had only prolonged the acceptance that Goldman's questions had prompted.

Butcher and mother, there was no conflict. She was both.

Silver stands surrounded her and the trunk, drifting in the faint breeze that slipped through the hayloft. Millie looked in the small polished brass mirror. She trimmed her hair short along either side of her head. She left longer strands along the top, teased into a braided mohawk with the help of a small tin of wax.

The coat was a comforting weight around her, open at the front and held in place by a woven sash tied at her waist. The leather leggings hugged her calves comfortably, tied in place by woven bands similar to her belt.

She remembered making all of it. Sewing hides that had cost an entire month's pay into leggings. Over the war she had extended them, reinforced her coat, and eventually, before the Battle of Marigot, beaded in her Sergeant's chevrons. These were more than garments; they were a second skin, holding her history in every stitch and bead.

Millie had expected it would feel too small, her waist no longer the wasp-like thing it had once been after having Fenna. To her surprise, it fit well. A little snug around her thighs, perhaps, but the reinforced leather of her leggings would ease with a few hours of wear.

At the bottom of the trunk waited an open wyvern skin bag, the bumpy leather worn to a shine at the loop she used to tie it shut. Inside were pots of kohl and pigment, each in a felt pouch to keep from clinking when she moved. The mirror and the straight razor had come from the bag, the razor still sharp enough to have cut Millie's hair.

It was in the mirror that she glimpsed the man walking up the steps to the loft. Millie turned, her ears flattening against her freshly shaved head as she met Goldman's stare. He had stopped on the stairs the moment he saw her, eyes wide.

"I need to thank you," she said, turning to face him. "Hal was right, you know. What the town needs right now is the war dog, not the deputy." She watched his reaction, curious about how he felt about the change. "But I wasn't ready until you reminded me of who I was."

His steps were light, but the loft's floorboards creaked all the same as Goldman walked into it.

"Well, I was coming to apologize," he said. "I needed to know if you were the Butcher or the deputy."

"And now you know," Millie said, putting away the razor and mirror. She slung the bag over her shoulder and adjusted her gun belt. Would he throw more insults? Her tongue was ready, no longer caught by the past. "Does that bother you?"

Gilbert shook his head, stopping just out of her arm's reach. Millie watched the banker's expression as he looked her over, taking in the coat, the hair, the weapons on her hips. He wasn't angry or disgusted, she realized. He was fascinated.

"No," Gilbert said, eyes meeting hers. "Fred's always been a liar. I can't see you hurting children. But it was a war. I know boys signed up. And a boy can pull a trigger as easily as a cranky elf can." Slowly, he reached out, giving her plenty of time to knock his hand away. She didn't.

His touch on her scalp was soft, feeling the soft fuzz left behind by the dry shave. She watched him; hands ready if he moved for her weapons. He didn't. Instead, he ran his thumb along the length of her ear, sending a little shiver through her. Her ear flicked on reflex, breaking the seriousness of the moment, and Gilbert smiled.

"Ticklish?"

Millie scowled. "No."

"I wanted to know who would look after my little girl if I get killed tomorrow," Gilbert said. "It will be tomorrow that Rousseau arrives, won't it?"

She nodded once, taking a half step toward him. "It's the full moon tomorrow night. He'll ride hard so he can come at us then. Probably use some flash fires to make it hard for us elves to see."

Gilbert nodded, his hand slipping back into the tangle of braid and hair that formed her mohawk. The smile was still on his face and still was as annoying and smarmy as it had been the night he rode into town. Still as handsome, too.

"I'm going to keep my promise, deputy. Your girls will be looked after, though I have a hard time imagining the old drunk being able to lay a finger on you."

She stiffened, shoulders twitching backward. Fred had, frequently. Even as he grew soft from drink in those last years, bleary-eyed and slovenly, he'd still been able to hurt her.

To his credit, Gilbert noticed the change, and Millie watched his smile fade into a frown.

"The scars weren't from the war," he said. It wasn't a question; he had already figured that out. He'd said Millie had been the first Blonde Elf in Fred's life. That meant there had been other blonde elves who might not have gotten away.

"Some were," Millie said. "Most aren't. That's why the stories about me aren't important right now. Fred is coming here and I'll die before I let him hurt anyone in this town. *He* has no qualms about hurting a child." She had made Fred into the man he was, as much as he had made her into the Butcher. They'd both ended up broken and twisted, but Millie had made her choice to rebuild. From what she heard of Fred; he had chosen to wallow.

"Most men would already be running away," Millie said. "A war hero riding against a war criminal, that won't end well. So, why are you staying?"

"He tried to kill me," Gilbert said. "But also, I have terrible taste in women," he admitted, sounding almost embarrassed. "And you are terribly fascinating. But I'm afraid my previous lover out-evils you. Sorry to disappoint."

Millie rolled her eyes. Then she reached up and caught the lapels of his coat and pulled Gilbert down into a kiss.

30

GHOST TOWN

Plainfield to Scorched Bluffs was two days' ride if you wanted to arrive rested, but 'Mister Rivers' had no interest in rest. The Captain, because that's what they all still called him, had the whole posse on the road before dawn the next morning. Forty-odd men and carts with supplies that were covered by tarpaulins lashed down tight, hiding whatever was stashed there.

That one-eyed bastard hadn't let any of the Willards near the carts and kept staring over Josie's way with an expression that Jeb didn't much appreciate. Josie had her hackles up. It was sly, but Jeb had grown up learning how to read her moods. Josie was afraid.

Nudging his tired horse into a gentle trot, Jeb caught up to his little sister. He greeted her with a grunt and looked over the trail of men behind them.

"You doing alright?"

He was met with a stony glare, the kind only the lady Willards ever mastered. Jeb cleared his throat and shifted in his saddle, well aware that look meant 'no'.

"Well, I reckon we're close to where we'll be camping," Jeb said.

"You know who that is, don't you?" Josie asked, her voice a low murmur. She flicked her eyes toward the head of the column, where Rémi rode alongside the captain.

"Yup," Jeb said. His teeth hadn't stopped hurting since they'd walked into Plainfield the other day. He'd gotten almost no sleep and not even Diamond's soft embrace had helped the ache go away. "Never thought I'd meet a real 'War Hero'," he said, unable to keep the disdain from his voice.

Josie tipped her chin down in the smallest of nods.

"I'd read the book once," Josie admitted. "I thought that man sounds so dashing and brave. Taking a risk and breaking the law to help win the war." She made a face and spat to the side. "I don't know why I believed that. I ain't seen him do anything heroic."

They rode in silence for a minute before Jeb spoke.

"Do you think that elf is the one who killed Isaiah?" he asked, looking at his sister. Her face grew tight, and she nodded.

"Now that I do believe," Josie said, looking at him. Dark circles ringed her eyes. Jeb wasn't the only one who had gotten little sleep the night before. "Soulless. That elf was soulless. If joining this sad excuse for a captain means the Butcher will get what she deserves, I'll do it. For Isaiah."

From ahead of them, Rémi split off to one side, making a real show of it. Slowing his horse, he waited until Josie and Jeb caught up with him. With a smile to Josie that made Jeb's skin crawl, the one-eyed man tipped his hat, a battered wool thing that moths had gotten at.

"Couldn't help overhearing," he said. He ran his tongue along his sharpened teeth. "That you think the Ghost killed your brother. How is it that this man died?" The man's remaining eye flicked between Jeb and Josie, lingering longer on the lady Willard. Josie stared straight ahead, refusing to so much as glance at Rémi.

"He was shot," Jeb said. "Shot dead between the eyes." Unlike his sister, Jeb kept a close eye on the one-eyed man. What else had he overheard?

"That's it?" Rémi asked. The man lifted his eyebrows, the one under the eyepatch wrinkling against heavy scar tissue. "No cuts, no marks, no brands?"

"Whoever did kill him put him in a fire," Jeb said. "Didn't leave much behind other than bones and boots, sir."

"That doesn't sound like her, then?" Josie asked, willing to suffer the man's interaction for some information.

Rémi shook his head and spit. "Nah, not one bit. The Ghost, she did not do little kills. She liked—how to explain it—the Ghost, she liked *spectacle*." He reached up and scratched at the scar that poked out from his eyepatch.

"She cut this out, you know?" He said, voice as bitter as laudanum. "Thought I was looking at her funny, so she cut it out in front of everyone. Said if I was looking at *her* funny, I'd have to look at *everyone* funny." Rémi's lips twisted, and he scrubbed his sleeve across his mouth.

"But burning a body," he said, his single eye focusing on Josie. "That sounds like her. The Ghost, she likes fire."

The kiss was interrupted by the loud clang of a cowbell from outside.

"Mildred, get down here." Annie bellowed. It might as well have been a bucket of cold water. Millie pulled back from Gilbert's lips, ears perked, and tilted toward the doorway.

"He can't be here yet, can he?" Gilbert asked, settling for kissing along her neck up to the base of her ear. His mouth hot and distracting, enough to send a delicious little shudder through her.

"No," Millie groaned. She was probably going to die tomorrow night, and the spirits couldn't even let her have one last distraction? "But I need to see what's going on." Millie, Bayou

Butcher and Mother of Two, did not pout... but her current expression was extremely close to one.

"Then I hope, after the meeting," Gilbert said, punctuated with little nibbles up her ear. "That we can continue this particular negotiation." His breath was hot on her skin, and as much as she hated the rich, smarmy persona Gilbert liked to wear... it was the kind of hate that she wanted to dissolve into a puddle under the heat of his touch.

"After," Millie agreed, extracting herself. Hurriedly fixing the coat and sash, she hurried down the barn's stairs. Gilbert could follow behind, but if she stayed even a moment longer, Millie knew she wouldn't be able to leave.

Striding out into the evening's golden sunlight, Millie straightened her shoulders and kept her head high. Annie stood by the door to her farmhouse, arms crossed. Next to her stood Eyota and Grannie Whitewing, with opposing expressions. Eyota's mouth fell open and their eyes went wide, while Grannie's face split into a pleased grin.

"Oh, my goodness, Mildred," Grannie said, beckoning her to come closer for inspection. "Look at you. I am so proud of you." Grannie reached up to fuss with the coat lapels, which were still slightly askew. "There you are," she whispered to Millie. "You've stopped hiding."

"What is this?" Eyota asked, looking Millie over. "Are you osaugan now?"

"Me," she answered, adjusting the sash around her waist. "It's just me, Eyota."

Gilbert cleared his throat as he descended out of the barn, brushing bits of hay from his woolen suit.

"Shall we?" He asked, smiling directly at her.

"Ah, and there *he* is," Grannie said. "Come here, come here, Gilly boy."

Gilbert's steps faltered for a moment, and from the twinkle in Grannie's eye, Millie knew that name meant something.

"You two will not have time to marry tomorrow," Grannie announced. "So, we will need to perform the ceremony now."

Millie blinked. "I'm sorry, Grannie, what's going on?"

"The war hero arrives tonight, so we must perform the ceremony now." Grannie's smile faded into a grim expression and she held out her hands, one to each Millie and Gilbert. "This is the way you keep all three girls safe, Fenna, Rasha and Sarah. All three."

Millie felt Gilbert staring at her, and Millie glanced up at him, ears dipping low.

"Has she been wrong?" he asked, uncertain. "She knew- she knew Sarah's name. Did you tell her that?" He asked. Millie shook her head. Gil looked around, spotting Hal emerging from the farmhouse. "Did any of you tell her that?"

Gently, Millie took Gilbert's hand. She gave it a small squeeze. "We promised to keep each other's daughters safe. We don't need a ceremony to keep that.

Millie *felt* the heads of those gathered turn to stare at her, even though she was still looking directly at Gilbert. She felt her ears grow hot, but she didn't let go of his hand. The banker was looking down at their clasped hands, a thoughtful frown on his face.

"No," he breathed. "Your grandmother's right. Legally, this is how we keep them safe. We can figure out what happens after tomorrow when we both survive. Mildred Berry, will you marry me?" he asked, taking her other hand.

"Excellent!" Grannie said, clapping her hands. "Eyota, go get a blanket from inside."

Millie held onto Gilbert's hands tight, unsure how or what was happening. Around them, friends gathered, including Eyota, who had found an old quilt from inside Annie's home that was large enough to wrap around them both. Hal's mouth hung open while Ryan had her hands on her cheeks and was beaming. Everything was surreal.

"You didn't say yes," Gilbert whispered. "Do you want this?"

"What?" Millie asked, looking back up at him as Eyota wrapped the quilt around their shoulders, pulling them close together. "Yes. I mean yes, I will. If it keeps the girls safe. All three."

"What do we do now?" Gilbert whispered, wrapping his arms around her as Eyota tucked the blanket in tightly, holding them in a cocoon.

"I don't know," Millie whispered back. "I haven't been to many weddings."

"You two wait while I pray," Grannie whispered to them both, and then giggled. Clearing her throat, she pulled out a braid of smokegrass and passed her hand over it, igniting the tips of it with a hushed whisper. She passed the smudge over them both, cleansing and blessing the blanket and the union itself.

"Spirits of the North, we honour you and welcome you to witness this marriage. Bless this couple, bless their family and keep them safe as they build their home together," Grannie said, inviting spirits from each direction in turn. Millie felt her ears prickle upon each invocation, and as she glanced around, she was certain she could catch shadows at the edge of her vision.

"Mildred Claire Berry, you are a warrior. A protector. Will you keep this man and your family safe?" Grannie asked.

"Yes, I will." Millie said, slipping her arms around Gilbert.

"Gilbert Brian Goldman," Grannie said. "You are a provider, a nurturer. Will you keep this woman and your family fed and warm?"

"Yes," Gilbert said. Millie could feel his voice rumble in his chest. "I will."

Millie looked up at him, craning her neck back due to how tall he was. Noticing her looking at him, Gilbert smiled down at her. He nodded slightly, as if to repeat his vow. He would. She knew that in her bones. He would keep the girls warm and fed, if the worst were to happen. And she would protect his little girl with everything she had.

"You can kiss now, if you'd like," Grannie said.

Lifting up onto her tiptoes wasn't enough, so with a huff of laughter, Gilbert picked her up and lifted her so they were eye to eye. Taking his face in her hands, Millie kissed him. He tasted as good as he had up in the hayloft, but there was something else there now. A thrum of magic made Millie's ears tickle, and she wondered how many spirits had shown up.

"That was lovely and all," Annie said, impatient as ever. "But if Rousseau is arriving tonight, we need to get back to town and get everything ready. Also, Mildred, you owe me a new blanket."

The ride into town felt like it took twice as long as it normally did, but Millie was grateful for Gilbert's presence for once. Instead of allowing an uncomfortable silence, he asked Annie about the business of ranching. If she was being honest with herself, Millie had to admit something had changed after the ceremony. Instead of annoying, she found his chatter was comforting, keeping her from thinking too much about Fred.

What *was* annoying was how Ryan kept glancing back at her on the ride and smiling. It made Millie's ears turn pink, and no matter how much she flicked them, they stayed that way. Fenna and Rasha had watched the ceremony without understanding what it was, but they seemed pleased that they had a new friend in Gilbert, especially since he had given them a puppy.

Everything else could be sorted out once Fred had been dealt with. Reaching the Hotel, Millie dismounted and gathered her girls from the wagon they'd been riding with Annie.

"Hey baby girls," she whispered, bending down to kiss each of their foreheads. Fenna was already reaching up to wrap her arms around Millie's neck, so she scooped up the shyer of the two girls, and settled her on one hip. Rasha hurried over to Gilbert, asking to get picked up. After a moment of surprise, he scooped her up and smiled at her mother. Millie's stomach fluttered, and she told herself it was just worry over how high up Rasha now was.

Rasha giggled wildly, waving at Fenna and Millie from her new perch on Gilbert. Millie waved back, following them both into the hotel's saloon. They were among the last to arrive and get settled. Hal sat next to Gilbert; brow knit in worry. She didn't blame him. If Fred arrived tonight, they had only a few hours to prepare.

Millie tightened her arms around her daughter and pressed her nose to Fenna's hair. This was what was at stake tonight. Little girls that deserved a better life than their mother had. Women who deserved a quiet life, if that's what they chose. People who only wanted to exist deserved a chance to do just that, but Fred was never good at leaving people alone.

Ryan caught Millie's eye and nodded. It was time for the town meeting to begin. Flanked by Fyodor on one side and the marshal Allan on her other, Ryan walked up to the small riser that had once served as a stage for performers.

"Citizens of Scorched Bluffs," Ryan said, her voice strong and carrying to every corner of the saloon. All chatter ceased immediately, and every pair of eyes settled on their sheriff. "The day we've been preparing for is here. We estimate that sometime tonight a group of armed men will arrive on our doorstep to take one of our own."

Guilt twisted in Millie's gut as some of the townspeople looked her way. A small voice whispered that it was her fault that the town was at risk, but she knew that wasn't true. It wasn't even close to being her fault. The blame lay at the feet of the man that had forced her out to the fringes of society. A man that would refuse to just take her and leave everyone else alone.

This was Fred's doing.

"This is the worst scenario. Frederic Rousseau and the Willards are on their way here as we speak," Ryan continued. She looked over at Millie, and the two exchanged a solemn glance. "As a result, I, Sheriff Ryan Collins, herby deputize every soul in this room. Every one of you is now an agent of Amelior law, sworn to uphold Justice and defend rightful settlers against armed incursion."

Millie saw Hal and Gilbert's eyes widen, and she glanced over at them, a tiny smile touching her face.

"Do you accept this burden of justice?" Ryan asked, voice rising. "Do you swear to uphold Amelior law and protect the people of this town?"

The reply was deafening. Chairs clattered as every woman within the room stood and shouted "Aye". After a moment, Gilbert and Hal both stood. "Aye" they said. Gilbert glanced down at her and nodded. He would help.

"We don't have much time," Ryan said. "Teams one through three. Report to the jail for your weapons. Four and five, report to the mines to prepare the shelter. Berry, you need to set the traplines, Sweetpea, you do your thing."

Hal and Gilbert looked dumbfounded as they watched the saloon mobilize. Women of all sorts moved in a practised unison. Some formed lines to file out of the hotel, while others made for the stairs or kitchen.

"What is this?" Hal asked. "When the Sheriff said you were preparing..."

"Exceptional women often attract exceptional circumstances," Millie said quietly, stroking Fenna's soft blond hair. "And exceptional enemies. I'm not the only one here with something or someone to hide from." Looking out at the crowd, Millie felt a deep pang of sadness.

"I had hoped..." she trailed off, looking around the room. "I'd hoped the first problem to arrive would have been someone else's."

31

WHITE NIGHTS

THINGS MOVED QUICKLY. HAL, back already aching from loading crates of ammunition at the ranch, was press-ganged into 'unit four' by the lovely Miss Sweetpea. Unnerved at the military precision with which the gathered women set to work, Hal had glanced at deputy Berry as the arroyan shopkeeper grabbed his arm. Berry had one daughter perched on her hip, the other wrapped around her thigh, and caught his eye and as Hal was pulled away.

This wasn't just some frontier town. Berry and Collins had put together a goddamn *militia*.

"Do you know how guns work?" Miss Sweetpea asked. Her grip around Hal's wrist was impressively strong.

"I do, I'm a—"

"Stratton?" Sweetpea interrupted with a bright smile his way. Sure, it had extra sharp canines, but it was warm and friendly. Sweetpea's demeanour was a pleasant change of pace after being stuck with Gil and the deputy for days on end. Watching them argue and flirt and argue while flirting without any reprieve was exhausting. "Yeah, Millie told us. You're one of those fancy detectives people keep hiring to find us." Halfway out the door of the saloon, Sweetpea stopped and turned to face him fully. Her gold and blue eyes searched his face, looking for an answer to a question that she had yet to ask.

"Who is 'us'?" Hal asked. "Berry?" Hal wracked his brain. How many other Strattons had come out this way? He couldn't remember that many cases coming into the Agency involving Scorched Bluffs. He scratched at the stubble on his chin, trying to match any cases of missing people with the residents of the town.

"She'll kill you if you hurt any of us," Sweetpea said. Her smile was worried, now. "You won't hurt us, right?"

A week ago, Hal would have been shaken by such a warning. He might have put it down to bluffing, or an overreaction by some paranoid friend. After watching Berry deal with the dragon, the Willards, after seeing what she and Collins had turned the town into... Hal was convinced that yes, Berry *would* kill him if he hurt anyone and not lose a wink of sleep after.

Hal thought of the telegram he had sent a week ago, letting Rousseau know they would reach the train wreck within a few days. A telegram he had asked Sweetpea to send to the Stratton office at Wyndford. His guts twisted, and Hal realized Fred must have used that telegram as a notice to head out west.

"No, I won't hurt anyone here. Not intentionally," Hal said, his throat tight. It felt like a thread had stuck along his windpipe, leaving him to clear his throat in vain, trying to dislodge the guilt there. He wasn't responsible for Rousseau's poor choices, but had he played a part in the captain's plan? He hadn't killed those farmers in Beaulieu. He hadn't let war criminals run free. He hadn't chased down an elf that thought nothing of bluffing to an outlaw gang that outnumbered her four-to-one. No, he told himself. This was not his fault, but it would be easier if he could believe that himself.

"Well, don't hurt us *un*-intentionally either," Miss Sweetpea warned. "Or Miss Millie might *un*-intentionally shoot you and her aim is really good." The shopkeeper patted his hand and tugged him forward, out of the saloon and across the dirt road to the church.

The church was simple, built of wooden planks and with a crooked looking wheel placed above its spire. Any true house of the Messiah would be ashamed to have such a sad-looking wheel on display, but Hal was starting to doubt that anything in this god-forsaken town was real.

"Ah," Sweetpea said, glancing at him, then up at the spire. "It turns out making wheels is a lot harder to make than it seems? That's the fourth one we did. Millie kept saying we had to try harder to make it look real."

Hal, already halfway across the road to the church, shook his head and dug in his heels.

"What do you mean 'make it look real'?" he asked, belatedly realizing the little arroyan woman was stronger than he was. Sweetpea didn't notice a difference and simply dragged him forward.

"Well, like a church people worship at!" Sweetpea said, reaching the steps of said church. She paused, looking back over her shoulder at him, brows knit. "Don't you know that's usually the first thing men like Rousseau burn? Why would we make it *nice* if the bad men are going to come along and burn it down?"

The question hit Hal like a sledgehammer. How many reports of burnt churches had he looked into? Women, children, elders, all packed into a place that had offered them sanctuary in the face of trouble, and inevitably, the gang of outlaws or rebels or *whoever* would barricade the doors shut and set the church alight. The sanctuary the Messiah provided only extended to true followers that respected His will. Unfortunately, many men and women in this world only cared about their sins when on their deathbeds.

"Don't any of you worship there?" Hal asked. Miss Sweetpea had dragged him to the steps leading into the building. Although the setting sun made it difficult to see inside, the detective could hear the scrape of wood on wood. Were they moving the pews? If the less capable citizens of Scorched Bluffs weren't going to shelter in the church, where would they go?

"Sure," Sweetpea said with a little shrug. "The sheriff does, so does Lyddie and Nylah, our blacksmith."

"Three... three people?" Hal asked, following the arroyan up the rough steps. He could see the inside of the church more clearly now. Benches that had been used as pews were now being tilted up onto their end and nailed to cover the windows. There was a pulpit at the front, but little else.

"Well," Sweetpea squinted at the church as she thought. "Four, if you count Fyodor."

"Who is Fyodor?"

"The sheriff's dog," Sweetpea said happily. "He's a real gentleman. Now come on, you can help hold the benches while I set the wards."

Oh, Hal thought as he was directed over to the nearest bench. *Wonderful. A full quarter of the congregation is a single dog. Marvellous.*

We're all going to die.

Something prickled along the back of Millie's neck as the saloon emptied. Slowly, she looked away from the Stratton over to Gilbert to find him grinning from ear to ear.

"Dearest wife," he said, crouching a little to look her in the eye. "Did you hear that?"

Oh, no.

"I'm a deputy!" Gilbert said, eyes twinkling. "That means we're equals!" His smile and boyish excitement were infectious, and as much as Millie tried to be mad at his enthusiasm, she felt the corners of her lips tug upwards. She tried to press them back down, but it was too late. He'd seen her almost-smile and now his was even wider.

"So, no more ordering you around, huh?" Millie said, watching as Gilbert draped one arm across her shoulders. Surprising even herself, Millie didn't mind. "Not that you listened."

"I listened," he said, placing his free hand over his chest in a show of being hurt. "I chose to disregard most of those orders, but I heard you say them." He winked at her. "I'll behave for now, though. How can I help?"

Millie took a deep breath. "The girls will need to go with Annie into the mines to stay safe. We take them there, then you can help me with the traplines."

"Mama, I wanna help with the traplines," Rasha said. "I don't wanna hide."

Millie pulled both girls into a tight hug, trying to memorize every detail of what it felt like to hold them. Rasha's knobby little shoulder blades, the way Fenna always pressed her face into Millie as if she could shut out everything scary in the world, the way their breathing almost always aligned when they were held like this. Reluctantly, Millie pulled back and planted kisses on each of their foreheads.

"You know that ceremony Grannie did?" Millie asked. The girls nodded. "That means Mister Goldman is going to help keep you very safe." Her throat was getting tight, and Millie had to clear it to keep from crying. She didn't want her girls to see that, especially not if it was their last memory of her. "I want you to know I love you both very, very much."

Gilbert crouched next to Millie's girls and rested a hand on Rasha's back.

"Your momma has this all planned out. But she needs you to help protect the people in the mine," he said. Rasha looked up at him and nodded solemnly. Then, ever the protective sister, she took Fenna's hand and gripped it.

"We can do that." She said, shoulders back. "Right Fen?"

Millie smiled at Fenna, who looked up at Gilbert, then at Millie. Her serious golden eyes fixed on Millie's and Fenna's lower lip trembled slightly. "Okay." she said. "Like Momma. We keep them safe."

Sweeping both of her brave girls back into a tight hug, Millie gave them each a last kiss on their cheeks. "Alright babies, you go with Annie and do everything she tells you to."

She stood and ushered the little girls and their puppy toward the rancher. Annie took their hands and nodded to Millie. They would be safest in the mines, where Annie could protect them, but seeing them go made the heat in Millie's throat spread to her eyes, a few tears slipping past her lashes. Wiping them away, she took a shaky breath to steady herself.

"You keep mentioning trap lines," Gilbert said, wrapping an arm around her and giving her a gentle squeeze. She was grateful that he didn't ask if she was alright. That question would have destroyed what was left of Millie's tenuous composure. "Are you planning to trap the horses?"

"It's easier to show you," she said. Sniffing back the rest of her tears, Millie motioned for Gilbert to follow. Millie grabbed a faded red haversack from behind Lyddie's bar. It was deceptively lightweight as she slung it over one shoulder and stepped outside.

The night air was cooling rapidly, but Millie's old coat kept the chill at bay. Stars were already sparkling overhead and to the east, a heavy moon was just peeking over the horizon. The last glow of sunset had already disappeared behind the mesas that cradled the town.

Across the road, the yellow flicker of lanterns illuminated the windows of the small church. The sound of hammers filled the air, and already some of the church's windows were blocked off by pews being nailed into place.

"So," Gilbert said. "I think your town might have broken Hal a bit. He had a dazed sort of expression before Miss Sweetpea pulled him away. I haven't seen him look like that since we were boys."

"Just him?" Millie asked, nudging Gilbert in the side, leading Gilbert to where Max was hitched at the hotel's hitching post. "We'll take Max. He's the fastest, and we might need to hurry if Fred sends scouts."

"Just Hal," Gilbert agreed. "As far as my personal, educated, and extremely important opinion goes, I think this is wonderful!" Millie looked up at him in surprise. He grinned, still able to see her expression in the dim castoff light of the church and saloon. "It is! I'd dream about punching Frederic sometimes, but being a Carpenter and not nobility, it wouldn't have ended well for my family. Seeing people actually stand up to him is cathartic. I hope you kick his ass."

Millie smiled up at him despite herself.

"Well, if all goes well, he won't be a problem for either of us after tonight." They climbed up onto Max, with Millie tucked in front of Gilbert. He wrapped his arms around her, and she kicked Max into a canter, heading for the entrance to the town.

The 'traplines' were set along the edge of the bluffs that rose above the road, offering shelter from the harsh sun and a lee from windstorms. It was difficult to spot from the road into town, but the bluffs had holes pre-drilled into its craggy rocks.

Dismounting, Millie set down the pack and pulled out a bundle of paper-wrapped cylinders. She held them out to Gilbert, who froze.

"That's dynamite," he said, gingerly taking the sticks from her. Face pale, Gilbert held the dynamite as though it might explode if he so much as breathed. Millie bit back a smile, reminding herself that not everyone had experience setting up explosives.

"Sure is," she said, digging out the fuse line from the haversack. "Our mutual enemy had those packed in a few bullet crates on the train. I think he was hoping if someone didn't rob it, the train would explode."

The stick of explosive was no larger than a candle. It was hard to imagine something this small could cause so much destruction, and Millie spotted a bead of sweat form on his brow.

Millie looked up from her work and bit her lip to keep from laughing. "Relax," she said. "The blast caps are inserted, but unless you light the fuse, they won't go off," she added, slinging the pack onto her back. "The blast caps shouldn't have been inserted before they arrived at wherever they'd get used. I didn't know why they'd do that when we found them, but I think Fred is forcing someone's bank to pay out."

Gilbert looked back down at the sticks of dynamite with a scowl. The poor man had been sent on a fool's errand. Millie was certain Fred never meant for Gilbert to find the missing cargo. Why else send the Willards after him?

"Shoot him dead for me, will you, darling?" he said, handing back the dynamite he'd been holding.

"That's the plan."

The climb up the bluffs was second nature by now. Millie knew which handholds were secure and where every blast hole had been placed. Originally, she had made do with some old sticks they'd found in the silver mine, but that dynamite had started to sweat nitroglycerin, making it too unstable to use. Finding Fred's failed attempt at sabotage had been a blessing.

Millie worked quickly, connecting fuse lines to the fresh explosives and sliding them into place, hiding the holes with loose rocks on the bluff's face.

Halfway along the line, Millie paused to stretch out her back and look out over the town. The small shapes of townsfolk hurried back and forth. There didn't seem to be any sign of panic yet, which was good. They had less time to prepare than she'd hoped, but the years of drills were paying off.

Turning to the northeast, Millie spotted the faint glow of campfires on the horizon. Her heart dropped, taking with it any hope she'd let herself have.

Fred was already there.

32

GIVE NO QUARTER

RÉMI DIDN'T LEAVE THEM alone again. For the rest of the ride, he hung near Jeb, or tried to talk to Josie. She ignored him as best she was able, replying with vague sounds that could have meant anything.

The captain called a halt as they reached a fork in the road. The sun had set. The town's namesake bluffs swallowed it early, casting darkness over the road ahead. If Jeb squinted, he could make out a few pinpricks of light that must be lanterns.

"Jebediah Willard," Rémi called out, nudging his horse to ride ahead to join with the captain. "Come with me."

Belly twisting into knots, Jeb followed. It seemed there would be no rest tonight. A nearly full moon was climbing up into the sky, though Jeb wasn't sure how well it would illuminate the cursed town that was hiding in the shadows. His molars ached. Nothing good would happen tonight. Capturing the Butcher was a worthwhile cause, but Jeb couldn't shake the feeling that the captain was walking into a viper pit, expecting hognoses.

"Right," Rémi said, "You n'me, we will be the ones to offer the elf the chance to surrender herself." Pulling a bottle from his saddlebag, Rémi cracked it open and took a long swig. He held it out to Jeb. "You'll want this. That way, if the pale bitch kills us, at least we had a fine breakfast, eh?"

Jeb laughed because he felt like he was supposed to, saying a silent prayer to the Messiah that Rémi wouldn't talk much on the ride into town. He took the bottle and tried not to think of Rémi's shark-like teeth clashing against the spout. The bourbon was strong and cheap, but it did the job it was meant to. Passing the bottle back to the swampman, Jeb could already feel heat spreading through his chest.

A fool might think this was courage, but Jeb knew better. Rivers or Rémi had chosen him to draw the elf's attention from them. As far as the Butcher knew, Jeb was the one who'd sold her out. He would be her first target.

"You are nervous, my friend," Rémi said, picking up on Jeb's unease with shark-like precision. He sniffed, loudly. "Good. You should be."

They rode into the small town of Scorched Bluffs as the warmth of the day faded. The horses were tired, heads low as they plodded forward, past the cabin on the outskirts, past the burnt-out husk of a home that had yet to be rebuilt after the fire years ago.

The town was quiet. No shutters closed nervously, no women grabbed their children from the road and hurried them inside. There was nothing on the main road save for the men, their horses, and a single wooden bucket that skidded forward a few inches; stopped, then skidded toward the other side of the dusty road.

"Hold, Jebediah!" the swamp man hissed, reining in his horse the moment he saw the bucket. Jebediah, confused, did as he was told, following the other man's lead. "That bitch laid a trap. Look." Pulling his revolver from his belt, Rémi aimed at the bucket and squeezed the trigger.

The dry wood splintered as the bullet punched through the bucket, nearly splitting it in two. Jebediah squinted at it as the report of the revolver echoed against the mesa, sounding almost like there were multiple shots instead of only one. As Jebediah watched, smoke poured out of the cracks in the bucket and flames followed.

"What is that?" Jebediah asked, but when he looked back at Rémi, the man had slumped back in his saddle, arms hanging limply by his sides. A very small, very neat red hole was placed in his temple.

"No need to panic, Mister Willard," the Butcher said, cocking the hammer of her revolver. She watched him through half-lidded eyes as he froze in place, shoulders hitched up by his ears. Her own were perked, like a damn hellhound waiting for an excuse to strike. Jeb wasn't certain where she'd come from. He hadn't heard a single step or click of her revolver.

"Rémi and I had some unfinished business," she said, those cold eyes fixing him in place. In the light of his lantern, they seemed to glow red the way they reflected his lantern's light.

Josie was right. This woman was unnatural.

"But I don't have any problems with you. So how about you get down from your horse nice and slow and we can talk like reasonable people?"

Jeb lifted his hands up so she could see them and nodded slowly.

"I need to know; did you kill my brother?" he asked. "Isaiah Willard. Were you the one who shot him?"

The ghost watched him, and Jeb could feel his heart thud in his chest.

"Yes," the Butcher said. He watched her face soften into sympathy. This was a trick to lull him into complacency. It had to be. "I gave him the chance to leave, and he didn't. He didn't leave me a choice, Jeb. But you can. Now, you get on down and let's have a proper talk."

Her words knocked the air out of him, leaving Jeb unable to speak. Isaiah, hotheaded and full of confidence that he couldn't back up with grit. How often had he seen his brother start a fight he couldn't finish? Jeb knew Isaiah would have seen the elf as an easy mark. Small, a lady, too little to be a threat.

Isaiah, you dumbass.

"Di told us you were coming," the ghost said. "She said you and your family aren't part of this. So don't be part of this, Jebediah."

Hearing the name of his fiancé pulled Jeb out of his thoughts, and he blinked at the elf. Had he heard that right?

"Di told you?" When had she managed that?

"We can talk inside; you must be thirsty. Come on down now," the ghost said gently.

"Alright," he said, placing his hands on the horn of his saddle. "I'm not going for my gun."

He dismounted slowly, keeping his hands held up and to the sides whenever he could. This was Di's hometown, her sister worked here. She'd been telling him since this mess began that he needed to treat the lady elf with respect, that she was dangerous. But Di had never called her a monster, not like the captain. Maybe the elf had softened over the years.

"Good man," the Butcher said, walking forward. "Now. I'm sure the boys back there told you a lot of stories about me. I want you to know that *everything* they told you was true... except the sacrifice." He watched as she huffed and her ears flicked up and down. Jeb was too scared to say anything. He swallowed hard and nodded to show he understood.

"You turn toward the hotel and start walking. Someone's gonna meet you there and take your guns, so we all feel nice and safe. I don't want to feel unsafe. When I don't feel safe, my finger twitches. Understand?"

"Yes, ma'am," he croaked.

Jeb rested his hands on the top of his hat and walked toward the hotel. He couldn't hear the elf behind him, but from the way his teeth ached, he could tell she was there. No wonder he hadn't noticed her at the entrance of town. She didn't make a sound. He wasn't sure what Rémi had been thinking, riding in as bold as brass.

At the door, dressed up to the nines in a blue dress with fancy lace ruffles, a demon stood with a sabre strapped to her belt. Spotting him, the demon-thing smiled and waved.

"A rotkin—" he hissed, recoiling. Something cracked against the base of his skull, and the world fell into blurry starbursts.

"Millie!" Sweetpea gasped. "That wasn't very nice."

"He called you rotten," Millie said, placing a foot on the nape of Jeb's neck. Some assholes thought the horns meant arroyans were demonic, as though deer, cattle, and bison couldn't possibly grow horns without being the bastard children of demons. The slur was one that only made sense to the people who used it. Rotkin: the kin of something rotten. It was all bullshit.

"That wasn't nice of him either," she pointed out.

"Oh." Sweetpea looked at the downed outlaw for a moment, then turned to shout up the Hotel stairs. "RY! What do we do with this guy? He's only a medium bad buy, not a really big one?"

Millie heard muffled voices talking the situation over and then Ryan's head appeared over the parapet of the hotel, one hand holding onto her hat as she looked down at the scene in the street. Millie stood, one foot on the back of Jebediah's neck, the revolver pointed at the back of his head.

"Lyddie?" Ryan called down. "He's your sister's friend." Lyddie's answer was muffled, but it was still audible.

"Fiancé, she's getting married to that idiot."

Ry motioned to bring Jeb inside. Millie rolled her eyes. She'd have preferred to just shoot him, but Diana had pulled through for them this time. Without Di warning the marshal, they would have been caught unaware by Fred's arrival. The least they could do was not kill her fiancé. Sweetpea hurried out and grabbed one of the man's arms. Throwing Jebediah's gun belt over her shoulder, Millie grabbed the other.

"You know, I don't really mind what people call me," Sweetpea said quietly to her as they pulled Jeb over the steps to the building.

"I mind, Sweetpea," Millie said. "They made up names for me, too. But at least I *earned* those. You, though, you're not rotten. You're wonderful." She glared down at the semi-conscious Jebediah. "Hear that asshole? She's *wonderful*."

The man groaned something that might have been an apology, words mushy in his mouth.

They passed him off to Lyddie and Nylah, the latter of which hefted him over her shoulder with a single arm. The orc made a face and turned her nose away from his body.

"He smells," she muttered.

"We'll lock him in the root cellar," Lyddie said, hurrying ahead to get the door for the blacksmith. "Should hold until this blows over."

"Your sister has terrible taste in men," Millie muttered to Lyddie as she passed by. Her own taste was probably worse, though. The banker seemed to be the best of the bunch, a fact that Millie would never, *ever,* disclose to him.

With the oldest Willard secure, Millie jogged up the steps to check in with Ryan on the hotel roof. *Trust Fred to show up too damn early*. Millie stayed fighting fit, but she wasn't a kid any longer. Her knees ached by the third storey, making her mood worse. Elves were supposed to last longer than humans, weren't they? Or maybe that was only a Ghost Eye thing she hadn't inherited.

"Millie," she identified herself before poking her head over the edge to look at the roof. Crouched by the hotel's parapets were Ryan, Marshal Al, Hal and- "Why are you here?" she asked, squinting at Gilbert. Who had given him that gun? Could he even shoot? He should be with Annie and the girls, *hiding*.

"Hello darling," Gilbert said, offering her a broad smile. He was up to something; Millie could see it in his eyes. Ears flicking back and forth, revealing her discomfort, Millie climbed the rest of the way onto the roof. She glanced at Ryan, who was trying to keep her expression straight. Allan had dissolved into a bout of coughing that sounded suspiciously like laughter.

"I'll fall back to the mine if they get close," Gilbert promised, motioning her over. "I learned to shoot in school. A bit." At his side, Hal rolled his eyes.

"He's not a bad shot," the Stratton admitted. "Better with a sword, though."

"Captain of the fencing team," Gilbert said with a little salute. "But that was years ago."

Millie looked at her new husband and reluctantly nodded. She had to trust him. He'd had many chances to let her down since the night at the train wreck, and he hadn't.

"Fine," she said and crawled over to join them. Once in place, Millie peered over the edge of the hotel's roof to surveil the situation. She spotted the enemy immediately.

The lanterns of Fred's small army moved down the road like a regiment of fireflies. Millie held up one hand, fingers splayed. They had to wait until enough of Fred's men were near the traplines. Too soon, and the losses would be minimal. Too late, and some of Fred's supply wagons might get through. They couldn't afford Fred's men having access to the spare ammunition those wagons carried.

Measuring time in hearts, Millie counted lanterns. When enough reached the chokepoint, she closed her hand into a fist.

Ryan yanked off her glove and placed her finger and thumb between her lips. Her whistle was shrill, echoing off the mesa that towered behind them. In tandem, the women leaned over the edge of the hotel's parapet to watch the mesa.

A puff of dust erupted from the rock, lit up briefly by the explosion that had caused it. The puffs repeated over and in a line along the mesa's edge with the last explosion directly above

Millie's little cabin. The sound came a moment later: rapid-fire cracks that sounded like a gunfight. The rock at the mesa's tip slouched for a heartbeat before it slid down the mesa wall in a rumbling cacophony of dust that spilled over the road.

"What was *that*?" Shouted Hal, covering his head.

"Traplines," Millie said, wiggling her ears to try to shake off the dull ringing that filled them. A dumb grin split her face, and she felt giddy at the rumble that shook her bones. "They trap the ammo carts *behind* the line of rock."

"Fireworks for our wedding?" Gilbert shouted over the cacophony of falling rock. He wrapped an arm around Millie and gave her a little squeeze. "Darling, you shouldn't have. I'm all *verklempt*."

They watched the mesa wall slide into the road, sending up plumes of pale limestone dust. Shrieking dragonets wheeled overhead, displaced by the initial explosions and upset by the rockslides. Turkey-sized, the dragonets weren't much of a threat to anyone, but that didn't stop Millie from hoping they covered Fred and his men in guano. Dragonshit was particularly pungent.

"You're insane," Hal said, looking back over his shoulder at Ryan and Millie. "You just... *blew up* part of your town?"

"That was *amazing*," Ryan breathed, still staring out at the dust cloud in awe.

"You are *all* insane," Hal corrected, squinting at the marshal. "You, for not flagging this as an illegal use of explosives, you two for setting the damn charges," he said, jabbing a finger at Millie and Ryan. "And you for *marrying* one of them," he added, settling on Gilbert.

"You're just jealous that my wife is terrifying," Gilbert countered smugly.

"Gil! they dropped—"

"Frederic Rousseau killed my family," Ryan interrupted, voice even as she met Hal's eyes. "And if we don't stop him, he'll kill both of yours, too."

The ringing in Millie's ears had yet to fade, and Millie wiggled a finger in one to try to ease the discomfort. She stopped dead as she heard what Ryan said.

"Ry," Millie said. "Are you sure you want to share this?"

"He sent Millie and other assassins to kill each and every one of us. My father, my mother, my brother, his wife and his son. Me. Everyone." Ryan's face was hard. Her voice was clipped, eyes icy. It took a lot for Ryan to get angry, but Fred was a hair trigger for both of them.

Millie felt Gilbert's arm slowly slip off her shoulders. He and Hal were staring, open-mouthed, at the Sheriff. The marshal, however, seemed distracted by the lacing on his jacket, and his ears had gone scarlet.

Allan already knew, Millie realized. *Did Ry tell him?*

"Frederic Rousseau owes many of us his life for what he's taken," Ryan said, looking at her. The icy glare melted a little, and Ryan reached out to take Millie's arm. "I refuse to let him take any more of my family." Millie was certain that Ryan's voice cracked ever so slightly. "Don't you dare let him, Millie."

"I won't," Millie promised. She pulled Ryan into a tight hug; nose pressed into the sheriff's coat. The baked-in smell of Fyodor just made the hot lump in her throat worse. Millie hadn't planned on surviving the day. Getting at Fred involved a great deal of risk, and Millie had plenty to atone for. But Ryan—that brilliant, *manipulative* woman—knew exactly what to say to make a sacrifice like that impossible.

"Be safe, *please*," Ryan whispered back.

"This is all very touching," Allan said, clearing his throat. "But there's some people coming over the rocks who have guns. So, probably *not* friends?"

Millie gave Ryan a last squeeze before letting go. She expected a raunchy joke from Gilbert, but he said nothing. That wasn't like him at all. Telling herself she wasn't concerned, Millie picked up her rifle and slung it over her back, checking that the rest of her kit was in place.

"Alright," she said, taking a deep breath. "Here we go." When was the last time she'd said that? Had it been at Marigot all those years ago? Millie twitched her ears, flicking the questions away for the time being. She couldn't afford to be distracted; she'd promised to be safe. As safe as possible, anyways.

"Where are you going?" Gilbert asked, frowning as he noticed her moving to the roof's trap door.

"Ryan's the sharpshooter," Millie said, climbing down the ladder. "Sweetpea and I are the brawlers." She hesitated halfway down. Looking up at the frowning face of her now-husband, she swallowed the pride she normally held so tightly to her chest. "Be safe, Gilbert."

Down the road, Fred's men began shouting for Rémi. Hurrying down the rest of the hotel stairs, Millie realized the man's body was still in the street. She flattened herself next to a shuttered window and peered through it's slats at the road below.

Shit.

Rémi's horse had spooked with the explosions, but instead of falling to the ground, the dead man's leg had caught in a stirrup. As the nervous horse pranced around, the body dragged along the ground behind it, smearing red in the dirt like a morbid paintbrush.

A few men were approaching the horse to calm it, while two others were looking nervously between the buildings. The one nearest to the hotel had a rifle. The others seemed to be a mix of revolvers and short guns, but the prancing horse made it difficult to be certain without wasting more time.

Millie crept down the remaining stairs to the saloon, making as little sound as possible.

Sweetpea waited for her there, skirts hitched up to reveal pink hooves and a swishing tail normally hidden by ruffles. The dainty blouse she had worn earlier was now folded neatly on the saloon's bar. Her chemise and corset left her arms bare and battle scars marked the arroyan's shoulders and upper arms.

Unlike Millie's, Sweetpea's scars were mostly from blades, white against pink skin, smooth and flat.

Sweetpea smiled and lifted the sheathed sword she held in a little wave as Millie joined her. A golden silk rope was tied around the curved sheath in intricate knots, ending in a beautiful silk tassel that fluttered with every movement.

"Ready?" Millie mouthed, keeping silent. She could hear the men's shouts about Rémi through the hotel's thick wooden doors.

Pulling her tomahawks free, Millie realized she almost felt bad for Fred. Almost. No one in all of Amelior had yet to face an Imperial War witch in a fight. Hell, Fred might be the first human outside the Arroyan Empire to face one in a battle. He deserved it. The *sonnovabitch* had it coming since he'd bought a tiny pale elf for a half barrel of bad wine.

Millie lifted her fingers up to signal that there were six directly outside. Sweetpea unsheathed her sword and lifted it in a salute. The highly polished blade seemed to crackle in the open air and Millie could swear she tasted ozone.

Some mages used staves as a focus, some used no tools at all, and channeled their power through their bones. Arroyan war witches carried swords that cut through the threads of reality itself. The energy released fuelled spells that no mortal had any business casting. It also let Sweetpea successfully cast if Millie was nearby. She'd explained to Millie once, but the terms had been too technical for the elf to understand.

Something about a waterlogged sponge couldn't absorb a puddle, basically.

Using the spike on the back of a tomahawk, Millie unlatched the saloon door and pushed it open, ducking around to flatten herself and the door against the front of the hotel. Sweetpea stepped forward into the doorway, sword flashing as she spun it in the air and slashed up. The sword released a blast of air that crashed into the men, slamming half of them into the dirt.

The horse reared, adding to the chaos as it lashed out blindly with its hooves. One clipped the shoulder of a half-elf Millie recognized from the war. He spun, clutching his shoulder, and caught her tomahawk in the forehead. He blinked and looked at the handle that stuck out in front of him, going eyes crossed.

Sprinting forward, Millie eliminated one man still in the dirt with the spike of her remaining axe. She tucked and rolled, hearing the crack of guns as more of Fred's men spotted what was happening. Bullets whizzed past, one sending a spurt of red up from the poor horse's withers. Scampering over to it, Millie cut the stirrup free and slapped the animal on the rear, sending it back toward the rockfall.

Sweetpea, a vision in blue skirts and flashing sword, conjured an orange fireball and lobbed it at the column of men. It exploded on impact, splashing flames out onto screaming soldiers and the cart they had taken cover behind.

No, Millie reminded herself, kicking the legs out from the man nearest to her. *These were not soldiers*. Not this time. These men were nothing more than thugs. Her tomahawk bit into his throat, and she was moving forward again, snatching up her other axe from the forehead of the downed half-elf.

The report of Ryan's rifle echoed off the remaining mesa walls, sharp and distinct among the cracks of small arms fire that sent bullets back and forth. Instinct told Millie to sprint at the oncoming force and slaughter anyone between her and Fred. But there were people who wanted her to come home, people who needed her to survive this fight.

"Take cover!" Millie shouted at Sweetpea. With a flick of her sword, Sweetpea sent a hurricane-like gust of wind down the road and sprinted over to join Millie in ducking behind the General Store.

Amid the gunfire, Millie heard a bottle smash against the far side of the building. Either Fred hadn't been able to hire any mages, or Marigot had finally taught him to stop relying on them. Millie tugged her bandana over her nose and mouth and slipped her tomahawks back into her belt. Shrugging her rifle from her shoulder, Millie chambered a round with the repeater's lever.

"Head to Nylah's," she shouted at Sweetpea over the sound of gunfire. "I'll cover you. Take out whoever's got those bottles."

Sweetpea nodded and fell into a low crouch, waiting for Millie's signal. Stepping out from cover, Millie fired at the corner where she'd last seen one of Fred's men. Her first bullet punched into his shoulder, and he dropped the bottle by his feet. The second shattered the bottle, splashing whiskey and shards of glass him and his squad. The lit wick turned it into a fireball that bloomed out in beautiful orange and yellow.

These were not soldiers. Millie knew she had to stay present and keep her head clear. She was fighting for her home. This was not the war. These men were not soldiers, they were just hired thugs.

Ducking back behind cover, Millie glanced over to see Sweetpea had made it safely across the street. She gave a thumbs up, which Millie returned.

Smoke stung Mildred Berry's eyes, making them water until tears spilled over her pale lashes. The bandana she'd tied tightly around her face kept some of the smoke from her lungs, but not enough. Crouched in the meagre shelter of a burning building, the elf reloaded her rifle.

The sharp cracks of rifle-fire punctuated the roar of the flames above Millie. She could pick out Ryan's measured shots from the spattered chaos of the attacking men. Glancing up at the roof of the hotel, she caught a glimpse of dark hair through thickening smoke. Of the two of them, Ryan was in a better position. The brick-built hotel had weathered worse fires, though the smoke would soon become a problem.

Reloading her rifle, Millie peeked around the corner. Once again, the town of Scorched Bluffs lived up to its name. Half the town was burning, and the fire was spreading quickly. She hadn't expected it to go up so fast, but the makeshift firebombs Fred had equipped his men with made short work of the dry wooden buildings.

Fred's men had claimed control of the main road, though Ryan was picking off any that were brave enough to leave cover.

Things weren't looking good, but Millie had faced down longer odds. Stepping around the corner of the chapel, she shouldered her rifle and lined up her shot.

A downdraft slammed into her, knocking Millie into the dirt. She threw an arm up to shield her eyes from the dust and embers the wind burst kicked up.

Peeking under her arm, Millie prayed to every god in existence that the downdraft had been a spell cast by someone on the other side. Next to her, the chapel no longer burned. Its timber smouldered, but the flames had been extinguished by the wind. Her prayer shrivelled in her throat as a furious shriek tore through the night.

Bathed in the orange glow of fire, the blue dragon wheeled around to make another pass over the town. Her head snaked back and forth, dragon's lone good eye searching for something. The echoes of the dynamite blast could have sounded like a stormbird's thunder, or maybe the glow of the fire had caught her eye. The 'why' the blue had arrived was insignificant. She was here, and she was a bigger problem than Fred was.

"Well," Millie muttered, tugging her bandana down. "Shit."

33

LINE OF FIRE

THE DRAGON'S ROAR SHOOK rocks from the mesa walls. The fighting ended at once, with every combatant diving for cover.

After the barrage of gunfire, the sudden quiet felt like someone had shoved cotton into Gilbert's ears. Hell, it felt like someone had shoved cotton into Gilbert's brain. He prided himself on being a quick thinker, but in the middle of a shootout with magic sizzling and a town burning, it was difficult to think. The chaos on the road was impossible to understand, even though he could easily pick out Berry from Fred's hired thugs.

Gilbert liked rules. He liked understanding how the game of life worked, how he could exploit its loopholes and twist rules to his favour. He did *not* like the chaos of fighting. There was only one rule out there, and it was 'kill the other side'. There were no tactics, no brilliant formations in the field that he used to read about in military books.

His cotton-brain screamed at him to run and hide.

Heavy wingbeats passed overhead, and Gilbert looked up to watch the dragon fly past. Smoke stung his eyes, but he could see she was bigger than he had first thought. When he'd seen her at the trainwreck, she had been curled up around herself like a cat, hidden by darkness and rain. Tonight she had unfurled like a deadly blue sail, her massive wings outstretched as she circled the town. The orange light from the fire illuminated her perfectly. She was a nightmare.

"We need to get to the mine," Gilbert heard himself say. The thought forced its way through the cotton and fear clogging his thoughts. Underground was the safest place with an angry dragon stalking the sky. Shaking himself free of the strange sense of being somewhere else while in his own body, Gilbert grabbed Hal's shoulder.

"Get to the mine. We need to get everyone to the mine," he shouted. "And we need to find Millie." Scrambling over to the hotel's parapet, Gilbert peered over it, looking for any sign of his tiny murder-wife. Smoke from the burning town made it difficult to see much, but Gilbert caught a glimpse of a white mohawk ducking into the General Store.

Overhead, the dragon wheeled, circling back toward them.

"Get down!"

Gilbert wasn't sure who shouted. It didn't matter. The dragon swooped down; legs extended to land on the hotel roof. The downdraft of the blue's wings alone bowled Gilbert over, sending him tumbling into Hal. The parapet caught them, knocking the breath from Gilbert's lungs and re-awakening sharp pain in his bullet wound.

Slumped against the brick parapet and trying to catch his breath, Gilbert risked looking up.

She was immense, beautiful, terrifying. Azure scales gleamed across her sides, deepening in colour as they spread up to her ridged spine. Lines of crimson marked her sides, some spreading out along her wings, which she ruffled and flapped in agitation. The webbing there was thin enough that Gilbert could see the dragon's veins throb. Fresh scars pocked the delicate skin, as shiny and angry as the scar on Gilbert's chest.

The hotel creaked under the blue's weight. While the roof was strong enough to support several people, the plaster-covered wood had never been designed to carry the weight of a dragon, let alone one this large.

The dragon occupied the entire roof and seemed unbothered by the sounds of slowly cracking wood under her. Instead, her massive head swung around to where Gilbert lay crumpled against the parapet, with Hal on one side and Ryan on the other.

A large golden eye studied him as she lowered her head to sniff at them. In books, the hero was supposed to slay the dragon and say something witty. But he was no hero, and this was no book. Instead, Gilbert held his breath and prayed. Next to him, he could feel Hal tense up next to him, and Gil crept his fingers over to grab his friend's arm to keep him from bolting.

Sarah had known. She'd asked him not to get hurt by any dragons and, like an idiot, he had laughed the idea off. His little Storm cloud would be inconsolable...

A bullet ricocheted off the dragon's side, shattering into sparks upon impact. Quick as a snake, the dragon lifted her head up and let out a furious hiss. Her wings lifted, ready to launch her into the air.

"HEY!" Mildred Berry shouted. "Get the hell away from my family."

Her first shot must have been a warning, because the next few punched through the dragon's scales in rapid succession, causing spurts of red to erupt from the dragon's neck and shoulder. Mildred Berry had promised under a quilt to keep him safe, and now she was doing just that. His new wife's bravery was breathtaking, but so was her stupidity stupid.

What was she doing?!

The dragon coiled, wings lifting to launch herself at her quarry. The roof cracked, its supports finally snapping under her weight. Thrown off balance, the blue shrieked, flapping her wings to regain her footing. Scrambling past Gilbert, the dragon threw herself off the front of the hotel, knocking out the bricked parapet as she went.

He ducked, shielding Hal as the dragon's spiked tail whipped over their heads, scoring deep grooves in the brick as she went over. The roof groaned. Gilbert reached up to grab onto the parapet behind him. The top brick gave way, tumbling down onto the ground below.

"This is going to all come down! We need to get out of here." Looking down over the side of the hotel, Gilbert blinked. The stables. If they crept along the edge of the roof to the back of the hotel, they could jump down onto the stables. It'd be a drop, and it'd hurt, but it was better than being buried by a hotel roof.

"Come on," he said, grabbing Hal and dragging him toward the back of the roof, praying to God that they could get there without being crushed, or shot, or eaten by a goddamn dragon.

"The explosions," Hal stammered. "The dragon must have—"

"Topic for later," Gilbert interrupted, hauling his friend along. "When the dragon is gone."

The drop to the stables was further than Gilbert had expected, even with the hayloft's added height, but what choice did they have? Lowering himself over the parapet, he grunted as the scarring in his chest pulled on still-healing muscle.

White heat exploded in his hip, setting every nerve in his body afire. Gilbert dropped, landing hard on his back. He gasped, struggling to suck down a breath even as the smoke and ash made him choke. Looking down at his chest, he could see red blooming on his shirt. But it wasn't from the scar on his chest. The red was spreading from just above his hip.

"Fuck," he mumbled, pressing a hand against the wound. Looking over to the side, he saw a familiar face through the smoke and dust. Standing by a burning home, rifle to his shoulder, was Frederick *fucking* Rousseau.

Jeb wasn't sure how long he'd been lying on the cellar's dirt floor. What he did know was the ghost elf had chosen not to kill him, and for that, he was grateful. She'd hit him hard enough to set his ears a-ringing, and the muffled cracks of gunfire from above made his head throb.

The first time Jeb pushed himself up to his knees, he vomited. He lay back down to one side, avoiding his own sick. The second time Jeb tried to get up was better, even though the world tilted under him like a damn bronco. Staggering up to his feet, he braced a hand against the nearest barrel. There was some writing on it, but the letters blurred and swam as he squinted at them.

Cradling the swollen back of his head with one hand, he made his way over slowly to the lantern someone had left by the door. Careful not to fall, Jeb picked up the lantern and listened at the cellar door.

There was a steady stream of yelling and gunfire until something inhuman shrieked.

Even through his scrambled brains, Jeb knew what a dragon sounded like. He looked at the cellar door, then at the dirt floor and walls around him. Very carefully, and very slowly, he set the lantern back down and lowered himself back onto the dirt to wait this whole mess out.

Let the creepy ghost elf and the dragon kill each other. He was staying right here.

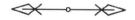

Mildred Berry had made plenty of dumb decisions in her life, but her first as Mildred *Goldman* made all the others pale in comparison. Then again, the goddamn blue dragon had landed on the hotel roof where Ryan and the men were stationed and she'd be damned if she let it hurt any of them.

"Millie!" Sweetpea hissed, hurrying out from their hiding spot. "What are you doing?"

"Shooting lizards."

"Are dragons lizards?" Sweetpea asked, swishing her sword through the air.

"Looks like a lizard to me," Millie said, squeezing off another round. The dragon reared back to take off. Instead, it staggered and tumbled forward, scrambling down the front of the hotel as the building gave way under its weight. Millie cocked the repeater to reload and fired. The bullet struck the dragon in her damaged eye. The blue's shriek was deafening, and she clawed at her snout. This was not an arrow that could be pulled out.

"You know," Sweetpea said, calling up a swirling wind that kicked up dust and smoke. "I don't think the dragon likes you very much?"

"Thanks, Sweetpea," Millie muttered, slipping bullets into the rifle's magazine tube one by one. When it was full, she cocked it and lined up her next shot. "I was worried she wanted to be friends." The explosions might have caught the blue's attention, but it had been looking for something. Did it associate Millie with danger after the last two encounters? If it wanted to kill her, the dragon would have to get in line.

"Hey 'Pea?" Millie asked, taking a half step backward as she watched the dragon pull herself back upright. They had her full attention, now. "Do you know any storm spells? Lightning? Thunder?" Millie could hear her voice creeping up in pitch. "Anything like that?"

"Uh," Sweetpea said. "I think so. Hold on. It'll take a minute to cast, though." With a flick of her sword, Sweetpea dropped the wind spell. Millie felt the air begin to crackle.

"Do it. Find somewhere safe," Millie said, squeezing off a shot. This time, the bullet bit into the dragon's shoulder. "I'll keep her busy."

Sensing magic, the blue reared back, throat rattling as she took a deep breath.

"*Run!*" Millie screamed, sprinting in the opposite direction of Sweetpea. She had to lead the dragon away from everyone.

Spotting an open door at Sweetpea's shop, Millie dove inside, tucking and rolling as she hit the wooden floor.

Heat washed over Millie as the blue spat fire at her heels. Flames splashed over the doorway and into the store at an angle, narrowly missing her. Someone screamed. Millie blinked in the smoke-filled shop. A cluster of frightened men huddled in one corner, some scorched and others trembling. One poor soul had been hiding in the line with the door. His scream had been mercifully short.

"Hey boys," Millie said with her sunniest smile. "Where's Fred?" The shop was too cramped to use her rifle, so Millie drew a pistol and shot the man by the shop counter, dead.

The men jumped as the crack of the revolver was echoed by a roar from the road.

"I said," Millie said calmly, pulling back the hammer on the revolver. "Where. Is. Fred?" She punctuated each word with a shot, leaving two men huddled together in a corner. The others slumped to the floor or cradled their chests, not yet realizing that they were dead.

"The rocks," one blurted. He was young, too young to have fought in the war. No doubt he'd believed all Fred's 'Hero of the Union' bullshit until this very moment. "He hung back at the rocks."

Flames licked at the painted walls of the shop, and Millie knew she couldn't stay. How long did she have before the dragon could flame again? Ten seconds? Twenty? She had to keep moving. Millie's ears swivelled, listening to the angry huff of the beast still outside.

"Good boy," she said, hopping up to her feet and scampering deeper into the store. "You should run now." Sweetpea's kitchen was still tidy despite the smoke and there was a tray of cookies that had been left out to cool. Cookies with thumbprints in them meant to hold dobs of jam. Passing them, Millie felt her throat close. The thumbprints were too small to be Sweetpea's.

Millie trembled, her fingers dropping the handful of rounds she was loading into the revolver. They scattered over the kitchen floor and several rolled out of reach. Forcing herself to take a deep breath, Millie pulled another handful of rounds from her bag and loaded the revolver, one bullet at a time.

Losing control right now would be deadly. Not only for her, for everyone. For Ryan, who had made her promise to survive; for Gilbert, who was supposed to take care of her daughters. For Allan and Hal, neither of whom she had given a chance.

Wood splintered at the front of the shop, and Millie peeked around the corner to see the blue clawing at the charred door frame at the front of the shop. One eye was ruined, weeping a mess of blood. The other was sharp and fixed on the cowering men.

They weren't men; they were just *boys*.

"Goddamnit," she hissed, grabbing one of Sweetpea's kitchen knives. "I told you boys to run." She threw the knife, but it was balanced for chopping, and it wobbled in the air. The handle struck the dragon's snout instead of the blade. She blinked and shook her head, pulled back from the doorway. Her inhale was audible, and Millie desperately looked for something she could use. A ceramic jar of honey sat next to the cookies, and Millie grabbed it. Honey wasn't flammable, but if she could smash it over the dragon's good eye...

As the elf leaned around the corner, honey pot at the ready, something white slammed into the side of the dragon. The dragon's breath came out in a pained wheeze, spitting out a few pitiful sparks instead of a gout of flame.

Darting forward, Millie launched the honey at the blue's face. The pot, thin ceramic, shattered on the blue horned brow, splashing honey and over her good eye. Millie ducked out of the burning doorway and reached for her gun.

A pale bison shook its head as it backed away from the dragon's side. Its horns were bloody, and Millie could see the dragon's hide had been pierced. The bison bellowed and pawed at the ground, readying for another charge. A pale wolf streaked past, running up to the dragon's wing and sinking its teeth into the thin membrane there. It shook its head back and forth, tearing at the sensitive skin.

"Uh," Millie mumbled to the two Ghost Eye shifters, eyes hot with gratitude. "Thanks." Spirits, what was happening to her? Millie had never gotten emotional during a firefight, but here she was, about to cry because someone from the clan actually came to help.

Millie knew Fred would already be retreating. A small, nearly forgotten voice in her mind whispered that she could take off after him. She could kill him. Make sure he never hurt her or her girls again. In the chaos of the dragon, no one would be able to stop her from going after him.

Millie levelled her revolver and walked toward the blue. Fred could wait. These people were her family, and some things were more important than revenge.

"Hey!" she shouted again to draw the blinded dragon's attention. The blue swung her head toward the sound, mouth opening in a furious hiss. Millie squeezed off all six rounds into the softness at the back of the dragon's throat. Some part of her hated the pained shriek the dragon let out, shaking her head back and forth as she tried to shake off the pain.

Dark clouds swirled overhead. Thunder rumbled.

Pulling her tomahawks from her belt, Millie sprinted forward and leapt onto the dragon's neck. She slammed the spike of one axe into the dragon's flesh, using it to haul herself up toward its head. She knew she wouldn't be strong enough to pierce the thing's skull, so she didn't try. Instead, Millie swung the remaining tomahawk into the space behind the dragon's ruff of horns.

The blue screamed, whipping her neck to one side to shake the elf off. Millie let go, rolling as she hit the ground. She tumbled into the base of Sweetpea's store, knocking the air from her lungs. Wheezing, Millie looked up at the sky. She saw the heavy clouds overhead glow and tried to cover her ears in time.

The flash of light blinded her and the clap of thunder was deafening. Unable to see or hear, Millie flattened herself to the ground, plugging her ears and her eyes squeezed shut. Sunspots danced in her vision; multiple jagged lines of light etched into her eyes. The world flashed again and again, the cracks of thunder rolling into one another until Scorched Bluffs might well have been a nest of stormbirds.

The rain followed, cold and hard as it pounded down onto her. Millie, dazed and unsteady, slowly opened her eyes and blinked to try to clear the afterimages of Sweetpea's lightning. Sucking down a ragged breath, Millie looked up.

The dragon lay in the middle of the road, wings fallen to either side. One had caught on the roof of Sweetpea's shop, creating a sluiceway for the rain to run down. Her neck was completely blackened, the skin and flesh burnt away by something much hotter than fire. The lightning struck the tomahawks Millie had planted there.

The blue was still.

Grannie and Eyota stood where the bison and wolf had been, just a moment before. Grannie leaned on her staff, one hand pressed to her back. Eyota hurried over to where Millie lay in the mud, sliding into a crouch as they reached her.

"Who did *that*?!" Eyota shouted, though Millie could barely hear them over the ringing in her ears.

"So," Millie said, staggering to her feet. "Have you heard about arroyan war witches?"

34

As Dust Settles

Jeb knew he'd made the right decision to stay where he'd been put. The rapid cluster of thunderclaps, sharp and loud even from in the cellar, cemented it. He wasn't about to mess with a dragon, but a stormbird? He would wait in the cellar until he starved to death if it meant avoiding one of those.

He waited, tucked against some barrels in a corner of the earthen cellar. Staying awake was difficult, but Jeb was worried. He might be safe, but his siblings were still out there, stuck with the stupid captain who'd gone and challenged a cursed town full of demons and ghosts. Josie and Zach would be smart enough to find cover, but Eli... it depended how much Eli had to drink.

He blinked, starting awake as the cellar door opened with a bang. The quick movement sent the cellar dipping under him, and he grabbed onto the nearest barrel to steady himself.

"Jeb?"

He looked up to see Josie hurrying over to him. Her hands were tied up with rope, linking her to others that stumbled after her into the cellar. He searched their blurry faces for Eli, for Zach. Maybe they'd gotten away?

"Josie, are you alright?" Jeb muttered, sitting up slowly. At the door to the cellar, two women walked into the room, standing on either side of the door. One he immediately recognized as Di's sister. They had the same nose, and while the half-elf's hair was auburn instead of red, the resemblance was strong. This had to be Lyddie. The second woman was an orc with a bandage on one shoulder, the cloth already stained red.

"She killed it," Josie hissed, helping Jeb right himself.

"The stormbird?" Jeb asked, blinking.

"No, idiot," she huffed. "The dragon. She killed the *dragon*. The Ghost. She jumped onto its face and called down lightning," Josie shuddered, each word becoming a hiss between her teeth. "Zach's dead, shot by their sheriff from near a mile out, and Eli got burnt by the Rotkin they got here."

Josie was talking too fast for his frazzled brain. Zach was the best shot in the West, or so they'd thought. Suddenly dizzy, Jeb leaned his head against the cool earthen walls of the cellar. This town was definitely cursed. Women who fought dragons, women who could pick off a man at a mile out, women who had horns and hooves.

"Heads up, Willard," Lyddie said.

Jeb opened his eyes and tried to focus on the cellar door.

The Ghost walked down the steps without even needing to duck. Her coat, an old blue Union uniform, was scorched and the skin along one side of her head and over an ear was bright pink and shiny. Jeb thought about the scars he'd seen back at the shack when he'd first met her. Those had been from war, he realised. She'd told him when taking him in, all the stories he'd heard, all the rumours, they were all true. He believed her.

"I warned your brother about using those kinds of names about my friends," the hellion elf said, looking at Josie with a smile that would've frozen a hearthfire in hell. "Tell me what I want to know, and there won't be any problems. Understand?"

One of the Captain's men tried to jump at the elf, but Di's sister intercepted him and smashed an iron frypan into his face. The man crumpled and lay still.

"Now," the Ghost continued, as though nothing had happened. "I know Frederic Rousseau. I know him better than any of you do. I know he lies, gets folk like you lot to do his dirty work. I know he sent you into a death trap and told you it'd be easy. He's done it to me too." Those unholy eyes looked them over, sending a shiver down Jeb's spine.

"You want to know where he's going?" Josie asked. She sounded cautious, but Jeb knew she was building a plan. He hoped it wasn't a stupid one.

"Fuck no," the elf said, letting out a bitter laugh. "I know where he's *headed*. I want to know how many men he had with him and what weapons they have. First one to tell me will get healed by my friends." The elf tilted her head back toward the two that flanked the door.

The one orc smiled, Lyddie rested her bloody frypan against her shoulder.

"I'll tell," Josie said. "But it's my brother that needs the healing. I can see his head ain't right."

The ghost bitch seemed to think about that, then nodded. She stepped forward and cut Josie free of the rope, and motioned for Jeb to get to his feet. He tried, staggering before Josie steadied him, her hands still tied together. Jeb was barely holding himself upright, even with his sister's help.

"Before any of you try to escape," Lyddie said, glaring at the gathered prisoners. "I would suggest you don't."

Jeb followed along with Josie, stumbling on the steps out of the cellar. A strong hand grabbed his coat before he could fall and lifted him back upright. Looking up, he saw the orc with an injured shoulder had caught him. When the orc smiled, her tusks gleamed in the light.

"Don't give me a reason, Willard," the orc whispered.

Gilbert drifted in and out of sleep, unsure if the conversations around him were dreams, or if they were real. He was familiar with the fuzzy tingle of laudanum on his lips. His spirit floated in his body, safely removed from the pain of being flesh.

Slowly, through the ebb and flow of sleep, Gilbert returned to himself. The first sensation he noticed was a pressure on his chest. Though it was certainly not pain, it was confusing. Had he been shot there too? He remembered the white-hot pain in his back and hip... then falling.

His body twitched; remembering the fall better than his mind could.

"Is he awake?" A soft voice whispered.

"I thought he was supposed to be asleep," another whispered back. "Do we call Cousin Eyota?"

Peeling his eyes open, Gilbert blinked a few times to focus on the scenes above him. There were three faces, each watching him with wide eyes. One set was gold, another brown and fuzzy, and the third grey like his Sarah's. Gilbert smiled, his lips half numb.

"Hello," he croaked.

The two little girls sat up immediately, their ears flapping up and down in excitement. The blond, hair as pale as her mother's, looked to the redhead for guidance.

"Yeah," Rasha said solemnly. "We should get Eyota."

"What about Grannie?" Fenna asked, glancing back down at Gilbert. Her ears flapped up and down again, and a little hand, still chubby with baby fat, reached out to pat at his cheek. "Grannie knows more."

Freckle, the treacherous and treasonous puppy, was snuggled up on Gilbert's chest, and crept forward to lick at his jaw. The sensation was strangely amplified while also numbed, and Gilbert grimaced, closing his eyes to keep himself from being overwhelmed.

"Oh," Rasha said thoughtfully. "Get Grannie. I'll stay in case he dies."

"Good God," Gilbert groaned, cracking one eye open to look at the little elven girls (and puppy). "Did your mother teach you to be so morbid?"

"No," said the blond.

"Yes," said the redhead. They looked at each other.

"Yes," they said together. The puppy barked, happy to be included.

"Thought so." Another slow blink, and Gilbert was able to turn his head to look at his surrounding environment. This was certainly no hospital. Instead, he recognized the hotel room that he initially stayed in. There was even the mostly empty bottle of whiskey on the bedside table, and cleaned glasses sat next to it. A note was propped up between the two glasses, with his name written down in simple letters... but whoever had written it had spelled 'Gilbert' right, which was impressive given the environs.

"Miss Gingersnap," he said, looking back at the redhead. "Could you please bring me that letter on the table?"

The two baby girl elves looked at each other and leaned their heads together, conferring in stage whispers about the nature of a 'gingersnap'. Ultimately, they determined gingersnaps were reddish, and that Gilbert meant Rasha.

Watching all of it, Gilbert couldn't help but feel homesick. He missed his little storm cloud of a daughter. He missed his snarky but loving father, and he missed Arnaud's cooking.

The two girls crawled down from the bed, one heading for the door to get their grandmother, and the other hurried over to the little table by the bed, reaching up to pull the note free.

"Where's your mother?" Gilbert asked, carefully lifting his arm up to hold his hand out for the little girl. He could feel a tightness in his hip, the simple movement pulled at something on his side. He glanced down for the first time, realising something weighed down on him, heavier than the blanket.

His shirt was gone, and a wool blanket had been pulled up to his chest. Gilbert lifted the blanket gingerly to peek underneath. He still wore his trousers, though they had been undone at the fly to allow for a thick bandage wrapped around his hip and side. It seemed to be soaked through with some kind of ointment, and smelled medicinal.

"Grannie and Auntie helped," the little redhead said, placing the note into Gilbert's hand. "They're *real* good at making ouches go away. Even *big* ones, like yours." He took the letter and watched as the little elf climbed back up onto the bed, careful not to jostle the mattress under him.

Her face grew very serious, and despite the flaming red hair, despite the freckles, she reminded him of her mother.

"Momma said you have a little girl," Rasha said. "Just like us."

Gilbert nodded, holding the note for the time being. It could wait. Right now, a little girl needed reassurance.

"Her name is Sarah," he said. "She's a little younger than you and your sister."

"Momma's gone to keep her safe," Rasha said, her pudgy little face grim. "From the bad man who hurt you."

Gilbert blinked, trying to understand what the baby girl meant. What bad man? He fumbled with the letter, opening it with a single hand, and stared at the message it held.

Gilbert,

I'm sorry I couldn't stop him. Fred got away. I know where he's going and I'm going to stop him. I promised, like you did. Sarah will be safe. Your father, too.

I promise.

—Mildred.

Rousseau had shot him, and the bastard would know that Gilbert had still been alive. Fuck.

He stared at the letter until someone knocked at the door. Looking up, he saw the elderly elf who had married him at Annie's ranch. She held Fenna's hand and wore a gentle, knowing smile.

"I apologize for not coming sooner," Grannie said, hobbling into the room. "These old bones don't shift back as easily as they used to." She eased herself into a chair next to Gilbert's bed, grunting as she settled.

"Sarah will be safe," the old woman said, her pale eyes creasing in a smile. "And your father, too. Now, let's take a look at that hip of yours."

Fenna hurried over to take Gilbert's hand and gave it a squeeze in both of hers.

Their departure had been hasty. Throwing supplies and ammo into bags, hoping it would be enough. Each hour spent in town was one that Fred had to gain distance on them. Norbert, loyal and dependable, was left behind in favour of the faster Max.

This time, Millie wasn't alone. Alongside her rode Ryan and Hal, and Sweetpea took up the rear on the horse that Rémi had ridden into town. Millie knew four people against a dozen wasn't nearly enough, but as they rode toward Plainfield, they passed bodies.

During the war, Fred had never cared if injured men needed care. If they couldn't fight, they were as good as dead to him. It seemed little had changed in the years since.

The Plainfield station was filled with steam as it came into view. The train to Wyndford started to pull away from the platform and whistled twice. Millie knew Fred was on it. She could feel it in her bones.

"Find Fred's house," she shouted over her shoulder before she kicked Max into a full gallop. The next train could be a full day away, and Millie couldn't risk letting Fred have that much time to plan for her arrival.

Ryan was shouting, but her words were lost between the chug of the train and Max's hooves. The locomotive was older and didn't accelerate out of the station nearly as quickly as the Blue Bullet had. They had been riding since midnight and Millie could tell Max wasn't going to be able to catch it. His gait was tired, and if she pushed him, he would collapse under her.

Watching the train pull away, Millie reined the mustang out of his gallop. Slowing him to a walk, Millie swore and turned him around to meet the others.

"We need to talk to Diana."

35

GOING HOME

THE TENSION IN THE air was palpable when Hal walked into the Plainfield Saloon with the Scorched Bluffs ladies. The noisy chatter and clink of glasses and mugs died, leaving out-of-towners asking what was going on in whispers that were far too loud.

Diamond dropped the tray of mugs she had been collecting onto the nearest table. She stared at Deputy Berry; eyes wide. Hal thought for a moment that Diamond would run. Instead, she hurried over and made to throw her arms around Collins.

The dopey, friendly dog that hung tight to Ryan's side jumped between Diamond and the Sheriff, hackles raised and a deadly growl ripping from his throat.

"Sit," Ryan said, and the dog did so, licking his chops and leaning his head against his master's hip.

"You got my message? Everything is alright?" Diamond asked, keeping her distance from the dog. She looked at Berry. "How is she? Is she safe?"

"Lyddie? She's fine." Sweetpea said, looking around the saloon with wide eyes. "This place is nice."

"Not Lyddie, Sweetpea," Millie said, walking over to an empty table and taking a seat. "She's fine, Di. A bit scared, but fine. Why? Are you growing a conscience all of a sudden?"

"Hal, why don't you and Sweetpea go look through Rousseau's room? We'll talk to Di here and find out what else we need to know," Collins said with a faint smile. Hal noticed the twinkle in the Sheriff's eyes was icy rather than warm.

"Which room is it?" Sweetpea asked, watching the goings-on with the dog, wide-eyed.

"The one that smells like whiskey and puke," Millie said from her seat.

"I feel like I should stay," Hal started, but a warm hand grabbed his arm and started to drag him toward the stairwell that led to the hotel. Glancing down, he saw Sweetpea's gloved hand holding onto his elbow. "I guess we're going to investigate Rousseau's room," he said, defeated. Sweetpea smiled brightly and nodded encouragingly at him. Her freckles glinted in the lamplight of the saloon. Regular freckles didn't glint.

"Exactly!" Sweetpea said, dragging him up the stairs. Between realising how physically strong she was, and the display of lightning back in town, Hal was starting to suspect that Sweetpea was more magic than mundane. "Let Ryan talk to her," she said over her shoulder. "Diana has a history with Millie. Ryan can get a bit protective when it comes to the Berries."

"The redheaded girl, that's Diana's daughter, isn't she?" Hal said, letting Sweetpea lead him up the stairs.

"Nope," Sweetpea said firmly. "Diana gave birth to her, but Millie's her mother. There's a difference." Her hooves clip-clopped on the wooden stairs as she hurried up the steps.

Hal was trying to listen, but he was distracted by the sounds of an evacuation from the saloon downstairs. Chairs scraped on the sawdust floor, complaints were shushed and boots clumped on the sawdust-covered floor as patrons hurried away from the women downstairs. Hal realised he was being uncharitable. The patrons were also probably running away from the dog.

"How well do you know the deputy?" he asked, turning his attention back to Sweetpea. She'd kept talking, but he had only caught enough of her chatter to know that Rousseau was not the first to try to leverage the town into turning over one of its residents. Just the most effective.

"Do you mean Millie? Because we're all deputies right now, Deputy Hal last-name-unknown," Sweetpea said.

"Stratton."

"No, that's what you call yourself. You had a name before that," Sweetpea said. "I learned that from the last Stratton I met. You're much nicer than he was." She sniffed at the air a few times and Hal realized he could smell whiskey. Good whiskey. No puke, though.

"Do I want to know why you've met Strattons in the past?" Hal asked, catching up to her.

He thought about that as they approached the rooms. "Probably not," he admitted. "That door's ajar. It might be Rousseau's." He pointed at the third door on the right, noticing the door jutting out slightly from the frame. Whoever had been through last hadn't quite closed it, and as he walked closer, Hal could see a smear of red on the door's handle.

Hal inspected the scene. The blood was still red, only going rusty at the edges. They had just missed Rousseau by a matter of minutes. He grit his teeth. If the dragon hadn't shown up, they would have caught the bastard. Now, Rousseau would have a full day's headstart on them. He hoped the Goldmans could last that long.

He frowned, trying not to think about what would have happened if the Deputy and Sheriff had caught him before he reached the train.

"You didn't answer my question earlier," he said, glancing up at Sweetpea. "How well *do* you know Deputy Berry?"

Sweetpea, still in her ruffled skirts and bloodied shift, shrugged. "Well, enough. I'd heard of her and she wasn't afraid of me and the town's been wonderful aside from the people that try to get at us."

"But she's killed so many people..."

"Like I said," Sweetpea answered, repeating her words more slowly. "She was not afraid *of me*. A lot of us have had to do stuff we didn't want to. I heard the stories, but war brings out the worst in everyone. Humans, elves, arroyans. Amelior is hardly the first country to fight among itself."

Hal glanced at the scars that marked Sweetpea's upper arms and decided for the first time in his life that now was not the time to ask more questions. He had watched, perched above the fighting on the hotel roof, as the woman next to him had kept up with the famed Bayou Butcher. The two of them had cut their way through Rousseau's men and taken down a greater dragon.

"Let's check the room, shall we?" he said instead, smiling too brightly.

It was undoubtedly Rousseau's room. Empty whiskey bottles that were nearly all empty lined one wall. A bottle by the bed was still a quarter full and had to be the source of the fumes that filled the room. Much like their rooms when Hal and Gilbert had stayed in the same hotel, there was a single bed that was flanked by a bedside table with a lantern and washbasin. An open trunk sat at the foot of the bed, emblazoned with Rousseau's initials.

Clothes and maps were tossed across the bed and onto the floor haphazardly. Rousseau must have been in a hurry to find something specific. He must have known that Berry would be hot on his trail, but what was it that he had been looking for?

Hal frowned as he studied the room. If he was a drunkard like Rousseau, where would he keep things that were important?

He walked over to the empty whiskey bottles and smiled as he spotted a thin leather notebook that had been slipped between the bottles and the wall. Pulling it free, Hal undid the leather tie and opened it. A tintype photograph on thick celluloid paper fell out, landing at his feet facedown. On the back, Hal could see a list of names written in a careful handwriting. All but one had been crossed out, with a date written next to the name. No doubt it was the same Mildred that was downstairs, though using a different surname.

Crouching, Hal picked up the photo and looked over the names. 'Mildred Argent' was the only name left untouched. Hal flipped the photo over to look at its front. A regiment of Unionist soldiers stared back at him, grim-faced. Front and centre knelt a familiar elf, her pale hair spiked into a mohawk and her face painted dark from forehead to cheekbones. She wore buckskin leggings under her infantry coat, a sash tied around her waist. In one hand, photo-Mildred held a tomahawk, and in the other, a rifle.

Hal looked back at the notebook and frowned as he scanned the writing there. It was a language similar to something studied at the Seminary, but he could only make out every other word.

"Find something?" Sweetpea asked, already elbow-deep in the opened trunk.

"I did, but it's all in Orman informal tense," Hal muttered, trying desperately to remember his lessons. Something about the leading vowel being soft meant... family? No. Talking to a family member.

"I never got the hang of informal tenses," Sweetpea said. "*Infernal* though? That's my mother tongue!"

Distracted, Hal looked up at the woman. He must have looked concerned because when she glanced up at him from the contents of Rousseau's trunk, Sweetpea's brow wrinkled.

"Because of the horns?" she said, pointing at them. After a moment, she sighed and rolled her eyes. "It was a joke. *Millie* gets my jokes," she added, not quite quiet enough for Hal not to hear it. "Millie also knows Orman. We should bring that downstairs with us." Standing up in a ruffle of blood-splattered skirts, Sweetpea held up something silver. Something familiar.

"Is this yours?" She asked, holding up Hal's Stratton badge, complete with Berry's dried blood still on it.

The next train wouldn't arrive in Plainfield until the following morning.

Diana had offered her room to rest in, but the smell of the saloon had begun to get to Millie. It smelled like puke, piss, and alcohol. It smelled like Fred. Unable to stand it any longer, she'd stepped out to get fresh air and made her way to the train platform.

Her knees ached and her shoulder kept locking even though she kept moving it to keep loose. War was a young person's game. She'd heard the old brass say that all throughout the war, but she'd thought they meant it was because the young were bolder. Now, feeling the aches settling in, Millie realised it was because war destroyed your body.

Sitting on the fresh-hewn wood of the Plainfield train station, Millie let her head hang into her hands. If she'd pushed Max a little more, would she have caught the train? Would she have been able to stop Fred before he reached Wyndford, where Gilbert's little girl was?

Someone cleared their throat behind her.

Turning, Millie saw it was Ryan and Fyodor. Ryan was holding one of the trays from the saloon, and upon it was a pair of cups and a pot of coffee.

"Ready for some company?" the Sheriff asked, with a tiny smile. Fyodor, ever the gentleman, was waiting for the okay, frozen in place with one paw hovering over the platform.

Millie nodded.

"Good, because if I drink this much coffee on my own, my heart might stop," Ryan said. She nodded at Fyodor, and he bounded up onto the platform. He trotted over to Millie and flopped down next to her, his head falling into the elf's lap.

Millie patted his neck. Her girls had the spitz puppy, and Grannie was still in town. They'd be safe until she got back. They were used to her travelling away from town for a few days, but Wyndford was further than she'd ever been from them. Had this been how Gilbert felt the whole time he'd been gone from his daughter?

No wonder he'd been such an ass for the first few days.

"You probably could," Millie said encouragingly. "How are you doing? Are you okay after-"

"Mildred," she winced as Ryan used her full name. "You jumped on a dragon's face. How was I supposed to be okay with that?" Setting down the tray next to them, Ryan took a seat on the platform on Millie's other side. She handed the elf a mug of steaming black coffee, and then a letter.

"I was trying to stop it," Millie said, feeling sheepish. "And I jumped onto its shoulder, not it's face." The argument sounded thin even to her. Millie abandoned it and looked at the paper Ryan handed her. "What's this?"

"Sweetpea and the Stratton found it," Ryan said, picking up her own mug and pouring herself a cup of coffee. Plainfield had things like sugar, cream, but after going without either in Scorched Bluffs for so long, neither of the women considered those as options. Sometimes, it was nice to have a cup of coffee made from fresh grounds.

Millie took a small sip of the bean juice and opened the letter. Here was the familiar handwriting that had been missing from the paper Gilbert had. Neat, well-formed letters written on a near-perfect level in informal Orman. Millie read through it twice, slowly setting down her mug of coffee for the second read through.

"Did they *read* this?" Millie asked, looking up at Ryan. The human shook her head.

"They couldn't. Most schools up north only teach Orman formal tenses. What does it say?"

"It was a letter to Rémi from Fred, from a month ago. Rémi was that one-eyed guy who came into town first. He always wanted to be Fred's second in command, and I guess he became that after the war."

Ryan waited; blue eyes fixed on Millie's face. Feeling her ears get hot, the elf realised she still hadn't explained what the letter said.

"Ryan, this was blackmail." She lifted the letter and pointed to a specific phrase. "Someone wanted the banker dead or ruined. They bought up all Fred's debt and told him it would be forgiven if he took care of Goldman. If that person tried to kill Fred, Rémi was to air the man's secrets." Millie blinked, staring back at the paper in her hand.

"This was never about us," she breathed. "Not even because of the train."

"Who could afford to do all of that?" Ryan asked, but the answer hit her almost as soon as she'd finished asking the question. "Wait," she said, a hand fluttering to her mouth. Ryan grew pale. "Is it the same person who said his debts would be forgiven if he got rid of a certain family?"

Millie nodded.

"He doesn't say the name, so it'd be harder to realise what this letter was, but he describes him perfectly. Rail tycoon, Harrold Colfield."

They sat there quietly for a while, watching the sun's light turn golden as it sank lower into the sky.

"I thought," Ryan said, voice cracking. Millie reached over and took her hand, giving it a gentle squeeze. "I thought he must have found out we were there, and that was why the train's manifest had been leaked. I thought he must have heard rumours about you, or about me. That this was his way of catching us."

"Me too," Millie said, gently pushing the tray of coffee back and out of the way. She pulled her friend into a hug, and from his position next to her, Fyodor lifted his head to lick at Ryan's hands. "I thought that too. But I think he put it here because of the robberies. He knew Goldman would be a target the moment he stepped foot in Plainfield. I mean, you see how he dresses."

Ryan rested her head against Millie's, returning the embrace.

"I wish," Ryan said quietly, "That I could have seen Rousseau's face, when the Willards told him they'd encountered you with the banker. I bet he nearly pissed himself."

Millie snorted. She hoped he had.

"So," Ryan said, "I guess it's finally time to go home." If Millie hadn't known Ryan as long, if they didn't know each other as well as they did, she might have missed the way the other woman's voice broke on the word 'home'.

"I guess so," Millie said, nearly whispering. "Well, Rhiannon Colfield, are you ready to take your inheritance back?"

Ryan sniffed and looked out at the prairie in front of them. Though tears welled up in her eyes, her jaw was set.

"Yes," she said. "And I'm going to send a telegram and get us a goddamn train. We've waited long enough. I'm not going to wait until tomorrow because of some damn schedule." Giving Millie a last squeeze, Ryan pushed herself to her feet.

"You stay here. I'll be back once it's done."

Fyodor got to his feet and trotted after her, tail wagging. Left alone with the coffee, Millie picked up her cup and blew the steam from it.

The prairie was beautiful at this time of day. The grasses were painted gold and orange by the setting sun, the sky open and wide, and the air fresh.

Ryan was right. It was time to go home. Fred and Harrold had enjoyed their ill-gotten status for too long. There would be no more girls left without fathers because of those two. She hoped Harrold Colfield pissed himself when he heard Rhiannon was still alive.

A train arrived at midnight, a locomotive pulling a single passenger car. The orc driving it was old, his hands stained with as much grease as ink, and he fumbled with grimy spectacles as he hurried down from the locomotive. It was the same model as the Blue Bullet, though it was painted a plain black.

"Miss Rhiannon?" He spotted her and Millie watched as his face crumpled into tears. "My word, you look so much like your mother."

Standing next to Hal and Sweetpea, Millie waited as Rhiannon pulled the man into a gentle hug.

"Do you know who that man is?" Sweetpea asked. Millie shook her head. Hal stood still, a hand over his mouth, eyes wide.

"She's Rhi—"

"Yup," Millie interrupted. "Keep *up*, Stratton." She said it without any venom, though.

Pulling back from the hug, Rhiannon smiled, and Millie could see her own cheeks were glistening in the lantern light.

"Gervais, I'd like you to meet my friends. Mildred Berry, Sweetpea, and Hal Stratton. Everyone, Gervais was my father's chief engineer. He designed all the trains. I used to follow him around the workshop asking questions nonstop."

The engineer, Gervais, smiled and wiped at his face with a stained handkerchief. "She knew those trains better than I did." He sniffled and took a shaky breath. "I'm so glad to see you, Miss. By the Messiah, look at how strong you've gotten."

"I can explain everything on the way," Rhiannon said gently. "We need to get to Wyndford as soon as we can."

"By all means!" Gervais said. "Lucky Penny here will get us there by morning. She's not as sleek as her sister Bluebell was, but she's just as fast."

Sweetpea leaned over to Millie and whispered: "Are you gonna tell him you blew the other one up?"

36

WYNDFORD

THE SKY WAS JUST starting to lighten as the black locomotive pulled into the West-Colfield Rail trainyard. Unable to sleep, Millie had spent the ride tearing out every insignia from her coat. The sergeant chevrons, the Union's patch at her throat, everything. The wool was dark and fresh where they'd been taken off, but the absence of the insignias was an improvement compared to leaving them on. She had been proud of them, once. Back when she'd thought of herself as a sergeant who took care of her people. Someone who did what she could to keep them fed and safe.

Then she'd failed them all when she let Fred arrest her. A quiet whisper in the back of her mind asked if she had even earned the promotions, or if she'd been given them because she was Fred's girl. But she hadn't survived on the Frontier because she was 'Fred's girl', she hadn't rebuilt a town from ashes because she was 'Fred's girl', and she certainly hadn't killed a dragon because she was 'Fred's Girl'.

It didn't matter if she'd earned those promotions properly or not. She'd done greater things since. While she might still be the Bayou Butcher, she was no longer 'Fred's girl'.

The train yard was already busy, with trains of all kinds being taken apart, cleaned, and repaired. The air smelled of coal and grease, and sparks flew as a spell was cast to rivet one piece to another. A few of the workers looked up as Gervais pulled 'Penny' into the yard, but not many.

Millie might have found the train yard fascinating, but at the moment all she could think of was Gilbert's little girl and what Fred might do to her.

"Everyone ready?" she asked, pulling her coat on and tying it into place with her sash. Hal and Sweetpea nodded, and Millie noticed Sweetpea was wearing Hal's jacket. Arching an eyebrow, she let it be for the moment and turned to Rhiannon.

"Yes," Rhiannon said, shouldering her rifle. "No more hiding." She had braided her hair, but let the thick dark plait hang over her shoulder. No more hiding. The woman stepping off the train would be Rhiannon Colfield, not Ryan Collins.

Millie nodded.

"After you," Sweetpea said, pulling open the door. Rhiannon climbed down from the passenger car and hopped down onto the gravel of the train yard. Millie watched as she strode forward, knowing exactly where she was going. Workers glanced up, some doing a double take as they realised who she was. From there, word rippled out like wildfire.

Following behind, Millie watched as some workers hurried over, greeting Rhiannon by name like Gervais had. Some watched, pale faced like they had seen a ghost, while others whispered amongst themselves, trying to figure out what the fuss was about.

"She's famous here, isn't she?" Sweetpea whispered, coming up alongside Millie. The elf nodded, surprised by the level of reverence the workers were showing. She had assumed, perhaps rudely, that the Colfields had acted like every other rich family. Making their money off the backs of their workers at the expense of their workers. Yet, the way tears cutting through the coal dust on some old timers' cheeks, Millie wondered if perhaps working for the Colfields had once been a point of pride among these people.

Rhiannon led them to the main office, her mouth twisting as she spotted the name on the door. 'Harrold Colfield'. With a single blow, Rhiannon kicked down the door. Inside was an opulent room, and it was covered in a thick layer of dust.

"Figures," Ry muttered, heading past the massive desk to a safe tucked against the wall. "Uncle Harrold never used to visit the yard. Why would he start now that he runs the place?"

She crouched by the safe and spent a moment staring at the dial.

"What are we looking for?" Millie asked. "How can I help?"

"Proof," Ry said, starting to spin the safe's dial. "Uncle was the type to hold on to old letters to use in arguments. I can't imagine he could throw away any agreements he had with Rousseau. He never comes here, and everyone else who knew the combination to this safe is dead. This is where he'd keep those papers."

The safe door swung open, so well made that the hinges barely squeaked after years of disuse. Rhiannon pulled out a folio of papers.

"This might take a while..." she said, shoulders sagging. As she stepped back from the safe, Millie could see at least a dozen more folios equally packed with letters.

"We'll each take one," Millie said, walking over to the safe and pulling out more. "If it's here, we'll find it."

Wyndford Central Station was bustling with passengers waiting for the train to begin their journey out west, while families waited for the return of loved ones. It was chaos, and more people than Millie had been around in almost a decade.

Heart in her throat, she took a deep breath as she watched the ebb and flow of people from her corner of the station. Tucked behind a brick column, she watched for Fred among the crowd, but it was someone else who she spotted first. High above the heads of the crowd, a little girl perched on a half-orc's shoulders arrived on the platform. Her dark curls were a mess and her eyes were puffy and red from crying, but Millie recognized her from Gilbert's photograph immediately.

Around the girl and man were a handful of Fred's thugs, trying and failing to blend into the crowd with their scraped and burned faces. Five, enough to make a banker comply, but Millie was no banker.

She slipped from her hiding spot, weaving through the crowd toward the little girl and her keepers.

They didn't notice until she pressed her knife into the back of the only one of Fred's men who didn't have any marks on him. Fred, for all his inept leadership and willingness to throw others underfoot, inspired impressive devotion among some of his goons.

The man in front of her stiffened as Millie slid the knife through layers of wool and cotton to nick the skin underneath.

"Hi Lenny," she said quietly. "You're going to give me the girl now, and once you do, I'll play nice. If you don't, I will cut out your kidney."

Turning his head to look down at her over his shoulder, Lionel sneered. He'd been Fred's steward when Millie had first been brought into the Rousseau home. He'd seen what Fred had done, and did nothing to stop it.

"I see you have done that *thing* to your hair again, Mildred." He sniffed and held his hand up. Around her, the goons closed in.

"They could kill you," Lionel said. "Are you certain that coming alone was a smart idea?"

"They could *try*," Millie corrected. "Give me the girl, and I'll come with you to see him. If you order them to come at me, I'll make sure you die last." She smiled up at him. Once upon a time, she had thought of Lionel as a father figure. He had helped bandage her up after sparring lessons. He had brought her broth when she was ill.

And then he had kept her locked in a cellar for years under Fred's orders.

Lionel's eyebrows raised at her offer. He waved the men down and motioned for the half-orc to approach.

"She wants the girl. You can go now, greenskin."

"I'm not giving Miss Goldman to some thief," the half orc said, scowling.

"Oh, I'm not a thief," Millie said, pushing Lionel around so the little girl and her protector could see her. "I'm a friend of your papa. He sent me to make sure you're safe. You must be Miss Sarah, the storm cloud, correct?" Her smile softened as she looked up at the girl. At the mention of her nickname, Sarah Goldman's eyes widened, and her hands, still chubby and small, tightened where they held fistfuls of the half-orc's lapels.

"You are a friend of Mister Goldman?" The man holding Sarah asked, a minty eyebrow lifting in judgement. He glanced down at Millie's coat and leggings, then back up to her mohawk. "You don't look like his type," he said reluctantly.

Millie's heart twisted as Sarah's arms wrapped tightly around the head of the man holding her. Her little chin wibbled, and Millie released Lionel, tucking her knife back into her belt.

"I'll keep you safe, baby girl," she said gently, reaching out to take her. "Your papa told me all about you, you know. That you like lullabies, and that you can count real high." He hadn't mentioned those specifically, but back in the smuggler's shack he had asked her to sing his daughter lullabies.

"I would rather stay with Miss Sarah, Ma'am."

"No," Millie said, meeting the half-orc's eyes. "You should go home and make sure it's ready for her to come back to." She couldn't tell him anything, not in front of Lionel. Here, in a crowd, he and Sarah were the safest they could be. It would be best if the half-orc remained safe. Whoever he was, he was important to Sarah.

Reluctantly, he lifted the little girl down from his shoulders and passed her over to Millie. Sarah whimpered and began to cry, reaching out for him. It broke Millie's heart, and she adjusted Sarah onto her hip, murmuring a few soft lines of a lullaby.

The surrounding men stared at her, and Lionel's expression changed from disgust to unsettled horror. Millie stroked the little girl's back, soothing her as best she could, given the situation.

"I heard a dragon had killed you," Lionel said. *"Shame it didn't."*

"You know me, Lenny," Millie said, staying in tune with the lullaby. "Always a disappointment."

37

SOUL CYCLES

HAL AND RHIANNON WAITED for Millie and Rousseau's men to leave before they approached the half-orc. Arnaud stood alone on the platform; head bowed in defeat. The man's pale green hair was mussed, rather than being slicked back with pomade like usual. His hands were clenched at his sides, and as Hal got closer, he could see that one held a little leather shoe.

Closing the distance, Hal reached out to tap the man on the shoulder. The half-orc turned on him, furious- until he saw who it was. One of Arnaud's eyes was swollen, a large bruise darkening under his pale green skin.

"They took her," Arnaud hissed. "That *monster* took Mister Avrom and little Sarah." He glanced from Hal to Ryan and the dog, who had caught up. Fyodor shoved his massive head at Arnaud, sniffing at the shoe he held.

"Mister Stratton, what's going on?"

"We're friends," Rhiannon said. Fyodor wasn't a hound, but Hal wondered if he could still track scents. That could be useful.

"Gil is safe, but he's recovering from being shot. He sent us instead," Hal explained.

"You, did you know that elf?" Arnaud said, glancing back at Hal. "Pale, like a whitefish and dressed like she was out of some penny dreadful?"

"Ah," Ryan said, pulling Fyodor away from the poor man. "That is actually Mrs. Goldman, now. It's a long story, but we're happy to tell you once it's safe to follow them. I'm Rhiannon Colfield," she said, putting out a hand to shake Arnaud's.

The half-orc stared at her, then looked at Hal.

"Where did you *find* these people?" Arnaud hissed. "They're insane!"

Hal cleared his throat, nodding to Sweetpea as she made her way through the crowd toward them.

"Actually," Hal said. "Not insane despite appearances, and Miss Rhiannon is right, it's a long story. But the safest place Miss Sarah can be right now is in the arms of that elf, Arnaud. We would appreciate your help with getting everyone back safely."

Arnaud tucked the little leather shoe into his pocket. He looked at the gathered crew and sighed, running a hand through his pale green hair.

"They were at the Goldman residence," Arnaud said, trying not to stare at Sweetpea. "But as Sarah and I left to come here, there was another carriage there waiting. I do not expect that Mister Rousseau and Mister Avrom will still be there if we return. But I know where they might have gone. I've had to drop off that blond bastard far too often."

Hal glanced at Rhiannon, hoping he was able to keep the worry off his face. Gilbert was a grown man and Avrom, as grouchy as he was, hadn't survived so long without a sense of self-preservation. But Sarah was only a little girl...

"Millie will keep them safe," Ryan said, reaching out a hand to clasp Arnaud's arm. "The elf. She promised Goldman that she would."

"Who is this elf that can keep our Sarah safe?" Arnaud asked, jaw trembling. "I saw how small she was."

"She's the Bayou—" Hal started to say.

"She served in the war with Rousseau," Rhiannon interrupted and elbowed Hal in the side, *hard*. He wheezed, gripping his side with a hand.

Arnaud was staring at Ryan with suspicion, and it took Hal a moment to regain his breath.

"No, she's right. They called her the Ghost, and she's one of the most terrifying women I've ever met," he said. "She'll protect Sarah until her last breath."

Her breath kept hitching, and it took a conscious effort for Millie to keep her breathing slow and calm. It wasn't for her benefit, but for the little girl clinging to her in the carriage. Sarah had stopped crying, but Millie knew any disturbance, any twitch could set her off again. Holding the little girl and stroking her back, Millie had sung soft lullabies the entire ride.

Surprisingly, Lionel and his goons allowed it. One, a bruiser with the burns down his jaw, even seemed to relax slightly. Lionel, however, knew better.

"We'll be arriving momentarily," Fred's lackey said with a prim sniff. "He'll want you bathed and dressed..." he trailed off, looking over the borrowed saloon dress with obvious distaste. "*Properly* before you are presented."

"Presented to who? Fred's seen me worse than this," Millie asked, stroking Sarah's hair.

Lionel smiled, cold and bitter. Millie wished she could kill him right there. But she had a little girl to keep safe, so she smiled back, putting on a mask of misunderstanding. It felt tight, brittle. She hadn't needed the masks in a long time, and trying to put them on again was uncomfortable.

The collar was warmer than she thought it would be. It'd been in his hand though, for how long?

"The day you can open the lock on this is the day you can stop wearing it," Frederic said gently. He cupped her cheek with his

hand, callused and warm. "I want to make sure you can get out of any trap someone might put you in."

Her breath caught again, and Millie tried to hide it by kissing Sarah's dark hair. Lionel's smile widened, and she knew he'd seen. Fuck.

"Again."

Battered, bruised, bloodied, Millie lay in the dirt, her hands worn raw. The kick was swift and strong enough to send her rolling toward to the knife he had knocked out of her hand.

"Again, or you go back to the cellar."

Taking as deep a breath as she could, Millie pushed herself up to her knees and reached for the knife.

"Oh, has the little pet remembered what it's like to disobey its master?" Lionel asked as the carriage rolled to a stop.

A battle field, one conquered. The supplies of the rebels had been burned; their wells poisoned. Millie sat by the campfire, grimacing as the healer stitched closed a slash on her shoulder. Next to them, the captain's tent waited. He demanded she was presentable first. He never liked seeing her dirty and bloodied.

"Here we are," Lionel said, watching her with unbridled glee. "After you, Mildred."

The carriage door opened, and the thugs stepped out first, flanking the carriage door. Millie cradled Sarah close, whispered a promise that she'd keep her safe, and descended from the carriage. There were men waiting at the manor's entry, but none of them were the blond captain she had once known so well.

"Do you love me?" He held her jaw in a single hand. They were so close to home now. The stink of the bayou was familiar, but kept twisting her stomach in a way that Millie wasn't used to.

"Always."

"Then trust me. I will keep these people safe after the battle. The sooner you get O'Leary, the more slaves we can save."

She smiled like an idiot.

"This way," Lionel said, walking past her briskly. "A bath will be drawn and some proper attire found. You were not expected, but I'm certain that Captain Rousseau will be far happier with your arrival than who he *had* been expecting."

Keep breathing. Keep breathing.

"I don't understand. These people saved everyone, they let us—"

He was still fast, even drunk. Strong, too. He knocked her down, but he had done that so often before that it meant nothing. Millie pushed herself back up to her feet, like he had taught her.

"They're slaves, they mean nothing," Rousseau said, voice slurring.

He hit her again.

She got back up.

"We promised them," she said, spitting blood from her mouth. "I promised them."

"And now they learn that the promise of an elf is worth nothing." He lashed out again, and this time, she didn't let him hit her. The guards came running as he screamed, her knife buried in his shoulder.

"Treason!" he screamed. "Lock her up. Away from the rest."

She should have killed him.

Lionel disappeared once they were inside, and the goons led her to a fortified room. There was a violin there, a bed and vanity that held various cosmetic tins. It was lived in, but there was no sign of its occupant. Looking around, Millie noticed that there were no windows and only the one door that led out of the room. Fred had only grown more paranoid, it seemed.

Millie hummed another lullaby to the little girl in her arms, holding her tight. She turned Sarah away from the little bin filled with bloodied tissues and waited, facing the guards.

She was back in a cellar.

Everyone else was dead. All her contacts in Beaulieu. Her friends. All the orcish mages in the field. Millie wished she had died there too, before she had been returned to the cellar. Before she was reminded how hunger ate away at your belly until it burned.

Before the scars.

Fred loved the scars. He said that they would tell anyone who she really was if she escaped. He loved reminding her of what she had done during the war. Loved promising that when she learned to be good again, that she could leave the cellar.

Millie had promised herself that she would never be 'good' again. And that, unlike the promises to the slaves in Beaulieu, the promises to Fred and the promises to any gods or spirits that might exist, was a promise she intended to keep.

A bath of hot water was drawn, and a dress found that was nearly her size. One of the servants tried to take Sarah, but Millie caught the woman's hand before it could reach her.

"She stays with me," she said, quiet and low. "Or I snap your wrist like a twig. Do you understand?"

The servant nodded, face pale and sweaty. Lionel must have told her who Millie was. Instead of arguing, the servant hurried away, eager to get out of the room.

"Let's get ourselves cleaned up, Miss storm cloud," Millie murmured to the girl in her arms. "I bet those old tears feel icky."

"This is your last chance to prove to me that you still love me," Fred said, holding her by the chin. His fingers dug into her jaw, and it hurt. There was no more softness to her cheeks, no fat left on her emaciated body. The only reason her muscles hadn't atrophied was that he still insisted on training, even as she starved.

"I promise," she whispered, desperate for the meal the mission would bring. For the chance to see daylight again, and feel a breeze in her hair. "Please."

"Good. No Survivors, or you'll find yourself back here, no meals. No water. Nothing."

She trembled, nodding in his hand like the beaten puppy she was.

Millie remembered everything, and hadn't realised she had started to cry until a little girl's hand reached up to wipe away the tears.

"I'm sorry," Millie whispered, smiling at Sarah as she scrubbed away the dirt and tears from both of them. "Can you keep a secret?" Wide, serious eyes watched her, and then Sarah nodded. Millie leaned in to whisper into the little girl's ear.

"I have two little girls, and I miss them very much," she said, "Just like you must miss your Papa."

The Colfield manor was grander than the Rousseau home. There were dogs, but Fred had promised that they would be taken care of before they arrived.

The hallways were wide enough for a full military parade to pass through, and the portraits of long-dead rich men and women watched as the assassins crept through the home.

Of all the rooms, Millie stepped into the room of the youngest daughter, Rhiannon. And that night, everything changed.

"He's mean," Sarah whispered. "Rousseau. He hit Grandpa *Tata*."

Clean, dressed in a pale pink gown that was too long for her, Millie smoothed the scowl on Sarah's face.

"I know," she whispered. "But I'm going to make sure he doesn't hurt you or Grandpa *Tata* again, okay?" She kissed a chubby cheek and wiped away the last tear on Sarah's face. "I promised your Papa and now I'm promising you."

A heavy knock on the door announced that their small respite was up. Millie gathered Sarah up onto her hip and lifted the borrowed dress's skirts with her spare hand. The small knife that had been tucked into her boot was now stowed in her bodice, warm against her skin like a second heart.

The Cycle of pain and evil ended tonight, even if Millie died breaking it.

"You almost look presentable," Lionel said, hands clasped behind his back as he waited in the hallway. "I suppose it will have to do. Come, we'll be late."

38

GHOSTS

"Hello Fred."

Millie stepped into the parlour, holding Sarah on her hip and stroking the little girl's back to keep her calm. The manor was bare, and only certain rooms were decorated at all. They were a sad shadow of the old manor in Marigot, where paintings in gilt frames hung on most walls, and everything was upholstered in plush velvet.

Fred's current parlour was one such room. Velvet horsehair sofas were spotless, but threadbare. The orman rug underfoot was worn thin and sun-faded.

Standing in the middle of the parlour with a crystal decanter clutched tight in his hand, stood Frederic *fucking* Rousseau. He wore a pressed formal suit that strained at his waist where a sash wrapped around him in a poor effort to hide the fact his shirt could no longer close at the bottom. His temples were greyed now, his moustache and beard freshly trimmed, but his hair was still full of grease and soot from Scorched Bluffs.

He watched her with jaundiced eyes, his swollen face going slack. For a moment, she wavered as her body pulled toward him from a lifetime of conditioning.

"Grandpa *tata*!" The little girl in Millie's arms squirmed and kicked until Millie set her down. The little girl ran across the room and threw herself into the lap of an old man that Millie hadn't noticed. He looked older than in the photo Gilbert had, and the bruises along one side of his face did him no favours. But the look he sent Millie as Sarah buried herself into his arms was grateful, if confused.

There were others in the room as well. A slight elf with blonde hair that sat by a harpsichord, hands in her lap. She watched Millie with a mixture of envy and hatred, a strangely familiar feeling that Millie herself once had felt whenever other women were near Frederic.

"I was certain that the dragon—" Fred closed the distance between them with two large strides, and swept Millie up into his arms. Bloated and softened with drink, he was still impossibly strong. The embrace was crushing, and Millie flinched away from the smell of bourbon on his breath and nausea rose up, hot in her throat.

Kill him. Kill him, Kill him, Kill him, Kill him.

She couldn't move, even as he relaxed his hold on her and set her back on her feet. Her body wouldn't work, her hands gripping handfuls of the too-large dress and trembling so badly she was certain she would only drop anything she grabbed.

It was hard to breathe. She could still feel the crushing pressure in her lungs, even after Fred had let her go. Hitches kept interrupting her breaths, and worst of all... her eyes had started to well up.

She didn't want to let him see her cry. He had too many years of this, of making her feel weak and worthless. She'd escaped him, been free. He shouldn't have this kind of power over her anymore.

But he did, she realised. He had her frozen in place.

His touch was gentle as he cupped her cheeks, wiping away the tears that rolled down. He smelled like he used to. The spicy soap he used to shave every morning nearly drowned under the stale stink of alcohol on his breath.

"I missed you, too," he murmured. "I was crushed when you left. I made stupid decisions." She was trembling. Not just her hands now, but her whole body. "I tried to replace you, to heal," He smiled, lips wet.

"Then the Messiah brought you back to me. You are such a strong girl, Mildred. I don't know what I was thinking." He let go of her cheeks and reached into his coat.

She couldn't breathe. This was it.

Fred pulled the revolver from his pocket and turned, squeezing off a shot. The elf at the harpsichord cried out, slumping back and then falling off the bench with a whimper. Fred fired a second shot, and the whimpering stopped.

"I could never replace you," he said, turning back to her. "There was only ever one Mildred Argent."

"Berry," she forced out, the sob locked in her throat choking her. She couldn't breathe. Her hands twisted in her skirts, balled into tight fists that were useless against him. He didn't even have to lift a finger against her. She was helpless. Useless.

"I'm Mildred *Berry*." But no, that wasn't right anymore, was it? She sniffed aggressively, reaching up and wiping away the tears with the heel of her hand. She was angry, furious, and she was stuck in place. The words helped, though, and she leaned into them.

"I'm Mildred Berry, daughter of Mathis Berry." It would have made far more of an impact if she wasn't crying, but her body wasn't responding right now. It was difficult enough to get the words out.

Fred watched her, a half-amused smile on his face. But the smile faded as he realized that she wasn't joking, and she wasn't going to apologize for speaking up. His face darkened, flushed with fury and murder in his eyes. There he was. The real Frederic Rousseau.

"No," he said with strained patience. She could see the veins in his neck pop out of the softness that drink gave him. "That *was* your name. Before I bought you."

"Why'd you try to kill him?" Millie interrupted. "The banker. He didn't know a thing when he showed up." She watched

Fred's jaw flex, and Millie knew she was reaching the limits of his matchstick patience. But she had to know, and he used to tell her everything. Maybe he would tell her one last secret.

"A favour for a friend. Goldman never could keep it in his pants. My friend didn't want him around after finding out Goldman fucked his fiancée." He took a deep breath, and Millie watched his nostrils flare. They were red, irritated.

"Well," Millie said, choking out her words. "I don't appreciate you shooting my husband." Seeing him, smelling him, had brought back old habits. But. She wasn't his pet anymore. She was Mildred Berry, dragon killer. Mildred Berry, mother of two. Mildred Berry, protector of the Goldman family.

Mildred Berry lifted her chin, looking at Fred with as much defiance as she could muster. If she could provoke him, maybe her body would break out of this horrible stasis. Maybe the Goldmans could get to safety. Maybe she could keep her promise to Gilbert.

"You bitch," Fred said, and raised his free hand. He was still strong, still fast... but he had grown sloppy over the years. He telegraphed his strike, and Millie was able to force herself forward and under his swing.

She threw a haymaker, knowing that Fred wouldn't give her the same opportunity twice. She was too short to land a solid strike on his jaw, so she aimed a few inches lower and slammed her fist into the softness of his throat. He stepped back, dropping the revolver on the carpet as he reached up to claw at his throat. The gun, hammer cocked, went off on impact. It blew a hold into the wall next to her.

Scrambling forward, Millie grabbed the revolver. Three bullets left. She cocked the hammer back and the parlour door burst open behind her. Turning, she squeezed off two shots, taking down Fred's guards, who had rushed in. One left.

"Can you run?" She asked the old man, her breathing still catching on every rib. She forced herself to take as deep a breath as she could to slow her racing heart. She couldn't lose her head right now, or everyone here would die.

"I'll have to," the elder Goldman said, standing and gathering his granddaughter tight against him.

On the floor, Fred was trying to pull himself upright, hands at his throat. Millie knew she could kill him right there and then. There would never be a better chance... but that would leave her empty. Millie checked the two men she had just shot, but they only had nightsticks.

"Follow me as quickly and quietly as you can," she said to Gilbert's father. Little Sarah was watching her with eyes puffy from tears, but the tiny thing nodded bravely. Millie returned the nod and gathered up the ungodly amount of skirts in one hand. With a last glance at Gilbert's father that tried to convey the promise she'd made, Millie stepped out into the hallway.

Lionel was running toward them, flanked by more of the dusty and haggard men from Scorched Bluffs. Spotting her, they dodged to either side of the hallway, flattening themselves against the walls. There was nothing to hide behind in the manor, only a stray console table or vase. Neither of which would stop a bullet.

Glancing up, Millie spotted the gas light between her and the men. Hissing as it lit the empty hallway. She raised the gun and fired.

The lamp exploded, the bullet punching through the gas line and letting the fuel escape with a menacing *hiss*.

"Out the front, go!" Millie shouted, grabbing the elder Goldman's arm and hauling him along with her toward where she hoped the foyer would be. The Marigot manor was tattooed into her brain, but Millie had only known this building's cellar.

Behind her, the escaping gas reached one of the other gas lamps. Heat flashed along Millie's back and stinging the still-unhealed burns on her ear and neck from the dragon. Shouts of alarm and one of pain told her that most of the men behind her were held back. Good.

She glanced over her shoulder and saw a bright gout of flame was shooting out into the hallway. Lionel and the others were on the far side of it and would have to find another way around or risk serious burns. That bought them time. Hopefully, it would be enough.

The coach was a little full, but somehow everyone fit inside and Ryan's dog trotted along outside. Sitting next to Sweetpea, who held a bundle of cloth to herself, Hal tried very hard not to think about how terrified Sarah must be. Deputy Berry was with her, though. Deputy Berry was a mother. Hal hoped she could spare the little girl from the worst of the trauma that would happen tonight.

"Have you been inside Rousseau's home?" Rhiannon asked Arnaud. She'd been peppering the poor man with questions since they climbed into the coach.

"No, Madam, I have not. Only to the door where I would peel that drunk bastard out of the carriage and guide him to his door. He would not allow a 'greenskin' to enter his home, you see."

Everyone inside the coach frowned.

"Millie said that Rousseau used to pretend to be more drunk than he really was," Rhiannon said. "People let down their guard, make it easier for him to get the upper hand. He's awful. I know it was her idea to go in there, but I'm worried about her." The woman scowled, looking down at her hands clasped in her lap.

"She'll be okay," Sweetpea said quietly, tugging at the knots of rope that held the bundle closed. "This is *Millie*."

"And this is Frederic Rousseau," Rhiannon countered. "She never told anyone about how we met." Hal watched as the

Sheriff looked out the window of the carriage. He realized, far too late, that Rousseau must live near to the Colfield Manor.

"Rousseau had kept her in a cellar for a year, maybe more," Rhiannon said. "She was fed, watered, but forced to train until she was skin and bones. She was only let out to kill me, but... she didn't. She risked her life to get me out of there and spent the next six years keeping me safe and training us how to survive. If she was facing anyone else, I wouldn't be worried... but some wounds are soul deep." Rhiannon took a deep breath and held it for a moment, slowly letting it out.

"He just has a way of getting inside her head," she whispered. "I don't want that to happen again."

"May I ask a question?" Arnaud said, after a long moment of silence. "Who *are* you? The elf, you two ladies?"

Hal held up a hand, stalling any explanation.

"Looks like we're here," he said. "Miss Sweetpea, what do you have in that bundle of yours?"

Next to him, Sweetpea smiled and pulled out her sword. The air grew fizzy and tasted strange, like a storm was brewing. Hal blinked and felt the little arroyan's thumb pressed to his forehead.

Murmuring a minor spell, Sweetpea released her touch, and the coach grew bright as daylight. Like the spell she had cast on him and Gilbert before, she'd given him the ability to see in darkness.

"Ry!" she said, leaning over to do the same for Rhiannon.

"The Rousseau Residence," the coachman announced, slowing the carriage to a stop. "Good Messiah what is-" Hal glanced out the coach window to see a bloom of light inside the manor, lighting up several of the first storey windows. It seemed to have come from deep within the home, still a hundred or more yards from the road where the coach pulled to a stop.

Without Sweetpea's gift, Hal wouldn't have seen Fyodor take off toward the home, turning into a streak of muscle and teeth.

"I see she's already gotten started," Hal said, opening the coach door and hopping down. It seemed wherever Berry went, things caught fire. He turned back to help Sweetpea, only to find her pressing a revolver into his hand before she hopped down on her own, eyes glowing faintly golden.

"Find Millie and the girl first," Ryan said, following the arroyan. She held one of Berry's tomahawks and her rifle. Her pupils were dilated from Sweetpea's spell, making her eyes look almost black. "We deal with Rousseau after they're safe."

Arnaud followed; eyes wide.

"Can you fight?" Hal asked, catching the man's elbow.

"For Sarah? Of course I can fight."

Millie had not found the foyer. What she had found, instead, was a guest apartment, completely bare aside from a single chest that she immediately shoved under the door to slow Fred's men from breaking it down.

"Hi," she whispered to the elder Goldman and little Miss Sarah. "I'm Millie." She undid the skirts around her waist and threw them aside, peeling off the overly large bodice with stupidly poufy sleeves and hurried over to look out the apartment's windows.

"After this is all over," the old man huffed, stroking his granddaughter's hair, "I would like to know how my son befriended a murderous elf, of all people."

"Married a murderous elf, actually," Millie muttered. "It was for legal reasons, don't worry," she added, heaving open a window. Outside were overgrown gardens, a much better option than being trapped inside. An explosion boomed from somewhere deep inside the manor. The gas lines were starting to fail.

"*What.*"

Millie smiled at the old man and hopped out of the window. She lifted her hands up to take Sarah, visible over the windowsill. The drop itself was, at most, six feet. More than enough for her to not be able to see into the building.

"You, miss, have a *lot* of explaining to do," the old man said, scowling as he appeared at the window, passing the little girl down to Millie. Sarah fussed until Millie held her close, kissing soft cheeks as she ducked low and waited for Gilbert's father to climb down. It took a little longer, but for an old man, Mister Goldman was remarkably spry.

"He's watching my daughters," Millie whispered once he was safely out of the building. "We made a promise to keep each other's family safe. I'm here to uphold my half."

There was a row of hedges in the garden, flanking a fountain and strips of lavender. They were thick enough to provide some cover from prying eyes.

"We're going to run over to that, okay?" She said to the old man. "You go first. I'll keep an eye out for anyone."

The old man nodded and took Sarah back. Millie tried not to notice how the little girl grabbed onto her camisole tightly to hold on. Gently, Millie freed herself from Sarah's hands.

Something massive and dark was sprinting towards them. On instinct, Millie threw herself in between it and the two Goldmans, covering Sarah with her body. But instead of crushing teeth, she felt a wet nose shove into the crook of her neck, quickly followed by whines and desperate licks.

"Fyodor! Oh, you're a wonderful boy!" she whispered, throwing her arms around him. The mastiff licked her face, nearly knocking the three humanoids over with his happiness. Fyodor. That meant Rhiannon was nearby. That meant safety.

"The cavalry's here," Millie said, helping the elder Goldman right himself. "We head for the road."

39

COLFIELD MANNERS

"CAREFUL," RY SHOUTED OVER her shoulder as she strode across the lawn toward Rousseau's manor. She pulled her rifle from her shoulder and chambered a round with a satisfying click-clack. "I think this place is lit by gas."

Hal looked up at the windows that were glowing orange, and sniffed the air, catching the hint of the acrid smoke escaping the manor. It smelled more like the trainyard than the wood-smoke clinging to his suit from Scorched Bluffs. Hell. Even dragonfire smelled better than gas fire did. But gas had properties that were worse than its smell.

A dull boom from deep within the house confirmed Ry's guess and Hal's thoughts. The small group watched as the windows glowed brightly before slowly fading to a flickering orange. As Hal watched, the crackle of flames grew louder.

"Do you think Millie is still in there?" Sweetpea asked, her voice nervous. She'd sidled up to Hal, fiddling with the cord on her sword's sheath.

"Anyone else, and I'd say no," Rhiannon said, settling her rifle on her shoulder. "But this is the man who trained her. I don't know, 'Pea," she said with a small sigh. "We'd better see if there's anyone we can help."

Help? This was a household that had kidnapped a three-year-old girl, a household that had trained a war criminal, one that- Hal had to shake off the sudden need for vengeance. Ry was right. Not everyone in that manor would be guilty. Maids, stewards, cooks, and more, they weren't at fault for what their master had done.

"Miss Sweetpea, can you do something about the fire?" Hal asked, breaking into a jog toward the building.

"I can try," came her reply. "It'll take some time."

For a moment, the air crackled, and Hal was certain he could smell thunder. Glancing back, he saw that Miss Sweetpea had drawn her sword and whispered a spell over the blade.

"As much as I understand the allure of magic," Arnaud said, catching up to Hal. The half-orc grabbed his shoulder and forcibly turned Hal back toward the burning building. "We need to find little Sarah. She must be terrified."

Hal nodded and looked back toward the manor, spotting figures running from the sides and front door, some flailing at flames that had caught on their sleeves or pant legs. It wasn't only about Sarah.

Hal ran toward the nearest figure, a maid whose skirt was on fire. He whipped off his vest, using it to smother the flame. But there were others coming, and despite Sweetpea's spell, it was difficult to see who was a servant and who was a soldier that had tried to take Scorched Bluffs. There was too much soot, and most of the people escaping had been wearing plain clothes rather than a uniform.

"Get to the road!" Hal shouted, gently pushing the maid toward safety. He turned to find who he could help next and was greeted with a raised nightstick and the furious, burnt face of a man.

The man flexed, ready to bring the nightstick down, but a hand grabbed it from behind, stopping any momentum the stick had well before the man could apply it. Hal watched the man's expression change to confusion. The nightstick was twisted away and smashed into the soldier's head, knocking him down.

"Do *not* tell the Goldmans," Arnaud said, kicking the dazed man away. "I refuse to do the job of three men for the pay of one."

"You haven't spent much time with Gilbert's new wife, have you?" Hal asked. He *highly* doubted that the Goldmans would bother paying for security when Gilbert had just married the most notorious war criminal of the century. Still, Arnaud deserved a raise for all he did.

"The grubby elf?" Arnaud asked, confused.

"Don't... don't call her that to her face," Hal suggested, patting Arnaud on the shoulder.

A dark shape sprinted past them, ears back and white teeth bared. Hal turned to watch it leap onto a man who staggered out of the front door, wearing a long and battered coat. The dog—Rhiannon's dog—grabbed onto the man's arm and threw his massive head back and forth, tearing into bone and muscle.

"Arnaud?"

Both Hal and Arnaud turned toward the old man's voice. Avrom was holding tight to Sarah, who had buried her face into her grandfather's shoulder. Behind them, dressed in a shift and corset, was deputy Berry.

"Get them to safety," she shouted at Hal, grabbing the revolver from his hand, freeing it with a twist that seemed effortless. A quiet part of his brain thought that disarming a Stratton should pose more difficulty, but the rest screamed to help Avrom away from the burning building.

"Come on," he said, looping Avrom's arm over his shoulders. "You're safe now."

"I doubt it!" Avrom panted. "My idiot son married that harpy elf!"

Hal thought about explaining, but now was not the time. Instead, he nodded and helped Avrom hurry back to the road where the coach waited and where onlookers had started to gather.

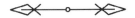

Millie raced over to Rhiannon, cocking the hammer back on her revolver, recently liberated from Hal. A last glance over her shoulder told her that Sarah and Gil's father were being helped away from the fire. That was good enough.

"Fyodor, *sit*," Millie shouted. At once, the mastiff let go of the man's arm and sat down on the human's back, tail wagging furiously.

"Millie?" Ry swept her up into a crushing hug, one that was returned immediately and just as intensely. "Are you alright?"

"Yeah," Millie mumbled into her friend's shoulder. "But my coat..."

A thin man staggered over to them and tried to pull Fyodor off of Fred. Millie squeezed off a single round and Lionel fell, grabbing his leg and screaming in pain.

"That's him?" Rhiannon asked, looking at the man under Fyodor.

"That's him," Millie answered.

In the distance, the wail of the fire brigade and the Wyndford Police force was growing closer. Millie's heart was in her throat, and she knew that whatever decision she made needed to be made soon. Before the men that were tucked into Fred's pocket arrived and took over.

"Frederic Rousseau," she said, forcing her voice to be strong. "You are under arrest for the unwarranted assault on the town of Scorched Bluffs, resulting in the death of innocents."

Ry joined in, bolstering Millie's voice with her own. She motioned for Fyodor to get off the man, and they continued.

"You also are under arrest for the kidnapping of one Sarah Goldman and her grandfather. You are under arrest for the torture and entrapment of one Mildred Berry and the murder of an unknown elf. You may hereby submit to the law, or face execution."

Frederic Rousseau groaned and wheezed, begging Millie for a second chance. If she'd just take him back, they could have everything. When she didn't reply, the entreaties turned to insults.

Millie stood still, heartbeat thudding in her ears. She could squeeze the trigger, and he'd be gone. No more people hurt, nor more little girls growing up without fathers because of him. No more nightmares about cellars.

"It's your call," Rhiannon told her, and looked away.

Millie shifted her aim and fired. Fred screamed as the bullet punched through his ankle. He wouldn't walk again without feeling an ache, a reminder of the evil he'd done. It wasn't enough. But if Millie killed him, no one would learn the truth. Taking a deep breath, Millie stepped forward and stomped on the shattered ankle as hard as she could.

Fred screamed, eyes rolling back as he blacked out from the pain. She wanted to stomp on him again, over and over, until he begged for forgiveness, until he admitted what he'd done. Feeling ill, Millie stepped back and wiped Fred's blood from her foot on the lawn.

"Murderers!" Lionel shouted, clutching his leg to his chest. "I saw it! *Murder!*"

"Oh, shut up, Lenny," Millie snapped. "He's still alive."

"Do you know who I am?" Rhiannon asked, loading another round into her rifle.

"Why would I care about you?" But Lionel's words faltered as he looked up at Ry's face for the first time. His despair was sweeter than Millie had ever dreamed of, but she rested a hand on Ryan's rifle, and slowly pressed it down, away from the man.

"Rhiannon Colfield," Millie said, eyes fixed on Fred's former steward. "Heir to the Colfield fortune and the woman who can decide your fate if you choose to testify on her behalf. Or, she could shoot you right now, and never face charges."

Lionel's eyes flicked from the two women to Fyodor, who was scratching at his ear. The mastiff paused, hindfoot still up in the air, and growled a warning. Millie felt her lips twitch into a smile. People didn't deserve dogs.

Millie's ears lifted in attention at the soft, distant cry of a little girl. Sarah. She glanced over her shoulder toward the road, then to Ry.

"I've got this," Rhiannon told her. "We drew up a warrant before leaving. Go."

The smile broke through, and Millie squeezed Ry's arm. "You're wonderful," she said, already heading toward the road, and the crying girl.

Behind her, Millie heard Ry promise Lionel she was the less forgiving of the two, and Millie didn't try to stifle her laugh as she heard Fred's steward surrender. But. Two realizations hit her as she hurried over to the Goldmans. The first was that Fred, Frederic *fucking* Rousseau, was finally going to face justice for all his crimes. The second was that regardless of all he'd done, of the proof that they had found, Millie would be required to testify. Millie's mirth faltered as she approached the elder Goldman and little Sarah.

To her surprise, the little girl spotted her through her tears and reached out, pudgy hands grasping for safety. The grandfather looked offended, but he still passed her over to Millie, who embraced the little girl, wrapping her arms around her and humming a soothing lullaby.

The rest of the night was a blur. Firemen and police officers arrived like ants on a picnic as Sweetpea's spell took hold. Cold rain poured down on the ruined manor and everyone near it. Soon as it started, Millie bundled up little Sarah into the coach that was still waiting on the road. The driver kindly pulled out a blanket to wrap around her and the little girl to keep them warm.

A police officer came to talk to her, flanked by a grim-faced Rhiannon and scowling Goldman Senior.

"Detective Stratton and I will be going to the Police station," Ry said, the rain bouncing off the brim of her hat. "We'll meet you at the Goldman house once we're done. Mister Avrom has kindly offered us shelter there for the night."

Ah, Avrom! That was his name. Millie looked at the scowling man and tried to smile appreciatively. He glared at her, but the expression softened as he looked down at the little girl nestled in Millie's arms.

"We're all exhausted, and you got us out of that hellhole," Avrom said, climbing into the coach. "It's the least I could do. Besides, your friend here is going to need someone to help her with that inheritance she's got coming!"

Millie looked at Rhiannon, who smiled.

"Do you need me to come to the station?" Millie asked.

"No, ma'am," the police officer said, tipping his hat, and inadvertently sending a stream of water down its brim. He shook it awkwardly, then placed it back on his head. "We'll come round to Mister Goldman's home in the morning. You take care of your little one and um," the man, a young thing, blushed. "Find some decent—I mean dry!—find yourself some dry clothing."

Millie glanced down at the shift she was wearing, only then remembering that city folk had *ideas* about propriety. How long had it been since she actually was part of normal society? Before the war started, if Marigot could even be counted as 'normal'.

"Pea will meet you at the house," Ryan said, closing the door to the coach. "They need the rain a little while longer so the fire doesn't spread."

Before long, the coach was bouncing along the cobbled streets, and exhaustion began to set in. Eyes drooping, Millie leaned back, letting out a slow, shaky breath.

"Married, eh?" Avrom said, shaking Millie out of her drowsiness. "He wasn't gone long enough to get you pregnant. Least that you know of. So, what'd you do to him? Drug him?"

"No, I didn't—okay, I did drug him once, but not like that," Millie said, ears flicking in embarrassment. "I have two little girls at home, a little older than your granddaughter. When Rousseau found out where I was, everything went to hell."

"And that's another question, but it can wait," Avrom huffed. He leaned forward, reaching out to stroke back some strands of hair from Sarah's face. She'd fallen asleep before the police officer had arrived and shown no signs of waking up yet.

"We promised to look after the girls, whoever survived. I didn't expect to walk away from this fight. To make sure my girls weren't taken away to be factory workers, we married," Millie pressed her lips together, deeply uncomfortable. It had made sense at the time. "Gilbert got hurt, but he's with the best healers I know. He'll be fine, but I was determined to keep my part of the promise."

Avrom squinted at her, searching her face for any sign of a lie. But... there was none.

"Hah, well," he said, leaning back into his seat. "That's not so terrible. And it can be undone? Presuming he hasn't gotten you pregnant?"

"I am *not* pregnant," Millie said dryly. "Despite your son's charms, there were plenty of other things to worry about than keeping warm at night."

It was hard to tell behind the old man's bushy eyebrows, but Millie thought she saw a small glimmer of surprise. Then again, if Annie hadn't interrupted them in the barn, Avrom might have been right. Millie needed to thank her once she got home. If there was much home left to go back to. The thought of rebuilding the town again was exhausting, and now there was a corpse of a giant dragon in the middle of it.

"You don't want to know about Rousseau?" She asked her new father-in-law.

"I know the stories," Avrom said. "A pale elf that the id-iot Swamp man dressed up all pretty in a horrid dress? No, I don't need to ask. I know who you are." He sniffed, wiping his pince-nez glasses on his collar. "No one better to protect my little Sarah. Don't you dare tell my son that I approve of you. I'll never hear the end of it."

40

LEGACY

THE CONSTABLE HAD BEEN pleasant enough, but now that Hal and Rhiannon were seated in the police station and talking to the Police Chief, Hal doubted the wisdom of going after the most powerful man in Wyndford.

"Do you have any proof of your allegations?" The chief asked, crossing his arms over his chest. They had roused him from sleep, and the man still wore his nightshirt under his uniform. It poked out around his collar, though neither Hal nor Rhiannon had bothered to mention it.

"Multiple forms of it. Would you like me to start by identifying my ancestors back four generations? Five?" Rhiannon asked, voice cool. "Or would you like to take a look at the letters I have in my possession that were sent between Rousseau and Harrold and detail the murder of my family and the attempted murder of Gilbert Goldman?" She smiled; eyes cold.

"Ah, but my dear, histories can be learned and letters can be forged," the Chief said, clearing his throat and tugging his collar. Hal said nothing, watching as faint beads of perspiration glinted on the man's temples. "False allegations of such things are a very serious matter, my dear. Mister Colfield is not a man to take slights upon his person with much... ah... grace."

To the Police Chief's credit, Hal wasn't certain if it was the damning evidence presented that was making him nervous, or if it was the dog that sat tall enough to rest his chin on the table. A small puddle of drool had formed under Fyodor's jowls. The big dog let out a deep sigh, causing the constable in the back to jump slightly. The very presence of a moorland mastiff should have been enough proof for the Chief.

"I have witnesses," Rhiannon said, unlacing her callused hands to reach over and stroke the big dog's head. A steady thump of Fyodor's tail on the floor drew the attention of every police officer in the small room.

"My dear, I'm afraid that dogs are not accepted as witnesses."

"I'm not talking about my *dog*," Rhiannon said, voice sharp and cold. "I'm talking about the assassin Rousseau sent to kill me, who has no reason to lie about why she was there. She's never met *Uncle Harry*," the Police Chief cringed at the familiarized use of Harrold Colfield's name. "And if you call me 'my dear' one more time, I will use my considerable wealth and power to remove you from your office the moment my rights have been restored to me."

Hal hid a chuckle by coughing into his hand. He wasn't sure where the Sheriff had learned her negotiating skills, but he suspected that her late father would be proud. The Colfields had a reputation for ruthlessness in the business world long before Harrold carried the ruthlessness over into their family life. Immediately, Hal's amusement soured.

"Well now, Miss, I think that sounds an awful lot like a threat. I'm not sure you understand that threatening an officer of the law is actually illegal."

"I'm a sheriff," Rhiannon said, opening the flap of her long coat to reveal the shiny star pinned to the inside of her lapel. "Not only am I well versed in the letter of the law, but I have no qualms about running for office here in Wyndford, and just *taking* your job from you by getting the popular vote."

The Police Chief burst into laughter so hard that his eyes began to tear and his entire face turned red, all the way up to his thinning hair. He rubbed at his eyes, laughter turning into wheezes as the man tried to compose himself.

Rhiannon sat still with a chilly, if polite, smile on her face.

"A lady sheriff? Now I've heard everything," the Police Chief wheezed.

"I have an idea," Hal said, speaking for the first time. He was certain if he didn't interrupt, the Chief would end up being savaged by Fyodor. He would deserve it, but it would hardly help Rhiannon's cause. "Why don't I and some of your officers go speak with Mr. Harrold Colfield?" He tried to ignore the icy look sent his way.

"And you are?" The Chief asked, squinting at Hal.

"Detective Hal Stratton, sir." He pulled out the badge Sweetpea had rescued and held it up. It still had a bit of blood in the letters, but that would have to wait until he had the time to clean it properly. "Of—"

"The *Stratton Detective Agency*," the Chief said, voice completely soured. "Wonderful. And this woman hired you?"

"Not at all, sir," Hal said, fixing his badge onto his shirt. "I'm a witness to all of this. Rousseau attempted to kill myself and my client, Gilbert Goldman, on Harrold Colfield's orders. Apparently, 'Uncle Harry' didn't want ex-paramours of his lovely new fiancée around in case she got bored of him. But I'm unable to let an opportunity to resolve such a widely known case pass without offering my help."

Hal knew the look in the Police Chief's eyes. It was that of a trapped man. No doubt the Chief had taken a 'donation' from Harrold Colfield to quash any deep investigation of the murders. It would all come out in the end, though. Of that, Hal was certain. Why else would the Messiah place him here, out of the Priesthood but in the thick of old lies but to cast light on the evils once left buried? Everything that hadn't made sense earlier was falling into place. This was where he belonged, where he could help people the most.

"I will go with another officer, but we cannot simply wake Harrold Colfield at such an hour. We'll go at daybreak," the Chief said, scowling.

The constable, young and awkward, cleared his throat.

"What?" The Chief snapped.

"Sir, it's dawn now, Sir," he said. "We've been talking for hours."

"That sounds lovely," Rhiannon said, smiling at the officers to devastating effect. "Let's go visit Uncle Harry, shall we? But we'll need one more person in our party."

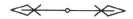

Someone was pounding on the door, and Millie groaned, burying her face into the pillow.

"Ry, no," she mumbled, hugging Fenna closer to her. No doubt Rasha was already up and already hurrying toward the door. "S' too early."

A sleep-soft voice answered. "Who's *'Ry'*?"

Right. Millie didn't have a pillow this soft. She had daughters, but they weren't dark-haired, with serious eyes like the one she opened one eye to see herself holding at that moment. Rubbing the crust from an eye, Millie looked around at the room she was in.

"Ry is my friend. She's very brave." Millie paused, stifling a yawn with the back of her hand. "She's the one with the dog." Slowly she remembered that she'd tried to put Sarah to bed only for the girl to start shrieking in terror. Naturally, she had sung lullabies to soothe the little girl. Apparently, she'd also sung *herself* to sleep.

"Miss Berry, Mister Stratton is here to see you with a disturbingly large number of police officers." A man's voice, one still strange but heard before. It took Millie's sleep-deprived brain to realize who was speaking. "Are you decent?"

"Never," Millie mumbled, pushing herself up to sit on the bed. The gloriously soft bed with a real mattress, not just furs covering a pile of straw. Going back to the cabin would be difficult after this, she thought. Then remembered her cabin had been crushed under falling rocks.

"Should I wait outside then?" The voice asked, slightly nervous. "I have clothes for you."

Millie squinted down at herself. While she'd crawled under the covers at some point last night, she was still in the shift from Fred. The memory made her shudder violently, and she leaned over the side of the bed, gagging.

"Miss, are you okay?"

She felt Sarah's arms press around her from behind, trying to help soothe Millie's own nightmares. She wiped her mouth and turned, offering the little girl a sleepy smile.

"Come in," she said, brushing Sarah's hair back from her forehead. "Miss Storm cloud, it sounds like I have to go do some adult things. Are you okay staying with your grandfather while I'm gone?"

Sarah nodded; big, dark eyes fixed on Millie's face. "But you'll come back, right?" she asked quietly. Her r's still a little too soft, like Rasha's had been until last winter. It tugged at Millie's heart, and she kissed the little forehead.

In the corner of her eye, Millie saw the door to Sarah's room open.

"Of course. Then, we'll go get your papa, and you might even get to meet my little girls too." Millie kissed Sarah's forehead again and slipped out of the bed, grimacing as several days' worth of aches and pains made themselves known.

The half-orc she'd met at the train station waited at the door, a hand over his eyes and a folded bundle of cloth draped over one arm.

"Please tell me you do not need assistance to dress," he said with a long-suffering sigh.

"I need coffee. Do you have some?" She asked, pulling the dress off his arm. It was grey, with a minimum of fancy trim and flounce. It'd do.

"We are no house of heathens, ma'am," the man said with an indignant huff. "I'll go prepare a pot immediately."

A massive dog shouldered the poor man out of the way and ran up to Millie, too excited to know if he wanted pats or to lick her hand. Overloaded, Fyodor leaned into Millie, knocking them both over onto the ground with a painful thud.

From the bed, Sarah gasped. Sensing a new friend, Fyodor was right back up onto his feet and trotted over to the bed.

"Fyodor, *gentle*," Millie warned. But he'd always been so good with her girls, she wasn't worried about him. But for Sarah, after such an ordeal the day before, a dog as big as Fyodor might be overwhelming.

"Is this the one that *saved* us?"

Millie resisted a frown, ready to say that *she* was the one who saved them, actually, and nodded. "The very same. His name is Fyodor."

She grunted, getting up from the floor in time for Ry to find the room where Fyodor had run off to.

"This is 'Ry'," Millie said, rolling her neck to try to pop it back into place. It was stubborn, and she knew it would take a while before her body stopped hurting. "Ry, this is Sarah, Gilbert's daughter."

Fyodor, paws wet from the outside dew and muddy from the Rousseau estate, climbed up onto the little girl's bed carefully. He snuffled at her face and hands before licking her happily, his tail wagging rapidly. The little girl squealed, and Millie saw her arms wrap around the dog's thick neck. Well, they tried to. It would be some time before she was big enough to reach all the way around.

"Fyodor," Ryan said, helping Millie gather the dropped clothing. "Why don't you stay here and guard Miss Sarah until we get back?"

In answer, Fyodor flopped down onto the bed, placing one paw over the tiny girl and whuffed. His tail thumped against the muddied quilt.

"One problem solved," Ry said. "I need your help, Millie. We're going to see my uncle."

"To ki—" Millie glanced at the little girl, who was back to giggling as the big dog washed her. "To 'convince' him to leave the world of the living?" She asked Ryan, peeling off the stained shift from Fred's home.

"No," Ryan said, closing the door behind her. She started undoing the laces of the corset that the half-orc man had brought. "To convince the police that I am who I say I am. And maybe just *punch* uncle Harry. In the face."

"I can do that," Millie said, pulling on the clean shift in the pile of clothing. "But do I have to wear this?" She asked, eying the dress with mistrust.

"Do you have any leggings? Or shirts?" Ryan asked, holding up the corset.

Millie frowned. "No," she admitted, and lifted her hands straight up. Everything she'd had was gone in the fire at Fred's home. Her coat, her leggings, her revolvers.

Dressing didn't take too long. There were fewer layers than there used to be back in Marigot and in Fred's hideous ballgowns. Corset, petticoat, pockets and then the skirt and top. She had no other boots and pulled on her own, still muddy and wet from the night before.

"If you laugh," Millie said, adjusting her hair in a vain attempt to look fierce, "I will disown you."

Rhiannon, biting her lip, nodded. "It's just, I've never seen you all *proper*," she wheezed. "You look like a lady. Aside from the hair, and the glaring," she added. "Pea brought what's left of your coat. It's in the parlour downstairs."

Millie glared at her friend, ready to complain. Instead, she stepped forward and pulled Rhiannon into a tight hug, burying her face in the other woman's shoulder. "I was so scared," she whispered. "I couldn't-"

Rhiannon's arms wrapped around her, holding her close. "It's okay. He's locked up now. One down–"

"One to go," Millie answered. "Okay." She took a deep breath and smelled the first hint of coffee brewing. "Okay. Coffee, then let's go finish teaching old men not to fuck with us."

A gasp reminded Millie they weren't alone.

"You said a bad word!" Sarah said, peering over Fyodor's paw.

"Don't tell your papa, okay?" Millie said with a nervous smile, hurrying to the door. "We'll be back soon."

As they exited, Ry laughed. "Adopting more little girls, are we?"

Millie declined to answer.

All Ry's teasing about being dressed well was worth it when Millie watched the doors to the Colfield Manor open, and the butler's expression of recognition as he looked at Ry. The elf let a smug smile spread over her face as she glanced back at the extremely sweaty Police Chief.

As Rhiannon and Hal entered first, Millie stepped up to the Chief's side and leaned in. "You're so fucked," she purred. He had realised who she was the moment she entered the Goldman parlour. Since that moment, Millie had made a point of making the chief as uncomfortable as she could.

"After you, sir," she said a little louder, sweeping into a curtsey. If she had to wear skirts, she was going to make everyone suffer for it. "Humans first."

"Miss Rhiannon? Is that you?"

"Good morning, Murphy," Rhiannon said, sweeping her hat off. She greeted the butler with a squeeze of his hands. "It's been too long. Would you mind making us some coffee? Uncle Harry and I have *so much* to talk about."

Turning to the police chief, Rhiannon smiled, bright and sharp. Pride welled up in Millie's chest at the sight. Ry had grown up into a powerful woman. Wyndford high society wasn't ready for her, and Millie was thrilled.

"Now, shall we?" Rhiannon asked, winking at Millie.

"After you," the elf said, doing her best attempt at a curtsey.

Rhiannon strode past the Butler, walking into her home like she owned the damn place. Her boots clicked on the marble floor, and Rhiannon shook her hair out of her braid. Hair loose, eyes sharp, Ryan slipped the rifle from her shoulder and chambered a round, letting the click echo through the home.

"Harrold Colfield," she bellowed. "Get the hell out of my house!"

41

LULLABIES, AT LAST

OVER THE LAST FEW days, Gilbert had realised why Eyota called Millie's daughters 'chaos spirits'. As he healed and moved around more, their desire for stories and attention only grew. Fenna had brought him a bucket of live salamanders, all lulled to sleep by her singing. Rasha had gone through every item he and Hal had in town, and not even Auntie Annie could get them to behave for long.

They were polite, though, and *terribly* endearing.

Word had come back that the venture to Wyndford had gone remarkably well. The Sheriff was now an heiress who had begun the process of transferring her investments to the Goldman National Bank, his father was in good health and only ominously referred to Gilbert's 'wife' as a 'remarkable addition to the family', and Hal reported that he was entering the running to take over as Wyndford Police Chief.

Things seemed to be going far too well, but the illusion only lasted until Gilbert and the Marshal tried to corral the two chaos Berrys on the long ride to Plainfield. Eyota had said they would stay behind to help rebuild, but Gilbert wondered if they would return to their clan before long. They seemed far more interested in learning more about how the delightful Miss Sweetpea could summon storms strong enough to kill dragons.

"So," Gilbert said, riding the black stallion Hal had bought back in Plainfield. It was a majestic animal, and he was growing deeply attached. "One last time. What are we *not* going to tell your mama about?"

"That we caught salamanders!" Fenna said happily from her perch on Berry's mule. Behind her, the little redhead grinned.

"That we caught a rattlesnake!"

"Or that we maybe found eggs," Fenna added, which was new to Gilbert. He twisted in the saddle and hissed as his hip protested.

"*What* eggs?" He asked.

At the rear, Marshal Allan was frowning. This was news to him, too. *How in the world did Millie manage these two on her own?!* Clearly, she needed help, and it was the least he could do to provide it. He owed her town a great deal, and Gilbert wasn't one to ignore his debts.

"In the dragon!" Rasha answered, holding her hands up to show how large the eggs were.

"What do you mean '*in the dragon*'?" Allan asked, his face growing pale.

"Cousin Eyota was cutting its skin off, and we poked around and found eggs. They're as big as Freckle!" The little pup barked happily from his saddlebag, this time with the flap tucked inside so he could watch the world go by.

"Let's add that to the list of 'do not tell your mother'," Gilbert said. He paused, then squinted at the two little elves. "You don't have any of those eggs with you, *do you*?" He had learned to ask the hard way. Always ask. God above and below, the elves were wonderful but also going to give him grey hair before he was thirty.

The little girls looked at each other. Not a good sign.

"Alright, we're almost to Plainfield," Gilbert said, rubbing the bridge of his nose. "When we get there, we'll need to take all the dragon eggs out of our bags, okay?" He tried not to think about how, after everything settled, these two little tornadoes would be gone from his life. Maybe he could help finance the rebuilding of Scorched Bluffs and visit. Sarah would enjoy having a few friends her age.

"Okay," two sad little elves said.

They arrived in Plainfield at midday. Grateful to get out of the harsh sun, Gilbert took the little girls to the hotel for some food and water while the Marshal managed the horses. The poor man had been shaken terribly when the two Berry girls started asking what his intentions toward 'Auntie Ry' were.

The Saloon was full, but as he entered, one little girl on his good hip and the other holding his hand and a fluffy puppy trailing behind, Gilbert noticed that the place went silent. The patrons stared at him, frozen to a one. Rather than letting it bother him, Gilbert put on his brightest smile and walked the Berries over to an empty table.

Diamond rushed over; eyes wide.

"Mister Goldman!" she said, smiling broadly. "Is this her? Rasha?"

"You look like *Lyddie*," Rasha said, climbing up into Gilbert's lap. Fenna watched from her chair, staring at the woman with haunted gold eyes. The puppy sat by her feet, vibrating from wagging his tail so much.

Gilbert watched the waitress grow pale, even though her smile stayed in place. "That's my sister," she said. "Lyddie's my—"

"You left my sister with *momma*," Fenna said, cutting into the conversation with a surprising coldness for a four-year-old. It might have surprised Gilbert, but he'd learned the small blonde elf knew things sometimes. Like how everyone in Wyndford was safe, well before the telegram arrived. Eyota had mentioned the pale colouring of Ghost Clan elves meant they were closer to the spirits, and Fenna had her mother's hair.

Diamond's mouth fell open, and she stared at Fenna. "Did your momma tell you that?" she asked Fenna. Now that Rasha was in the same room as Diamond, Gilbert could see the resemblance. She had Diamond's hair and freckles, but Millie's sharpness.

"You left her and said it was because you wanted money," Fenna continued. "We told Jeb. We told him that."

And just like that, Gilbert learned what it felt like to be evicted from a saloon. He bought some snacks at the general store and met Allan at the train station, settling a four-year-old elf on each knee and a puppy at his feet.

The train ride was peaceful compared to the chaotic days spent riding from Scorched Bluffs to Plainfield. The rocking of the train car lulled the little girls to sleep, which left Gilbert free to try not to think about how the dragon had so easily taken down the Stonecreek overnight. Or about how big the dragon had been. Or about how his tiny murder-wife and her similarly tiny friend had killed it.

"Allan," he whispered, looking at the Marshal who sat across from him. "How wise do you think it would be to annul a marriage with a dragon slayer?"

The marshal stared back and silently shook his head.

"Yeah," Gilbert said with a sigh, leaning back and looking down at the two little girl elves asleep in his lap. "That was my thought, too. I hope she agrees."

There could be worse wives, he thought. Bianca, who discarded her daughter like a bundle of trash. Diamond, who abandoned hers for the promise of money. Even his own mother, who had left her son on the steps of a church. Marriages were more of a business arrangement than about feelings, and Gilbert knew Millie would fight to the death to protect her daughters. She'd faced her own personal demon to keep Sarah safe.

"Are you going to ask the Sheriff?" He asked, looking back up at Allan. "To marry you, I mean."

"I don't know," the Marshal admitted. "She's an heiress now. Noble, there'll be plenty of suitors better suited—sorry. I didn't mean to make a pun." Allan sighed, looking glum. Gilbert understood the rules of society, even if he didn't understand the need to follow all of them. Hell, by taking an elf as a wife, he himself had accepted that his own social standing would be affected. Then again, his wife was a notorious war criminal, which would help offset things.

"You love her though, right?" He asked. "Tell her. Sheriff Coll- Colfield isn't some social climber. You loved her when she was nothing. A woman like that can tell," Gilbert said with a confidence meant to convince himself as much as to convince Allan. "If she says no, at least you know you've tried."

Gilbert watched as the Marshal thought, scratching his chin. He was smarter than he looked and certainly smarter than he acted. Gilbert had learned as much over the last few weeks. It was a good lesson that one could only infer a certain amount of judgement without risking being horribly, irrecoverably, wrong.

How many had Gilbert misjudged in the last few weeks? The sheriff, the deputy, Miss Sweetpea and the Marshal. It was a lesson that he was certain his father would gloat over, once the relief of everyone being safe had faded.

"You're right," Allan said, nodding to himself. "I'll tell her. And then at least I know the answer, no more wondering about what if I'd said something."

Gilbert smiled. "Good."

The train's whistle woke up the two little girls as it pulled into Wyndford Central, and Gilbert checked that both Fenna and Rasha were alright. Sleepy, yawning, but perfectly alright. It only struck Gilbert as the train slowed to a stop that he cared about them. The concern wasn't (only) about avoiding the wrath of their mother, but was from a genuine concern for the little girls who had drooled onto his shirt for the last five hours.

Scooping up Rasha, and taking the hand of little Fenna, Gilbert led the girls out onto the platform. Rasha spotted her mother first and shouted loudly as she pointed toward their welcoming party. Gilbert looked to where she was pointing and felt his heart thud hard in his chest.

Standing on the platform was his father, Arnaud, and with his little baby girl Sarah perched on one hip, Deputy Berry. Millie. His wife for now. Sarah held onto the grey bodice Millie wore, but broke into a wide smile the moment she and Gilbert locked eyes.

Hurrying over, Gilbert set Rasha down and let go of Fenna, letting them run over to their mother with the excited puppy weaving between them. Millie did the same with Sarah, and Gilbert scooped up his daughter, hugging her tight and peppering her forehead with kisses. She was safe! His little storm cloud, her dark serious eyes, her little hands, still chubby at the palms. He kissed each before hugging her tight, burying his face into her dark curls.

"Papa!" Sarah exclaimed, holding onto him tight.

"It's good to see you, son," Avrom said, closing the distance to hug both Gilbert and Sarah. The hug hurt his hip, but Gilbert was too proud to protest. He was home. He had his family, all thanks to one stubborn, terrifying elf.

"Hi," he said, letting go of his father to greet his wife. Fenna was already perched on one hip, and Rasha was clinging to her skirt. Gilbert tried not to think about how his heart had thudded when he saw her holding Sarah.

"Hi," she said, smiling back. Were those... tears in her eyes? The dreaded Bayou Butcher, crying?

Impulse took over, and Gilbert stepped in, swooping down to kiss his wife. For a moment, his heart was full to bursting. He had his daughter, his father, his friend and his bank. More than that, he had a terribly scary woman who had promised to keep them all safe who returned his kiss.

"Hi," he mumbled against her lips.

And he felt her smile into the kiss.

"Hi."

Avrom cleared his throat. Reluctantly pulling back, Gilbert found a newspaper thrust at his chest. Glancing up at his father, Gilbert noticed that despite a ripe bruise on his Tata's cheek, the old man's eyebrows were drawn down into a scowl just as fierce as ever.

"Read this!"

Glancing at his wife, Gilbert noticed her ears had gone red and dipped low. Offering an apologetic smile up at him, she winced.

"I'm sorry," she said. "Sweetpea isn't great at keeping secrets."

Gilbert blinked and looked back at the paper. Plastered over the front page was a headline about him. There was also a side-bar about Harrold Colfield being arrested, but the important part was printed in giant letters that took up half the page.

"'Local banker marries Bayou Butcher in Pagan ceremony,'" he read. He blinked and then looked at his wife. The doubt that had plagued him since leaving Scorched Bluffs evaporated. Gilbert beamed.

"We should get this framed!"

AFTERWORD

Thank you so much for reading No Land For Heroes.

If you've enjoyed following the adventures of Mildred and her friends, please consider leaving a review or rating the book on Goodreads, Storygraph, or the site you purchased it from.

Keep reading for an excerpt of *No Land For Heroes*'s sequel, *No Port in a Storm*.

ACKNOWLEDGMENTS

Thank you so much to the following people for supporting me in the writing of this book: Anne Novikova and Char M for letting me write about our idiot children and their poor decisions and for always being excited to read new chapters. Ebook Launch for the wonderful cover art and cover design, Alexia "Bookishends" for beta-reading and providing sensitivity feedback on Hal and Annie.

Thank you to Wattpad for awarding a Watty Fantasy award to the very first version of this story back in 2019. I wouldn't have thought this silly cowboy story had legs until you chose it. Thank you to my therapists over the years who introduced me to the concept of "Post-traumatic growth" and gave a term for what I wanted both Millie and myself to pursue.

Thank you, Mom, for the unending support through hard times, and thank you to Bird the cat, for sitting on every printed draft and reminding me when to take a break.

—❦—

SNEAK PEEK: NO PORT IN A STORM

Book Two of *Legends & Legacies*

Rattling Cages

Millie

IN THE DEAD HOURS of the night, Wyndford was as quiet as it ever got. The yowl of a street cat clashed with the clatter of cartwheels on cobbles, making the ghostly elf perched on the roof of a tenement building wince. Mildred Berry flicked her ears to shake out the sharpness of the noise and turned her focus back to the building next to her.

The Wyndford City Jail was built out of the same granite as the rest of the city, a four-storey block of a building in the centre of the city. It had a steady business for the first hour she'd watched, drunk after drunk was escorted through its doors. Some went quietly, others singing or shouting. A fog rolled in off the lake during the second hour, muffling the sharp edges of the city. A lucky break for her. The fog would help to obscure her in an already dark night: a few of the officers she had were elven, and their eyes could see in the darkness just as clearly as her own.

A narrow alleyway separated the roof of the jail from Millie's perch, littered with trash and squabbling rats. Once upon a time, Millie wouldn't have hesitated at the distance. She'd have leapt across it with the confidence that only came with young joints and the sense of invulnerability that got people killed. Instead, tonight she had a length of sturdy rope in hand and a plan.

Rising to her feet, Millie spun the loop of rope a few times to build momentum and released it, sending the lasso across the empty space and hooking it onto one of the jail's chimneys. Pulling the rope taut, she tied off her end onto one chimney on the tenement. She'd checked it over for any weakness, but the grout of the brick was sturdy and the bricks whole. It might not hold a full-grown human man, but a petite elf? Not a problem.

Pulling her newsboy cap low to cover her hair, Millie climbed onto the rope, arms held out to either side to keep her balanced. Her moccasins' thin soles let her feel the hemp rope as though she were barefoot. Millie tested her weight on the rope, and while she felt it sag slightly under her, it held. Carefully and quickly, she put one foot in front of the other until she reached the jail's rooftop. She crouched once she'd made it, ears perked for any sounds of commotion.

Somewhere in the jail, a drunk man was singing, his voice faint and surprisingly on key. Millie raised her eyebrows as she realised he was singing an old Union marching song, something she hadn't heard since the war. Either that was a good sign, or it meant exactly nothing.

Creeping across the roof, Millie found the trapdoor that led down into the jail's interior. She made out the runes and sigils of an alarm, and a magical lock, but there didn't seem to be a mechanical one. Then again, most jails were built to be difficult to break out of, not to break into.

She placed the flat of her hand on the runes and watched the faint glimmer of magic die. Most of the time, the way magic reacted around Millie made life difficult, so she was happy to use the strange effect to her advantage whenever she could. Lifting the trapdoor carefully, Millie heard the clink of a hook and eye latch. Pulling out a small knife, she slid it along the crack between the trapdoor and its frame until she caught the hook. With a little wiggle, she freed it from the loop of metal that had held the trapdoor in place.

Opening the trapdoor just enough to peer inside, Millie took stock of the situation. There was a ladder that led down to the attic, with bundles of cloth, dried rations, and more stored inside. She eased herself down, moving slowly and quietly down the ladder. The attic was dusty from disuse, and Millie pulled her shirt up over her nose to keep from sneezing. She crossed the floor, following the nails in the floorboards that told her there was a crossbeam underfoot. The floor wouldn't creak where it was supported, nor was it as likely to give way if a plank was rotten.

The man she was looking for was below, and the thought made her heart race. Millie could kill him tonight and end the cycle of suffering that he'd put her and so many others through. She wanted to do it, to make sure Frederic Rousseau would never hurt another person and give herself peace of mind.

How often had Millie waited for him, locked in a half-flooded cell in the Marigot jail? Crumbling brick walls that let the water in whenever it rained, it was a far cry from the dusty, dry Wyndford building. Her last stay in Marigot had been shortly before the war turned hot, and Millie remembered the feeling of rough scales coiling around her ankle as a palemouth viper soaked up her body heat underwater.

Millie blinked, realising that this was the first time that Fred was in a real cell. Every time she'd been tossed into the rat-filled bowels of the centuries-old fort that served as the Marigot jail, Fred had been put up in an inn across the street until he sobered up enough to retrieve his property.

Closing her eyes, Millie let herself remember what those nights were like. Rats were attracted to the smell of food and drink in her hair, or the blood that seeped from the cuts she'd sustained in the inevitable brawl Fred would start.

The rats attracted the vipers, who were far more palatable. The trick was to snap its neck before the snake realised you'd grabbed it. Its head tried to bite you even after you'd killed it and the snake started to stink badly enough to chase away the remaining rats. Marigot Jail didn't feed its prisoners the way Wyndford did. You had to catch your supper if you wanted to eat.

The stink of snake musk was only a memory now, though Millie could smell Fred through the dust of the attic. The rotten smell of old drink mixed with the regular prison smells of piss and unwashed bodies. Crouching by a floorboard, Millie used her knife to pry up the nails that held it down. Pulling the plank up, she peeked down to spot a familiar blond head buried in bandaged hands.

So he wasn't asleep, good.

Slipping through the space the removed board gave her, Millie climbed down the door of an empty cell until she was face to face with the man she'd spent so long hiding from. The sounds of the jail were quieter once she was inside. Someone was still singing, but it was muffled by the layers of stone and wood between them.

Frederic Fucking Rousseau looked up from his cot, his eyes searching the darkness of the otherwise empty cellblock. Lionel, Fred's ever-loyal servant, lay in the far corner of the cell, deeply asleep.

"Mil?" Fred asked in a whisper. "I know it's you."

There was no one to stop her if she sank the knife into his throat. She could do it, step up close to the bars and just—

"Have you come to gloat, then?" he asked, voice raspy. He smiled as she stepped into the light, and Millie crossed her arms instead of lunging at him like her instinct screamed to do. "The healer says I won't be able to walk again without using a cane."

"Are you saying I should have shot you in the head?" she asked, sinking her emotions deep into her belly. Away from the surface, away from him. The night she'd shot him in the ankle, she'd been too exhausted and shaken to keep her composure. He had kidnapped a little girl, and wanted to take Millie back. The thought of it still made her stomach churn.

"I was wondering what had made you go soft," Fred said, rheumy blue eyes fixing her in place. He was stone sober, she realised. Maybe for the first time in years. "But I've had a lot of time to think, Mil. I think you know deep down that I'm the only one who'll love you for what you are." He smiled again, but the expression was soft and sad.

"You're wrong," she started. This wasn't going right. She was supposed to have the upper hand, but a sober Fred was a dangerous Fred. It was so easy to underestimate Fred when he was sober. He still looked like a drunk, swollen and ruddy-faced, but somehow the drink had left his mind in pristine form despite the years of abuse.

"Am I?" He sniffed, and pushed himself up to stand on his good leg, using the bars of his cell for support as he hobbled closer. "I learned my lesson. You marked me the way I marked you. I shouldn't have forgotten who you are. I shouldn't have given so much of myself up to the drink. But you saved me by sending me here."

The blood drained slowly from her, leaving Millie cold despite the layers she wore. He was up to something, and she wasn't sure what he was getting at just yet.

"You think I shot you in the ankle to teach you a lesson?" she asked, her whisper getting dangerously close to a hiss. He was right, though. Millie had wanted to hurt him, to make him feel just a sliver of all the suffering he'd inflicted on her and her friend Rhiannon over the years. To leave him with a permanent reminder of what he'd done. He'd arranged the killing of the whole Colfield family, sending Millie and other assassins to eliminate any other claims to the family's fortune so that Rhiannon's uncle could inherit the whole thing. Millie reminded herself of why she was there. Rhiannon didn't know, but it was for her benefit that Fred wouldn't die tonight.

"Why did you come then, Mil?" Fred asked, resting his head against the bars. "If it wasn't to gloat, then why are you here?"

"I'm going to testify," Millie said, straightening her shoulders. "About what you did to the Colfields."

Fred looked through the bars at her, his brow knit slightly in confusion.

"And then what?" he asked. "They'll arrest you for Marigot. Or are you going to 'testify' against me for that, too?"

"Yes," she breathed. "About all of it."

Fred pushed himself up straight, grunting as his fresh scars pulled on healing muscle. Rhiannon's dog had savaged his arm, and the scars that peeked out from under his bandages were an angry red. It looked like a vishap had gotten at him.

"Well, if you're going to tell the *truth*," Fred whispered, his eyes fixed on hers. "You'll hang right next to me. I appreciate the romantic gesture, Mil. Together, we face death, just like old times. Us against the world."

Millie's hands gripped fistfuls of her shirt and it took every shred of composure she had left to stay rooted where she was, and not launch herself at the man on the other side of the cell door. Why had she come here? What was the real reason? It was hard to remember with his words bouncing around inside her head.

"If you plead guilty and testify against Harrold Colfield, they won't hang you." Millie took a deep breath, forcing her heartbeat to slow and her hands to still. "Rhiannon Colfield will arrive later today to make you an official offer."

Fred listened, eyebrows raised.

"And what life would there be for me? A known coward, left to rot in a cell until I die from sobriety?" He cleared his throat and shook his head slowly, eyes slipping from Millie to focus on the ground between them. "I'm surprised you haven't tried to talk her out of it."

"I tried," Millie said, and scowled at the smile that appeared on his face. "But she's a kind woman, Fred. Even after everything you did to her—"

"That we did," he corrected.

"Don't try that on me," Millie hissed. "I kept her safe for years. I taught her how to survive. I might have hurt a lot of people in the past, but I did right by her."

They watched each other in the weak moonlight, filtered through the fog outside.

"I never meant for you to take the fall for that," he whispered.

"But you did in Marigot," she countered. "You didn't even hesitate back then. The 'Butcher of the Bayou' was too perfect of an excuse for that fucking ritual we found O'Leary doing. Couldn't let a human be caught performing sacrificial magic, now could we?"

Fred's face fell, and if she were less familiar with his moods, Millie might have thought the grief there was genuine. Maybe it still was, but that meant nothing. It was easy to grieve a mistake when you weren't the one whose life had been ruined.

"That was an order," he said, rubbing his face with his newly scarred hand. "It came down from top brass. I hid you so you wouldn't be pilloried. What was I supposed to do, Mil? They would have labelled you a traitor, a heretic."

"You were supposed to set me free, Fred." Her voice was harsh, and Millie had to pull herself back from breaking out of her whisper. She wanted to yell at him, scream it until his ears bled. Instead she swivelled an ear toward the door "You were supposed to set us all free after, not kill everyone off one by one. Not keep me in a fucking cellar for three years."

Fred's shoulders sagged, and he eased himself back onto the cot, his injured leg stretched out in front of him.

"You're right," he said. He smiled at her, looking as tired and sad as she felt. Neither of them were young like they had been during the war. It had drained them both, leaving them broken and grim. "Better late than never, right?" he said, running a hand through his hair. "I'll tell your friend I'll testify. But I need you to promise me something."

"I don't need to do *anything*," Millie hissed.

"Well, then please promise me you won't forget. Once a master, always a master. I know that better than anyone. Your friend might act like she's grateful, but she's back in society now. She's the wealthiest woman this side of New Haven, and she's going to forget you the same way I forgot who you were to me."

Even after all these years, Fred's words could knock the air from her. Millie grit her teeth, refusing to let him see just how deeply that had cut. Rhiannon wasn't like that, she wasn't like Fred at all.

"No masters," Fred said. "No kings. Remember?"

"You don't get to say that," Millie snapped. She spun on her heel and climbed up the cell door to the hole she'd made in the ceiling. His words chased her up into the attic, and she wasn't fast enough to escape them.

"Don't let her make the same mistakes I did, Mil. You deserve better than that."

RETRIBUTION

THE RED HAND

THE PERSON WHO WENT by The Red Hand watched the pale elf emerge from the jail and cross her rope back to the building she'd used to surveil the police officers. Deep in the shadows of a tenement across the street, the Hand lowered the spyglass from their eye and checked that their hood was still drawn low over their face.

Curious. What had happened in the jail that made her less careful on the elf's exit? She hadn't checked for any witnesses other than a quick glance down the alleyway.

The rope was severed on the jail's side, though the figure hadn't seen how the elf had managed it. She didn't have her axes with her, and no gunshot echoed through the sleepy Wyndford streets. Magic, perhaps? Raising the spyglass to their eye once again, they watched the Bayou Butcher quickly pull her rope up, coiling it around her forearm and hand before tying it off. The clothes she wore were plain, a child's shirt and breeches that made her look like an underfed youth, but her skin practically glowed in the night's fog.

The Hand didn't need to follow the Butcher to know where she was going, but they would trail her back to the banker's home the same as they had every night since her arrival in Wyndford.

The children had been a surprise, but any doubt that Mildred Berry was the Bayou Butcher had evaporated the first night she had snuck out of the home to case the city jail. The Hand moved quietly, descending from their own perch, feeling clumsy compared to the silent movement of the elf. They had lost her those first few nights. She'd disappear behind a building and be gone when the Hand reached it, or the clatter of a late-night carriage passing by covered her scramble up a building where they did not yet dare to follow.

The years since the war had done little to slow her, it seemed. The Hand smiled under their hood as they slipped out from their hiding spot to follow the pale elf home. It was a relief that the elf had not gone soft like the captain had. It would have soured what the figure had planned.

Ten years ago, the elf had murdered someone dear to the Hand. Eight years ago, she had burned Marigot down, uncaring who was caught up in the flames. But soon, the Bayou Butcher would face the consequences she'd evaded for so long.

Made in United States
Troutdale, OR
07/16/2023

11303900R00224